TIDES
OF FIRE

TIDES OF FIRE

A Σ SIGMA FORCE NOVEL

JAMES ROLLINS

wm

WILLIAM MORROW

An Imprint of HarperCollins*Publishers*

HarperCollins books may be purchased for educational, business, or sales promotional use. For information, please email the Special Markets Department at SPsales@harpercollins.com.

FIRST EDITION

Library of Congress Cataloging-in-Publication Data has been applied for.

ISBN 978-0-06-289307-9 (hardcover)

ISBN 978-0-06-289314-7 (international edition)

23 24 25 26 27 LBC 5 4 3 2 1

To Steve Berry, the best friend any author could wish for. We started in the trenches together, and I'm happy to still be fighting alongside you. Of course, I should temper such praise with an insult—but for once, I will not. And only this once.

Acknowledgments

It's always a long road to cross the finish line at the end of the book. Like for any marathon runner, it's great to have a crew of friends cheering you on along the way, picking you up if you fall, offering encouragement at every mile marker. So let me give a special shout-out to a wonderfully supportive crew who have done all of that and more for me: Chris Crowe, Lee Garrett, Matt Bishop, Matt Orr, Judy Prey, Caroline Williams, Sadie Davenport, Igor Poshelyuznyy, Vanessa Bedford, and Lisa Goldkuhl. And a special thanks to Steve Prey for both his critiques and the production of the book's map. I also have to single out David Sylvian for all his hard work and dedication in the digital sphere. And Cherei McCarter, who has shared with me a bevy of intriguing concepts and curiosities, several of which are found in these pages. Of course, none of this would happen without an astounding team of industry professionals, whom I defy anyone to surpass. To everyone at William Morrow, thank you for always having my back, especially Liate Stehlik, Kaitlin Harri, Josh Marwell, Richard Aquan, and Caitlin Garing. Last, of course, a special acknowledgment to the people instrumental to all levels of production: my esteemed editor, Lyssa Keusch, and her industrious colleague Mireya Chiriboga; and for all their hard work, my agents, Russ Galen and Danny Baror (along with his daughter Heather Baror). And as always, I must stress that any and all errors of fact or detail in this book, of which hopefully there are not too many, fall squarely on my own shoulders.

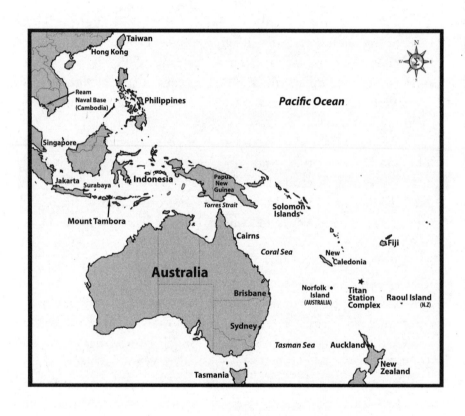

TITAN STATION COMPLEX

TITAN STATION UP

TITAN X

TITAN STATION DOWN

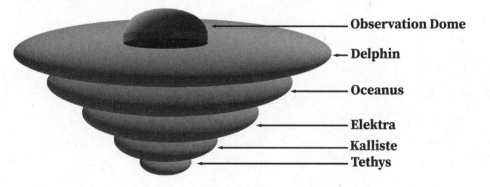

Observation Dome
Delphin
Oceanus
Elektra
Kalliste
Tethys

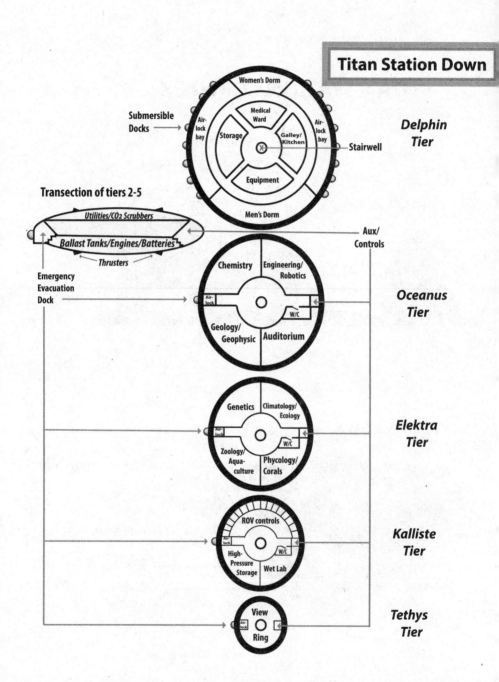

Titan Station Down

Submersible Docks →

Women's Dorm

Medical Ward

Air-lock bay

Storage

Galley/Kitchen

Air-lock bay

Equipment

Men's Dorm

Delphin Tier

— Stairwell

Transection of tiers 2-5

Utilities/CO$_2$ Scrubbers

Ballast Tanks/Engines/Batteries

Thrusters

Emergency Evacuation Dock →

Aux/ Controls

Chemistry

Engineering/ Robotics

Air-lock

W/C

Geology/ Geophysic

Auditorium

Oceanus Tier

Genetics

Climatology/ Ecology

Air-lock

W/C

Zoology/ Aqua-culture

Phycology/ Corals

Elektra Tier

ROV controls

Air-lock

W/C

High-Pressure Storage

Wet Lab

Kalliste Tier

View

Air-lock

Ring

Tethys Tier

Cast of Characters

Dutch East Indies

COMMANDER LELAND MACKLIN—British captain of the HMS *Tenebrae*

LIEUTENANT HEMPLE—second-in-command of the HMS *Tenebrae*

MATTHEW—aboriginal cabin boy aboard the HMS *Tenebrae*

DR. JOHANNES STOEPKER—physician/naturalist and member of the Royal Batavian Society

SIR THOMAS STAMFORD RAFFLES—Lieutenant-Governor of the Dutch East Indies and President of the Royal Batavian Society

CAPTAIN HAAS—Dutch commander of the Indiaman cruiser, the *Apollon*

DR. SWANN—ship's surgeon of the *Apollon*

THOMAS OTHO TRAVERS—aide-de-camp to Lieutenant-Governor Raffles

DR. JOHN CRAWFURD—physician and fellow member of the Royal Batavian Society

WILLIAM FARQUHAR—naturalist and governor of Singapore

Titan Station Crew

PHOEBE REED—marine biologist

JASLEEN (JAZZ) PATEL—post-grad student working alongside Dr. Reed.

WILLIAM BYRD—Australian CEO of ESKY and principal investor in the Titan Project

JARRAH—station security chief

ADAM KANEKO—geologist and member of *Tako no Ude*

Haru Kaneko—vulcanologist, uncle to Adam Kaneko
Datuk Lee—biochemist from the Universiti Sains Malaysia
Bryan Finch—submersible pilot
Kim Jong Suk—biologist, professor from Korea Advanced Institute of
  Science and Technology
Henry Stemm—captain of the *Titan X*

Sigma Force

Grayson Pierce—current commander of field ops
Seichan—former terrorist/assassin, now working alongside Sigma
Monk Kokkalis—specialist in medicine and bioengineering
Kathryn Bryant—expert in intelligence-gathering operations
Joseph Kowalski—specialist in munitions and explosives
Painter Crowe—director of Sigma Force in D.C.
Jason Carter—computer tech at Sigma Command

Duàn Zhī Triad

Guan-yin—mother to Seichan and dragonhead leader of the triad
Zhuang—second-in-command
Bolin Chén—an apprentice (a "blue lantern") with the triad
Yeung—a triad deputy

Chinese Contingent

Captain Tse Daiyu—commanding officer of the PLA research base in
  Cambodia
Luo Heng—bioengineer and physician at base
Zhào Min—molecular biologist and aide to Dr. Luo
Sublieutenant Junjie—worker at the base
Petty Officer Wong—patient at the base
Choi Aigua—former lieutenant-general with the PLA Strategic Sup-
  port Force, now a consultant with the China Academy of Space
  Technology
Choi Xue—major with the PLA Strategic Support Force (son of Aigua)
Captain Wen—head of the Falcon Command Unit
Yang Háo—lieutenant with the PLA Navy

Others

Aiko Higashi—director of *Tako no Ude*

Darren Kwong—head of the Lee Kong Chian Natural History Museum

Kadir Numberi—director of the Jakarta History Museum

Valya Mikhailov—terrorist leader of the new Guild

Jack Pierce—son of Gray and Seichan

Penny and Harriet—daughters of Monk and Kat

Notes from the Scientific Record

Are we alone in the universe?

It's a question that has puzzled and challenged humankind since we first stared at the stars and wondered who, if anyone, was up there.

In October 2021, a group of NASA scientists proposed a framework for assessing this question, compiling seven rigorous steps necessary to confirm the presence of "biosignatures" that might indicate extraterrestrial life.[*] They dubbed this list the "Confidence of Life Detection" scale.[†]

In a nutshell, here are those steps:

1. The detection of a signature of biological life
2. Rule out contamination
3. Rule out non-biological sources
4. Prove that the signature could originate from such an environment

---

[*] A compendium of biosignatures: "Cellular and extracellular morphologies, biogenic fabrics in rocks, bio-organic molecular structures, chirality, biogenic minerals, biogenic stable isotope patterns in minerals and organic compounds, atmospheric gases, remotely detectable features on planetary surfaces, and temporal changes in global planetary properties." National Academies of Sciences, Engineering, and Medicine. 2019. *An Astrobiology Strategy for the Search for Life in the Universe.* Washington, D.C.: The National Academies Press.

[†] "Call for a framework for reporting evidence for life beyond Earth," J. Green, T. Hoehler, M. Neveu, *et al.*, *Nature*, October 28, 2021.

5. Acquire additional observations
6. Eliminate all alternative hypotheses
7. Independent, follow-up observations

Plainly, NASA is already modeling for that moment when extraterrestrial life is discovered or detected, whether that be out in the stars or elsewhere.

In a similar vein, back in January 2021, the CIA declassified nearly three thousand pages of documents, known as the Black Vault, pertaining to UFOs and UAPs (Unidentified Aerial Phenomenon). Likewise, in July of that same year, the Pentagon produced an unclassified report regarding 144 UAP cases noted by military pilots between 2004 and 2021. Of those cases, only *one* had an explainable origin (a deflated balloon). Perhaps it's for that reason that the Pentagon established a new group in November 2021, to "detect and identify" unknown anomalies in restricted airspace, naming this outfit the Airborne Object Identification and Management Synchronization Group.

With all the recent declassifications, the continuing slow leak of data, and the congressional hearings with Pentagon officials in 2022—all pertaining to the possibility of alien life—it raises two questions:

What does the government already know?

And from the uptick in all these releases: *What are they trying to prepare us for?*

You're about to find out.

Notes from the Historical Record

We live on a volatile planet. A geological powder keg that has challenged the permanence of life on Earth throughout its history.

More than 250 million years ago, one of the greatest mass extinctions—the Permian-Triassic Event—wiped out 70 percent of life on land and 90 percent in the oceans. Based on this massacre, it has been dubbed the "Great Dying." What caused it? Extensive volcanic eruptions throughout Siberia surged magma to the surface, pushing lava through rock, igniting gas and oil deposits. It covered a land area half the size of the United States. The clouds of gasses released raised surface temperatures 18 degrees above today's average. It acidified oceans, disintegrated coral, and dissolved the shells of ocean creatures.[*] Life died around the planet, both on land and in the sea.

And that geological event would not be the last to threaten all life.

The Toba supervolcano erupted 74,000 years ago in Indonesia. It blasted two thousand megatons of sulfur dioxide and created a crater more than sixty miles wide by twenty long. The blasts resulted in a volcanic winter that lasted years and tore a massive hole in the ozone layer of the planet, frying life under ultraviolet radiation.[†] Humanity

---

[*] "The Great Dying: Earth's largest-ever mass extinction is a warning for humanity," Jeff Berardelli and Katherine Niemczyk, *CBS News,* March 4, 2021.

[†] "An Ancient Supervolcano May Have Zapped the Ozone Layer, Exposing Early Humans to Intense Sunburns," Isaac Schultz, *Gizmodo,* June 2, 2021.

was driven to a thin population of only about 10,000 to 30,000, a bottleneck that nearly ended us.

After that, Earth was not done trying to shake us off the planet. Almost seventy near-apocalyptic volcanic events followed, one of the last being the 1815 explosion of Mount Tambora in Indonesia. It was the largest ever in recorded history, witnessed by hundreds of thousands and shared with the world by British colonial ships plying the South Pacific. The blast was heard eight hundred miles away and was first attributed to cannon fire. It atomized the top three thousand feet of the mountain, sending a plume of ash and rock eighteen miles into the sky. Between the immediate explosion and the starvation that followed, 100,000 were killed in Indonesia alone, and millions more would die less than two weeks later when the ash cloud circled the equator, dropping temperatures in some areas as much as 20 degrees. It resulted in the infamous "year without a summer."*

Yet, under that smoky cloud, another story has been buried. It's a tale that bears on the geological instability of our volatile planet—and on a future playing out today, one that will challenge all we know about our place in this world.

Read on and find out the truth that's been kept hidden from us all. Until now.

---

* William K. Kingaman and Nicolas P. Klingaman, *The Year Without Summer: 1816 and the Volcano That Darkened the World and Changed History* (St. Martin's Press, 2013).

Let China sleep, for when she wakes, she will shake the world.

—attributed to Napoleon Bonaparte

All warfare is based on deception.

—Sun Tzu, *The Art of War*

"Earth must be warned!"

—Claudie Haigneré, the distinguished French astronaut who spent weeks aboard both the Mir space station and the International Space Station. She shouted these words before attempting suicide in 2008.

April 11, 1815
Off the coast of Sumbawa, the Dutch East Indies

From the bow of the HMS *Tenebrae*, Commander Leland Macklin stared into the fiery mouth of Hell.

Already it was high onto midday, but there was no sun. A low layer of ash and smoke fully cloaked the skies. The reek of sulfurous brimstone stung his eyes and burned his lungs. The only light came from the fiery island of Sumbawa. The coastline lay a half-mile off, but it remained indiscernible, except for the rivers of lava flowing down the blasted slopes of Mount Tambora.

The silence of the grave hung heavy over the surrounding seas—what little could be seen of them. The waves around the ship were covered solidly in a foot of ash, interspersed with floating reefs of pumice rock. Still, it couldn't hide the dead. Shoals of fish bloated in the hot ash, along with countless bodies. Hundreds of souls. Most were so burned and blackened that they were indistinguishable from the dark seas.

"Best we retreat, Commander," Lieutenant Hemple recommended with clear trepidation.

Seven years his junior, the lieutenant had been Macklin's second-in-command for more than a decade. Hemple was an abrupt, hard man with dark blond hair and beard, one seldom taken to histrionics. Presently, due to the stifling heat, he had shed his uniform jacket. He wore only his waistcoat, a white shirt, and blue breeches. Like all the crew, his nose and mouth were hidden behind a wrap of damp cloth.

"We've taken on a tonnage of ash already, sir," Hemple warned. "Some of it growing quite hot."

"We have indeed."

Macklin wiped a wet cloth across his steamy brow. He was similarly garbed to his lieutenant, except that he had kept on his blue jacket with its simple gold piping and gilt-brass buttons. He knocked ash from his black hat before replacing it over the salt and pepper of his hair.

Macklin turned to evaluate the state of the *Tenebrae*. His ship appeared to be as petrified as the seas themselves, a dark hillock rising out of these cursed waters. Ash covered all her decks and riggings and blackened the sails of her three standing masts. Masked members of the crew set about sweeping, brushing, and shoveling the hot ash away, only to be confounded by showers of powder and feathery flakes that continued to fall.

"Sir?" Hemple pressed him.

"Turn us about," Macklin ordered. "Back to Java. Lieutenant-Governor Raffles will be anxiously awaiting our evaluation. Still, keep the *Tenebrae* at half sail in these treacherous waters."

"Aye, Commander."

Hemple left to pass down his orders to the helm. Within minutes, the ship slowly swung away from the fiery island. As she did, the coarse pumice in the water scraped along her hull, sounding like the claws of the dead scratching to board the ship. A low hissing could also be heard in the distance, whispering eerily across the sea's stillness, coming from where the volcano's lava poured into the water.

Macklin was cheered to see the fiery glow of Mount Tambora slowly disappear behind him. The first eruption had occurred six days before. The blasts had traveled the eight hundred miles to the island of Java, sounding like distant cannon fire. Many believed it marked a fierce pirate attack on a merchant vessel, but when black thunderheads of ash swept across the islands, followed by a swamping wave, all knew it for what it was: a volcanic eruption of Biblical might.

At the time, the *Tenebrae* had been docked at Batavia, the capital of the Dutch East Indies on the island of Java. Two days after the eruption, the ship had been commissioned by the lieutenant-governor to sail off and determine the source and the extent of the regional damage.

The *Tenebrae* had been a good choice for such an excursion. She was a collier-class vessel, used for hauling cargo. She had a square stern, a broad bow, and a flat bottom perfect for sailing through shallow waters. The ship also had a wide main deck running from forecastle to quarterdeck, stretching to a total length of ninety-seven feet with a beam of thirty. And as these were pirate-infested waters, she sailed with six 24-pounder carronades on her deck and two 6-pounder guns on her forecastle.

Macklin rested a hand on one of the latter, appreciating the cool iron and its strength. He was glad to be heading back to port, filled with an uneasy dread, which was only heightened by the stillness of these seas and the continual scraping of stones against the hull.

Footsteps drew him back around as a tall, skeletal figure approached. Though the man's face was covered in a wet rag, it was easy to recognize Johannes Stoepker, a naturalist with the Batavian Society. He had shed both his jacket and waistcoat, wearing only black trousers and a white shirt, which by now was nearly as dark as his pants. The man had been assigned to the ship by Lieutenant-Governor Raffles, who was president of the same learned organization, whose goal was to study, preserve, and foster interest in the historical and scientific significance of the East Indies. So, for such an undertaking of exploration as this, the Batavian Society had wanted a member on board the *Tenebrae*.

Stoepker was shadowed by the ship's cabin boy, Matthew. The twelve-year-old was an Aboriginal lad—dark of hair and skin and admirable of spirit—who also served as powder monkey whenever they employed the ship's cannon, but during the past days, the boy had acted as the naturalist's aide. Clearly happy with the assignment, Matthew grinned and hefted a heavy leather satchel over one shoulder, laden with pumice stones that the crew had netted from the water.

"What is it, Mister Stoepker?" Macklin asked.

The naturalist pushed his mask down to his bearded chin. "Commander, as we're turning about, would it be possible to retrieve one of the bodies from the sea? Back in Java, there is an anatomist and surgeon with the Society who would be intrigued in the state of the dead."

Macklin grimaced at such a thought. "I won't have it aboard my ship, Mister Stoepker. The ill luck of it all will have the men in revolt."

Stoepker frowned and bunched a brow. He spun a gold ring absently around a finger, in deep thought. The ring was adorned with a garnet stone, carved deeply with the letters BG, an abbreviation for *Bataviaasch Genootschap*, the Dutch name for the Batavian Society.

Stoepker finished his contemplation and cleared his throat. "Commander Macklin, the *Tenebrae* has an iron-hulled tender for coursing over rocks and reefs. Could we lower it down, load a body into it, and have your ship drag both to Java?"

Macklin considered this request, appreciating its cleverness. "It is a reasonable accommodation. I'll allow it." He turned to Matthew. "Boy, grab Landsman Perry and see about freeing the tender."

The lad nodded, set his bag down, and sped off.

As they waited, Stoepker joined him at the rail and stared back toward the island's glow as it faded behind the ship's stern. "I never would've expected Mount Tambora to be the culprit, here. Maybe Mount Merapi or Klut. And if I were a betting man, I would've wagered Bromo, a peak that has been regularly smoking."

Macklin nodded grimly. "Everyone believed Tambora was dormant."

"Extinct, actually," Stoepker corrected. "At least, that was the consensus until now. Though, I heard rumors that the natives of Sumbawa felt occasional shakes or heard deep-earth rumbles. Maybe we should not have dismissed such tales out of hand."

"Clearly."

"And last night . . . I think that second eruption from Tambora was even fiercer than the first. Or maybe it only seemed that way because we were much closer."

"No, it had to be worse," Macklin countered. "The thunderous blast it gave off sounded like the very Earth had cracked in half."

"True. And the huge swell of the seas afterward did indeed feel monstrous. No doubt there'll be even more coastal flooding throughout these islands."

Macklin pictured the wave that had struck Java following the first eruption. The *Tenebrae* had been anchored in deep water and spared any damage. Along the shore, docks had been crushed by that surge, tossing ships and debris far inland.

"Let's just pray we have a port to return to," Macklin grumbled.

By now, Lieutenant Hemple had returned to the forecastle. He moved swiftly toward the deck, his legs stiffened by urgency. "Commander, the crow's nest reports fresh fires ahead of us."

"From one of the outlying islands?"

"No, sir. At sea. Starboard side. Half-mile out." Hemple lifted a brass spyglass. "I confirmed the same."

Macklin waved for the scope. "Let me see."

Hemple passed him the spyglass. Macklin carried it to the starboard side of the bow. As he crossed, he noted the faintest glow through the pall. He fixed the scope to his eye and took a few breaths to center and focus down upon it. He studied it for a full minute. As the *Tenebrae* swept toward the location, the sight grew clearer.

"It appears to be a ship," Macklin reported. "Aflame and listing badly."

"One of His Majesty's, sir?" Hemple asked. "Or an Indiaman?"

Macklin lowered the glass and shook his head. "Still too far off to make out any colors or flags. But we'll strike for it, nonetheless."

Hemple nodded crisply and left to alert the quartermaster at the helm.

"These seas remain hot," Stoepker warned. "It would not be hard to imagine an errant flake of flaming ash setting torch to a wooden ship."

"Not on the *Tenebrae*. My men know what to watch for. We'll not be caught unawares."

"Perhaps the other ship did not have as diligent a crew."

"We shall see."

Even at half sail, it did not take long to reach the foundering ship. By then, Macklin and Stoepker had joined Lieutenant Hemple on the quarterdeck. Master Welch manned the ship's wheel. No one was taking any chances. Especially as it had become clear that the vessel in distress was that of a Bugi pirate, the scourge of the Dutch in this region. The ship's masts had become torches, tilting crookedly out of the water. The hull smoked so thickly it nearly obscured the flames from view.

Several smaller boats rowed away from the wreckage through the heavy ash. Most were also burning, smoldering, or dancing with flames.

Two boats turned and headed for the *Tenebrae*, with oars desperately chopping the waters.

Macklin found it strange that such pirates would seek succor aboard a ship waving His Majesty's flag. They must know that they would only find the end of a noose if they made it here. Still, both fought hard for the *Tenebrae*.

One of them caught fire. The suddenness of it drew a gasp from Stoepker. Pirates crowded into the center of the boat, as if fearing the water more than the fire. But there would be no escape from either. Clothes quickly caught the flames and the boat broke out from under them. Men tumbled into the sea, vanishing below the layer of ash. One arm burst high, still burning, then drowned away.

"What's happening?" Hemple asked, his eyes huge.

Stoepker backed away from the rail. "We must leave these waters. Something is infernally wrong here."

As if punctuating the naturalist's warning, a thunderous boom erupted, shaking the waters. The gloom behind them brightened with fire. It marked yet another eruption of Tambora.

Macklin grimaced, realizing the ship's name was proving all too apt this day. Her first owner had run her as a convict ship and fittingly named the vessel after a Catholic ceremony of punishment. The celebration of Tenebrae marked the last three days of Holy Week, when a hearse of fifteen candles, representing Christ's travails on the way to the cross, were extinguished one after the other—until there was only darkness. The ceremony ended with a loud bang in the dark, representing the closing of Jesus's tomb.

Macklin stared at the sunless skies as the blast echoed away.

Are we about to be similarly entombed?

Moments later, the waters behind the ship swelled up, as if a great sea beast were surfacing and closing upon them.

"Hold tight!" Hemple bellowed to the crew.

The surge lifted the stern high, before rocking it down again, teetering the ship over the swell until she fell heavily back into the sea behind it. Afterward, the *Tenebrae* continued to jostle hard, waving masts and whipping sails.

Macklin returned his attention to the last of the fleeing rowboats. Only now it had swung away and had begun striking off, as if the pirates had finally noted the flag waving high as the masts flailed in the air.

But that was not the reason.

Hemple rushed to his side. "Smoke, sir. Rising all around us."

Macklin had noted the thickening pall, but he had attributed it to the burning pirate ship.

A boatswain and his mate burst out of the quarterdeck and hollered to all. "Fire in the bilge!"

Hemple directed several of the crew. "Sand buckets and water! Go!"

Macklin frowned at the sea, at the burning pirate ship.

Stoepker leaned over the rail and looked down. "What are those?"

Macklin followed his gaze. A tide of black stony branches clung to the lower hull. With each rock of the boat, more appeared. Smoke billowed around them, as if the branches were red-hot irons branding into the ship's planks.

Farther below, seen through breaks in the ash, something flashed and flickered down in the dark depths, like streams of glowing lights passing beneath and around the *Tenebrae*.

Macklin shuddered at the ungodly sight.

"Full sails now!" he ordered. "Get us out of these waters!"

As he shouted, he never took his eyes from the sight below. Those burning branches continued to spread, climbing higher, as if the fiery claws of some briny monster had nabbed the *Tenebrae*.

He now understood what had panicked the pirates.

Before the *Tenebrae* could truly gain speed, flames burst along the hull and swept along those branches, encircling the ship. Even a roll into the ashy water failed to douse the fire.

Behind him, Hemple bellowed and spread the commander's orders. Shouts and curses rang out everywhere as desperation and terror gripped the *Tenebrae*.

Macklin searched across the thickening pall toward the Bugi ship. The pirate vessel slowly sank into the ash-covered sea. He knew the same fate likely awaited the *Tenebrae*. It was only then that he noted

Mister Stoepker and the ship's cabin boy had vanished from his side, but he had no time to ponder their disappearance.

As smoke shrouded his ship and flames rose to the rails, his heart pounded in his throat. He remembered the last time he had attended a Holy Week mass at the church in Batavia. A song had been sung, composed by Gregorio Allegri centuries before, marking the Tenebrae service, those last three days of Christ's torture.

He recited the title now, *"Miserere mei, Deus."*

It was as apt as the ship's name.

Have mercy on me, God.

April 23, 1815
Batavia, on the island of Java

Stamford Raffles, the lieutenant-governor of the Dutch East Indies, followed the captain of the Indiaman cruiser, the *Apollon*, through the recovering ruins of the town's port. Captain Haas was accompanied by his ship's surgeon, Swann.

The two had appeared at the governor's palace with some urgency, carrying a letter from a man whom Stamford trusted. So, despite the late hour, with the sun sitting low on the horizon, he had set off with the men in a carriage to the docks. The group now crossed briskly down a long stone pier, one of the few still intact following the damage over the past weeks.

Hammering and sawing and shouting echoed all around the port. But, at least, the skies had mostly cleared of ash, though a thick haze persisted that turned the sun into an angry red orb and created a perpetual twilight. The early evening's breezes still sweltered and carried the reek of sulfur.

Stamford held a perfumed cloth to his nose against the stench. The heat further soured his mood. He had left the palace fully attired in a black jacket and stiff waistcoat as he was due to attend a dinner later with dignitaries from British Malaya, who had come to survey the damage from Tambora's eruption.

Captain Haas drew alongside Stamford. The sandy-haired Dutchman was less formally dressed in gray jacket and trousers, but he kept himself neat and carried himself with a measure of practical gravitas.

Haas waved to his ship anchored in the bay. "The *Apollon* was sailing from New Guinea, passing through the Java Sea, when we came upon a small boat, foundering and lost. We thought she might've broken free and been left adrift."

Swann nodded. He was a small, older man with a stern demeanor and dark eyes. "Then we spotted what the boat held. I recommended to Captain Haas that we haul it all here."

"We've not touched any of it," Haas added, raising a silver cross to his lips, then lowering it. "Not that any of us dared to."

The two men drew Stamford to the end of the pier, where a small tender had been tied up. It was covered by a tarp of sailcloth. Before it stood the man who had sent the letter with the captain. It was Stamford's aide-de-camp and trusted friend, Thomas Otho Travers. The dark-haired Irishman and former soldier kept a fit build, accented by a snug jacket and crisp trousers. He stood with a Scotsman of the same age, whom Raffles also knew, a physician of distinction, one associated with the Batavian Society, Dr. John Crawfurd.

Both men looked equally grim.

Stamford crossed past Haas to reach the pair. "What is it? What required such urgency?"

Travers turned to the iron-hulled boat, which looked weathered and dented. "This tender is from the *Tenebrae*."

"What? How can you be so sure?"

Stamford had dispatched the cargo ship, the *Tenebrae*, sixteen days before, but nothing had been heard from her since. All imagined the vessel had been beset by pirates, as the Bugi fleet were prowling the waters in greater numbers following the eruptions, like vultures picking at a carcass.

"We're certain, sir," Travers said and turned to the physician. "Perhaps it's best you show him, Doctor Crawfurd. I'll help you."

The young physician was dressed in black with a white collar, making him look priestly. He crossed with Travers to the tender and together they drew back the drape of sailcloth to reveal a ghastly sight.

Stamford wanted to step away, to refuse what was revealed, but Haas and his surgeon crowded behind him.

Two bodies lay across the bottom of the tender, one twice the height of the other. Both were blackened and featureless. Still, there remained an eerie polish to their surfaces, as if both had been carved of dark marble, with a slight prickling over their skin. The smaller of the two, clearly no more than a boy, lay curled under the arm of the other. Even still, the agonized contortion of neck and spine spoke to the pain of the boy's death. The lad had found no comfort under that arm. Still, the man had tried, even as the same torturous death afflicted him.

Even stranger, the larger of the two had not fully succumbed to the affliction. The quarter of his body farthest from the boy remained blistered and burned at the edges, but mostly untouched past that point. An ear and cheek still shone pale and blue in death. Part of a burned white shirt hid the upper torso, and one whole leg looked untouched, still clothed in a dark pantleg and a calf-high boot.

None of it made any sense.

Raffles raised a foremost question. "Who are they?"

Doctor Crawfurd stepped gingerly into the tender and over to the larger body. He pointed to the arm wrapped around the boy, then down to a blackened hand, which still bore a ring on a finger. "The stone bears the initials BG."

Stamford clutched his perfumed cloth tighter, knowing who had been aboard the *Tenebrae*. "Johannes Stoepker. The naturalist."

"We believe so," Travers acknowledged. "We suspect the lad must be a cabin boy from the ship."

"What happened to them? No fire does this to a body. It looks like they've been turned to stone."

Crawfurd stood again, rocking the tender enough that Travers had to reach over and steady him. "We don't know, sir," the physician admitted. "But I did a brief examination. Whatever afflicted them has indeed petrified their flesh. Turning it hard as a rock. But I cannot fathom how or why. I'll need the corpses carried to my rooms behind the town's apothecary, where I can better examine the bodies."

"But there's something else you should see first," Travers warned.

The aide-de-camp joined the physician aboard the tender and knelt next to Stoepker's other arm, which was held tight to his chest. His stony fingers clutched a small steel box.

"He clearly was protecting more than just the boy," Travers said. "We didn't want to disturb anything more until you arrived."

"Can you free the box?" Stamford asked. "And whatever it holds?"

"I can try."

Travers wrapped his hand in a handkerchief and grabbed hold of the steel, clearly trying to avoid touching the petrified skin. He attempted to slip the box free, but to no avail. Even in death, Stoepker refused to release the secret he held.

"With more force, Mister Travers," Stamford demanded.

"Yes, sir."

Travers planted his feet wider, then set about rocking the box and tugging hard at it. Finally, a loud *snap* cracked sharply, and Travers fell back to the gunwale. The tender nearly capsized under his weight, but Crawfurd balanced the other side to keep the boat from tipping over.

A splash near the stern drew Stamford's eye.

He flinched. "Did you lose the box?"

"No, sir." Travers lifted the steel container. "I still have hold of it."

Stamford's gaze remained on the water. He watched the remains of a blackened hand float to the surface, missing a couple of fingers. Despite its stony appearance, the hand clearly remained buoyant.

What devilishness is this?

Travers climbed out of the tender and carried the box to him.

Stamford crossed his arms, having no desire to touch the accursed object. "Open it," he ordered.

Travers popped the latch and creaked the lid open. A fold of paper fell out, fluttering to the pier. Likely a last message from Johannes Stoepker.

Stamford ignored it and leaned closer to the box. It held only one other object: a branched stalk of rock that looked like a piece of black coral.

"What do you make of it?" Travers whispered.

Stamford shook his head, unable to fathom any meaning to it.

Why would Stoepker go to such lengths to preserve such a thing?

Still, Stamford noted that the color and sheen of the fractured piece matched the blackened corpses in the tender. He also remembered a unique feature of *coral*: when broken and dried, their pieces often floated.

As he stared at the ruins of Stoepker's hand bobbing in the water, a cold certainty chilled through him.

These bodies hadn't been petrified into rock.

They'd been turned into coral.

FIRST

THE TITAN PROJECT

1

Phoebe Reed stared out in awe at the sunken Garden of Eden.

Beyond the nine inches of acrylic glass, the station's lamps lit the perpetual darkness. They cast out a unique band of red light that caused little disturbance to the surrounding marine life. Standing at the window, she wore image-enhancing goggles tuned to the light's wavelength to expand the view.

Even here, two miles down, life teemed in a kaleidoscope of riches. Giant crimson-legged crabs climbed over shoals of reefs, picking delicately into crevices. Ghostly white snailfish glided over open sands. A cookie-cutter shark—once called a cigar shark due to its cylindrical shape—glowed past the window, dark on the topside, bioluminescent below. A larger shark, a bluntnose sixgill, patrolled at the edge of the light.

Next to her, a hand pointed, noting the same. "Sixgills have never been recorded at these depths."

"Is that true, Jazz?" Phoebe asked, glancing over to her post-grad assistant.

Jasleen Patel gave her a scowl for doubting her expertise. Jazz had completed her master's degree in marine biology two years before and was finalizing her doctoral dissertation under Phoebe's mentorship. Jazz had been one of Phoebe's undergrad students and eventually her teach-

ing assistant at Caltech's marine lab. Since then, they had been working collaboratively for more than five years. So much so that Phoebe
and Jazz became known as PB&J by most of their colleagues.

Most believed the two had bonded because they were both women
of color. Phoebe had been born in Barbados but raised by her mother in
South Central after they immigrated to the States when she was eight.
Jasleen, eight years younger than her, was a native-born Californian,
but her heritage was East Indian. Her family, originally from Mumbai,
ran a chain of dry cleaners across the Bay Area.

But it wasn't the women's skin color or gender that drew them together. At least, not entirely. It was much more about their mutual
interests in the mysteries of the deep. That, and their respect for each
other.

"It's hard to believe *anything* could survive in this sunless bathypelagic zone," Jazz said, placing a palm against the glass. "The pressure
out there is more than two tons per square inch."

"It's exciting, isn't it. Life not only took a foothold out there, but it's
thriving in great abundance."

They both gazed at the wonderland beyond the glass.

A couple of anglerfish dangled their long rods, waving their luminescent lures. Clutches of squidworms squirmed through the light, feeding
on marine snow that fell from the sunlit levels, bringing energy down
to these midnight seas. Every glance around her revealed more: schools
of viperfish, a pair of vampire squids, a single dumbo octopus. Farther
out, albino lobsters crawled amidst waves of crimson anemone.

"Have you picked out the coral beds where you want to take our
first samples?" Jazz asked, checking her dive watch. "Our first allotted
window of ROV time is in ninety minutes."

"I've selected a few candidates, but I'd like to make another full pass
around the ring of windows at this level, and maybe on the tier above
us, too."

"Don't dawdle," Jazz warned. "We're not the only ones salivating for
ROV time. We've got a lot of competition down here."

"And above us."

Thousands of researchers, academics, and scientists had petitioned to be part of this great oceanic enterprise—but only three hundred had been chosen for the inaugural start of the Titan Project. Those hundreds were now spread across three zones.

Half the researchers remained topside, aboard the *Titan X*, the thousand-foot-long gigayacht that supported a thirteen-story glass sphere at its stern. The orb housed twenty-two state-of-the-art laboratories. It was a ship capable of servicing the station here, but it could also swiftly sail the seas, driven by a molten-salt nuclear reactor, to engage in studies around the globe.

Also topside was *Titan Station Up*, a floating platform designed after the FPSO system of oil rigs. It served as the staging ground, workstation, and permanent support facility. The station's two dozen submersibles—both HOVs and ROVs—were also docked there.

During the past two weeks, the specialized HOVs—human occupied vehicles—had ferried researchers and staff two miles deep to *Titan Station Down*. Some had described the inverted pyramid of the underwater station as the "world's most expensive toy top."

To her, as she had descended in an HOV two days before, it had been the most incredible sight. The station's uppermost level, with its large glass observatory dome, looked like a huge UFO that stretched a hundred meters across. The four tiers below it were the same circular shape as the first, but each shrank in diameter the deeper they went, forming that "toy top." The bottommost level—where she was now—was a mere twenty meters wide. It held no labs, just a ring of polarized black glass, making it as much an observatory as the dome on top.

Like the platform and ship above, this entire station floated, hovering above the seabed. Its position was maintained by ballast tanks and dynamically stabilized by thrusters at each level. The only point of contact with the fragile ecosystem below were a few anchors cabling them in place.

To make it easier for the researchers and workers to move about the three zones, *Titan Station Down* was maintained at a constant one atmosphere of pressure, requiring no acclimation or decompression as personnel arrived or left. Submersibles offloaded or took on passengers through a docking system similar to the one at the International Space

Station—which was appropriate, as the landscape around them was as hostile and as dangerous as any vacuum of space.

Still, such fears were hard to hold on to. Phoebe and Jazz, like most of the researchers, continued to walk around the sky-blue passageways in a haze of awe, nervousness, and excitement. They'd all had months of preparations, weeks of lectures, and days of safety classes. Still, nothing could prepare one for entering this world.

"Pheebs, you finish your survey down here," Jazz said. "I'm heading up and checking our assigned ROV terminal. I want to make sure that duo from MIT doesn't eat into our time."

"You do that. Keep breathing down their necks if you have to."

"Oh, trust me, this girl'll cut a guy if he doesn't move quick enough."

Phoebe smiled as Jazz headed toward the spiral staircase that led upward. Jasleen was barely five-foot, with a pixie cut of dark hair, but when it came to defending their workspace and schedule, she could become a veritable pit bull.

Knowing Jazz would hold *her* just as accountable to their schedule as anyone, Phoebe set about circling the Tethys Tier. This time, she focused less on the wonder of the abundant sea life that swam, crawled, or jetted across the reefs and more on her area of expertise.

Her doctoral thesis had been on the unique biology of deep-sea coral. Most people were familiar with shallow coral from snorkeling, where polyps derived energy from photosynthesizing algae that lived cooperatively within the coral. But her interests focused on those corals who made their home *below* the sunlit zone. Such deep-thriving corals continued to be a mystery and remained poorly understood. In these frigid, high-pressure waters, they matured slowly and were known for their incredible longevities, up to five thousand years by some estimates.

With no sunlight, such species fed on microscopic organisms—zooplankton and phytoplankton—along with the particulate organic matter from decaying plants and animals. To take up that abundance, deep-sea corals formed beautiful, fragile structures of fronds and fine branches that sifted the currents for food and oxygen. As a result, bathypelagic reefs looked more like forests, all feathered and fanned out.

Which is certainly true here.

Beyond the window, the sheer volume of coral was astounding. It was more of a fluorescent jungle than a forest. Brilliant gorgonian coral rose in towering stalks and branches, some climbing thirty or forty feet high. They glowed in yellows, pinks, blues, and soft purples. They were mixed with sea whips and sea fans. Elsewhere, tall stands of jet-black tree corals rose in dense, thick branches, looking like carbonized sculptures of meter-tall pines. In stark contrast, huge bushes of ivory-colored *Lophelia* filled gullies or crowned ridges.

She was momentarily daunted by the monumental task to study and catalog the breadth of this landscape, but she took a deep breath, remembering a Chinese proverb often quoted by her mother whenever Phoebe grew too overwhelmed, especially after they had first moved to the States.

A journey of a thousand miles begins with a single step.

She took a deep breath and exhaled it slowly.

I can do this.

11:08 A.M.

Forty minutes later, Phoebe completed her second pass around the windows of Tethys Tier. To navigate the space, she had to scoot past clusters of colleagues, who whispered in languages from around the globe. She carried an e-tablet that glowed with a map of the surrounding reefs. She had marked fifteen possible sites—three times too many for their first window of ROV time.

I need to whittle this down to the best five or six spots.

She clutched her tablet, frustrated but knowing she would have ample time later for additional sampling. In the months ahead, she intended to widen her search grid. The first week was intended to be about acclimation, about getting accustomed to the collection methods and learning how best to utilize the station's onboard labs. After that, her research could be expanded. She already had a booking on a survey HOV heading out next Tuesday, where she could explore sites farther afield.

As if summoned by this thought, a brilliant yellow submersible, with a huge glass sphere at its bow, glided past. Beyond the glare of its lights, which stung through her sensitive goggles, shadows could be seen moving behind the HOV's curve of glass.

She pressed a palm to the window and watched it disappear into the darkness, a slowly fading star. An ache of desire burned through her.

A man spoke, startling her. "What do you think of all this, Dr. Reed?"

Focused fully on the view, she hadn't noticed anyone approach. She turned, then stiffened in surprise at the presence of William Byrd, the CEO of ESKY and principal investor of the Titan Project. The fifty-year-old Aussie had made his fortune from shipbuilding—mostly container ships and freighters, but also for the Australian navy. His company continued to handle the bulk of international trade. His net worth was upward of $70 billion. Still, he currently wore a simple navy-blue jumpsuit and cap bearing the symbol of a trident, the official uniform for the station. The only sign of his wealth was a bulky gold pocket watch that hung from a chain across his chest.

She removed her goggles and struggled to find her voice. She finally waved to the seas beyond the glass, remembering her own first impression of the view. "Mister Byrd . . . you . . . were not wrong to describe these seas as a lost Garden of Eden. It's all truly astounding."

"Ah, so you heard my press conference last week?"

He gave her a rakish grin, making him look even more boyish. His face was deeply tanned—but not from any salon. It had the salt-scoured look of a rugged sailor, set off by thick blond hair, speckled with white from either age or the sun's bleaching, probably both.

"I doubt anyone missed it," she said. "Though I suspect Bezos, Branson, and Musk might've taken offense."

He shrugged. "Serves them right. Why spend billions sending rockets into space when there are so many mysteries left unexplored right here on Earth. Especially under the sea, where only *20* percent of the ocean floor has been mapped so far. And even those maps are of poor resolution. When it comes to discerning a level of detail necessary to detect items as large as plane wrecks, it drops to a paltry 0.05 percent—leaving nearly *all* the ocean floor unexplored."

"I hadn't realized those numbers were so low," Phoebe said.

Byrd nodded sadly. "It presents our greatest challenge. Humanity's future will not be discovered on the surface of Mars, but in that 99.9 percent of the Earth's oceans that remain a mystery. And we neglect it at our peril. The oceans are our breadbasket, our playground, even our pharmacy. More importantly, the seas are the true lungs of our planet, producing 80 percent of the world's oxygen and consuming 25 percent of the carbon dioxide. If even a quarter of the ocean dies, so does most life on Earth."

Phoebe nodded along with him, reminded of the overall importance of the Titan Project. It was funded by a conglomerate of non-profit groups, research grants, and corporate sponsors, but the lion's share of the investment had come from the man standing before her. She didn't know if this was his way of giving back after raking in billions from his thousands of cargo carriers plying the world's oceans. Still, at least he was giving back. It was his company that had overseen and financed most of the construction of the Titan Complex, spending $10 billion to see it come to fruition in a shockingly swift timeframe.

And I get to be part of it.

Yet, even the billionaire standing before her could not hold Phoebe's full attention. Her gaze kept slipping past his shoulders to the ring of windows. Her eyes followed the path of a Cuvier's beaked whale as it swept across the coral beds, likely as curious about them as they were about their surroundings. Such whales were the Cetacean deep-divers, known to hold their breath for hours.

Byrd must have sensed her restless inattention, which only broadened his welcoming grin. He turned to stare at the wonderland glowing out the windows.

"If this is truly a lost Garden of Eden," he said, "let's hope we don't get kicked out for seeking forbidden knowledge like Eve. We have much to learn down here. And a lot of work ahead of us."

"It's not work. Trust me. It's an honor. To be here at the edge of the Coral Sea. With all the discoveries that await us, I'm anxious to get started as soon as possible."

By now, the others on this level had all turned their way, ignoring the view outside. William Byrd seldom intruded upon the researchers. During Phoebe's weeks of training aboard the *Titan X*, she had spotted the billionaire only a few times, either across the deck of the yacht or as he was shuffled amidst an entourage throughout the science globe. At the moment, he had pared his staff down to a lone, stern-faced bodyguard, a tall Aboriginal man, who had a hand resting atop the pommel of a baton secured at his waist.

"Your enthusiasm inspires me, Dr. Reed," Byrd said, still staring out at the breadth of the sea.

"Thank you," Phoebe stammered, shocked that the man even knew her name.

Then again, she was one of the few Black faces aboard the Titan Complex and the only Black *woman* as far as she knew. She hoped that was not the reason for his recognition—or the fact that she stood six-foot-two and towered over most everyone.

While the Titan Project was an international effort, the majority remained white and male. There was a fair number from across Asia, along with a handful from Turkey, Pakistan, and the Middle East. Still, men outnumbered women twenty to one. But that spoke more to the lack of women in the sciences versus any prejudice.

At least, I hope so.

Byrd turned from the window to face her. "I look forward to your thoughts on the state of our reefs, Dr. Reed. I can only hope we discover a way to stop the destruction of the coral beds that gave this sea its name."

She had suspected this was the reason she had been selected to participate in the project. Deep-sea coral seemed especially resistant to the heat-induced bleaching of surface coral, an affliction threatening the Great Barrier Reef. Such deep-growing coral also withstood pollution far better. But no one truly knew exactly why. If it could be discovered, it might offer a solution to saving the great reefs of the world.

"I've read your journal articles from your research at the Monterey Bay Aquarium Research Institute," Byrd continued. "Related to the resilient ecology of Sur Ridge off the coast of California. It's why I place such hope on your work here."

She tried to hide her shock. *He read my work.* So, maybe the man's acknowledgment had nothing to do with her skin color or her towering height after all.

She straightened her back. "I will do my best."

"I have no doubt of that."

Byrd finally sighed loudly. "I will leave you to get fully settled, Dr. Reed. But I look forward to chatting with you again."

Before he could step toward the central stairs, a low rumble echoed through the station. Outside, the anchor cables swayed, but the five tiers of *Titan Station Down* barely moved as its rows of thrusters, all computer coordinated, compensated for the shaking.

Still, the other scientists gathered closer, shying from the ring of *windows.*

Even Byrd's bodyguard reached a hand toward his charge.

But the Aussie stepped aside and raised an arm, along with his voice. "Just a minor sea quake, everyone. Nothing to worry about. We're in a tectonically active region. This is the sixteenth—no, seventeenth—tremor we've recorded since we started this project. Such quakes are expected and have been fully accounted for by Titan's design team."

As the tremor subsided, Phoebe was the only one to step back to a window. She gazed out. Beyond the glass, the sea life looked as unimpressed by the shaking as Byrd. The fluffed-up sand was already sifting back down.

She tested a palm against the glass, feeling the slight thrum of the stabilizing thrusters but nothing else. She stared beyond the reach of the red lamps to the darkness beyond, toward the likely epicenters of the recent tremors. She pictured where this sea shelf dropped away into an interconnecting maze of deep trenches: the Solomon trenches, the New Hebrides, and farther out, the Tonga and Kermadec trenches. They marked the broken tectonic line where the Pacific Plate ground under the Indo-Australian Plate.

While the Mariana Trench to the north got more publicity and attention—being the world's deepest—it was only a thousand meters deeper than this chain. Because of their second ranking, these trenches had never been given as much scientific attention.

Until now, she hoped.

One of the reasons she wanted to join the Titan Project had been its proximity to those trenches and how it tied to her latest research. Deep-sea coral had been well documented in beds two miles under the sea. But no one truly knew if they thrived deeper, and if so, what they might look like or how they survived. Answers to those mysteries could be found in the neighboring maze of trenches.

She glanced back to William Byrd, who had been stopped by a trio of researchers before he could leave. It sounded like he was still reassuring them, speaking about all the troubleshooting and shakedown testing that the station had undergone.

She let him drone on, remembering instead his statement from a moment before, about how 99.9 percent of the ocean remained unexplored. There must be *deeper*-growing coral out there somewhere.

She turned back to the window.

And I will find them.

With her palm still on the glass, she felt a tremor that started in her hand and vibrated up her arm. Outside, the seabed shivered, casting up sand, shaking that vast forest. The sedate sea life flashed away with flickers of fins and tails. An army of crabs abandoned their scavenging and skittered away from the reef. Octopi and squids jetted off into the darkness, leaving behind a panicked fog of ink.

Her eyes widened, and her breath caught, stifling the warning in her throat.

Before she could exhale, the sea floor bucked under the station. The anchor lines thrashed violently. Two of them ripped away. Overhead, fire doors slammed shut between the levels, isolating each tier. As the station twisted and jolted, the rest of the cables were jettisoned with bubbling blasts from their attachments to the floating structure.

Once loose, *Titan Station Down* spun slowly like the top that it was—until the thrusters finally compensated and drew them back to a steady hover.

Phoebe glanced to the others. A few of the researchers had been thrown to the floor by the jarring of the station. William Byrd remained on his feet, likely due to the firm grip of his bodyguard.

The Aussie attempted a laugh, but it came out forced. "That was more of a *shakedown* cruise than I had hoped you'd experience, but as you can see, even under such a severe jolt, all is well."

Overhead, the fire doors slowly sighed open between the levels. An all-clear klaxon chimed throughout the station.

"As I told you," he assured them with a big smile, "there's nothing to worry about."

Still, his grin looked far less sure than it had a few moments before.

Phoebe turned back to the window. As the quake faded, the seabed settled. The sands sifted down and revealed the reef again, which appeared mostly intact. A couple of taller tree corals had snapped at their bases and crashed down into the sand. But that seemed the worst of the damage.

Still, she waited and maintained her vigil.

After a full five minutes, a cold wave of dread shivered through her.

None of the other free-wheeling pelagic life had returned, as if still avoiding this area.

She winced, suddenly worrying.

Should we be doing the same?

2

Commander Grayson Pierce knelt across from his two-year-old son and waited for Jack to make the selection that would determine his destiny.

For the moment, the boy's focus remained on the sulfur-crested cockatoo dancing atop a perch near a balcony door. Outside, the sun sat low on the horizon, illuminating a view that swept across the forested heights of Victoria Peak and down to the skyscrapers of Hong Kong and its harbor.

An exasperated sigh drew back Gray's attention.

"C'mon, Jack, pick one," Harriet urged the boy. Clearly the seven-year-old girl's patience had reached its limit. She knew there was a four-tiered birthday cake in the shape of Snoopy sitting in the kitchen.

"Don't rush him," Penny scolded her younger sister, portraying the tolerant older sibling, older by an entire year.

The two girls were the daughters of Gray's best friends and fellow Sigma colleagues, Monk Kokkalis and Kathryn Bryant, who were presently in the kitchen readying the small party that would follow this ceremony. Gray heard the easy comfort of their conversation, interspersed with quiet laughter and the occasional louder snort of amusement from Monk, which was a fair approximation of a goose's mating call.

He and the others had come to China from D.C. late last week to celebrate Jack's second birthday with the boy's maternal grandmother.

Guan-yin circled those sitting on the floor around Jack. Her name meant *goddess of mercy*. Though as the dragonhead of the *Duàn zhī* Triad, such a moniker was likely more ironic than apt. Gray knew that if he and Seichan had *not* come to Hong Kong with Jack, no *mercy* would've been afforded them. Guan-yin had been furious enough that she had missed Jack's pivotal first birthday.

Clearly, the boy's grandmother intended to make up for it.

The slender woman wore a hooded robe, revealing a long cascade of black hair with a single streak of gray along one edge of her face, the same edge that bore the curve of a deep purplish scar. It curled from her cheek to across her left brow, sparing her eye. She hid the disfigurement in public—not out of shame, but because it was a well-known marker of who she was. Her status, as both dragonhead and the Boss of Macau, invited both reverence and enmity. But in her villa atop the Peak, she could let her guard down. Not that she needed any protection—the grounds were heavily patrolled by the elite of her triad. Plus, even in her early sixties, she was wickedly skilled with the knives and daggers hidden in her robes.

Guan-yin settled another stack of money-stuffed red envelopes atop those already resting on a side table. Scores of wrapped presents also crowded there. Clearly, there were few in her organization who were not going to honor her grandson with a gift.

Protecting that pile was Guan-yin's ever-present shadow. Zhuang stood half a head taller than Gray. The older man's snow-white hair was pulled back and knotted into a long tail. His face was lineless and smooth. His every move had a silky power to it.

As one envelope slipped from the pile, the man deftly caught it without glancing aside and returned it to its proper place. Across his back, he carried the scabbard of an eighteenth-century Chinese Dao saber. The man never mentioned its history, beyond the weapon's age. But in the past Gray had watched Zhuang wield the blade and knew the centuries had not dulled its edge.

Guan-yin silently thanked Zhuang for rescuing the envelope with the lightest brush of her fingers across his upper arm. From the way Zhuang's eyes lingered on her as she crossed back to the gathering,

Gray suspected the man served more of a role than just a personal bodyguard.

Gray envied the quietness of their affection for each other.

He glanced to Jack's left, where the boy's mother knelt.

I wish the same could be said for our relationship.

Seichan looked seemingly calm, awaiting their son's decision. She was dressed in black slacks and a matching jacket, embroidered with flowers only a few shades lighter. Her hair fell in a smooth ebony plait past her shoulders. Despite her patient expression, Gray knew her well enough to recognize the tense pinch to her emerald eyes, the slight rise in her shoulders as muscles clenched across her back.

She was a tightly wound spring.

And not about Jack's future destiny.

Gray still felt the heavy weight in his sportscoat's breast pocket.

What was I thinking?

Guan-yin leaned down to kiss Seichan on the cheek. "*Chúc mừng sinh nhật, Con gái,*" she said in Vietnamese, her native tongue, wishing her daughter a happy birthday.

Seichan reached to her mother's hand and wished her the same. "*Chúc mừng sinh nhật, Mẹ.*"

Smoothly, Guan-yin knelt on Jack's other side, resting a palm atop his head, drawing his attention back from the cockatoo. "*Chúc mừng sinh nhật, Jack.*"

Seichan had already explained the Vietnamese tradition for celebrating birthdays. The actual date of one's birth was seldom acknowledged. All birthdays were celebrated, no matter the true date, on *Tet Nguyen Đan*, the Vietnamese New Year. The holiday fell on the first new moon after January 20. The same as the Chinese New Year, the eve of which had been celebrated wildly and raucously last night.

Jack's true birthdate was in another two days, but Guan-yin had insisted that her grandson be celebrated in the ways of Vietnamese, Chinese, and American traditions. There were still candles to be blown out atop the Snoopy cake—but not until the Chinese ceremony of *Zhua Zhou* was performed.

Still, like having his birthday cake two days early, Jack was a year late for this particular ceremony. While the Chinese performed this act on a child's *second* birthday, a Chinese child's *first* birthday was counted on the month after they were born. The Chinese considered the time spent *in utero* to cover the bulk of a child's first year.

Still, Guan-yin demanded that lines be blurred for her grandson. *Zhua Zhou*—or the birthday grab—would be performed today. An array of symbolic items had been arranged across the floor before Jack, each representing a predicted destiny. There was a jade abacus heralding a future in business or finance. A chicken leg for a calling as a chef. A small microphone for that potential entertainer in the family. In all, there were sixteen items for sixteen destinies.

The group all waited for Jack to pick an item.

Gray did not fail to note that Seichan had centered a tiny sword closest to Jack's left knee. It needed no explanation for the destiny it represented. Guan-yin, ever the grandmother, had snuck a toy stethoscope near Jack's other knee. Apparently, all grandparents wanted a future doctor in the family.

Gray hadn't bothered with such foolishness.

No one's fate is decided like this.

Still, Gray sat straighter as Jack leaned forward. The boy gained his feet and took his first steps into the future. An expectant hush fell over the room. By now, Monk and Kat had joined them, standing at the entrance to the kitchen. Even Zhuang, drawn by the suspense, stepped away from his post to watch the action.

Jack crossed through the cluster of objects as if navigating a minefield. He finally dropped to his knees, then his hands. He reached to an object at the very edge, shadowed by the arm of a couch and hidden under a drape of a velvet throw.

Once obtained, the boy dropped heavily to his backside, giggling at his new treasure and proudly lifting it for all to see.

Gray lunged forward and grabbed it. "Who put a grenade over here?"

The answer came from the hallway behind him. "That's my godson, all right."

Gray swung around and glared at Kowalski.

The gorilla of a man stood in boxers, flip-flops, and a T-shirt. From his red eyes and the pained set to his lips, he was still hungover from the New Year celebrations that ran into the early morning.

"Don't worry," Kowalski grumbled to them all. "It's a dud. From the Korean War. I picked it up at a night market a couple days back. Knew Jack would love it. Got future demolitions expert written all over him. Just like me."

Gray groaned. "Maybe we'd better try this again."

Seichan nodded, a rare point of agreement between them of late. "We're definitely doing it again."

10:18 P.M.

Seichan stood at the railing of the dark balcony and stared down at the walled garden below. A scatter of small lanterns glowed, illuminating dark ponds, arched bridges, and tinkling bamboo fountains. The scent of winter-blooming Bauhinia orchid trees sweetened the gentle night breezes.

Behind her, the villa slowly succumbed to the night. Gray was showering after getting Jack settled to bed. Monk, Kat, and the girls had retired to a private cabana within the walled grounds. Kowalski had set off into the city, trailed by a pair of triad guards—though their presence was likely less to protect the large man as to keep him from triggering an international incident.

Their group had traveled from the States under fake names and with forged passports. The goal was to keep a low profile. Since they were not here in any official capacity, they had to tread lightly. On paper, Hong Kong remained a special administrative region of the People's Republic, with a separate governing and economic system from the mainland. But the principle of "one country, two systems" had grown so blurred of late as to make the two nearly indistinguishable in governance, especially following the harsh crackdown of protests in 2019 and then the strict quarantines during Covid.

Despite these changes, their group's trespass into Hong Kong was facilitated by two factors.

First, Sigma remained a clandestine organization, operating at the periphery of military structure. Members were former soldiers with the Armed Forces, mostly special ops, who had been covertly recruited by DARPA, the Defense Department's research-and-development agency. The operatives were re-trained in various scientific disciplines to act as first-strike field agents and investigative teams whenever a global threat should arise. In that capacity, Sigma missions remained entirely off-the-books, operating in a shadowy realm that blurred the lines between intelligence services, military operations, and scientific research.

Second, even with all the subterfuge, their group in Hong Kong was undoubtedly under surveillance and their identity was surely known. It was a game intelligence services played, to pretend not to notice another agency's trespass, while keeping close tabs. Unless their group posed an immediate threat to Chinese security, their presence would be tolerated. No one would act against them without provocation.

At least for now.

Still, as Seichan stood at the balcony rail, she remained guarded, which was her steady state at all times. With the exception of the tiny lanterns in the garden, the only light came from the cold glitter of stars and the distant neon shine of Hong Kong's skyscrapers. The moon had already set, not that it would have cast any light. With the Chinese New Year coming to an end, the phase of the lunar cycle—the new moon—was but a dark shadow sliding across the stars.

It was how she had felt most of her life.

A shadow moving across the brightness of the world.

The curtains shifted behind her, allowing a sliver of lamplight to slice across the balcony. The slider glided open, and a silk-robed figure pushed out onto the balcony. Her mother crossed toward her, bringing along the awkwardness that had never fully cleared between them.

Despite being reunited four years before, a certain discomfort remained. A gulf of more than twenty years—when each had thought the other was dead—had proven to be a hard bridge to cross. After they had rediscovered each other, Seichan had spent considerable time with her mother, but during the last couple of years, the gaps between visits had grown. The last time she had come with Jack had been ten months ago.

Upon reaching the balcony rail, her mother kept silent, as if testing these waters before speaking. Guan-yin used the time to withdraw a crumpled cellophane pack from her robe and tap a cigarette loose. She slipped it to her lips. She patted her clothes, looking for a lighter.

Seichan sighed and removed an antique Dunhill lighter from a pocket. It was brass and plated in silver. She snapped it open, rolled up a flame, and offered it to her mother.

Guan-yin leaned down to light her cigarette. The flame illuminated her jagged scar, a wound carved across her cheek by an interrogator with the Vietnamese secret police twenty-six years before. Her mother had turned that wound into a badge of honor by incorporating it into an intricate tattoo, transforming it into the tail of the dragon now inked across cheek and brow. It matched the silver dragon pendant hanging from her neck. Seichan wore a similar one, but it was subtly different, sculpted from a childhood memory of her mother's pendant.

As her mother straightened, puffing out a stream of smoke, Seichan's hand drifted to her dragon. She pictured herself as a girl, sprawled on her belly next to a garden pond, not unlike one of those below. She remembered tracing a finger in the water, trying to lure up a golden carp—then her mother's face appeared in the rippling reflection, unscarred and perfect, sunlight glinting off the silver dragon resting at her mother's throat.

The moment felt like someone else's life.

Seichan still struggled to fully bring past and present together. *If they ever would.* Like their two pendants, their two lives had been forged and set into hard metal, leaving them forever similar, but never the same.

"Jack has grown so much," Guan-yin finally whispered to the night, breaking the silence.

Seichan heard the scolding edge in those few words, admonishing her long lapse between visits. "It has been hard to get away."

Her mother merely exhaled a stream of smoke, leaving the accusa-
tion hanging in the air as much as the pall.

Seichan waved aside the cloud, along with the tack of the conversation. "I didn't know you smoked."

"Zhuang doesn't like it. He keeps hiding my packs."

"Clearly, he takes his role as your *body*guard quite seriously. Maybe
you should heed him."

"I can take care of myself, Chi."

Seichan bristled at the use of her old childhood name. In Vietnamese, Chi meant *twig*. Her mother had christened her triad *Duàn zhī*—
which meant *broken twig*—after the daughter she had thought had
died. And in many ways, that girl had died.

"You know I prefer Seichan. Or shall I start calling you by your old
name, Mai Phuong Ly?"

Her mother stiffened. Neither of them were their past selves. And
neither liked to be reminded of the loss they had sustained or the misery that followed.

For the first nine years of her life, Seichan had lived in a small village
in Vietnam, raised by her mother. Those bright and happy years had
ended one awful night, when men in military uniforms had burst into
their home and dragged her mother away, bloody-faced and screaming.

It would take decades for Seichan to learn the truth, how the
Vietnamese secret police had discovered her mother's dalliance with
Seichan's father, an American diplomat, and of the love that grew from
there. The Ministry had sought to ply U.S. secrets out of her mother,
holding and torturing her in a prison outside Ho Chi Minh City. A
year later, she escaped during a prison riot, and for a short period of
time, due to a clerical error, she had been declared dead, killed during
that uprising. It was that lucky mistake that gave her mother enough of
a head start to flee Vietnam and vanish into the greater world.

By then, abandoned and alone, Seichan had been shifted through a
series of squalid orphanages across Southeast Asia—half starved most
of the time, maltreated the rest—until finally she'd taken to the streets
and back alleys of Seoul. It was there that a shadowy terrorist organization, called the Guild, found and recruited her. Their trainers had

systematically stripped away not only her remaining childhood but also much of her humanity, leaving behind only an assassin.

With the help of Sigma Force, she eventually took down the Guild. Afterward, she had been left adrift, orphaned once again, until she discovered a new purpose in Sigma—and a new home and family with Gray.

Her mother took another long draw on her cigarette.

Similar to Seichan's own path, her mother had turned her anger and grief into purpose, founding the *Duàn zhī* Triad in Hong Kong and carving her own place into this hard world.

"*Deui m hjyuh*," her mother apologized in Cantonese.

Seichan dipped her chin in acknowledgment. "It is late. I should be getting to bed."

Her mother touched her arm before she could leave. "I heard you declined Gray's proposal last night. That is why I came out to speak to you."

Seichan closed her eyes. "That is between us, Mother."

"He asked me for your hand. Two days ago. Before the eve of the New Year. I gave him my blessing. I wanted you to know. If it makes any difference."

"It doesn't."

Her mother looked down, but not quick enough to hide the wince in her eyes.

"I don't wish to be married," Seichan said. "Ever."

"It is a sentiment I understand. I'm glad you turned him down."

Seichan glanced sharply at her mother. "But I thought you gave Gray your *blessing*."

"A blessing is not *approval*. He is a good man. And a good father. I can see that. If you had accepted his hand, I would not have objected. But you are my daughter. I can see your heart has been hardened by all that you have survived. As has mine. That is nothing to be ashamed of. We can love—both a man and any child he gives us—but we have no need of a husband. We remain our own islands, inviolate and guarded by necessary shoals. That is who we are. Both mother and daughter."

Guan-yin fingered the unbendable silver of her pendant.

Seichan swallowed, both disconcerted and relieved to hear these words. She remained silent for several breaths, then challenged this cold sentiment. "What of my father?" she asked. "If he had offered, would you have married him?"

"You ask for an answer to a question that could never be put to me. You know that. Such a union was impossible."

"But if he had defied his family and asked you, what would have been your response?"

Guan-yin turned to the rail and looked a thousand miles off. "I . . . I do not know. I was young." Her shoulders sagged at some memory of her former self. "Better it was never asked."

Ready to leave her mother to this reverie, Seichan turned toward the balcony door.

"But you *were* asked," Guan-yin said behind her. "By a good man, with a proud heart. And with your refusal, you risk losing him."

Seichan continued to the door, forcing her back straighter. "If it takes a ring to hold him, then it's better he does leave."

Upon reaching the balcony door, she flashed to Gray down on one knee as fireworks cascaded across the Hong Kong skyline. Their dinner had been private—her mother took Jack and the others to watch the New Year celebrations aboard a boat on Victoria Harbour. He had worn a dark gray suit, with a crisply starched shirt and a silvery blue tie that matched the ice of his eyes. His dark hair had been slicked down, even the stubborn cowlick that always gave him a boyish look, masking the lethality in those firm muscles and quick reflexes. The only mark of casualness was the persistent dark stubble that shadowed his cheeks, courtesy of his Welsh heritage.

Then he had withdrawn a ring box.

I should've expected it before that moment.

But she had not. In the past, they had talked about marriage, both jokingly and at other times with some earnestness, more so after Jack was born. She had no desire to be married, content with matters as they were. She had believed the matter to be settled.

Yet, in hindsight, she also suspected the reason behind the sudden proposal.

Friction had been growing between them of late, accompanied by arguments and long silences. When Jack was younger, their focus on the boy had masked a growing frustration on both their parts. Gray wanted more from her, even talking about another child. But Seichan could not dismiss the feeling of being trapped. All her adult life, she had been under the thumb of the Guild, her actions directed and proscribed. And while she loved Jack with an ache that sometimes crippled her, she wanted more, especially as the boy grew older, heading toward independence. She felt pulled in two different directions, and the straining only grew worse over time.

So, when Gray had bent a knee in the villa's dining room, the ring he had offered her had felt more like a set of shackles. She had tried to explain what she was feeling, what she believed. He had nodded, accepting her at her word, but the wounded look never left his eyes. They had made love that night, slowly and passionately, as if both were trying to reassure each other and themselves.

But this morning, the tension continued. The various celebrations of Jack's birthday had allowed them some space to further put this behind them, but she was not sure if it was enough—or if it ever would be.

As she pulled the slider open, a low rumble rattled the door in its frame. She froze until the balcony began to jolt, and the chimes in the lower garden rang stridently in alarm.

She turned and waved her mother away from the rail. "Get back from there!"

Off in the distance, the neon skyscrapers of Hong Kong swayed and rolled. Patches of the city fell dark, first over in Kowloon across the harbor, then spreading to the island here. It looked as if the dark moon had descended out of the sky, obliterating the lights.

Her mother joined her, and they hurried inside, away from the windows. Zhuang came sweeping to them from a back room.

"Get everyone down into the open gardens," Guan-yin ordered crisply. "It'll be safer there."

"I'll get Jack and Gray," Seichan said.

But before she could take three steps, muffled gunfire erupted outside. She glanced back at her mother. The sharper blast of a rocket-propelled grenade exploded out in the garden, accompanied by a bright flash of fire and a concussion that rattled the balcony windows.

Her mother's features were preternaturally calm. "Go to the garage bunker instead," she ordered both Zhuang and Seichan. "We'll regroup there."

They both fled in opposite directions.

As Seichan ran, the quaking steadily worsened.

3

Phoebe stifled a yawn—but not out of boredom. It was well after midnight, and she was bone-tired. She and Jazz had managed to nab a late-night ROV time slot. There were still another three sites that she wanted to sample.

"Where to next?" Jazz asked, seated at the booth's control station.

Fifteen matching cubicles ringed Kalliste Tier, the fourth level of *Titan Station Down*. Each booth was separated by walls that ran from floor to ceiling and could be closed off by an accordion-style folding door both for privacy and to limit the ambient light when viewing the ROV's camera footage.

Phoebe leaned over Jazz's shoulder and studied the forty-five-inch monitor. It displayed a gorgeous high-definition view of the coral reefs sweeping past the vehicle. A window in the screen's corner plotted the ROV's relative position as it traveled across the illuminated fields. A trio of coordinates blipped crimson on the same map.

Phoebe pointed to one at the very edge, where the station's lamplight faded into darkness. "Let's continue to Loci A17."

"Got it."

Jazz manipulated the console's toggles and drove the ROV farther out. Other knobs and switches were spread in an arc before her seat. They operated the array of equipment aboard each ROV: claw and caliper attachments, cutting tools and sampling jars. Unfortunately, the ROV's range was limited to five hundred meters, the length of its fiber-optic tether.

As Jazz homed in on Loci A17, Phoebe studied the darkness beyond the station's lamps, where the ROVs could not travel.

Farther out in the sunless depths, the Titan Project had seeded forty-two AUVs. The autonomous underwater vehicles operated on preset programs, mapping the surrounding landscape. They ran on batteries that lasted for a week before needing to be recharged. Unfortunately, the AUVs were not good platforms for collecting samples. Instead, they were used for high-resolution mapping and had been in operation for six months, tracking the surrounding landscape, all the way to the very edges of the deep trenches to the east.

During the past weeks, Phoebe had reviewed the AUVs' camera and sonar logs. She had mapped the location of two dozen coral beds. None were larger than the one under the station, but several lay far deeper. She wanted to collect samples from there, too, but that would have to wait another three days, when she was scheduled to leave on a far-ranging HOV survey.

But until then . . .

"We're almost there," Jazz said, then whistled appreciatively. "And you picked out a beaut."

Phoebe returned her attention to the coral beds closer at hand. On the screen, a six-meter-tall sprout of coral waved in the deep-ocean current. Its branches were densely packed and feathered by fields of emerald-green polyps.

"I spotted this lonely giant on the first day," Phoebe commented. "It looks like a species of black coral."

"If so, it'd be a record breaker. It's easily twice the size of any that I've seen."

Excited to learn more, Phoebe leaned closer. Black coral came in hundreds of species, with polyps of every hue: brilliant yellows, shimmering whites, even dark blues and purples. Yet, all of them had the same characteristic jet-black calcareous branches, lined by tiny sharp spikes. It was for the latter reason that some black corals were also called *thorn* corals. And green ones, like this specimen, were sometimes named Christmas Tree corals due to their brilliant, dense branches.

So far, Phoebe had identified fourteen species of black coral sharing this reef, but her interest in this specimen went beyond its sheer size. "For it to have grown this large," she said, "it must be ancient."

Jazz nodded. "A veritable sequoia of black coral."

"Exactly."

Species of black coral were considered to be the longest-living marine animals. A polyp species in Hawaiian waters had been dated at 4,270 years old and continued to thrive.

Jazz manipulated the controls and circled the ROV around the tall specimen. She recorded it from every angle. "Did you ever get a consensus from the topside researchers about the age of these coral fields? I mean, how long has this oasis been hiding down here, waiting for us?"

"It's still not clear. A marine archaeologist up in *Titan X*'s science globe is repeating some preliminary studies. He cored out a deep sample from the thickest areas of the reef and is using laser ablation to date it. The same technique was employed to clock the age of coral beds in the Mediterranean. That study concluded the coral had been growing continuously for more than 400,000 years."

Jazz glanced back at her. "Wait. You said the archaeologist was *repeating* his tests. If he's doing that, then he must be double-checking something that *requires* double-checking." She must have read Phoebe's expression. "You've heard something already! And you've not told me?"

"Like I said, it's still preliminary."

"Tell me, or I'll crash this ROV straight into the sand."

Phoebe smiled. "According to the archaeologist's initial surveys, he's estimating these coral beds have been here for ten million years. Maybe longer."

"Ten million . . ." Jazz whispered in awe.

"Or longer," Phoebe repeated. "There's no telling what this coral might reveal about the ancient past."

This was what intrigued her the most about deep-sea coral and continued to be the focus of her research. Because coral grew so slowly at these extreme depths, their calcified skeletons incorporated ocean elements, creating an archive of marine conditions that predated human-ity. Studying those preserved records promised to offer valuable insight into how the changes in the ocean affected coral growth, both in the past and into the future.

She remembered her earlier conversation with William Byrd and his concern about the state of the world's reefs.

This is why I was brought here.

She didn't want to disappoint him. Though, in truth, that was only a small part of her motivation. She had always had a love and fascination with the ocean. It was her refuge and playground.

Back in Barbados, her father had been a hot-tempered Puerto Rican, prone to sudden angry outbursts, who had used his fists as much as his tongue to express his frustration. Her mother would do her best to shield Phoebe, sending her off when those storms grew too fierce. Phoebe had found solace and peace underwater, where the anger of the world grew muffled. She would stay down as long as possible, holding her breath, trying to get as deep as she could on a single lungful—what would later be called freediving.

After she and her mother had finally fled the abuse and settled in Southern California, Phoebe had kept close to the sea, taking up the sport with more seriousness—even earning a scholarship to help pay for her schooling.

She continued to practice the sport, still finding joy in the solitude.

She stared out at the dark depths beyond the station.

Only now I'm diving much deeper.

"Pheebs?" Jazz turned to her. "What do you want to do?"

Phoebe shook off her reverie, blaming it on her exhaustion. She pointed to the screen, to the unusual specimen. She was anxious to learn its secrets.

"Jazz, draw us closer. I want to pick out the best branch to sample."

"No problem, boss."

Jazz slowed and expertly nosed the ROV up to a dense cluster of branches and hovered the vehicle in place—or at least, tried to do so. "There's a pretty strong current. Do you want to perform the sample collection while I hold the ROV steady?"

"Will do." Phoebe shifted next to her friend. She squeezed over to the bank of controls that operated the ROV's claws, cutters, and collection equipment. She reached a fingertip to the monitor and circled a few branches of coral glowing on the screen. "Zoom in right here."

Jazz manipulated a lens toggle. A dense field of the emerald-green polyps swelled into view.

After some fine-tuning, Jazz flinched. "Boss, I think you might've been *wrong* around this being a species of black coral."

Phoebe grimaced, hating to be mistaken, but realizing Jazz was likely right. "From a distance, I was so sure," she mumbled. "The skeleton of this coral is jet black. And up close, you can even see thorny spikes along its bark, typical of such species."

"But you can't ignore the polyps themselves," Jazz warned. "Just count their arms. These each have *eight*. Just like little octopuses."

"Whereas black corals only have *six*." Phoebe sighed her concession on this point. "Still, it's intriguing. Maybe we'll learn more once we collect a sample."

"It could be a new species," Jazz said.

"Let's hope so."

Phoebe reached a claw toward a polyp-packed branch. As the jaws neared the stalk, dozens of the polyps unfurled long, thin threads. They stretched a foot long and battered at the approaching steel claw.

"Sweeper tentacles," Jazz said with clear amazement.

Phoebe moved closer, equally astonished.

Many species of coral came armed with such weapons. But their tentacles were never this long. Sweepers, like this, were used to hunt prey beyond the reach of a polyp's tiny circlet of arms. They were notoriously tipped with a potent nematocyst, a venomous stinger for stunning prey. Sweepers were also employed as a means of territorial aggression, to ward off the encroachment of any other coral.

"Whatever species this is," Jazz said, "it's clearly not keen on us sampling it."

Phoebe shifted the claw closer. "We'll remove just the tip of this stalk. It can't begrudge us that."

As the claw's cutter touched the coral, a flurry of motion drew a gasp from both women. Polyps burst out of their calcified nests, escaping like a startled flock of birds. Once free, they sped across the water with tiny spasms of their bodies and twirls of their arms. Several even attacked the claw, grabbing hold and clinging tight.

"What the hell?" Jazz asked. "*No* coral does that."

Phoebe squinted and noted a few polyps hadn't made their escape from the coral. Before they did, she quickly snapped off the branch and vacuumed the twig and its last few residents into a self-sealing sample jar.

Once done, Phoebe straightened from the console. "That was definitely strange."

Normally, a polyp remained sessile and rooted into the coral, living and dying in place. While it could periodically spin off tiny medusae of itself during its life cycle, it never abandoned the coral.

"I've never seen anything like it," Phoebe said.

"No one has." Jazz stared wide-eyed at her. "This may not just be another *species* of coral, but possibly an entirely new *subphylum* of Cnidaria."

Cnidaria encompassed a slew of different subphyla and classes, from jellyfishes to anemones, to all manner of coral, even strange parasites. If Jazz was right, they had just made an astounding discovery.

Still, she tamped down her excitement.

"Let's not get ahead of ourselves," Phoebe warned and checked her watch. "We're almost at the end of our allotted time slot. We can figure out *what* we discovered once we have it back at our lab."

Jazz nodded and began retracting the ROV.

As the vehicle retreated away from the specimen, Phoebe stared at the screen. Distracted earlier, she had failed to note another peculiarity of the giant coral tree. The sands around it looked devoid of any other life. No corals grew within meters of the emerald-green outcropping. No fish poked about its fringes. No crabs scuttled under its bower.

She pictured the jetting polyps, the whipping sweeper tentacles.

While much remained unknown about this specimen, one aspect was clear.

Whatever it was, it was highly aggressive.

4

Carrying his son in his arms, Gray rushed down the shaking concrete stairs toward the garage on the villa's first floor. Dust shifted from overhead as the earthquake's rumbling wave contorted the building.

He raced barefooted, wearing only a pair of sweatpants. He had been in the shower when the world had started shaking. He hadn't even had time to towel off when Seichan had rushed into the bedroom. She had come to secure Jack and to alert Gray about an attack on the villa. Only after her warning had he heard the muffled popping of automatic gunfire and a few louder blasts. Seichan had quickly got them all moving downstairs.

As he leaped off the last steps and into the cavernous eight-car garage, Guan-yin waved to him from a wall to the right. She was guarded by four men with Chinese QBZ automatic rifles, all carbine variants with shorter barrels.

"This way!" Guan-yin called to them.

Seichan crowded behind Gray. "Go!"

He ran toward Guan-yin, sidling along a row of Audis, Porsches, and Aston Martins. A million-dollar Bugatti Chiron rested on a turntable. It was plainly profitable to be the Boss of Macau.

When he reached Guan-yin, one of her men hauled open a secret door camouflaged into the wall's wainscotting. She pointed down the revealed ramp. "Get into the bunker."

Gray hesitated—and not just because he was reluctant to seek shelter underground during a quake. He rocked Jack in his arms. Despite the continual stomach-churning roll of the ground, the boy remained half asleep, exhausted from the long day of excitement, dead to the world as only a two-year-old could be. Jack rested his cheek on Gray's shoulder. But his son was not the only child in danger.

"What about Monk, Kat, and the girls?" Gray asked.

He was prepared to pass Jack to Seichan and go look for them. Monk's family had taken up residence in a guest cabana adjoining the walled garden. The girls had insisted on being close to the koi ponds and the many ducks that floated or patrolled the grounds.

"Zhuang went to fetch them," Guan-yin said. "He will keep them safe."

Her confidence was proven well founded when a side door crashed open on the far side of the garage. Past that door, a breezeway connected to the gardens. Zhuang and another triad guard rushed Monk and Kat into the garage. They hurried behind the row of cars. Monk and Kat each carried one of the girls.

Through the open doorway, the sounds of the firefight erupted louder. A war was being waged out in the gardens. A sharper blast echoed above, followed by the brighter tinkle of glass. Someone had shot a grenade into the villa. The attackers had mounted a full-scale assault, likely taking advantage of the quake's confusion to strike.

Gray knew street battles periodically broke out between the city's aggressive triads. The clashes were often as fierce as any urban warfare, but he had thought no one would dare assault the *Duàn zhī* Triad, which ruled Hong Kong and Macau with an iron fist and was respected and feared throughout Southeast Asia. An open assault upon the dragonhead's personal home was especially surprising. According to triad code, such an act was deemed dishonorable and was considered a blood sin, one that would require retribution, often spanning generations. Centuries-old feuds and vendettas were waged for far less of an affront.

From the anger shadowing Guan-yin's features, she would use all her resources to exact her revenge. She also had pacts and oaths with a dozen other triads. Whoever had attacked the villa had lit a powder keg that would soon rip across Hong Kong and beyond.

Monk rushed across the long garage with Kat. Monk was in boxers and a T-shirt with a Georgia Bulldog growling on it, which matched his expression. Kat wore a belted robe, her auburn hair disheveled and loose. The girls, both dressed in bright pajamas, were not taking the chaos and uproar as quietly as Jack. Both sobbed and clung chokingly to their parents.

Rage fired Monk's eyes. The furious flush to his face had risen over the top of his shaved scalp. The arm that carried Penny was bunched into a protective knot of muscles. Kat looked no less ferocious, only her expression was tempered by worry.

Before they had crossed half the distance, huge explosions blasted three of the garage doors off their tracks, sending panels flying inside. With reflexes born of his Green Beret training, Monk scooped Kat and Harriet under his free arm and ducked them all behind an Audi SUV. Debris crashed into windshields and across hoods and roofs. Smoke billowed heavily into the garage.

Zhuang dove next to them, cradling a SIG Sauer P226 in his hands. The other triad member was a step too slow and got struck by a twirling panel, nearly decapitating him in the process.

Gunfire strafed the garage. Outside, assailants blindly fired through the pall. Guan-yin's men returned the volley with chattering rips from their assault rifles. Unfortunately, her men shot just as wildly, but for the moment, it was enough to deter the attackers from entering the garage.

Gray turned to pass Jack to Seichan, ready to go help Monk and Kat. But Seichan snatched a rifle from one of the gunmen's grips and raced across the garage, firing one-handed. Gray had forgotten how lightning fast she could be, especially when fueled by adrenaline and fury. With no other choice, Gray retreated a few steps down the ramp to shelter Jack, but he kept the garage in view.

Seichan reached the others, gathered them up, and got them running low, sticking to the shelter of the row of vehicles.

They had nearly made it across when a figure came rushing into the garage, low, an FN SCAR at his shoulder. The battle rifle was outfitted with an undermount grenade launcher. Guan-yin's men fired at him, but the assailant ducked between an Aston Martin and the Bugatti, aiming his weapon straight at Seichan and the others.

Not even Seichan was quick enough to respond to the ambush.

Her mother was.

Guan-yin struck a fist against a large button on the wall next to her. The turntable under the Bugatti lurched as it was activated, throwing the gunman off balance. It was enough for Zhuang to bring his SIG around and fire three quick shots. Two to the chest and one to the head.

The man dropped, allowing Zhuang and the others to cross the last of the garage.

"Get below," Guan-yin ordered.

They all fled down the concrete ramp. The secret door sealed behind them. Sconces in the shape of winged dragons lined the walls. The ramp ended in a low-roofed space a quarter the size of the garage above. Gray had expected the bunker to be a fortified safe room, but it was another garage.

Only here there were no expensive sports cars or luxury sedans. Three armored and rivetted vehicles were parked side by side. Matte-gray plating sealed the exterior of a trio of Alpha Titans—armored Mercedes G550 4x4s. They sat on tall tires. The windows were surely bulletproofed and ballistically rated.

"Split up and get inside," she ordered them. "We're heading off this mountain."

"Can't we stay here?" Kat asked, clutching hard to Harriet. The girl's sobbing had quieted to shaking gasps. "The quake has ended, and you've got an army out there."

Monk nodded, hiking Penny higher in his arms.

Amidst all the chaos, Gray hadn't noted the ground had finally stopped rolling. He understood Monk and Kat's concern for their frightened girls. By now, even Jack had woken with a pinched expression, heading toward a wail.

Still, Gray stared up at the cracks in the concrete roof overhead. Dust and sand trickled from them. "No, Guan-yin's right," he warned.

"There could be aftershocks. We don't want to be in here if there are any strong ones."

Seichan hefted her rifle to her shoulder. "And we can't count on the enemy not finding this place. They clearly knew the layout of my mother's villa, well enough to purposefully herd us into the first-floor garage, to lead us into that ambush. They must have tortured staff to get such details."

"Two maids never showed up to work this morning," Guan-yin admitted. "I attributed it to too much celebrating on New Year's Eve."

Seichan turned to her mother. "Did either of them know about this bunker?"

"No, only Zhuang and a handful of my deputies know about it. But some of my staff may have heard rumors."

Gray waved to the Titans. "Then we can't stay here. The enemy likely only missed this bunker because they acted hastily, deciding to take advantage of the quake versus waiting for a fuller reconnaissance."

"Then let's not give them a second chance," Monk said.

They all got moving. Even with GPS, the Peak's roads formed a tangled labyrinth. Needing the expert guidance of locals, their group had to split up. Zhuang led Monk, Kat, and the girls off into one of the Titans. Gray got behind the wheel of another with Guan-yin riding shotgun. Seichan climbed into the back with Jack and another triad member. The third vehicle was loaded with more *Duàn zhī* gunmen.

Upon Guan-yin's signal, the bunker doors rolled up. The way opened out into an overgrown niche off Mount Kellett Road. The tangled roots of a huge rubber tree masked the camouflaged exit. The Titan packed with gunmen took the lead. Gray followed, with Zhuang and the others trailing behind.

The road was pitch black. Streetlights had been extinguished by the blackout. Their group traveled dark, with headlights off. The only illumination came from the Titan's brake lights. Still, it was hard to mask the throaty growl of their vehicles' V8 engines.

They rolled as fast as they dared down the tortuous road, with a wall of rock rising on one side and a precipitous cliff dropping on the other.

In the rearview mirror, the generator-powered lights of the villa were cloaked in smoke and brightened by flames.

So far, it seemed the enemy had failed to note their escape.

Let's hope it stays that way.

A portable radio on the dashboard squawked, then Monk's voice came over the air. "What about Kowalski?" he asked, a reminder that one of their group was still missing.

11:07 P.M.

And I thought cancer was going to kill me.

Kowalski forded across a street full of milling people. He held a bundle of napkins pressed to the side of his face, where a piece of broken glass had sliced his cheek.

Before the quake, he had been holed up in a SoHo-district bar called the Old Man. He had chosen the place for its name. He certainly *felt* old after his cancer treatments. The bar had also been small and dark, which matched his mood. It was open until two in the morning, and he had planned on closing it down. He had started with a drink called Men without Women, a coffee-tasting blend of clotted Irish whiskey, stout cream, and salted arabica.

The cocktail had seemed fitting as he was traveling without his girlfriend. Maria and her sister were in the second week of a six-week anthropological project outside Stuttgart, Germany. Before she had left, he and Maria had celebrated the New Year in D.C. Then Kowalski had realized he could indulge in a *second* New Year if he traveled to Hong Kong.

He could not resist.

Especially as he had plenty of reason to celebrate.

His last biopsy result had shown no sign of a relapse. Ten months ago, he had undergone a bone marrow transplant to treat stage-three multiple myeloma, a cancer of his plasma cells. Three weeks ago, he had finished a regimen of immunosuppressive drugs. From here, it was all a matter of regaining his strength, eating well, and limiting his intake of alcohol. He had followed those instructions diligently—or at least, two out of the three. A guy needed a little fun in his life, or it wouldn't be worth living.

He had been in the middle of his second cocktail—a rum and lemon soda concoction called Soldier's Home—when the entire bar started shaking. Bottles had rattled off shelves. Mirrors had shattered. He had ducked low, keeping his drink in hand, and rode out the five-minute-long temblor. Once it ended, he and most of the city had emptied out into the streets, vacating the tall buildings and skyscrapers, wary of an aftershock.

With his cheek on fire, Kowalski crossed the street, crunching glass underfoot. He climbed the steps under a sign that read 光漢台花園 and under it, KWONG HON TERRACE GARDEN. The elevated park offered some clearance from the neighboring structures and a bit of height to view the damage. As he reached the top step, he found he was not the only one to have picked this spot.

A mob crowded the grass and the children's playground. Still, at six foot four, he could easily see over most heads. His muscular bulk and deep scowl cleared a path ahead of him. He aimed for a rail that overlooked the lower street and across the dark city. A few areas glowed with generator-powered lights. Other areas flickered with patches of flames. Sirens blared all around, adding to the cacophony of honking horns, shouted calls, and spats of gunfire.

It reminded him of something that Painter Crowe, the director of Sigma, had once warned him: *Despite appearances, the world is only one disaster away from barbarism.* At the time, prone to creating those disasters, Kowalski had tried not to take the warning personally.

Reaching the park's rail, Kowalski surveyed the quake's aftermath. Across the dark city, all the skyscrapers appeared to be still standing, though the corner of a nearby building had crumbled into the street. Lamp poles and streetlights had toppled across roads. Vast swaths of windowpanes had exploded out of their frames.

As he stood there, a hand snatched his elbow and yanked him hard. He turned with a raised fist. Before he could punch down, he recognized one of the triad guards who had accompanied him down from the hilltop villa. He was a lean-faced strap of muscle.

"Must go now," he warned Kowalski.

"Where?"

"To meet the Mountain and the others."

Kowalski knew Guan-yin was sometimes called the "Mountain Master," an honorific for her position as the triad's dragonhead. The guard turned and led Kowalski back across the park. He shoved his way through the crowd. From the man's haste, Kowalski knew something was wrong, though he wasn't sure if this summons was just because of the quake or something more dire. He followed after the man, struggling to pick out his short form through the milling throng. He nearly lost him a few times. Then the guard swung around, clearly impatient. The guard raised an arm, as if ready to scold him, but blood poured from his lips instead.

The man staggered a few steps, clutching the hilt of a knife impaled through his throat. A hand reached from behind and ripped the blade out with a savage twist. The man fell to his knees. The attacker— his face masked with a wrap of black—knocked the guard aside and stalked toward Kowalski.

Another four masked figures closed from other directions. Kowalski back-pedaled and crouched lower, attempting to hide his height among the press of people, but it was like trying to bury a watermelon in a bin of oranges.

He spotted two more masked assassins driving toward him.

Seven against one.

Bad odds.

Especially as Kowalski had no weapon, except his fists. He balled them up, ready to fight. By now, others in the crowd had noted the dead man, the masked figures. People fled for the stairs on the far side of the park.

As the mob thinned around him, the lead attacker tossed aside his knife and removed a pistol from a shoulder-holster under his jacket.

The odds were worsening by the second.

Kowalski slowed, ready to make his stand. The gunman's companions closed to either side. By then, Kowalski had realized he was not entirely weaponless.

He reached into his jacket pocket and removed his only hope. He brought it to his lips—not to kiss it, but to pantomime a threat. He pretended to bite into it, then threw the spherical black pineapple toward the gunman.

"*Shǒuléi!*" he shouted.

Kowalski had learned the Chinese word for *grenade* when he had bought the Korean relic from a night market vendor. Kowalski was suddenly glad that Gray had forced him to remove it from the villa after Jack had picked it up earlier.

The effect of his ruse was immediate. The gunman flung himself away and dove toward the retreating crowd. So did his companions.

Kowalski turned and ran the opposite way. With the crowd cleared, he reached the rail of the terrace garden and leaped over it. He plunged to the street below. The impact threw him down hard, but he rolled over his shoulder and back to his feet.

He fled into the crowd, limping a bit, and ducked around a corner.

He had barely gotten two steps when another hand grabbed him. This time he did punch his assailant. The kid's nose bounced off his knuckles. The teenager's head snapped backward, and his legs went out from under him. Still, the guy refused to let go of Kowalski's arm.

Hanging there, the kid shouted, "Blue Lantern. Blue Lantern with *Duàn zhī.*"

It took Kowalski a few more steps, dragging the teenager along with him, to recognize the term for an uninitiated member of a triad—a Blue Lantern—someone who hadn't yet earned their stripes.

Kowalski pulled the kid back upright. "What are you doing here?"

"I followed you from the villa," he gasped out, blood dripping from both nostrils. "Saw the others attacked, then watched you fly down here."

Kowalski frowned. Someone must have tipped off the attackers about the two guards sent into Hong Kong with him. But obviously the bastards had missed *one*, and Kowalski could guess why.

"Guan-yin didn't send you," Kowalski said.

"No," the kid confirmed. "I came on my own."

Clearly, the teenager was trying to earn those stripes—which Kowalski especially appreciated at the moment.

"Do you know a way out of here?" he asked.

The kid finally let go of his arm and fled ahead. "This way!"

11:16 P.M.

In the backseat, Seichan cradled Jack under one arm and rested the butt of the Chinese carbine on her other knee. She held tight to her son as the Titan rocked with every sharp turn of the twisting road.

She sat on the left side, which offered a dizzying view down a steep drop. Across the Titan, the rocky side of a hill filled the far windows. The road was unnervingly narrow, especially accounting for the size of the armored tanks that rolled down it. Worse, they still ran dark, not taking any chances, even with the villa a couple of miles behind them.

Mount Kellett Road looped around this hilltop. Ahead, a Y-junction appeared, where the road circled back upon itself, forming a single road that descended into Hong Kong proper. Beyond the intersection, the roadway was packed with condominium complexes and smaller homes.

Behind the wheel, Gray clutched the handheld radio to his lips. "Any word about Kowalski?"

Zhuang answered from the Titan behind them. "No. I alerted the men who went with him, but I've not been able to raise anyone since. I've tried repeatedly. But cell signal is patchy due to the power outage and overloaded systems."

In the front passenger seat, Seichan's mother shook her head. "They must've been ambushed, too," she said, her voice matter-of-factly certain. "We must assume your friend is dead."

"You don't know Kowalski," Gray said.

Seichan silently agreed. The man was nearly impossible to kill.

Still, if Kowalski and the others were attacked in the city, it made no sense. The *Duàn zhī* Triad was seventy thousand members strong. *So, why bother with a handful in Hong Kong?*

Ahead of them, the lead Titan reached the Y-junction. It slowed to merge onto the descending road. A thin crowd lined the road after fleeing the precarious perch of the cliffside homes. Several groups milled into the street.

The Titan ahead honked to clear the way as it crossed the intersection. But Seichan noted a few pedestrians were already in motion, with panicked looks on their faces, seeing something their group couldn't.

She lunged forward to Gray. "Stop!"

From the other leg of the Y, a huge tractor-trailer slammed into the side of the lead Titan, sending it spinning away. Smaller trucks followed behind the tractor, closing off the junction. From their open beds, armed men leaped out.

At Seichan's shout, Gray had already begun braking.

Gunfire pelted the front of their armored Titan, sounding like golf ball–size hail. Bullets spattered against the bulletproof windshield.

Guan-yin pointed to the forest on the left. "That way!"

Gray gunned the Titan into a hard turn—aiming toward a wall of towering trees and a steep drop. A grenade struck the road near their flank. The blast jolted the Titan. A flash of flames and smoke washed across the side windows. As the concussion cleared the view, Seichan spotted the shooter lowering an RPG launcher.

It can't be . . .

Then the Titan slammed into the forest's edge and kept going. The front of the SUV tipped steeply. Only then did Seichan notice the thin trail descending from the road, too thin for their vehicle. The Titan crashed through saplings and bounced off larger trunks. More explosions and gunfire erupted behind them as the other Titan followed the path that Gray carved through the forest.

Belted in place, Seichan dropped her rifle and clutched Jack with both arms. He hollered and wailed, which stoked her fury to a red-hot blaze.

"Gonna get stuck!" Gray shouted.

"Keep going," Guan-yin insisted.

The large tires and portal axles drove them onward for another fifty yards—then the forest broke ahead of them, opening into a packed gravel trail nearly as wide as their vehicle. It was lined by dense ferns and tangles of tall banyan trees.

Guan-yin pointed. "Go right!"

Gray swung the Titan sharply. The vehicle lifted on two wheels before crashing back down. With four tires under it again, the Titan sped off. Behind them, the second vehicle crashed into view and made the turn more deftly. Zhuang must have known about this trail through the Peak's highlands.

"Where are we?" Gray asked as they got moving.

"Hiking path and fire road," Guan-yin answered.

To confound any pursuers, she directed Gray through a crisscrossing of other trails. With their vehicles still running dark, Seichan searched the surrounding forests for any other lights, for any sign of the enemy in pursuit. But the woodlands remained dark.

"These trails form a maze across the Peak," Guan-yin said. "With a half-dozen exits across Hong Kong Island and twice that number of lesser-known ones. Those damned *pok gaai* cannot cover them all."

The portable radio chirped from where Gray had tossed it atop the Titan's dashboard.

Zhuang's voice traveled from the other Titan. "I just heard from Hong Kong. From Bolin Chén."

Guan-yin leaned over and nabbed the radio. She lifted it to her lips. "*Bolin Chén? Shuí?*" she asked, inquiring about the identity of the person.

"*Guà lán dēng long,*" Zhuang answered in Cantonese, claiming the caller had been one of the triad's Blue Lanterns.

"What's happening?" Gray asked.

Guan-yin held up a palm and continued in Cantonese, while guiding Gray through more twists and turns.

Seichan used the moment to rock Jack, trying to calm his fear, which had settled to a quiet trembling, but it did nothing to assuage her own fury.

Guan-yin finally ended the communication with a sour expression.

"What?" Gray asked, plainly anxious about Kowalski.

"Your friend is safe. In the custody of one of the triad's youngest. I've ordered him to take your man and meet us at Deep Water Bay on the island's southern side, away from the main city. I have a catamaran moored at the Royal Hong Kong Yacht Club. No one knows about it, except Zhuang. We can take it to Macau. No triad will dare attack our stronghold there."

With Jack somewhat settled, Seichan leaned forward. "It wasn't another triad that attacked us, Mother. It was one of *our* enemies."

Gray frowned in the rearview mirror at her. "What do you mean?"

Seichan pictured the assailant who had lowered the RPG launcher back at the intersection. There was no mistaking the Russian woman. She hadn't even bothered hiding her pale features. Her snow-white hair had glowed in the darkness, reflecting the truck's lights. The tattoo across her right cheek formed a black shadow of a sun with kinked rays—only now the symbol was distorted by a scar across it.

"Who attacked us?" Gray pressed her.

"Valya," she answered, naming the Russian assassin. "Valya Mikhailov."

Seichan recalled their last encounter two years ago, just before Jack was born. Atop a blizzard-swept mountain in West Virginia, she had fired two shots at the Russian, a ghost out of Seichan's past with the Guild. One bullet had struck the assassin's chest. The other had grazed her tattooed cheek, toppling the woman off the cliff and into deep snow. The Russian's body had never been recovered.

Since that night, a fist of tension had knotted inside Seichan. She had been waiting for this moment, expecting it. When she had spotted Valya on the road, she had felt more relief than surprise.

Seichan had always known that snowy hilltop battle had never truly ended.

At last, it begins again.

5

Exhausted and bleary-eyed, Phoebe hauled her way up the spiral stair-case. She hoped she could sleep. The strange discovery of the hostile coral tree kept her buzzed and agitated, but any further study would have to wait until the morning.

She had left Jazz down below to secure the collected specimens from the late-night ROV run. They needed everything placed into one of the biology lab's high-pressure isolation tanks. To ensure the integrity of any sea life, the specimens had to be maintained at the same pressure as outside. Otherwise, the extreme change could instantly kill an organism, even destroying the tissue integrity as its cells exploded.

Can't let that happen.

Phoebe had wanted to stay and assist Jazz, but her post-grad student had chased her off, demanding she get some rest. Phoebe had offered only a half-hearted objection. So far, her sleep had been fitful aboard the station, especially as all the women shared a cramped dormitory on Delphin Tier. Everyone's schedules were cycled around the clock. No one had their own bunk. Instead, like on a military submarine, they shared beds across shifts, what submariners called "hot racking."

Between the warm bed and the constant clanking, humming, and echoing of the station, she had not slept well.

Jazz seemed unaffected by it all—then again, she was a decade younger.

Phoebe climbed past the thick hatch that separated Elektra from Oceanus Tier. Each level of the complex had been named after a Greek sea god or water nymph. As she cleared the hatch, she was blocked by a tall Asian man coming down.

Phoebe shifted aside to let him pass, but he stopped in front of her.

"Dr. Reed, I was headed down to see you."

"Me? Why?"

She did not recognize the researcher. He was definitely not with the biology contingent. She would not have missed him. He stood as tall as her and was strikingly handsome. His mop of black hair was faded tight on all sides. His almond-dark eyes glinted even in the subdued lighting.

She had to look away from that piercing gaze.

Woman, you have been alone for far too long.

The man looked Japanese, but she couldn't be certain. She also had trouble judging his age. Maybe mid-thirties, like her. He was wearing the typical navy-blue jumpsuit of the station, only his fit snugly over a muscular frame. She had also noted the icon on his breast pocket, of the earth superimposed by a pickaxe, marking him as part of the geology contingent.

No wonder I don't know him.

"Our team could use your input," he said and held out a hand. "I'm Adam Kaneko."

She shook it. "You're a geologist?"

"Seismologist, to be precise."

Ah, that's why he's up so late.

During the past five days, there had been periodic tremors, but nothing as severe as the one that had knocked the station off its anchors a few days ago.

"How can I help you, Mr. Kaneko?"

"Please call me Adam." He gave a small bow of his head. When he raised his face, his brows were knit with concern. "I don't know if you've heard, but a massive quake struck Southeast Asia, with an epicenter in the South China Sea. It only happened within the past hour, so details are sketchy."

"I hadn't heard. But why do you need to consult with a biologist?" *Especially me.*

"For the past two weeks, our team has been mapping the epicenters of a cluster of tremors. They all seem to be rising from the Tonga Trench, about four hundred miles from our location."

"Should we be concerned?"

"Not at the moment."

Phoebe was not reassured, especially at the hesitancy in his voice.

"It's better if I show you," he said. "If you can spare a few minutes."

"Of course."

Adam led her off the stairs and across Oceanus Tier. The two levels below were the domain of the biology departments; this level was dedicated to chemistry, engineering, and geology. It also had a large lecture hall for cross-disciplinary discussions.

Up until now, Phoebe had barely set foot on this tier. Adam guided her past one of the emergency docking sections. Each level had them. Beyond a thick airlock hatch, four steps led down to a circular docking ring. With all the talk of quakes, she was suddenly all too aware of the two tons of pressure squeezing down upon every inch of the station.

"This way," Adam said, noting her slowing.

He took her around the central hub and to a door marked with a pickaxe crossed by a hammer. Inside, the geology lab was laid out similarly to all the others. The space was divided into a warren of cubicles, booths, and workstations. Across the back wall, a curve of polarized black glass glowed with the rosy shine of the exterior lamps.

Even at this late hour, men bustled about worktables and computer stations. Sifters rattled and shook. Something rhythmically thumped. The air had a bitter taint to it, likely from reagents and acids used to analyze core samples.

Adam walked her past all of it and over to a wide arc of monitors with a trio of ergonomic chairs before them. Two people were already settled there, and Adam waved her to the empty seat.

Phoebe sank warily into it, confused by the strange summons. An older Japanese man, with neatly combed white hair, sat in the center. He greeted her with a small bow of his head. Still, he kept working at a set of controls, studying his monitor, peering through a slim pair of reading glasses perched on his nose. On the screen, a glowing topographic map slowly shifted over a rocky landscape, shining in a rainbow of hues. A towering cliff rose on one side.

Past the old man, the third seat was occupied by a familiar figure.

"Thank you for joining us, Dr. Reed," William Byrd said, leaning forward to meet her eye. "I hope we don't have to keep you for long, but I suggested we consult with you on what we discovered."

"I'm happy to help." She glanced over to Adam, who stood behind the older man. "I was told about the continuing swarm of quakes, but I don't understand what the geology department needs from me."

Byrd sighed. "After that large jolt a few days ago, I've directed considerable resources to assessing the threat level, both to the station and to the general area. For now, the epicenters all seem to be rising along the Tonga Trench."

The older man glanced over the top of his glasses at the billionaire. "Not just *along* the trench, Mr. Byrd. But from one small stretch of it."

"I'm not sure I'd call a hundred-mile section of the trench *small*."

"Still, the patterning remains strange," the older man insisted. "And worrisome."

"It's too early to state that with any certainty." Byrd waved over to Adam. "Even your nephew agrees with me."

Phoebe looked between the older man and Adam, only now recognizing the resemblance between the two.

Adam noted her attention and made the introduction. "My uncle. Dr. Haru Kaneko. Department head of volcanology at Kyoto University."

"It's an honor to meet you," Phoebe said, still unclear why she had been summoned here.

Byrd twisted in his seat. "Adam, while we continue our sonar scan, can you catch Dr. Reed up on the geology team's assessment."

"Of course."

Adam shifted next to Phoebe and tapped at a keyboard before the monitor in front of her. He brought up a regional map.

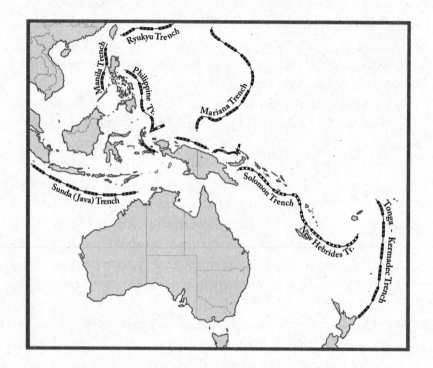

"This chart shows all the major trenches throughout the area," Adam explained. "A veritable maze, as you can see. It's why Southeast Asia is one of the most tectonically active areas of the planet. The Tonga Trench alone is the source of two-thirds of the world's deep-earth quakes. Such volatility is due to the collision of four major tectonic plates. The Pacific, Indo-Australian, Philippine, and Eurasian plates."

She nodded, aware of this through her own interest in deep-sea life.

Adam tapped a finger near the middle of the map. "Those big four meet at one point near the center of the Indonesian islands."

Haru waved an arm at his nephew. "Adam, please show Dr. Reed the latest seismology map. That will make matters clearer."

"I'm bringing it up now," Adam said as he tapped a few more keys. "There."

A new map of the same region appeared, only now it was dotted by crimson stars of various sizes.

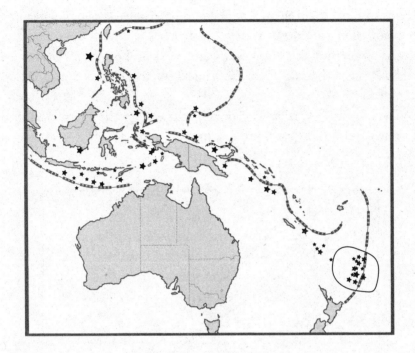

"The stars mark all the seaquakes recorded over the past *four* days. I restricted the mapping to only those tremors *greater* than 2.0 on the Richter scale. The larger the star, the stronger the quake." He had used a stylus to circle a celestial cluster in the middle of the Tonga-Kermadec Trench. "As you can see, the activity in this section of the chasm is extraordinarily volatile."

"And has been for the past two weeks," Haru added.

"But swarming of quakes is not uncommon in this region," Byrd clarified, likely to reassure her.

"True," Adam said, "but these tremors have been growing steadily. Both in numbers and strength. My uncle has been aboard the *Titan X* for the past three months, monitoring seismic activity during the finalization of the complex. He was the first one to note the disturbing clustering that started two weeks ago."

Haru spoke up. "I've kept a log of each tremor. Dates, durations, strengths, and locations."

Adam nodded. "I used my uncle's data to build a force vector map. It seems to show that the quaking here in the Tonga Trench is spreading outward along the regional maze of trenches and fault lines, amplifying in strength as it sweeps westward. Let me show you." He tapped again at the keyboard. "Here are the main vector lines that my program compiled."

The same map was now overlaid by three large arrows that spanned Indonesia and the surrounding countries, aiming for the coastline of Asia.

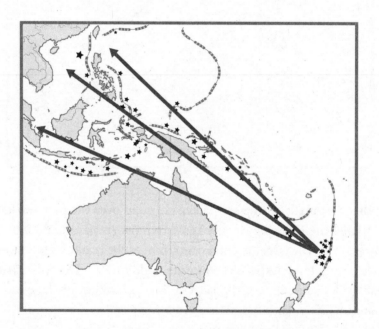

"What does this mean?" Phoebe asked.

Haru answered, "From the models that my nephew projected, if the current escalation of quakes continues, the entire Sunda Arc of volcanos could destabilize, possibly erupt. Maybe across all of Southeast Asia."

"How many volcanos are you talking about?"

Adam drew Phoebe's attention back to his screen. "There are more than seven hundred in Southeast Asia, both active and potentially active. I've marked the ones that are the most threatened if the current pace of escalation in volatility continues."

He pulled up another map with small triangles dotting the region.

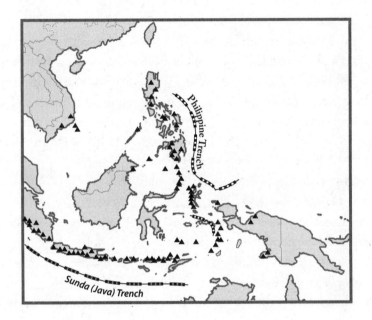

Phoebe choked down a gasp. "There's still close to a hundred."

"One hundred and twenty-two," Adam corrected. "Some of those triangles mark clusters of two or three volcanic peaks."

Phoebe glanced to the map that showed the force vector arrows. They all ran straight through the volcanic areas. "What's causing this to happen?"

Byrd shifted forward. "That's what we're trying to determine. It might simply be a normal pattern of stress relief between Tonga's tectonic plates. Everything could quiet once enough pressure is released."

Haru cast the billionaire a doubtful look. Clearly this was an ongoing point of contention between the two men.

Byrd ignored him and continued, "I deployed a pair of DriX USVs along the Tonga Trench. They're unmanned surface vehicles that can perform high-quality sonar surveys. We can operate them remotely from this station."

"I'm familiar with the vehicles from my own research," Phoebe said.

"Of course." Byrd nodded. "Late this evening, we reached the problematic section of the trench. Then a short time ago, we came upon an unusual discovery, one that we'd like your input on."

"My input? Why?"

"Can you show her, Dr. Kaneko?"

Adam's uncle nodded. "Give me a moment to set this DriX on an autonomous course along the trench. We don't want to miss anything."

On his screen, a high-definition topographic map of the Tonga Trench glowed in a rainbow of colors. The high tops of seamounts shone in bright yellows. The lower slopes and rifts were an emerald green. The deepest regions glowered in shades of blue.

She noted the depth reading on the map.

More than six thousand meters. Twice the station's depth.

She knew the deepest section of the Tonga Trench—Horizon Deep—reached depths of ten thousand meters. Even there, life persisted, though it was limited to worms, shrimp, and sea cucumbers.

What else could be down there?

Phoebe suspected the answer, which only heightened her anticipation.

3:04 A.M.

As they all waited, Adam watched Phoebe's knee bopping up and down. She squinted at the screen, while absently rubbing her palms together. Her dark hair had been bunched back from her face with a bright tie, which made her singular focus imposing, like a thunderstorm threatening to break.

He recognized that intensity. Before enrolling at the University of Tokyo, he had served six years with the Japanese Special Defense Force, much to his father's ire. He had worked alongside soldiers, especially snipers, who could maintain such a determined focus.

Phoebe had their same flinty concentration.

"All set," his uncle said. "I'm switching over to the other DriX, the one I left circling over the anomalous region."

The screen went dark, erasing the glowing landscape of silt, sand, and cliffs. Uncle Haru worked a mouse's cursor through a series of menus, then the monitor bloomed back into brilliant colors. For the moment, it looked no different from the other scan. Seamounts shone as if lit by a sun. A towering cliff face on the left dissolved through a spectrum of prismatic shades—from bright yellows near the top to darker blues and purples as the depths fell away.

Adam leaned toward the screen. "*Oji*, I think the DriX drifted off course."

"I can see that." Haru shifted his glasses higher on the bridge of his nose. "There's a storm brewing out there, challenging the vehicle's telemetry and seakeeping. I'll get it back into position."

As his uncle worked the controls, the view swung around, bringing the cliff face closer on one side. The DriX then continued along it. "We're about a half-kilometer off target."

Byrd rolled his chair closer. Phoebe followed his example. Adam crouched over her shoulder, squinting at the screen.

The view continued to sweep along the trench. According to the depth gauge, the dark purple patches marked regions that were more than nine thousand meters deep. Almost six miles under the water, three times the station's depths.

"Almost there," Haru said. "Though, we're approaching from a slightly different angle than the first time. The region covers two hundred square miles, stretching forty miles along the trench."

A shadow rose to the right of the screen. It appeared and faded as the DriX sped along the trench.

"Is that Tonga's other cliff face?" Phoebe asked.

"It is," Adam answered. "While the average width of the trench is around fifty miles, it's pinched here. Ranging from five to seven miles across."

"The tightness of this spot might explain why this section of the trench is so volatile," Byrd said. "It could be a stress point."

"Maybe," Adam admitted. "But the sheltered nature of this region might also explain *what* we found."

"What did you—?" Phoebe's question died as the view on the screen changed.

The dark purples of the seabed slowly turned black, as if oil had been spilled across the trench's bottom, seeping down its length.

She pushed closer, nearly shoving his uncle out of the way. "It can't be."

The three men looked to her for confirmation.

"It's coral," she said and motioned to Haru. "Can I take over the driver's seat for a moment?"

"Certainly." Haru rolled his chair aside and allowed her to push in front of his controls. "Are you proficient with the operation of a DriX?"

"I used one to explore the Sur Ridge oasis off the coast of Monterey. Besides building 3D maps of the ocean floor, a sonar's backscatter can differentiate between rock, sand, and coral." She glanced over to Haru. "Has this DriX been equipped with a sub-bottom profiler?"

"*Hai*, an Echoes 3500 T7, which can penetrate up to eleven thousand meters of water column."

"Perfect."

Byrd frowned. "Dr. Reed, what do you want with a sub-bottom profiler?"

"I've run into this issue before. Cursory sonar scans often mistake dense outcroppings of coral for boulders or a part of the seabed floor." She pointed to the uniformly black spread on the screen. "The DriX's sonar is bouncing off the canopy of that coral forest, making it look like that's the bottom."

"It's not?" Byrd asked.

"No."

"Then where is it?"

"That's what I'm going to find out. A profiler can penetrate *into* sandy seabeds, even through layers of clay. I've used this technology before to peek under the tops of dense coral fields."

She slowed the DriX and brought the Echoes unit online. She manipulated the software to get a real-time feed. As she did, the screen split. One side continued to display the sonar's ongoing mapping of the trench. The other half showed what the sub-bottom profiler revealed.

Both Haru and Byrd gasped. Phoebe remained silent, maintaining her concentration. Her only reaction was a slight widening of her eyes.

On the screen, the profiler displayed a cross-sectional view through the featureless black expanse. It sliced down into the darkness. Phoebe took a moment to focus the unit's chirping, and the image grew clearer. It revealed layers of coral stems and stalks, all densely tangled and woven together. It looked like a film negative of a woodland deadfall. The resolution blurred out before reaching the bottom.

Phoebe released the controls and let the DriX drift onward autonomously. "That's not possible," she finally said.

"What do you mean?" Byrd asked.

"That coral forest is gigantic, at least a thousand feet tall. Which means this section of the trench is far deeper than it appears. Previous sonar scans of this area must have confused the coral's canopy as the trench's bottom."

"But it was a false bottom," Adam said.

"Then how deep does it go?" Byrd asked again.

"I don't know," Phoebe admitted. "The sub-bottom profiler couldn't penetrate any deeper. It failed to reach the bottom." She pointed to the gradient scaling on the sepia-colored screen. "We lose resolution after three hundred meters below the coral's canopy, which is about ten thousand meters below the surface. Depending on how much farther down it goes, this section of the trench could be its deepest sounding."

"It could threaten the Mariana Trench's record," Adam added. "That trench is the deepest known point on the planet, just shy of eleven thousand meters. This trench could be even deeper in spots."

Byrd's eyes shone, likely thrilled at the possibility of breaking that record. Still, his lips drew thin. "But as amazing as all of this is, does it offer any explanation for the clustering of quakes in this area? Or is this discovery just incidental?"

All eyes turned to her.

She shrugged. "I'm not a seismologist. But we're not talking about a *small* bed of coral. That's a lost jungle down there, a veritable Brazilian rainforest. And at these extreme depths, it must have been growing exceptionally slowly. It must've taken hundreds of billions of years to achieve this height and expanse. It could even date back to the first corals, which appeared half a billion years ago."

"But what about the recent quaking?" Byrd pressed her.

"If you're right about this tight section of the trench being under stress, then perhaps the weight of all this coral—two hundred square miles of it, all pinched between tight walls—maybe it proved too much. Maybe its growth passed a threshold, crossing a breaking point where the underlying fault line couldn't handle it anymore."

Adam shook his head, unconvinced. "With the tectonic pressures we're talking about, I can't imagine that's the answer."

Haru stiffened in his seat, drawing all eyes to the screen where his gaze was fixed. "What's that?" he asked.

They all gathered closer. By now, the dark expanse of oil had spread to the cliff walls on either side, but near one edge, that featureless landscape was interrupted by a jagged rip that stretched at least a quarter mile through the pristine coral.

Phoebe guided the DriX closer and followed that torn path. As she reached the end, a smoother shape appeared under the sonar scan, buried in that oily darkness. Even crumpled by pressure and nosed deep into the coral, the silhouette was easy to identify. The cylindrical shape stretched more than four hundred feet long, topped by a prominent conning tower.

"It's the wreck of a submarine," Byrd said.

Haru gave Adam a sharp look. Clearly his uncle was wondering if the submarine's presence might account for the localized tremors. The tail end of the boat looked like it had imploded with considerable force.

Adam had his own concerns about this lost submarine. "Is there any way to estimate its age?" he asked Phoebe.

"Not with sonar alone. Not at these depths. We'd need eyes on it to say with any certainty when it sank."

"Then that's what we're going to do," Byrd said. "I have a submersible that can reach depths of—"

A loud klaxon cut him off, rising from a computer across the lab.

"It's another quake," Adam said, straightening with concern. That workstation's alarm only sounded when there was a seismic event greater than 7.0 on the Richter scale.

Another of the geologists rushed to the computer. He studied its screen, then called over. "An eight point two!"

Adam winced and shouted back. "Where?"

"South China Sea! Near the Manila Trench. Not far from the one reported forty-five minutes ago. Only this one's much stronger."

"So it can't be an aftershock," Haru said.

Adam nodded. "The first one—as bad as it was—must have been a *foreshock*, a precursor to this one."

"Or this could be another foreshock, too," Haru warned dourly. "With worse yet to come."

Adam turned to the neighboring monitor, which still glowed with the maps he had devised. He stared at the large arrows pointed straight at the South China Sea. A second window displayed the hundreds of volcanos throughout the region.

"I fear this is just the beginning," Haru said.

From the cold certainty in his uncle's voice, they could all guess what was left unspoken, what Haru feared stating aloud.

It could be the beginning of the end.

6

Gray kept a vigil at the end of the pier with the other men. Across the breadth of Deep Water Bay, dozens of boats were moored throughout a buoy field belonging to the Royal Hong Kong Yacht Club. The vessels ranged in sizes from small sailboats to midsized cabin cruisers to a hundred-foot superyacht. The clubhouse itself was on its own island out in the bay, but it required a ferry to reach it, and it was not operating due to the quake.

Instead, a lone Zodiac sped across the flat midnight waters, heading away from the bayside pier where Gray and the others waited. The pontoon boat was piloted by Zhuang and carried Seichan, Kat, Guan-yin, and the three children. The Zodiac aimed for a forty-foot catamaran—a Leopard Powercat—moored far out in the bay.

Gray hated to be separated from the others, but the small skiff could not hold any more people. Once the women and children were offloaded onto the catamaran, Zhuang would return for the men.

Monk shifted closer to Gray, glancing back toward shore, plainly still worried. "If Seichan is correct about Valya leading the attack, why ambush us here? And why now after so long?"

Gray took a deep breath of the salty air, trying to shed the anxiety that kept his muscles taut. He tugged the windbreaker tighter across his shoulders. After Gray had reached Deep Water Bay, Kowalski had arrived shortly thereafter with a pair of triad members who had secured a change of clothes for all of them: hooded sweatshirts, loose pants, light Gore-Tex jackets, and boots of various sizes.

"I don't know," Gray answered, having wondered the same thing about Valya.

Monk scowled, his voice growing heated. "Of course, it was too much to hope that she had died. Still, maybe now I'll get a chance to pay her back for what she did to Kat and the girls."

Two years before, Valya had led an attack on Gray's house. She had kidnapped Seichan and Monk's two girls, while also shooting Kat. Monk's wife had barely survived the encounter. Earlier, when Kat had heard about the Russian assassin's reappearance, she had looked ready to return to the Peak and exact her own revenge—not for herself, but for her girls, whom Valya had put in danger both in the past and now.

Kowalski grunted his own assessment, fingering the taped cut over his cheek. "Someone needs to put that bitch in the ground once and for all."

Bolin Chén winced, searching around. The fourteen-year-old wore a dark blue hoodie and a ballcap. He was far too young to be here, but he kept his place next to a fully vetted member of the *Duàn zhī*, a steely-eyed triad deputy named Yeung. The latter was a tattooed wall of muscle, a tank on two legs.

The pair had hauled in a load of scrubbed weapons. Gray had nabbed a SIG P229, now holstered under the flap of his jacket. Monk had grabbed a Glock G45, fitted with a thirty-three-round magazine. Kowalski had claimed a snub-nosed Israeli Tavor X95 bullpup. The large man didn't even try hiding the assault rifle. It was slung across his massive chest.

Monk frowned at the bay. "For Valya to show up now, she's gotta be here for a reason. Especially after playing dead for two years."

Gray nodded. "While the ambush could've been her attempt at exacting her long-delayed revenge—for us taking down the Guild, for the death of her brother—I doubt it. She's more calculating than that. The attack felt hasty, a kneejerk attempt to use the quake as a cover. Something else is going on."

When Sigma Force had first encountered the former Guild assassin, she had been gathering forces, filling the power vacuum left behind after the terrorist group's destruction. In the fierce encounter that followed, her twin brother, Anton, had been killed. Though he had died protecting a Sigma asset, Valya continued to harbor a vendetta, especially against one of them.

Gray stared across the bay toward Seichan and Jack. The Zodiac had finally reached the stern of Guan-yin's catamaran. The group gathered to board with the children.

Thank God, they're all—

The pier jolted under Gray, then again even harder. He and the others were all thrown to the planks. Gray fell to his hands and knees. Across the bay, the waters rippled into a huge chop. Off in the distance, the catamaran bobbled and rocked, but it was moored in deep water, where the quake's effect was muted. Zhuang had managed to secure a line and got everyone climbing aboard the larger boat.

Relieved, Gray concentrated on his own situation. The pier continued to buck and roll under him. Behind him, the town of Deep Water Bay rattled and shook. As he watched, a bayside building collapsed, spilling bricks and sections of wall across the neighboring beach. A fiery explosion blew deeper in the town as a gas main burst.

Gray and the others kept low, not even attempting to get to shore. It took all their effort just to hold their place as the writhing pier tried to throw them off. They had no choice but to wait it out.

A loud splintering cut through the quake's low rumble. Ten feet away, the end of the pier ripped off its stone pilings and toppled sideways into the sea.

The teenager, Bolin, panicked and burst to his feet.

Kowalski yanked the kid back down. "Stay put!"

After another five minutes, the fierce jolting tempered into quieter trembling. Gray risked sitting up, making sure the catamaran had fared all right. By now, the Zodiac was already on its way back. It sped and bounced over the quake-driven ripples.

"Look!" Monk called over.

His friend drew his attention to the water on either side of the pier.

The levels were rapidly receding down the pilings, exposing more and more of the beach.

Despite the continued tremoring, Gray stood up. He recognized what was happening and pointed toward shore. "Run! Get to higher ground!"

The others gained their feet.

Gray continued to face the bay as a massive tide pulled the waters out from under the pier. He lifted both arms and crossed them over his head, trying to warn Zhuang. But the Zodiac continued toward him.

Gray cursed and snatched the SIG from its holster. He fired two shots into the air.

Finally, the Zodiac slowed, the bow dipping as it did. Zhuang finally recognized the danger—either from Gray's warning shots or the sight of the widening stretch of starlit beach. The Zodiac made a hard turn and swung away from shore, then raced off toward the catamaran, chased by the receding waters.

With nothing more he could do, Gray turned and pounded down the planks after the others. As he did, the water piled higher and higher out in the bay, building toward a tidal wave, a tsunami that would crash through town in a couple of minutes.

The only blessing was that Seichan, Jack, and the others were safely aboard the catamaran and out in the deep water. Gray had only one mission from here.

Stay alive for them.

12:38 A.M.

From the stern of the catamaran, Seichan watched the shadowy shapes of the men fleeing down the pier toward shore. The quake had subsided, but the new danger was evident as the waters retreated from the shoreline. Tsunami sirens echoed over the bay, rising into a wail of warning.

Closer at hand, Zhuang fought the Zodiac across the water as the tide rose under its pontoons. Seichan felt the catamaran lifting, too. It floated higher and higher. The bow—still tied to the mooring ball and its anchor—dipped. The chain down to the seabed must have reached its limit. The deck continued to tilt under her.

Not good.

Fearing the worst, she headed forward. She passed along the narrow promenade that ran alongside the main salon. Kat had taken the children inside there, retreating to a cabin to try to calm them.

As Seichan headed for the bow, Guan-yin called down from the flybridge. Her mother had gotten the engines started, but she had also recognized the danger as the boat continued to tip steeply forward.

"Get us off the mooring!" her mother called down.

Seichan reached the foredeck and skidded across its fiberglass surface. By now, the boat had tilted to nearly thirty degrees. Once near the bow rail, she dove on her stomach to the starboard cleat. The catamaran had been tied down on the portside, too, forming a secure bridle at the bow. She hit the rail with her shoulder and tugged at the nylon line wrapped around the cleat. The tension jammed it in place. She couldn't loosen it.

"Seichan!" Guan-yin yelled to her. "Cut us free!"

Seichan heard a sharp *thunk* to her left. The hilt of a dagger vibrated two inches from her cheek, proving her mother's deft skill with her throwing knives. Seichan snatched up the dagger, noting the serrated lower half to the eight-inch blade. She twisted around and sawed at the trapped line.

Her shoulder ached as she frantically worked. The tilt of the boat rushed blood into her head, pounding her ears. She got three-quarters of the way through when the line snapped free. Now untethered, the starboard side shoved high, tossing Seichan off the deck for a breathless moment.

When she landed, she rolled across to the portside cleat. She hacked and sawed at the second line. All the while, the water rose higher, swelling into a huge surge under the catamaran, rolling the boat sideways.

Guan-yin yelled, "Hurry!"

Seichan clenched her teeth and bit back a curse. Then the nylon line broke and ripped away. The portside hull bobbed up hard, throwing Seichan high. She tossed the knife and grabbed the railing with both hands before she flew overboard. She struck the deck hard, knocking the wind from her.

The catamaran rocked wildly. Her mother throttled up the engines and got them moving. The forward motion settled the boat better in the water. Guan-yin piloted the catamaran away from shore and headed for deeper water, escaping the pending wake of the tsunami.

As the deck evened out, Seichan rolled to her knees and searched toward shore. She prayed the others had reached higher ground. With the rising water, the catamaran now sat above the town, but she saw no sign of Gray or the others. The boat reached the other side of the swell and rode down its far slope as the surge rushed toward shore.

As it did, Seichan realized another of their party was no longer in sight.

Zhuang and the pontoon boat had vanished.

12:52 A.M.

Gray fled across the seaside promenade. It separated the beach from the spread of a dark golf course. He and the others hit a chain-link fence that ran down the street's median. Gray mounted and leaped over it. Monk followed, while Kowalski practically tossed the teenager over, then the big man and triad deputy, Yeung, clambered after them.

A glance back revealed a huge band of churning whitewater, bright under the stars, rushing toward the beach and gaining speed, thirty to forty miles an hour, impossible to outrun.

With less than a minute before it struck the shore, they raced across the street and reached a towering, netted fence that kept golf balls from hitting passing cars.

"Where now?" Kowalski gasped.

The golf course stretched hundreds of yards in either direction. Towering apartment buildings climbed the surrounding cliffs, but they could never reach them in time. The only high ground nearby—and it wasn't much—was the course's clubhouse. It rose two stories, with a dining terrace on the upper level.

Gray pointed through the netted barrier at it. "There."

The teenager, Bolin, leaped high and threw himself against the netting. He clutched a blade in both hands and jammed the point through the mesh. He used his falling weight to rip a hole through it—then held the gap open.

"*Fǎi dī, fǎi dī,*" he urged them.

They all burrowed through and sprinted across the manicured lawns. Water roared behind them as the tsunami's surge crested toward the shoreline. The dark clubhouse, fifty yards away, was locked up tight for the night.

Luckily, they had brought keys.

As they closed the distance, Kowalski shouldered his rifle and fired at the row of tall windows across the first floor. The panes shattered under his barrage. Without slowing, they reached the building, crunched through the broken glass, and dashed into the dark interior. Kowalski's weapon was fitted with a tactical flashlight. He switched it on and swept the beam around the interior.

Gray spotted steps leading up. "With me!"

A grinding roar erupted behind them. A glance back showed a huge surge tearing across the street, ripping down the golf course's netting. It was moving at incredible speeds.

Gray sprinted to the stairway. He made it halfway up and reached the first landing, when a churning wall of water slammed through the broken windows behind them.

"Go!" Kowalski hollered.

Gray sped around the landing and climbed the turn of the stairs, taking them two at a time. Water chased them. It surged up the stairwell, churning with a meat grinder of debris. Gray dashed down a short hall that led to a set of glass doors out to the dining terrace.

Water flooded after them, swamping over his new boots, rising toward his shins.

Kowalski raised his rifle and fired past Gray's shoulder. The deafening rounds splintered the door's thick glass, but it failed to break. Gray sped faster and struck the weakened pane with his shoulder. He crashed through it to reach the terrace.

As he did, he tripped and struggled to regain his footing. The others barreled through—Monk grabbed Gray's shoulder and got him moving.

They fled farther from the door, pursued by the flood, but its strength was already ebbing as the surge receded back down the throat of the stairwell.

Still, they were not out of danger.

Past the balcony's edge, the black tsunami swept around the clubhouse, climbing a story high. As it flooded across the golf course, the current carried shattered trees, floating cars, broken boats. The terrace trembled underfoot, then jolted harder as the fierce currents tore at the walls below. The front of the building started to sag, succumbing to the tidal forces that ripped through its foundations.

Gray got them all moving across the terrace. More and more of the clubhouse broke apart behind them, ripped down into the flood. The far side of the terrace started to collapse and fell into the churning maelstrom. The destruction ground its way inevitably toward them.

They all backed to the farthest edge, but they had nowhere else to go.

Monk shouted and pointed past the balcony rail. "A light!"

Gray turned and spotted a small glow against the black tide. It rode through the surge, dodging debris, tossed about by the currents.

The Zodiac . . .

Zhuang must have failed to clear the surge in time and had gotten caught in its tide. With no other choice, he had to surf the tsunami as it made landfall.

Gray hurried to the rail, tugging Kowalski with him. "Wave your flashlight high."

The big man obeyed, recognizing the Zodiac was their only chance of rescue.

Zhuang, likely focused on his own survival, didn't notice their signal. Gray freed his SIG and emptied the magazine into the air. Zhuang heard him. The Zodiac spun and fought toward them.

Gray continued to hold his breath as the clubhouse disintegrated toward their position. The surrounding water filled with an apron of debris. Even if Zhuang made it, they would have only seconds to leap aboard before the jagged maelstrom below tore the pontoon boat apart.

Zhuang struggled through the current. He dodged larger obstacles and bounced over others. Finally, once close enough, he opened the engine's throttle and shot toward the clubhouse, riding across the debris field.

"Get ready!" Gray hollered to the others. "Leap once it's under us."

The Zodiac rode through the churning border of whitewater around the clubhouse. At the last moment, Zhuang swung the boat sideways and slammed broadside into the building.

"Now!" Gray bounded over the rail.

The others followed with him. They all plummeted in a tight knot and struck the Zodiac in a heavy tangle of limbs. The impact bounced them high. The lightest of them, Bolin, flew over the pontoon toward the grinding water.

Kowalski lunged out, grabbed the kid's leg, and yanked him back aboard. "Quit trying to get away from me!"

Zhuang didn't wait. Standing at the helm, he roared the engines and sped off. As he did, a section of the portside pontoon ripped, collapsing a section of it. It added drag to their maneuverability, but Zhuang compensated.

Behind them, the last of the clubhouse broke into the tide.

By now, the tsunami surge had bled away most of its momentum. The tide of water reversed, rushing the other way, returning to the bay.

Zhuang surfed along it again. He sped around a capsized sailboat that spun in a riptide. They passed between two of the golf course's net pylons that were still standing, as if clearing a pair of goalposts.

Zhuang raced them across the street and over the flooded beach.

Gray should have felt joyous, but a drowned body bumped against the damaged pontoon and rolled away. There were likely thousands more across Hong Kong and its outlying islands.

As they reached the bay itself, a lone patch of light shone out on the water.

Guan-yin's catamaran.

As Gray stared at it, he took solace where he could.

We survived—at least for now.

7

Seated in the catamaran's salon, Gray rested his head in his hands, exhausted and troubled. Seichan shared the leather banquette. Across a small table, Monk leaned against Kat with an arm around her.

Kowalski had retired below into the main cabin, joining the three children who found great comfort in his size and weight, as if he were an enormous teddy bear. All four of them had fallen asleep on the king-size bed, nestled in a big pile.

Above them, in the flybridge, Guan-yin and Zhuang piloted the Leopard Powercat. They guided the catamaran across the channel that separated Hong Kong from Lantau Island. They were all headed to Macau, thirty miles farther west.

Though they were all tired, Gray wanted to report in with Painter Crowe at Sigma Command after the attack by Valya Mikhailov. The director needed to know what had transpired. Also, Gray was certain Painter had heard about the quakes and the tsunami that had struck the region. The director would want an update on their status, especially in a country where Sigma was not welcome.

Luckily, Guan-yin had spared no expense in outfitting the boat's communication equipment—which was no surprise for a woman who led criminal and legitimate enterprises across Southeast Asia. Once Gray was alone with his group, he had dispatched a code on the salon's desktop computer, requesting an encrypted connection to Sigma. They now waited for Painter to reach out to them.

Gray sighed, wondering what was taking so long. While it was the middle of the night here, it was midafternoon in D.C. Painter was surely at Sigma Command. Gray glanced at the computer's monitor on the neighboring workstation. A tiny hourglass spun on an open window.

More than ten minutes had passed.

Monk looked equally frustrated. "Now is not the time for Painter to be taking a long lunch."

A minute later, the computer finally chimed and the hourglass transformed into a ten-second countdown. Gray climbed to his feet and crossed to the workstation. The others followed and crowded behind him as he sat down before the computer.

When the countdown reached zero, a view into Painter Crowe's office pixelated onto the screen. The director sat behind a wide mahogany desk with a trio of flatscreen monitors glowing on the walls behind him.

One blazed with a map of Southeast Asia.

Clearly, Painter had prepared for this discussion. He had shed his jacket and rolled the sleeves to his elbows, a sign that he had been working hard, possibly on this very matter.

The director leaned forward and combed fingers through his black hair, shifting a single white lock behind an ear. Painter looked exasperated, which darkened the burnished planes of his face.

"About time you all reported in," the director started. "I've been trying to reach you for hours."

"We ran into a bit of trouble. And not just earthquakes and tidal waves."

"What sort of trouble?"

"Valya Mikhailov."

Painter grimaced. "In Hong Kong?"

Gray nodded and filled the director in on all that had transpired this long night. As he did, Painter listened, asked a few questions, and nodded, almost as if he were unsurprised.

"That attack might not have been coincidental," Painter said. He glanced back to the map on the screen behind him. "There's trouble brewing across Southeast Asia. And like you said, not just earthquakes and tidal waves."

"What do you mean?"

"Two weeks ago, the Chinese lost a nuclear submarine. One of their latest. A Type 096 SSBN. The Tang-class variant had been kept under tight wraps. The only sighting of it was a grainy photo taken by a geospatial intelligence satellite. It was docked at the Huludao Shipyard, in Liaoning province of northern China."

"This new sub?" Monk asked, leaning over Gray's shoulder. "What's its capabilities?"

Painter shrugged. "No one can say with any certainty. I consulted a naval expert for the latest intel. The consensus is that the sub was equipped with a new pump-jet propulsion system to compensate for its predecessor's noisiness. That grainy photo also showed rows of VLS cells—vertical launch systems for twenty-four Julang-3 ballistic missiles, all equipped with nuclear warheads. As you might imagine, China does not want anyone else to recover their sub—especially *where* it was discovered."

"Discovered?" Kat said. "So we found it?"

"Actually, it wasn't us. A competitor beat us to the prize. Still, they reached out to Sigma for help. Especially as they knew you all were in the area. I also imagine—as young as their organization is—they felt more confident with their older, more experienced, brother getting involved."

"Who are you talking about?" Gray asked, rubbing a temple, too tired for riddles.

Of course, Kat figured it out and sighed. "You're talking about TaU. Did Aiko reach out to you?"

Gray glanced back at her. Three years before, they had dealings with Aiko Higashi, during a mission in Hawaii and Japan. She was the leader of a covert Japanese intelligence group, called TaU—or *Tako no Ude*—which stood for "Arms of an Octopus," an apt name for a burgeoning spy agency. Gray also knew that *tau* was the next letter in the Greek alphabet after *sigma*. The name was possibly a tip of their hat to their American counterpart. Or maybe it was meant as a challenge, that TaU intended to be one step ahead of Sigma.

Which in this case, proved to be true.

"It's why I was delayed in returning your call," Painter said. He tapped at his keyboard, and the image on the screen split. "I thought Ms. Higashi should be part of this discussion. Especially as she might be partly to blame for the attack against you last evening."

Gray frowned. *What did he mean by that?*

On the other half of the computer monitor, a new office appeared. The desk had an ebony surface over blond wood that matched the framing of the white Shoji-screen paneling behind it. A bookshelf of the same vertical-grained wood was full of journals and texts, a majority of which were titled in Japanese.

Seated behind the desk, Aiko gave them all a nod. "*Kon'nichiwa*," she greeted them, her voice perfunctory and serious. She kept her back stiff, carrying herself like someone with a military background. Her navy suit looked starched as firmly as her manner.

Gray knew her background—though Kat knew the woman far better. The two had run up the respective ranks of their intelligence agencies. Aiko had started with the Japanese Ministry of Justice, then later joined the Public Security Intelligence Agency.

According to Japan's constitution—written after World War II—the country's intelligence operations were restricted from operating on foreign soil. But with the rising threats from China, North Korea, and Russia, along with terrorist incursions, Japan had been bolstering its intelligence services, centralizing them under CIRO, the Cabinet Intelligence and Research Office. But more was needed with rising world tensions and threats. So, as Sigma operated under the auspices of DARPA, TaU now served the same covert role under CIRO. The new agency was only three years old, and any mission far from their homeland required delicacy and international cooperation.

Like now.

Aiko did not look particularly happy about it, but she was sharp enough to recognize when necessity required such cooperation. "I assume you've been informed about China's loss."

Gray nodded. "A nuclear submarine."

Aiko's eyes narrowed. "The escalation of China's saber-rattling has grown unnerving throughout the region. It grew worse after AUUKUS, a trilateral treaty between Australia, the U.K., and the U.S. And the situation with Taiwan grows ever more tense. During the past few years, the PLA Navy has increased its number of live-fire exercises and patrols. Including conducting incursions into territorial waters, especially around Australia of late."

"Is that where they lost their sub?" Kat asked. "Somewhere off the coast of Australia."

"That's what we had initially suspected. Two weeks ago, leaked intel revealed frantic Chinese naval activities north of New Zealand. It soon grew clear that one of their new subs had sunk, possibly during a seaquake."

"U.S. military intelligence had heard the same chatter," Painter confirmed.

Aiko continued, "Rumor was that there was a recovery operation. A handful of submariners were said to have been evacuated and promptly whisked away."

Gray frowned. "Evacuated how?"

Aiko matched his frustrated expression. "Intel suggests that the new sub was equipped with a pair of escape chambers, likely based on Russia's Oscar-class VSUs. Small chambers that could hold a dozen men and be blasted to the surface. But the rumors of such a rescue could just be naval propaganda. Especially as the Chinese didn't seem to know exactly where the sub sank. If there had been survivors, it seems likely the rescued men would have known where their sub went down."

"And how did TaU get involved?"

"Through a bit of serendipity and happenstance. We had not truly planned on being drawn into the matter. But there was already an international research project underway in the waters four hundred miles away. To get some boots on the ground—or in this case, underwater—we dispatched an agent to the area. He was a former sol-

dier with our SDF. TaU recruited him two years ago, while he was finishing a degree in geology and seismology, topics of particular interest
to Japan's safety."

Kat nodded. "And you sent him out to be your eyes and ears in the
area?"

"We did, especially as he had a personal connection. An uncle—a
volcanologist who had been already working at the Titan Project nearly
from the start."

"And what has your agent heard?" Gray asked.

"He didn't just *hear*. While investigating an unusual swarm of
quakes along the Tonga Trench, he and the geology team discovered a
wrecked sub, in waters ten thousand meters deep."

Monk whistled. "At those depths, the story of any survivors seems
even more unlikely."

Kat reached to her husband's shoulder. "Not necessarily. They could
have escaped before the boat hit bottom."

Gray had never stopped frowning. "But I don't understand. All of
this seems like a matter for our respective militaries. What can TaU or
Sigma hope to accomplish? And more importantly—" He stared hard
at Painter. "How does any of this explain the attack on us in Hong
Kong?"

"I'll let Director Higashi answer that," Painter said.

She nodded. "Before the sub was discovered a few hours ago, our
agent had reported a possible regional threat last week, one posited by
his uncle. He believes the swarm of seaquakes that drew them to the
sub could be the source for the escalating number of tectonic events
throughout the region. Let me share their research data."

Aiko ran through a series of maps, showing the maze of fault lines
and deep-sea trenches throughout the South Pacific, followed by the
epicenters of quakes, then a chart dotted with hundreds of volcanos.

"Our agent and his uncle," Aiko continued, "believe whatever is
happening in the Tonga Trench—something possibly connected to the
sunken sub—could threaten all of Southeast Asia, destabilizing the
region's fault lines and volcanic arcs, leading to a catastrophe beyond
measure."

Gray sank back in his seat. "How certain is your agent's data and extrapolation?"

"We've consulted with a dozen other seismologists. Ten of them concur. Two do not." Aiko stared straight out at them. "It's why—a few days ago—when I had heard of your group's arrival in Hong Kong, I had thought perhaps you were already made aware of the threat and had come to investigate. I made some discreet inquiries."

"Inquiries that reached the wrong ears," Painter added. "Especially as Chinese intelligence surely already had you on their radar. They must have believed you posed some threat to their own efforts to recover the sub."

Gray sighed. "So, the Chinese outsourced our assassination, hiring mercenaries."

"To mask the Chinese government's own involvement," Kat added. "To give them plausible deniability for our deaths."

Gray rubbed his forehead. "And, of course, if Valya's outfit heard about it, how could she refuse to take it up? It offered her the perfect chance to carry out her long-festering vendetta—and get paid to do it."

"What do we do now?" Kat asked.

Painter sat straighter. "First, we need to get your children out of harm's way. That's already being arranged. Kat, I'd like you to accompany them and join me back in D.C. We're heading into deep water—both literally and figuratively—and I could use your intelligence expertise in coordinating TaU and Sigma's efforts. Plus, with the threat of something catastrophic happening in such a politically volatile area, it's going to take someone with your experience and contacts to keep this from escalating into a global war."

Kat nodded. "Of course."

"Monk, you're to take Kowalski and head out to Titan Station and join Director Higashi's agent. He is heading out on an exploratory trip to that area in the morning. I want you both there. Something strange is going on in that trench, and we need to know what it is before it's too late."

"What about me?" Gray asked.

"I'll let Director Higashi explain. It might be a wild goose chase, but if not, I want you involved. Seichan, too, if she's willing."

"Involved with what?" Gray asked.

Aiko answered. "Six hours ago, word reached us of another avenue of pursuit by the Chinese, from an operative with Cambodia's General Directorate of Intelligence."

Kat's brow wrinkled. "Cambodia?"

Aiko explained. "The search for the lost submarine is being orchestrated out of Beijing, but from the start, there has been a flurry of communiqués with a Chinese installation at the Réam Naval Base in Cambodia. Despite denials by both Phnom Penh and Beijing, it's a poorly kept secret that China constructed a secret military research installation there, a strategically significant site in the Indo-Pacific region. The scientists at the site are said to be testing new weaponry and equipment."

"And your Cambodian contact?" Gray asked. "What has he told you?"

"It was from him that we learned about the supposed recovery of a handful of submariners. But then, a short time ago, he also reported that a strike team had been dispatched to Singapore to secure something from a museum there."

Gray scowled at the unusual tack of this conversation. "From a museum?"

"On the campus of the National University of Singapore. The Lee Kong Chian Natural History Museum."

"What could they want from there?" Gray asked.

Aiko shrugged. "We don't know."

Painter lifted a brow. "That's what we want you and Seichan to find out. And if possible, to secure it instead."

Monk did not look happy with their assignments. "I'm off to the high seas with someone who likes to blow stuff up. And you two get to go on a museum heist."

Gray glanced to Seichan, who hadn't spoken a word. She stood with her arms crossed. From the hard set of her lips, she was still furious at the attack. From the pinch in her brow, she was already calculating, weighing the odds. If the Chinese had dispatched a team to Singapore, there was no doubt who Seichan hoped to find there.

She finally uncrossed her arms and gave Painter her answer.

"Sounds like fun."

8

Captain Tse Daiyu climbed from the backseat of the black Xpeng G9 SUV, while her driver idled the vehicle. Its electric motor was as darkly silent as her mood. The sun had yet to rise over the Gulf of Thailand, which bordered the Réam Naval Base. The morning was still warm and humid after a sweltering night.

She took off her glasses and used a handkerchief to wipe the fog that had immediately steamed her lenses after she had exited the air-conditioned interior. She dabbed the same dampness from her brow. She hated the heat. She had grown up in the city of Mohe, in the northern province of Heilongjiang, where the aurora borealis would often shine and the weather was cold and dry year-round.

Not like this infernal sweatbox.

She headed across the parking lot. Men and women—a mix of enlisted and officers—bustled throughout the fortified corner of the Cambodian base. They all wore blue fatigues in oceanic camouflage, which showed only a few insignias, in an attempt to keep their ranks hidden. It was a cynical ploy to mask the depth of PLA involvement on Cambodian soil. Not that anyone was fooled. The role-playing was more for the benefit of the Cambodian government than any real worry from Beijing.

As the commanding officer of the base, Daiyu refused to participate in this game. She wore crisp gray pants and a white, open-necked coat with hard epaulets and bar insignia of her rank. She carried her hat under one arm. Her hair was neatly trimmed to her collar. Her only concession to vanity was the dye that masked the few strands of gray.

At forty-eight, she was only the second female in the PLA Navy to reach the level of captain, and she did not intend to stop here. She aspired for an admiralcy.

As the only child of factory workers, she carried the burden of her family's honor. Her parents had wanted a son but had to settle for a daughter, trapped by the "one-child policy" of the time. Still, afterward, her parents had doted on her and loved her, instilling self-confidence, along with pride of country, family, and self—if not necessarily in that order.

When her mother died twelve years ago, it had been the impetus for her to join the PLA. Her ambitions could not be fulfilled in the civilian sector. By then, she had already made her parents proud. She had graduated from Sun Yat-sen University with a PhD in geosciences, then worked at the Guangdong Southern Marine Science and Engineering Laboratory. There, she worked on deep-sea research projects for the navy. So, her transition into the military had been an easy one. After a post as a navigator aboard an aircraft carrier, she returned to the same lab.

Since then, for the past decade, she had overseen the advancement of China's bathyscaphe project. Her crowning achievement, though, had been the completion and testing of an AI-driven ship, the *Zhu Hai Yun*. The marine research vessel needed no crew. It served as the mothership for a collection of unmanned drones and submersibles, allowing it to operate independently, with minimal human involvement.

Her goal was to usher the PLA Navy into a new era of oceanic dominance. If she was successful, the rank of admiral would be within her reach. Still, much resided on her new role here in Cambodia. She intended it to be the next jewel in her crown of achievements. She had orchestrated the installation's construction, both the base shown to the world above and the layers of engineering labs buried and insulated deep underground.

She crossed toward a steel-roofed warehouse, rising four stories, and looming over the neighboring water. The only sign on it was the number 零八 above the entrance, but it was the most important structure on the base. Two armed guards flanked the door, but neither saluted her, though it clearly strained them not to do so. They were all under orders to adhere to the role-playing while in the open.

She swiped a keycard and entered the humid warehouse. Immediately, the dank smell of seawater and diesel fuel struck her. The structure contained two floors of offices and open workspaces, all centered around a deep-water bay in the middle. It opened out onto the Gulf of Thailand, but its huge doors were currently closed. A research ship was tethered at the dock, along with a prototype submersible that floated next to it.

Daiyu's office was on the second level. Though she had a long day ahead of her—and an important one—she aimed instead for an elevator near the warehouse entrance. She wanted to see if any progress had been made while she had been gone the past two days.

Another swipe of her card opened the elevator doors. She entered and tapped the bottommost button, glowing with the number 五, marking the fifth subbasement of the installation.

The doors slid closed, and the cage dropped thirty meters into the subterranean concrete bunker. It lay mostly under the neighboring parking lot. The cage bumped to a stop and the doors whisked open with a slight hiss of pressurized air. She entered a long gray hallway, with sealed airlocks opening into various labs.

She crossed along it, glancing into the first room. Past the windows of its airlock, she spotted the three naked bodies on steel gurneys. Their corpses were blackened as if charred by a fire, each contorted in shapes of agony. She had once visited the ruins of Pompeii and had seen the chalk-plaster casts of ash-covered victims from Mount Vesuvius's eruption. The trio inside the morgue looked much the same.

Only these are not plaster casts.

The three crewmen had been recovered from an escape chamber jettisoned out of the missing Chinese submarine, the *Changzheng 24*. It had taken the PLA Navy three days to hunt down the small pod bobbing in the South Pacific. A fierce storm had challenged their efforts, driving the chamber far from where it had been dispatched. The beacon, damaged during its ascent, had also fluttered on and off, further confounding the recovery. When the pod was finally discovered, it was found to be half-submerged, flooded by a pressure crack through one side, bodies floating inside.

With a shudder, Daiyu continued past the door and entered the next airlock. She savored the cool blast of recycled air, then entered the biolab. It had been hastily outfitted ten days before, after the discovery of the strange state of the bodies. To study them, she had brought in microscopes and centrifuges, along with an ultra-low temperature freezer and a CO_2 incubator. She had also commissioned a next-gen sequencer and a PCR system for genetic assays. Additionally, at the request of the lead researcher, an electron microscope and an X-ray diffraction system had been installed in an upstairs lab.

After all the expense and effort, she wanted answers.

She headed to the man who was expected to have them.

Dr. Luo Heng bowed at her arrival. He was a brilliant bioengineer and physician from the University of Shanghai. At only thirty-two, he had garnered a slew of accolades for his research and was the current director of CSCB, the Chinese Society of Cell Biology.

When Heng faced her, she noted the obstinate hardness to his eyes. He had not wanted to come here. At first, he had foolishly believed he had a choice.

The man had grown up in Hong Kong. He was a child when the region was handed back over to China. Yet, he carried himself—all six feet of him—as if he remained caught between two worlds: between East and West, between civilian life and military authority. A stubborn and belligerent streak persisted in him, one she had already butted against since his arrival.

Around the lab, four others worked at various stations, looking as if they were trying to avoid her gaze. Two had been handpicked by Heng. Daiyu had selected the other pair, a lieutenant and sublieutenant, to assist the doctor and watch over his efforts.

But, ultimately, the responsibility for any progress lay with Heng.

She crossed to the bioengineer. "How is our patient?"

"Come see for yourself, Captain Tse." Heng led her to a window that looked out into the next room. "I don't think he'll last the day."

Daiyu stared at the figure propped up in a hospital bed in the sealed room beyond. A lone nurse decked in a white biohazard suit checked a morphine drip that ran into his arm, the only limb still unafflicted. Tubes passed through his lips and nose, connected to a respirator that rhythmically rose and fell.

The submariner was a petty officer second class with the *Changzheng 24*. He was the only survivor found in the escape pod when it had been recovered ten days before. But he had not escaped unscathed. His legs were afflicted—hardened, blackened as the corpses. It was as if his lower half had been dipped in oil. Pain and delirium had kept him from answering any questions or explaining his condition.

Over the past days, the affliction had spread and climbed his body. It now covered half of his chest and left shoulder and had seeped halfway down the same arm. No regimen of drugs or radiation therapy had been able to stem its spread. Only one treatment showed any efficacy. It required lowering the patient's body temperature in ice baths and acidifying his blood. Still, it only slowed the progress and did not stop it.

"We've had to resuscitate him twice overnight," Heng reported with a lilt of fury. "He won't last much longer, not even with the heroic efforts we've employed."

Daiyu read sympathetic pain in the doctor's face. Heng had requested that she let the man die three days ago, but she had instructed Heng to keep him alive for as long as possible—or at least until they had more answers. At this point, no one knew if his affliction was due to the accidental exposure to an unknown toxin or if it was evidence of the deployment of an exotic bioweapon against the crew. Answers were needed, especially as recovery efforts were about to start on the lost vessel.

"What progress have you made while I've been gone?" Daiyu pressed him.

"It's a mixed bag at best. We've made some headway in terms of *what* is happening to his body. As to *why* or *how* it's happening, that continues to defy us."

"Show me what you've learned," she ordered him.

He drew her to a computer station. "His body is clearly undergoing a process of biomineralization. Take a look at this centrifuged sample of cerebrospinal fluid."

A pair of microscope images appeared on the screen. One showed a close-up of small crystals floating in a diffuse haze.

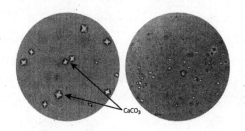

"What are they?" she asked.

"Calcium carbonate crystals."

She frowned. "Are those normally found in cerebral spinal fluid?"

"Definitely not." Heng glanced at her. "While carbonate naturally makes up about eight percent of our bodies, that's not where these crystals are coming from."

"Then where?"

"They're derived from the victim's *bones*."

"What?"

"The process seems to dissolve and scavenge the calcium from skeletal bones to produce these crystals—which are then densely deposited into the cell membranes throughout the body. The interior of the cell remains intact, but it makes the outer walls brittle and hard."

"Turning the body stone-like."

"Exactly. There's a condition called scleroderma, an autoimmune disease that produces too much fibrous tissue between cells, making the sufferer's skin and organs turn hard and unpliable. But in this case, it's not fibrous tissue that's causing it, but calcium deposits."

"And what of the bones themselves?"

Heng turned to the petty officer in the other room. "We took multiple scans of his legs. Though his limbs are stiff and solid, there are *no* bones beneath that hard shell. It's as if the process is terraforming his body, turning his internal skeletal structure into an exoskeleton."

Daiyu grimaced. "And you have no idea how this is happening?"

"All I know is that it's a brutal process, deriving most of the energy to fuel it from the victim. When Petty Officer Wong arrived here, his body temperature was 107, but as his condition worsened, it rose to 122 degrees. It's what sent him into a deep coma and maybe why the ice baths helped. Still, whatever is happening seems capable of unleashing the potential energy stored in a body—which is a tremendous amount. Our bodies are very efficient batteries for storing energy. It would take a car battery weighing a full ton to hold the same amount of energy retained in the fat stores of a healthy man."

"And something is tapping into it?"

"Not just tapping into it but unleashing it all at once—a biological nuclear explosion."

"But why? What's causing it?"

Heng shrugged in confusion. "I have no idea. I've identified no bacterium, virus, or chemical agent that could be triggering all of this. I don't know if what's happening is some form of bodily *preservation* or a new form of *predation*. Maybe both. I've studied the crystal's microstructure, looking for answers. The results were puzzling."

"How so?"

"Calcium carbonate is mainly found in two polymorphs, two different configurations of crystalline structure. It most often forms as *calcite*, like in limestone, where the crystals have a trigonal configuration." He pointed to the screen. "But using X-ray crystallography, it's clear these crystals are orthorhombic, a form called *aragonite*. This shape is less stable, but it's how calcium carbonate crystallizes out in the presence of *seawater*."

"Seawater?" Daiyu pictured the *Changzheng 24* sinking and crushing in the ocean depths. "Is that significant?"

"Maybe not. The concentration of salt and other ions in seawater is remarkably similar to what's found in our blood's serum. It might explain why the carbonate crystalizes into aragonite. But I can't be certain."

Daiyu nodded, feeling far more shaken up than before she had come down here.

But Heng was not done. "There's one last detail you should be aware of." He returned to the computer and moused through various menus and windows. "Again, I don't know the significance of what I found yesterday, but it's unusual enough that you should be alerted."

"What does it concern?"

"I told you before that the calcium crystals were being distributed throughout the cell membranes of the afflicted. That's not exactly true."

"What do you mean?"

He brought up a video clip onto the monitor. It showed him and another researcher in the neighboring morgue room, decked in biohazard suits. Someone else manned a camera and zoomed in as Heng took a vibrating bone saw to one of the corpse's calcified heads. He carved through the top and lifted it away. The camera shifted to reveal what was exposed.

Daiyu gasped at the gruesome sight.

The convolutions of a gray brain glistened under the light.

Heng explained. "While the rest of the body's cells—in every organ and tissue—underwent the biomineralization process, the central nervous system remained unaffected. The brain and spine seem largely untouched."

Swallowing down her horror, Daiyu fought to keep her voice steady. "Why do you think they were spared?"

Heng didn't bother answering. He gave a shake of his head. "What is most strange is that we tested the brain shown on the video. When we did, we picked up a faint EEG, as if there was some ongoing electrical energy."

She looked at him, aghast. "Are you saying the tissue is still alive?"

"No . . . certainly not," he insisted, though he sounded disturbingly hesitant. "I imagine it's just some residual heat energy from the violent process that's randomly stimulating nerves and synapses. But it's baffling, nonetheless. I intend to dissect out the brain and spine later today. Maybe then I'll—"

A sharp alarm rose from the neighboring room, loud enough to make Daiyu flinch.

Beyond the window, the nurse waved for help as the petty officer's body seized on the bed—or at least the part of him that was not frozen in stone.

Heng looked at Daiyu, his eyes pleading for her to let the patient go. She glanced to the macabre video paused on the monitor, then back to the physician. "Keep him alive."

Heng scowled but did not challenge her. "*Duì.*"

She turned and strode out of the lab. Half in a daze, she headed back to the elevator and took it to the second floor of the warehouse. She crossed in stiff steps toward her office.

Before she could reach it, her secretary rose from her desk and bowed before her. "*Hǎijūn shang xiao Tse,*" she greeted her. "I had a call from Beijing a short time ago. They are sending someone over this afternoon to consult with you on . . . on the project below."

"Who?"

The secretary looked down at the scrap of paper clutched in both hands. "Dr. Choi Aigua."

Daiyu frowned, not recognizing the name. "Who sent him?"

"The deputy head of the *Zhōngguó Guójiā Hángtiān Jú,*" she answered, naming the China National Space Administration. "Dr. Choi is an astrophysicist with the Academy of Space Technology."

Daiyu scrunched her brow in confusion.

Why are they sending an astrophysicist?

Still, a trickle of trepidation iced through her. She remembered Heng's earlier description of the biomineralization process, calling it a *terraforming* of the petty officer's body. She also could not shake the last image from Heng's video—of a glistening brain in a hard shell.

One that still shivered with energy.

She again pictured the damaged submarine sinking into the dark depths.

What is truly happening out there?

SECOND

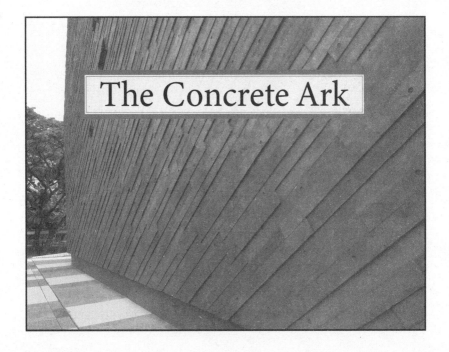

The Concrete Ark

9

Three hundred miles off Norfolk Island (Australia)

Phoebe climbed out of the submersible's upper hatch. The bright sunlight stung her eyes after a week underwater, but she refused to even blink. A wind buffeted her hair. She inhaled the fresh air and lifted her face to the sun in a cloud-scudded sky. It felt as if she had finished a free dive—and in some ways, she had.

Titan Station Down lay two miles under her feet. The ascent had taken twenty-two minutes. She had left Jazz down below to continue their research while she was gone. The new specimens collected last night needed to be analyzed, catalogued, and DNA sequenced. Phoebe trusted her grad student to handle it while she was away for four or five days on the excursion to the Tonga Trench.

She was excited for the trip, nearly breathless at the chance to be the first to explore that giant coral forest in the sunless abyssalpelagic depths of the trench. She clambered off the submersible, making room for Adam Kaneko, who would be coming on this trip with her.

She hopped down to the floating dock, where scores of other yellow subs were tethered around the massive pylons of *Titan Station Up*. She studied the two-tiered platform far overhead. This part of the Titan Project had been modified from the design of a floating oil rig. It served as the perfect staging ground for operations both on the surface and below.

Adam joined her, landing deftly on the planks. He ignored the colossal structure rising overhead and stared at the surrounding seas. "Are we too late?"

She followed his gaze. It took her an extra moment to realize one vital part of the Titan Complex was missing. The huge gigayacht—the *Titan X*—was no longer docked on the rig's far side.

She frowned. "Did the ship leave without us?"

She and Adam had been scheduled to board the massive research vessel this morning. The *Titan X* was supposed to ferry her and Adam the four hundred miles to the trench. The huge ship had a deep-sea submersible aboard that was rated for hadal dives. Plus, William Byrd— never one for half measures—had wanted to haul the yacht's scientific contingent over to the site of their discovery.

So where is it now?

"There you are!" a voice shouted to them.

They turned to find Byrd crossing from the elevator that rose up one of the legs of the rig. Anxious to find out what had changed overnight, Phoebe hurried to meet him with Adam at her heels.

"Ah," Byrd said. "I hope you are both well rested."

"Where's the *Titan X*?" Phoebe pressed him.

Byrd shaded his eyes and stared across the waves. "I sent her off four hours ago."

"Why?" Adam asked.

"To get a jump-start on the voyage. Even with her molten-salt reactors, it'll still take the ship nine hours to reach the trench. Didn't want to lose half the day." He pointed up. "I have a helicopter ready to hop you both over to her. Once you're aboard, it should be only another two or three hours until you're on site. We could have you diving into the Tonga by late afternoon."

Phoebe stammered, both excited to hear this and slightly irked that no one had warned her about the change in itinerary.

"There's another reason for the accelerated timetable," Byrd said as he led them toward the elevator. He glanced over to Adam. "I'm sure your uncle informed you about the devastation from the quake and the tsunami that struck the coast of China."

Adam winced. "He did."

"The death toll will surely rise into the tens of thousands before everything is cleaned up. If the cluster of quakes in the Tonga is truly to blame, then we can't waste any time getting there and discovering what's causing this tectonic instability."

Adam nodded. "My uncle is still below monitoring continual temblors throughout the region. He believes we've not seen the worst of it yet."

"It's why I'll be staying here. To assist your uncle and ready *Titan Station Down* to be evacuated if the threat level escalates."

"Are they in any danger?" Phoebe pictured Jazz. "Should you evacuate now as a precaution?"

"Even Haru thinks such a course is premature. Plus, there are multiple fail-safes to protect those aboard."

Phoebe was not reassured by his words, but she also recognized the importance of the endeavor ahead. If there was an answer in that trench, they needed to find it.

Byrd led them to the elevator, which would whisk them up to the topmost platform. The rumbling noise of an engine drew her attention out to the water. A seaplane ducked out of the sky and dove toward the waves.

Byrd stared toward it, too. "That should be our new guests. Arriving just in time."

Phoebe squinted. "Who are they?"

"The U.S. requested that two DARPA researchers join us. To judge the level of threat to the region and to help identify the submarine we found."

"Word must've traveled fast," Phoebe said sourly, perturbed that any military were getting involved, even if it was just a pair of DARPA scientists.

Byrd nodded. "As I understand it, they were already in the area. In Hong Kong. They were there for the quake and flooding. So it's little wonder that DARPA's taking our discovery seriously."

Phoebe frowned and glanced to Adam, expecting him to be equally irritated. Instead, his eyes had narrowed as he watched the seaplane course across the waves in a fan of spray. He did not look irked, only expectant and wary. One of his hands had balled into a fist, as if readying for a fight.

She suspected the truth.

He knew they were coming.

10:55 A.M.

Adam stood at the edge of the helipad with Dr. Reed. Phoebe had a backpack slung over her shoulder. His bag rested at his feet. They were not the only ones waiting.

An ESKY corporate helicopter—an AgustaWestland AW119 Koala—warmed its engines for the flight to the *Titan X*. With an extended flight range of more than six hundred miles, it would make the hop to the research yacht, then serve as a transport between these waters and the Tonga Trench.

Adam took advantage of the delay to bask in the warmth and take deep breaths. The scrubbed air and artificial light boxes paled to the real thing. He had been submerged at *Titan Station Down* for ten days. Still, he regretted leaving his uncle far below.

Phoebe shifted on her legs, bending one knee, then the other, clearly anxious to get underway. Under the bright sky, she looked like an Amazon preparing for war. She stood as tall as him, but there was no lankiness to her. Even the bagginess of her jumpsuit could not hide her curves.

She caught him staring. "That seaplane landed half an hour ago. When are we getting out of here?"

He shifted closer. "I'm sure Mr. Byrd is giving them his usual sales pitch for the Titan Project, likely trying to encourage DARPA to reach deeper into its pockets to further fund this enterprise."

"No doubt." Her eyes sparkled with amusement. "But I'd prefer the military stay as far from this project as possible. Still, I get why they're involved. Do you think the submarine could be from the U.S. Navy?"

"I . . . I don't know." He felt a twinge of discomfort at lying to her.

He swallowed and glanced toward the elevator as its doors opened. "But it looks like we'll finally be underway."

Byrd led the two Sigma operatives across the deck. The billionaire's head was bowed toward the shorter of the two men. Director Higashi had already passed a brief dossier to Adam on the newcomers. Aiko had assured him that the two could be fully trusted and had told him to give them his full cooperation—though she had also cautioned him to be discreet when sharing any details about TaU.

Despite Aiko's assurance, Adam resented involving a foreign covert group. He was proud of all that TaU had accomplished in a short time. In the past six months, they had thwarted a bioterrorist attack in Kyoto and exposed a Russian hacking scheme against the Japanese Ministry of Foreign Affairs. But those operations had all been on home soil. He understood the necessity for Sigma's involvement here—both as support and to address the caveat in Japan's constitution that limited intelligence operations conducted abroad.

Still, it doesn't mean I have to like it.

Byrd reached them and made introductions, offering Phoebe and Adam's names and backgrounds. He then waved to the shorter of the two men, who wore a gray hoodie and a black pair of tech trousers with multiple pockets.

"This is Monk Kokkalis, who has a PhD in biology with an emphasis on biomedicine, which hopefully will prove valuable as you all dive into that trench."

The man doffed a black cap, exposing a bald scalp. He shook Phoebe's hand, then offered his palm to Adam.

Adam gripped it hard to assert his place. Still, it was like trying to break rocks with his fingers. The Sigma operative might only stand to Adam's shoulders but every inch of him was steel.

Monk's expression never changed from its genial grin. "I hope we're not intruding."

"Not at all," Adam answered, trying not to grit his teeth.

They backed from each other as Byrd motioned to Monk's towering companion, a beast of a man. His gruff face was gnarled by an old break of his nose. He bore a cut across a cheek, taped over but clearly fresh. He wore a long wool duster over black jeans, boots, and a T-shirt. He hauled a heavy duffel over one arm.

"This is Joseph Kowalski. Former Navy man, with a degree in mining and demolition."

Adam was happy the man failed to offer his hand, fearing that massive mitt would crush his bones to dust. Kowalski merely nodded to each with a small grunt of acknowledgment.

"As there's very limited space in the research submersible that'll descend into the trench," Byrd said, glancing at the larger man, "especially for one this size, Mr. Kowalski will be staying here to assist Dr. Kaneko and me in monitoring the ongoing threat."

Monk gave Adam and Phoebe a big smile. "Looks like it'll just be me joining you."

"With that settled, let's get you on your way." Byrd waved to the waiting helicopter. "Safe travels. Stay in communication at all times. And we'll do the same."

The group split off in opposite directions as the helicopter's rotors spun up.

Monk called back to his companion. "Don't break anything!"

Kowalski shrugged, clearly promising nothing.

Adam frowned between the two, even more certain about one detail of this mission.

I'd be better off on my own.

10

Under a dreary drizzle of rain, Gray headed over a pedestrian bridge that crossed the Ayer Rajah Expressway. He carried an umbrella and wore a blue windbreaker against the weather. The day was warm, in the mid-eighties, and sticky.

Below the bridge, traffic was sparse for the normally vibrant and bustling city. The entire region seemed to be holding its breath, hunkering down. Singapore had felt the quake and caught the edge of the tsunami, but it had experienced little of the devastation suffered along the coasts of China, Vietnam, and the Philippines. The death toll steadily climbed as rescue operations continued.

And the worst might not be over.

Gray hoped that the geologists' warnings of a greater cataclysm to come proved to be overblown. For now, all he could do was focus on the task at hand. Monk and Kowalski had already reached the Titan Complex in the Coral Sea. He had also confirmed that Kat was in the air, headed home in a private jet arranged by Painter. Jack and the girls, with the resiliency of the very young, were already recovering from the night of chaos and terror.

With the kids out of harm's way, Gray felt more centered on the mission. As he reached the end of the pedestrian bridge, he studied his target as it loomed into view.

The Lee Kong Chian Natural History Museum rose like a seven-story dark gray boulder sitting at the edge of the National University of Singapore. The monolithic structure was nearly windowless, covered from top to bottom in molded concrete planks. The angular shape of its roof and sides made it look as if a giant ark had beached itself on the campus.

To Gray, it was a concrete safe that he needed to crack in order to solve a mystery.

What did the Chinese want with this museum?

Behind him, Seichan murmured with her mother, while Zhuang kept alongside Gray. The two triad leaders had accompanied them to Singapore to assist in the investigation. Guan-yin had a slew of contacts in the area. With the timetable so short, Gray had accepted their help—not that he could have persuaded Seichan's mother otherwise.

Guan-yin had already proven herself valuable by helping them ferry weapons into Singapore. Gray carried his SIG Sauer P229 at the base of his back, hidden under the fall of a light sweater and a windbreaker. Seichan had Monk's pistol, a Glock 45, secured in a Kevlar ankle holster.

No doubt, Guan-yin and Zhuang were similarly armed—though the triad lieutenant had left his saber at the hotel on the other side of the expressway. As an extra precaution, Guan-yin wore a crimson silk niqab that wrapped her head and neck, with a gauzy veil over the lower half of her face, hiding her tattoo and scarring.

Zhuang shifted closer to Gray. "What do you hope to gain from coming this early? If the Chinese strike, it will surely be after hours, under the cover of night. And we can already see inside the museum via its security cameras."

"Cameras are not as good as one's own eyes."

While they had been traveling here, Sigma's resident tech guru, Jason Carter, had hacked the camera feed, offering them a continual view into the museum. But Gray had not been satisfied. There remained too many blind spots. Before nightfall, he wanted to get a better lay of the land, which was best done on foot.

Painter had already confirmed that nothing out of the ordinary had happened at the museum so far. Apparently, it remained unmolested.

Sigma's director had also delivered a care package to their hotel. It held encrypted sat-phones and e-tablets, radios and throat mikes, but most importantly it contained a quad of IVAS military goggles. The Integrated Augmented Vision System eyewear not only came with the latest night-vision tech, but it allowed the hacked camera feed to appear in the heads-up display inside the goggles.

Before leaving the hotel, Gray had them all insert radio earpieces and tape throat mikes in place. The devices were nearly invisible unless one looked closely. He wanted the group in constant communication. He split the remainder of their gear into shoulder packs, which they all carried.

Gray checked his watch and got them all moving more swiftly. "We need to pick up the pace."

At noon, they were scheduled for a private tour arranged by Sigma's contacts at the Smithsonian Institution. It had not been difficult to arrange. Sigma's headquarters were buried beneath the Smithsonian Castle on the National Mall. The site was chosen due to its proximity to both the extensive research labs of the Institution and to the neighboring halls of power in D.C. The location had served the group in the past—and did again now. This tour would allow his team access to the museum's private spaces, while also bypassing the metal detectors and bag searches at the public entrance.

Gray continued around to the front of the museum. Its façade changed dramatically. The far corner of the building had been carved away, forming a reef of exposed balconies. They were overgrown with trees, shrubs, and ferns, all cascading down in a fall of leafy vegetation. It was meant to represent the lush cliffs of Singapore's outer islands. Other gardens also surrounded the museum.

Seichan joined Gray, allowing Zhuang to drop next to her mother. "Where are we supposed to meet the museum director?"

He pointed away from the wide steps leading up to the public entrance. "There's a group entrance around the side. That's where Professor Kwong should be waiting."

They all strode briskly through the midday bustle. Gray continued to watch all around. So did Seichan.

"You were doing a lot of reading during the flight," she whispered. "Did any of it offer a clue as to what the Chinese might be searching for here?"

"No. The museum contains more than a million specimens. But only a fraction is displayed in the museum's galleries. Everything else is stored in dry and wet labs on the upper floors. Areas that are off limits."

This was the other reason Gray had wanted to arrange a behind-the-scenes tour. The museum covered more than ninety thousand square feet, but the public galleries encompassed only a quarter of that space.

Gray searched up at the towering structure. "Odds are that whatever the Chinese are after is in one of those restricted areas."

"That's still a lot of ground to cover. Didn't that strange mind of yours narrow anything down for us?"

"I'm not a miracle worker."

Still, Gray knew he had been recruited into Sigma for that *strange mind*—far more than for his military background with the Army Rangers. While growing up, Gray had always been pulled between opposites. His mother had been a deeply devout Catholic who staunchly challenged Church dogma. His father had been a roughneck oilman who had been disabled in midlife and forced to assume the role of a housewife. Maybe this upbringing made Gray look at things differently, to try to balance extremes. Or maybe it was something genetic, ingrained in his DNA, that allowed him to see patterns that no one else could.

After a decade with Sigma, he had come to realize his talent wasn't so much a matter of thinking *outside* the box as it was throwing everything *into* that box and shaking it until some semblance of order revealed itself.

"And you remain entirely baffled?" Seichan challenged him.

He glanced sidelong at her.

She studied his face. He tried to keep his features stoic, but she knew him too well. "You *did* figure something out."

"A hunch at best," he admitted.

"What?"

"Singapore's museum may have an extensive collection, but China has its *own* natural history museums in Shanghai, Beijing, even Hong Kong. All with similarly vast collections. So why dispatch a team here? What's so important about this museum?"

Seichan shrugged.

"I had Jason cross-reference the various databases of regional museums, looking for items that are unique to this location. And while there are many specimens found nowhere else, nothing struck me as overtly unusual or that could be tied in any way to a wrecked submarine and strange quakes."

"So you hit a dead end."

"I did—until I studied *where* this collection originated. The history of the museum itself is more intriguing than its contents."

"How so?"

"Both the founding of Singapore and the founding of this museum tie back to a man named Sir Thomas Stamford Raffles. In 1819, he established the port city that would become modern Singapore. But he was also an avid naturalist who loved this region's flora and fauna, making countless discoveries. To preserve and showcase the biodiversity, he started the Singapore Institution in 1823, which was the first incarnation of the museum here. It was later renamed the Raffles Museum in his honor, then again changed to the National Museum of Singapore in 1965. Even now, it remains the oldest such institute in all of Southeast Asia. Eventually, though, its natural history section—and all its specimens—were moved here to this new location in 2015."

Seichan frowned at him. "Why does any of that matter?"

"History always matters."

Her frown deepened. "Get to the point, professor."

"Within this building, at the heart of the collection, are legacy artifacts that trace directly to Sir Stamford Raffles, to when he first started the collection, to before he ever set foot in Singapore. His interest in natural history preceded his arrival here, going back to when he was the lieutenant-governor of Java. There, he had been the president of the Batavian Society, a scientific group interested in preserving and promoting the natural history of the East Indies. Some of the artifacts in the museum date back to that time period."

"And why's that important?"

"It might not be, but while Raffles was lieutenant-governor, the region suffered one of the world's most devastating tectonic events. The eruption of Mount Tambora. It triggered quakes, swept a series of tsunamis throughout the region, and darkened the skies with an ash cloud that swept around the world." He looked at her. "Sound familiar? With the apocalyptic predictions made by the geology team at Titan Station, the Chinese could be looking for something preserved from that catastrophic event, something they deem important enough to warrant raiding the museum."

Seichan lifted one brow, questioning this line of supposition. "Is that what your strange mind led you to?"

"Like I said," he countered with a shrug, "it's only a hunch."

Still, he left unsaid what he truly believed.

My hunches are seldom wrong.

1:34 P.M.

Seichan climbed behind Gray as they followed Professor Darren Kwong, the current head of the museum, up a curving stair to the mezzanine level. The curator was a short Malaysian man with a ready smile and an open manner. He wore a knee-length lab coat over a white shirt and red tie, likely representing the two colors of Singapore's flag. The man clearly took great pride in his country and this establishment.

"Now we come to our Heritage Gallery," Kwong exclaimed with a sweep of his arm toward a section of the museum that looked like a turn-of-the-century library. The gallery was lined by tall wood-and-glass cases full of old books, artifacts, and curiosities. "Here we have on display the museum's earliest history. Feel free to open some of the cases and drawers. We wanted to make it feel as interactive as possible."

Gray did just that, lingering over each glass case as he walked down the row. From their prior talk, Seichan knew this was an area of special interest to Gray. The same could not be said of her.

Seichan tried not to exhale her impatience as she lagged behind the pair. Their group had spent an hour touring the main floor's fifteen zones, which hallmarked the region's biodiversity—from the origin of life through all its branches, stems, and leaves. The span covered millions of years.

And it had felt like it.

Her mother and Zhuang remained below, waiting for a light show that would further highlight the three towering sauropod skeletons, whose long necks and skulls rose beyond the mezzanine level. With everyone's radio earpieces and throat mikes in place, they could stay in communication. Guan-yin and Zhuang also surreptitiously watched the public entrance, keeping alert for any suspicious visitors.

Gray straightened and faced Kwong. "I see you've divided the Heritage Gallery into two sections, covering Sir Stamford Raffles on one side and William Farquhar on the other. The timelines of their contributions and discoveries overlap extensively. Why are they kept separately?"

Kwong's smile broadened. "Because otherwise we might be haunted by their ghosts. Sir Raffles and Major-General Farquhar both helped found Singapore and were equally avid naturalists. They competed for discoveries, fought over recognition, and disparaged each other at every turn, sometimes quite heatedly, all the way until their deaths. So, we dared not put them into the same cabinet together."

Gray shifted to the cabinet with Farquhar stenciled at the top. "How did the two become so embittered? According to his placard, it was Raffles who appointed Farquhar to oversee Singapore after the city was founded?"

"Ah, you see, Raffles wasn't happy with the lax manner in which his appointee undertook the assignment. Farquhar failed to follow the instructions that Raffles had left. Under Farquhar's helm, slave-trading flourished in Singapore, along with the spread of opium and other vices. Friction grew between them, worsening with every passing year. Then Farquhar committed an act so heinous that Raffles abruptly dismissed him from his post."

Gray frowned. "What did he do?"

"Stories vary, but it's said that their animosity had grown so fierce at the end that Farquhar had sought to dig up some dirt on Sir Raffles, something that would drive his competitor out of the region. Hearsay at the time was that Raffles was harboring some great secret, but no one knew what it was. Rumors abounded of a great treasure or some shameful truth. Farquhar enlisted allies from local criminal elements, mainly among the Chinese who facilitated the opium trade in the city, to root out his secret. When Raffles learned of this ploy, he sacked Farquhar immediately."

Gray glanced Seichan's way with a raised brow, as if scolding her for doubting him. He turned back to Kwong. "Did he ever find out *what* that secret was?"

The curator shrugged. "Not that I know of, but Farquhar continued to have good relations with the Chinese, who awarded him a departing gift, a silver cup that cost seven hundred dollars, an exorbitant sum at the time. It was also the Chinese who assisted him with his naturalist efforts, supplying artists who completed nearly five hundred illustrations for him." Kwong led Gray down the case on that side. "You can see a few here."

Gray followed, bending down to study an intricate plate of a brightly colored bird. "If Farquhar had learned Raffles's secret, then the Chinese would have likely known about it, too."

"I would imagine so, but nothing ever came of it."

"At least, not yet," Gray mumbled.

Kwong glanced his way. "What was that?"

"Nothing." Gray straightened. "When did this all take place?"

"Back in 1823."

Gray frowned at the curator. "That's the same year the museum was founded, when it was called the Singapore Institution."

"That's true."

"Who did Raffles assign to take Farquhar's place? To oversee the city. And his new museum."

"A physician, a man named Dr. John Crawfurd."

"A physician?"

"And fellow budding naturalist. Crawfurd had worked under Raffles when he was the lieutenant-governor of Java."

Seichan drew closer.

Gray and his damned hunches . . .

Gray kept his focus on Kwong. "So Crawfurd was in Java with Raffles when Mount Tambora erupted in 1815."

Kwong's brow pinched in confusion. "I suppose he was. Though I can only imagine what that horrible event must have been like for the two men."

Gray glanced at Seichan. "Let's hope we only have to imagine it."

2:09 P.M.

Gray rose up in the elevator with Seichan and Dr. Kwong. The director tapped a keycard to allow the cage to access the five floors of the museum above the two public ones. They were headed into the working heart of the museum.

As the elevator climbed, Gray pondered the puzzle in his head. Had Raffles and Crawfurd discovered something during the Tambora eruption, a secret that Farquhar later uncovered and shared with his Chinese conspirators? Clearly whatever it was hadn't made any sense at the time because Farquhar had never exposed what he had learned. Neither had the Chinese, but they were notoriously detailed record-keepers. Some account could have been preserved over the passing two centuries. Whatever secret Raffles had kept, he had placed Dr. John Crawfurd, a trusted friend, to act as its steward, hiding it in a museum that would come to bear his name.

But what was so important that it required such secrecy?

The elevator door hissed open onto the third floor, and Kwong led them over to a door that also needed a keycard to open. As they stepped through, a sharp tang stung Gray's nose. Ahead and spreading across the breadth of the museum were shelves upon shelves of glass specimen jars of various sizes.

Kwong drew them along the rows. "These first two private floors hold our *wet* collection, both vertebrate and invertebrate species, all suspended in ethanol."

Gray now recognized the source of the tang in the air. They passed a researcher wearing a face shield, bent over a table. A coiled, striped snake had been freshly decanted from a bottle next to it. The specimen lay sprawled on a tray. A fume hood hummed over the workstation, but it failed to completely vacuum away the alcohol evaporating off the soaked specimen.

Kwong drew them to a shelf and stopped before a collection of tiny jars that looked far older than the others. The handwritten labels were faded and peeling. The bottles held a collection of tiny crabs, some no larger than a thumbnail.

"You showed interest in our museum's history," the curator said. "These crustaceans were collected by a Royal Navy ship—the HMS *Alert*—from a Singapore beach back in 1881. Yet, they look as fresh as the day they were caught."

"Impressive." Gray peered closer, then straightened to face Kwong. "How far back in age does your collection go?"

"That's hard to say. In the early days of the museum, specimens were often donated by the public. They came from explorers and adventurers or were sold to the Singapore Institution by locals. Oftentimes with poor provenance. Confounding matters, many of the labels disintegrated long ago."

Gray glanced back to Seichan, who trailed them. Her lips were sealed tight with distaste as she looked across the drowned collection.

Kwong led them onward to the far side where a door opened into a stairwell. They headed up again.

Gray climbed alongside the director. "In regard to those historical specimens, were any of them contributed by Stamford Raffles?"

"Of course. We have a few on display in the Heritage Gallery downstairs."

"Yes, but none were dated as far back as the museum's founding in 1823."

"Ah, those treasures are kept in a locked vault."

"Really? You still have them? I'd love to see them."

"We can end the tour there if you'd like. The specimens inside are not of any real scientific importance. We have better examples in the greater collection. They're simply locked up due to their age. So, I hope you're not disappointed."

Gray nodded.

Me, too.

When they reached the next floor, Kwong led them into a sprawling labyrinth of tall metal cabinets, all stacked tightly against one another, forming solid walls. Each cabinet had a steel wheel affixed to its end, which allowed it to be rolled right or left down a track.

Kwong waved as he passed along them. "This floor houses our *dry* collection. These compactors allow us to efficiently use the space, to store as many specimens as possible. The cabinets hold thousands of drying shelves where specimens are preserved."

He continued past a room where several researchers bustled about, pinning insects to boards. One woman concentrated on delicately pinning and separating the legs of an arachnid the size of Gray's palm. As they forged on, Kwong elaborated on the drying, freezing, and preservation methods for the specimens. Gray let him drone on, not wanting to press him too hard or risk raising warning bells by being too direct.

Still, time was running short.

"The historical vault you mentioned before," Gray said, "is it on this level?"

Kwong glanced up. "No, above us are offices and a research lab." The director looked at Gray with a raised brow. "And our historical vault."

Gray glanced at his watch, less to check the time as to silently communicate that the tour needed to come to an end.

Kwong got the message. "I can take you there right now."

He turned abruptly toward the stairwell and nearly collided into the petite researcher who carried a huge spider pinned to a cardboard tray.

"*Maafkan saya,*" he apologized in Malay to the young woman.

She tossed her tray aside and revealed the pistol clutched beneath it. She jammed the weapon into Kwong's ribs. The other researchers from the pinning room rushed out with weapons in hand. Boots pounded up behind them.

Kwong's captor glared at Gray and Seichan.

The woman had dark hair, bobbed short, with smoky eyes. Her features were a shade of almond. Gray knew all of it was fake. In his mind's eye, he stripped away the wig, the make-up, the contact lenses, even the sculpting latex that widened her cheekbones. He pictured the pale woman beneath, the blank canvas over which she had layered her disguise.

"I think your tour has come to an end," Valya said.

11

Captain Tse Daiyu intended to defend her turf. She had expended considerable time and energy to establish this research installation on Cambodian soil. She refused to let another division of the military commandeer the project. To be shoved aside would be a blemish on her record, carrying with it a measure of dishonor.

Still, she greeted the astrophysicist with respect. She stood behind her desk as her secretary led the man into her office. She offered a small bow. "Welcome to Cambodia, Dr. Choi."

"*Xièxiè nín,*" he responded formally and crossed to the seat offered to him.

After being alerted to his pending arrival, Daiyu had already read up on the visitor. Choi Aigua was in his late sixties, two decades older than her, and had served most of his life in the PLA, specifically at the Jiuquan Satellite Launch Center, where Chinese taikonauts were flown into space. He had risen to the rank of *zhōngjiàng*, a lieutenant-general with PLA Strategic Support Force, before retiring from service. Still, he stayed on as a consultant with the China Academy of Space Technology.

And now he's here.

She waited for him to sit before she settled behind her desk. She was suddenly all too aware of the spartan nature of her office. Beyond the utilitarian steel desk, which supported a desktop computer and a neat stack of folders, there were two file cabinets and a spare chair pushed into a corner. Daiyu seldom greeted visitors in her private space. There was a conference room down the hall for any organizational meetings.

The only bit of drama in her office was the large window that over-looked the warehouse's docking bay.

Aigua cleared his throat. "I'm sorry to intrude, Captain Tse. And thank you for allowing me to bring my son." He waved to a young man leaning on her secretary's desk with a hat in hand. "Xue is a major with the Strategic Support Force."

She nodded, hearing the pride in his voice. Clearly, his son had fol-lowed in his father's footsteps, likely gaining his rank at such a young age due to his paternal connection. Irritation shot through her, know-ing how hard it had been for her to gain her captaincy.

Still, she kept her voice even. "How may I help you?"

"My son and I have come to view the bodies recovered from the *Changzheng 24*. It seems the goals of the PLA Navy and the Strategic Support Force have grown aligned in this matter."

"How?" she asked, voicing the question that had plagued her all day. No amount of research had revealed any explanation. "Of what interest is this to the space agency?"

"Because we were the ones who sent the *Changzheng 24* to its doom."

Daiyu failed to hide her surprise and rein in her reaction. "I . . . I had not been told."

"Very few in the PLA were informed. Most believed the new subma-rine was on a shakedown cruise, to test its capabilities."

Her jaw muscles clenched, but she spoke calmly. "That is what I was informed."

"And now you will know the truth."

"Which is what?"

"The *Changzheng 24* was dispatched to investigate an aberrant radio signal rising from a deep-sea trench, where it eventually sank. It had on board a bevy of drones, autonomous ROVs that you yourself developed while designing the *Zhu Hai Yun* research vessel."

She sat straighter, proud of her accomplishment. Still, a worry settled in her gut. *If something went wrong with one of my drones, will the blame for the sub's sinking be placed on me?*

She kept her voice guarded. "What were you searching for?"

Aigua looked down, clearly organizing his thoughts, before finally speaking. "Captain Tse, how familiar are you with the Chang'e-5 project, the lunar mission back in 2020?"

Daiyu blinked at the sudden change in the conversation's direction. "Only that the spacecraft traveled to the moon and brought back a payload of lunar rocks."

Aigua sighed. "Then there is much you don't know—can't know, in fact. What has generally been reported is that the Chang'e-5 landed atop an old lava plain on the moon's northern edge, a region called Oceanus Procellarum. The lander drilled into the volcanic plain and brought home two kilograms of mare basalt. It was the first such lunar sampling in more than forty-five years."

Daiyu frowned, still failing to see what this had to do with a sunken sub.

Aigua continued. "The purpose of the mission was to get a better understanding of the moon's *evolution*. According to current consensus, the moon was formed when a Mars-size planetary object—called Theia—smashed into the infant Earth, some four and a half million years ago. The ejecta of that collision—a mix of rock, gas, and dust—coalesced into a hot magma ball that would eventually cool into our moon."

"I still don't see what this has to do with—"

Aigua cut her off. "The sample collected by Chang'e-5 proved to be far *younger* than the rocks from earlier lunar missions, showing evidence that they had cooled much slower. This demonstrated that the moon had been volcanically active for far *longer* than previous estimates. The results made no scientific sense. For the moon to still be hot for such an abnormally long span, it would require the presence of an unknown heat source—some element or process that delayed the moon's cooling."

"Like what?"

"Theories abound." Aigua shrugged. "It is a mystery that continues to baffle scientists. Some initially believed the heat source could be an unusually large concentration of decaying uranium or thorium. But the rocks recovered by Chang'e-5 ruled this out."

"Then what could it be?"

"I have my own theory, one I've been trying to substantiate since the spacecraft returned to Earth."

"Did that substantiation involve sending a submarine to its doom?" Daiyu asked with a note of bitterness. She had dealt with scientists in the past who grew so focused that they failed to see the larger picture, or the real-world cost of their research. "What discovery on the moon could possibly justify such a mission?"

"A discovery that could change the world," Aigua said with a coldness to counter her anger. "While we sent lunar rocks to labs around China, we kept the most exciting bits at the SSF labs."

"What bits?"

"A tiny fraction of dust. It took us a while to separate out those exotic particles. At first glance, they appeared to be ordinary basalt, a mix of silicates and metal oxides. But the particles were in a state of radioactive decay and were isotopically different from any other rock. Even their crystalline structure was unusual."

Daiyu flashed to Dr. Luo Heng's computer, showing the strange crystals that had coated the cells of the afflicted submariners. For now, she kept silent about it.

Aigua reached to the side of his chair and lifted a briefcase to his lap. He snapped it open. "If you'll allow me, let me backtrack for a moment." He rummaged inside the case while he continued. "For the longest time, many assumed that the moon was formed out of a piece of Theia, the planetoid that struck Earth. But we now know through isotopic studies that the moon and the earth are made of the same material."

Daiyu sensed where this was headed. "But according to you, that exotic dust you discovered was isotopically *different*."

Aigua nodded. "While it's clear that a majority of the moon is derived from Earth, I believe a small fraction of the planetoid Theia got mixed into the moon's formation, too."

"You think those exotic particles came from Theia."

"Exactly. The particles are elementally strange and radioactive enough that they could be the unknown *heat source* that kept the moon hotter for far longer than it should have."

Daiyu shook her head. "That's intriguing enough, I suppose, but it still doesn't explain why you came to Cambodia."

"I'm here because—while the exotic particles from Chang'e-5 prove that a bit of Theia got incorporated into the moon—*massive* slabs of the planetoid have been found elsewhere."

"Where?"

"Right here on Earth. Under our very feet." He looked hard at Daiyu. "And they may soon destroy us."

2:44 P.M.

Dr. Luo Heng breathed heavily through his respirator. He stood in the sealed morgue with Zhào Min. The thin-limbed studious woman was a colleague of his, a molecular biologist from the University of Shanghai. The two had coauthored five papers together. When he had been commandeered for this monumental task, he had recruited her.

A pang of guilt etched through him now. He regretted involving her in this covert investigation. There would be no papers published on this research. They had both signed ironclad nondisclosure documents. Breaking their silence would likely end with a punishment far worse than any bankrupting fine or imprisonment. It would likely end up with them both dead and buried.

And regardless of our pledged agreement, we may still end up there.

He pushed down that fear and inserted another electrode into the occipital lobe of the brain that he and Min had dissected out of the body.

As they worked, Junjie videotaped them with a handheld recorder. The tall sublieutenant barely fit his biohazard suit. Even with the chill in the air, his face streamed with sweat behind his face shield. His eyes looked glassy, his mouth tight, likely fighting against a sickening churn of his stomach.

He had been forced to watch as Min and Heng had cut into the blackened corpse, the same body upon which they had performed a craniotomy the day before. Heng had rolled the subject onto its stomach and spent two hours cracking open the back of the skull and slicing down the spine. He then had delicately dissected out the brain and spinal cord, along with many intact nerve bundles.

It had proven to be surprisingly easy. With the surrounding bones dissolved away, the brittle calciferous flesh had parted cleanly around the neurological tissue. He had described it at the time: *like peeling a hardboiled egg from a shell.*

Junjie had coughed and clutched his stomach at this analogy.

After placing another electrode needle, Heng straightened and studied his handiwork. The brain and spine were all in one piece, soaking in a saline-filled plastic tub. He had needed the tissue insulated from the steel table under it to run an intracranial EEG. Thirty needles had been implanted across the stretch of the brain and spine.

"That should be the last of them," Heng reported.

Min nodded and attached tiny clamps to the final two electrodes. Wires ran from all of them to a portable encephalogram. They crossed together and activated the EEG. Bent shoulder to shoulder by the monitor, they waited for it to warm up.

Heng noted how Min leaned heavily on him. He knew she had more than an academic interest in him. That affection was likely the larger impetus for her agreeing to come to Cambodia. Suspecting that—and unable to return her passion—only sharpened his guilt at involving her in this project. He had never been honest with her regarding his sexuality. In the academic world, especially following the handoff of Hong Kong to China, anything outside the ordinary could end one's career. So, he remained deeply closeted, playing the role expected of him.

On the screen, glowing lines finally stacked across the monitor. The image flickered as the system fully engaged. The rows vibrated up into jagged spikes and troughs, but the amplitudes remained low.

Just like yesterday.

"It's still there," Heng whispered. "I was sure the electrical activity would've faded by now. With no blood flow and no oxygenation, none of this should be happening. It makes no sense."

"Could the leads be responding to some electromagnetic radiation from the installation around us?" Min offered. "The engineering projects above us surely require great amounts of power."

Heng shook his head. "No. We're decently insulated down here. And look at the pattern. The rhythms and waves are too much like normal brain activity." He ran a finger down a few of the lines. "These are clearly alpha, delta, beta, and gamma waves. Interference noise wouldn't randomly produce them."

Min leaned closer. "Then what are we looking at?"

Heng studied the screen. He absently lifted a hand to his chin only to have it bump against his face shield. He lowered his arm. "I can't say with any certainty, especially as weak as the signaling is. But it looks like there is a marked decrease in alpha waves and an increase in theta and delta."

"What does that mean?"

"The brainwave pattern looks like what you'd see in a coma patient."

Min glanced at him. "Petty Officer Wong fell into a coma when his temperature spiked. Surely these men suffered the same before dying. Could this be some ghost of that event? A pattern burned into their brains and still somehow persisting after death."

"If that was even possible, something would still have to sustain the tissues, keeping the neurons oxygenated and alive. Whatever is happening here is too important to ignore."

He had planned on sectioning the brain and studying the tissue, intent to determine *why* the CNS had been spared the calcification. But with this sustained electrical activity, he decided against it for the moment.

First, he wanted to explore one other avenue.

"I'd like to see what happens if we stimulate the tissue with more energy." He turned to Junjie. "Can you use the intercom and ask Nurse Lam to bring over the pulse generator from Officer Wong's bedside?"

The sublieutenant nodded, looking relieved to step away.

The portable EEG had come from the same room. They had been using it to monitor Wong's comatose state. Heng had also requested that a neurostimulator be brought into the lab. Pulse-generating units were used to treat neurological disease, even comas. They had tried it on Wong, but it had no effect.

Heng stared across the drape of brain and spine, peppered with needles as if attacked by a mad acupuncturist.

"What do you hope to learn from deep brain stimulation?" Min asked.

"If it is ghosting, as you suggested, a surge of electricity should disrupt it, erasing this pattern. But if this is truly a coma pattern, I'm wondering if neurostimulation might reset a normal rhythm."

Junjie met the nurse in the airlock and returned with the handheld pulse generator. Loose wires hung from it. Heng accepted the tool and attached the unit's leads to electrodes across the brain.

Once done, Heng returned to the EEG. Its screen continued to run with whispery waves and small jagged lines. He clutched the battery-powered neurostimulator and twisted the dial. "I'm going to start at the lowest setting."

Min watched the monitor.

"Here we go." Heng pressed the button and a light blinked green for two seconds, then turned red as the pulse ended. He turned to Min. "Anything?"

She pointed to a spiky scrabble of lines that marked the jolt of electricity. "Give it a moment."

The lines quickly faded back to quieter rhythms and waves. It all looked the same. The surge had failed to erase the pattern or reset a normal pattern. The only difference was perhaps a slightly increased amplitude to the rise and fall of the tracings.

Heng turned the dial to its midpoint. "Trying again with a bit more vigor."

He pushed the button, waited for the green light to turn red, then faced Min. Again, the results were the same. No significant change, only some greater swings in the heights and valleys of the waves on the screen, as if those seas were growing more agitated.

"I'm going for a full pulse," he warned and twisted the dial until it stopped. "Here goes."

He pressed the button—and all hell broke loose.

3:02 P.M.

Daiyu gaped in disbelief at Aigua. "You truly believe that huge pieces of an ancient planetoid can be found beneath the earth?"

"Bear with me," the astrophysicist urged her. He rummaged through the briefcase on his lap and removed an e-tablet. He unlocked it with his thumbprint. He spoke while swiping and tapping at its screen. "Since the 1970s, we've known of the existence of two massive blob-like structures within the earth's viscous layer of its mantle. They were identified using seismic tomography, which revealed that earthquake waves would slow when they tried to cross through those regions. Because of that, scientists called them *large low-shear velocity provinces*, or LLSVPs. Eventually due to their shape, most simply call them *blobs*."

Aigua leaned forward and placed his e-tablet on her desk. "These blobs are the size of continents and a hundred times as tall as Mount Everest. One lies under Africa."

He brought up an image on his screen that showed an amorphous shape lurking under Africa.

"And another LLSVP lies on the other side of the world," Aigua explained. "Under the Pacific, with its edge extending into this region."

He swiped his e-tablet's screen and rotated the world until Australia and Southeast Asia appeared. A second continent-size shadow appeared, spreading under the Pacific.

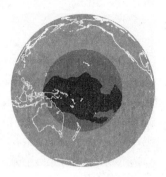

Daiyu straightened after studying the screen. "You think these two blobs are the remains of the planetoid Theia?"

"Not just me. It's the growing consensus of the scientific community. The latest geodynamic research further confirms this supposition."

Daiyu leaned back in her chair, trying to imagine shattered bits of an alien planet buried under the crust of Earth. "You mentioned these blobs posed some threat. That it could destroy us all. How?"

"Whether or not these LLSVPs are truly from Theia, what is known is that they're the cause of tectonic instability, especially at their edges. The African blob has been the source of violent volcanic activity throughout Africa's history. It's also the reason the continent has slowly been rising, pushed up from below by the mass beneath it."

Aigua pointed to the schematic still on his tablet. "The Pacific LLSVP has been equally problematic. It's one of the main engines that drive the volcanic Ring of Fire around the Pacific Ocean. Throughout Earth's history, these blobs have driven up millions of cubic kilometers of lava, oozing upward in huge plumes. It's believed one such plume triggered the Great Dying at the end of the Permian Period, an extinction event that wiped out most life on the planet. And even today, those blobs remain geological time bombs. Especially if they're disturbed."

"How do you disturb a continent-size chunk of an ancient planet?"

"That's why I'm here. Because we did just that."

"What? How?"

"That's what I'm trying to find out. If we can discover the answer, it could lead to a weapon that would make the world's nuclear arsenal obsolete. To cement China's dominance for centuries."

Daiyu cast him a doubtful look.

Aigua continued, "When Chang'e-5 was drilling into the lunar plain, we momentarily lost satellite contact with the lander. When it was re-established, the drill had stopped and appeared inoperable. We told the world that we had hit a layer of shale that restricted us from digging deeper, but that was not the reason. When we examined the lander's drill after it returned, its electronics had been melted."

"What happened?"

"We don't know. But what we did detect—and it took us years to even recognize the significance—was a faint radio burst at the same time. It was picked up and recorded by our WEM sensory array in the Dabie Mountains of Huazhong. At the time, the operators judged the incoming signal to be insignificant, especially as it only lasted seconds. They had attributed it to radio interference."

Daiyu frowned. She knew of the WEM installation. She had toured the highly guarded facility back in 2019, shortly after the project—the Wireless Electromagnetic Method—had become fully operational. Its purpose was to produce ELF transmissions, extremely low-frequency signals that were capable of traveling through water and rock. The array allowed the military to maintain communication with Chinese submarines, even when they were deeply submerged.

"It was Xue, my son," Aigua continued, "who noted the correlation between the radio signal and the issue with the lunar lander. He's currently involved with the Chang'e-6 and 7 projects. He had been studying all the events surrounding that moment when we lost contact with the Chang'e-5's lander and when the drill malfunctioned. He hoped to discover the cause of the failure, to protect those future missions."

"Why does your son think the signal was significant and not coincidental, especially when the WEM operators had already dismissed it?"

"Two reasons. First, because of *where* it originated. Other radio telescopes and antennas had also picked up the signal. Their records allowed us to triangulate its origin. The signal came from a location north of New Zealand, along the Tonga-Kermadec Trench. In the middle of the ocean. And it couldn't have come from any ship passing through the area."

"Why not?"

"Because of the second reason. The signal received was in the ELF range—which as you know takes a massive transmitter to generate. It's nothing that could be carried on a ship."

She nodded. The WEM mountain array covered four thousand square kilometers. It took something that large to be able to produce ELF transmissions.

"It's why we sent out the *Changzheng 24*," Aigua explained. "To search for the source of the signal. It would take something *huge* to generate that ELF signal." He pointed to the large shadow lurking under the region. "Something the size of a continent."

"You're saying the signal came from the LLSVP."

"That's what we were trying to determine when we dispatched the *Changzheng 24*. It could be a natural phenomenon. We know lightning strikes and earthquakes can also generate ELF waves. Over the past year, geologists have been testing the WEM array as a means of early quake detection."

"And what did you find in that trench?"

Aigua shrugged. "That's just it. We don't know. When the *Changzheng 24* was over the trench, I had the WEM array transmit an ELF signal, an exact mirror to the one recorded in 2020. The submarine verified it had received it—then we lost all communication."

"Like with the Chang'e-5."

Aigua nodded. "Minutes later, a large seaquake was detected. With the epicenter near where the submarine had last been reported."

Daiyu frowned, beginning to understand the *weapon* that Aigua had mentioned. "Are you suggesting the ELF signal somehow triggered the quake at that location?"

"We did something. Because since then, the trench has been swarming with quakes, all localized at that one spot. They've been growing worse and spreading wider, threatening to destabilize the entire area.

Projections and modeling suggest the region may be headed toward an unprecedented apocalyptic event."

Daiyu wanted to belittle such a claim, but the man's earnestness was hard to dismiss.

"That's why we must leave no stone unturned, and why I've come here. The inexplicable state of the submariners could be important. My son is convinced of it. Especially as there is a possibility this is not the *first* time that such bodies have been found in this region."

"What are you talking about?"

"After learning of the fate of the submariners, Xue did a deep search for anything that corresponded to such a strange affliction—much like he did when he uncovered a signal that everyone else had ignored. Two days ago, he discovered a historical record. An account of another near-apocalyptic event, when Mount Tambora erupted back in 1815. It was written by Chinese traders living in Singapore during that time."

"What was in those records?"

"It was a sketchy account, but it told of bodies turned to stone during the Tambora eruption."

She sat straighter. "What?"

"It also told of a cure discovered and kept secret by a former lieutenant-governor of Java, Sir Stamford Raffles. In addition, it hinted at a means of appeasing quakes and eruptions. The knowledge was said to be locked in a steel box, along with a sheaf of papers, and secured in a museum he had founded."

"Surely that account must be some opium-induced fantasy," Daiyu said.

"Many must have believed the same over the centuries. And I might have, too, except for one detail that my son dug up."

"Which was what?"

"The current incarnation of the same museum *does* list among its inventory of historical artifacts a *metal box and private papers belonging to Sir Stamford Raffles.* The entry is dated 1825, shortly after the museum was founded."

Daiyu pictured the state of the submariners, the agony of the petty officer. Beyond any cure, she recognized the desire in Aigua's eyes.

A weapon that would make the world's nuclear arsenal obsolete.

The man hoped to be able to control quakes, to turn those continent-size chunks of ancient planetoid into earth-shaking weapons.

She slowly nodded. "If those papers can offer any answers . . ."

Aigua collected his e-tablet from her desk. "That's why I hired a strike team to secure the artifacts over in Singapore."

Before Daiyu could respond, a loud klaxon rang from outside.

Her secretary rushed in with Aigua's son. "There's a major problem down in the med lab!"

12

Held at gunpoint, Seichan could not prevent her attackers from yanking her Glock out of her boot holster. Her hands were zip-tied behind her back. She glared at Valya the entire time.

Gray was also bound and stripped of his weapon.

Next to him, Kwong breathed hard. The museum director's wrists remained free. Valya clearly did not consider the small man a threat. Plus, the pistol grinding into his ribs encouraged his continued cooperation.

Their capture was all done swiftly and surreptitiously. A glance around revealed no cameras pointed their way. They had been ambushed in a blind spot. She and Gray likely only lived so they could be questioned later. The Chinese would want to know how deeply the U.S. was involved in all of this. Or maybe the strike team feared leaving any bodies behind for a roving security guard to stumble upon and raise an alarm.

Still, from the glee in Valya's eyes, Seichan guessed the likeliest reason for their capture: to make their demises more painful and prolonged.

Once they were secure, Valya turned aside and spoke into a wrist radio. "Lock down the security control room. We're hard out in ten minutes." She then waved her SIG Sauer to the others. "Get them moving."

They were hustled quickly toward the elevator. Guns were kept out of direct view. Several men split off and headed for the stairwell on the far side, to cover the museum's other flank.

"What are you looking for?" Gray asked as he was pressed into a corner of the elevator.

Valya rolled her eyes at him, clearly not willing to share anything. She tapped a stolen keycard to allow them up to the floor above. Either her team had been supplied with the security cards, or they'd dispatched a few researchers to obtain them. Seichan failed to understand why Valya hadn't already completed her task.

Why wait to ambush us?

The answer came as the assassin's eyes narrowed on Kwong.

Valya needed him.

Their lengthy museum tour must have stymied her raid. She had been forced to lie in wait, keeping hidden, until she could secure the director. Everything had been on hold until this moment.

As the elevator opened, Valya herded them into a small lobby. She stopped before a door that led out onto the fifth floor. Beyond it, Seichan heard a muffled *pop-popping*, accompanied by a single strangled scream. The other half of the strike team must be sweeping and securing this level. From the gunfire, the assailants were no longer concerned about leaving dead bodies in their wake.

The door flung open ahead of them. A student researcher burst out, trying to escape the gunmen behind him—only he ran into Valya's blade. She thrust the dagger deeper into his chest, twisting the hilt. The young man fell to his knees. Valya ripped her blade free and slashed his throat, silencing his rising scream. She kicked him aside.

Kwong choked and tried to back away, but his captor pressed the pistol's muzzle harder into his spine.

With the floor cleared, they were marched down a hall. It opened into a research lab sectioned by long rows of workbenches. Microscopes and photographic mounts lined the tops. Three more bodies draped the floors in pools of blood. Ahead, one of the gunmen guarded the far hall that led into a suite of offices. Valya left another man behind them to protect that flank. The other seven closed ranks around their group.

Valya pointed to a door at the back of the research space. "Over there."

Their group hurried across and pushed into a cavernous storage room. Crates and boxes climbed shelves. The place smelled musty. Dust motes hung in the air. Valya led them unerringly to the back wall, to a six-foot-tall circular door of black steel. A large wheel fixed its center.

The vault door had an antiquated look to it, like something out of the turn-of-the-century. Only from the glowing red pad next to it could one tell that the door had been retrofitted with a biometric lock.

No wonder Valya had needed to secure the director.

One of the guards nudged the curator forward.

"Open it," Valya ordered him.

Kwong glanced to Gray, who nodded at the man. "Do as she says."

The director fumbled and swiped his keycard through a reader, then placed his palm atop the glowing pad. The screen buzzed, then turned green. A rumble of gears sounded, accompanied by a sliding of metal.

A gunman grabbed the wheel, spun it, then heaved the foot-thick steel door open. Past the threshold, a large space opened. It was the size of a two-car garage and looked like a microcosm of the larger museum. To the right, rows of open shelves were crowded with bottles of every size. From the yellowing of the glass, Gray surmised that the collection was old, going back to the museum's earliest years. To the left stretched rows of tall steel drying cabinets.

Valya left them outside and passed into the vault by herself. She consulted a scrap of paper and searched down the rows of cabinets, studying the dates on them. She crossed all the way to the back, to the oldest section, and bent down by one of the cabinets. With her back to them, she opened its door and ran a finger down a stack of wooden drawers. She tapped one and drew it out, sliding it fully free so she could carry it forth.

With the drawer in her hands, she crossed back to the door with a hard, satisfied smile.

Seichan glanced at Gray.

He nodded and said one word. "Now."

3:17 P.M.

Upon Gray's signal, gunfire strafed into the storage room through the open door behind him. He leaped headlong and bowled into Kwong. He knocked the curator behind the nearest shelf of crates. Seichan dove along with them.

"Secure!" he radioed to Zhuang and Guan-yin.

The barrage intensified.

Men twisted and writhed, caught in a crossfire from the two shooters. Guan-yin and Zhuang had taken up positions on opposite sides of the research lab outside, firing through the door into the storage room.

Earlier, as soon as Gray had been ambushed, he had dipped his chin, activating the throat mike taped over his larynx. During the captors' rush to secure their prisoners and get them moving, the gunmen had failed to note the nearly imperceptible radio gear. With the device activated, Gray had been able to alert Zhuang and Guan-yin of the attack, letting the two listen in on them the entire time.

In turn, Zhuang and Guan-yin had kept Gray abreast of their own journey upward. Zhuang had lifted a keycard from a passing guard. Guan-yin obtained the same from a researcher eating lunch. They had split up, coming up opposite sides of the museum to ambush Valya's two posted guards. Their attack was aided by the team's IVAS goggles. Using the feed from the CCTV cameras on this floor, they were able to spy on their targets. The two had waited until the guards were looking the wrong way, then silenced them with slashes to their throats. Afterward, they took up positions outside the lab and waited for Gray's signal.

As the barrage continued, Gray covered Kwong with his own body.

By now, Seichan had snapped her ties free on a sharp bolt in the shelves.

Gray rolled off Kwong. "Keep him safe," he called to her.

"Where are you—"

He didn't even have time to free his wrists.

"Hold fire!" he radioed as he lunged up.

The gunfire ceased for a breath, and he dashed over to the open vault. He shouldered into the heavy door and swung it closed, intending to trap Valya with her prize inside. Before it could seal completely, she rushed out sideways.

She matched eyes with him, her hate shining brightly. To escape through the narrow gap, she had tilted the wide tray in her hands. She also struggled for her holstered SIG. As she did, the tray's contents spilled to the floor.

Valya dove for them.

Gray did the same, skidding low, feet first, as if sliding into home plate.

"Resume fire!" he hollered.

Gunfire strafed over them. Gray's toe kicked aside a clear envelope of yellowed pages. It slid under one of the shelves. He tried to do the same to a dented steel box, but Valya nabbed it one-handed and rolled away. She came up with her SIG in her other hand.

She pointed at Gray and fired—but a bullet from outside grazed her shoulder and threw off her aim. Her round pinged off the vault door near his ear. Valya was forced away as the gunfire focused on her. One of her men, bloodied but alive, rounded the shelves on the other side where he had been sheltered. He came to her aid.

Together, the pair rushed the storage room door, firing nonstop. As they reached the exit, Valya grabbed the man by the collar and shoved him ahead of her. Using his body like a shield, she fled across the research lab. His body jolted and jarred under the impact of rounds.

With the assailants gone, Seichan dashed out of hiding and retrieved a weapon from one of the dead men. She fired at Valya's back, but the assassin had reached the end of the row and rolled out of view, tossing the dead man aside. Valya had also somehow gained another weapon—maybe from the assailant she had used as a shield.

She fired in both directions, driving Zhuang and Guan-yin into hiding, and fled for the stairwell to the right.

Zhuang shot after her, but Valya pounded through the far door and vanished.

By now, Gray had followed Seichan's example and snapped off the wrist ties on a bolt in the shelving. He grabbed the sheaf of old papers and tucked it into the back of his pants under his windbreaker. He also armed himself.

To the side, Kwong stumbled out of hiding. The director clutched a hand to his neck. Blood poured between his fingers. Gray cursed himself for failing to note the man's injury.

He crossed and gathered Kwong under an arm. He carried the man toward the research lab. At the door, Seichan noted the director's state and came up on the man's other side. They headed out together.

Zhuang ran up to them, hefting a Glock 18, a fully automatic with an extended magazine. "Your mother," he gasped to Seichan. "She ran after that *biaozi*."

Seichan glanced at Gray.

"Go," he ordered her, then passed the director to Zhuang. "Take him down the elevator. Get him help."

Seichan took off, and Gray sprinted after her. They could not leave Guan-yin chasing after Valya. Not alone. Seichan's mother could not comprehend the lethality and cunning of the Russian assassin.

They fled past the offices and burst out into the stairwell. Gray listened for any sound of gunfire below, but all was silent. With pistols in hand, they raced around and around.

As they reached the third floor, voices echoed up to them, sounding furtive. Gray knew Valya had more men. He overheard when she had ordered another group to lock down the security control room in the museum's basement.

"Careful," Gray warned.

Seichan barely slowed, anxious to reach her mother, too furious for caution. She swept down the next turn, only to be met by a torrent of automatic gunfire. She stumbled back. Rounds gouged into the concrete wall near her. Boots pounded up toward them, coming fast.

"This way!" Gray called to her.

She ran back to him.

He turned off the stairs and rushed to the door that led out onto the third floor. They ducked through it. Gray had barely closed it behind them when gunfire erupted. The door shook under the barrage.

He pointed across the breadth of this level. "Run!"

They fled, knowing they had only seconds before the men, armed with assault rifles, burst inside and caught them in the open. The far door looked an impossible distance away. A few rooms opened on the left, but if they sought shelter inside, they'd be trapped with no place to hide.

Gray placed his hope on what lined the other side of the third floor.

The wet collection.

Thousands of bottles packed the rows of shelves.

Gray pointed his pistol and fired as he ran, shooting down the length of the shelves. Each round shattered scores of bottles, splashing their contents to the floor. Pools of ethanol spilled and spread in a widening lake.

The door slammed open behind him.

As she ran, Seichan fired back to discourage entry.

"Your lighter," Gray called to her.

With her free hand, she tugged out an antique silver lighter and tossed it to him. He thumbed it open, while still firing at the shelves. He flicked a flame and tossed it low at his heels.

It landed in the pool of ethanol as a pair of gunmen dashed through the doorway and splashed into the pool's far edge.

The lake of alcohol ignited with a whoosh of red flames. The heat washed Gray's back. The fire swept across the room in seconds, engulfing the two men.

Their screams chased Gray and Seichan.

But Valya's team were not fools.

Another two men kept a post at the door, well away from the flaming lake. They fired after the fleeing pair. The unfortunate problem with alcohol fires was that they burned smokeless, leaving Gray and Seichan still exposed.

But Gray also knew the standard fire suppression for such conflagrations. Plain water would not work. From the hundreds of sprinkler heads, an alcohol-resistant foam sprayed across this level. The thick jets frothed a heavy lather through the air, immediately obscuring the view.

As deafening fire alarm bells rang out, Gray pulled Seichan low and to the side. He ran and skidded over the slippery floor, shading his eyes from the downpour. Gunfire blasted after them, but the rounds found no targets through the thick wall of foam.

Gray struck the far door, shoved through it, and slammed it behind him. He breathed heavily, catching his breath. They had reached the elevator lobby, but with the fire on this floor, no cage would stop here.

Instead, they dashed to the emergency stairs that ran alongside the shaft. They sprinted down, leaping steps. Gray counted on Valya only guarding the main stairwell on the other side, the one she had retreated down. With a limit to her manpower, she would use the last of her resources to protect her back, to aid her escape.

Gray was proven right when they safely reached the bottom of the stairs and exited out onto the main exhibition floor. The space had mostly cleared out. An intercom cut through the bleats of the alarm, warning everyone to evacuate in multiple languages.

Gray and Seichan ducked into the last of the crowd, hiding their weapons.

They hurried outside, where sirens added to the cacophony of shouting and alarm bells. They searched for the others.

Zhuang found them first, shoving through the crowd to join them.

"How's Kwong?" Gray asked him.

Zhuang stared down at his bloody hands. "I got him to an ambulance. But know no more."

"And my mother?" Seichan asked.

"I've not seen her," Zhuang answered, his voice sharp with panic.

Seichan looked at Gray.

He had no words to offer her hope. They both knew the truth. Either Valya had her mother, or Guan-yin had died on those stairs.

Gray didn't know which fate was worse.

13

Standing inside the airlock, Dr. Luo Heng stared into the morgue. Min crowded next to him. Junjie pointed his camera between their shoulders.

A loud klaxon rang out in the hall behind him. Heng had struck the emergency alarm as they fled the morgue. He had also used the phone in the airlock to alert Captain Tse.

"Keep filming," Heng ordered Junjie when the sublieutenant started to lower his camera. Heng wanted every second to be recorded, not trusting his eyes to take it all in.

Inside the morgue, the length of brain and spinal cord still lay in the saline bath. Only now the cord writhed in the solution. From the brain's gyri and sulci, hundreds of foot-long tendrils thrashed the air.

The neurological tissue had burst to life after Heng had shot a strong jolt of electricity through it. Heng had immediately driven everyone into the airlock, putting glass and steel between them and the horror inside.

"What's happening in there?" Min gasped out.

Heng glanced to the portable EEG. It was still operating inside. Its leads remained attached to the implanted electrodes. On the monitor, the waves and troughs of its lines swung wildly. He had never seen such violence, not even in a patient in the midst of an epileptic seizure. The brainwaves overlapped and ran roughshod over one another, as if the EEG were registering a legion of readings.

Footsteps pounded out in the hall. Heng looked past his shoulder. Captain Tse appeared in the window behind him, her face stern and reddened. She carried a pistol in her hand. She was flanked by two men, a gray-haired gentleman in a crisp suit and a young man in a PLA uniform with the double stripes and single star of a major.

"What's wrong?" Tse called to him.

Heng pushed Min aside to open the view into the morgue.

Junjie also shifted a step, then flinched. "Look!"

Heng turned back. Inside, nothing had changed. The brain and cord continued to contort in the tub. It took him another breath to realize what had alarmed the sublieutenant.

Beyond the wire-draped table, the other two calcified bodies now trembled atop their steel gurneys. The skull of the closest fractured like a ripe melon. Tendrils writhed through the cracks, waving and battering. The fissures widened. Chunks of calcareous pieces fell to the floor.

From within, the brain pushed out of its casing, like a butterfly from a chrysalis. The gray lump toppled free and fell over the table's edge, but it remained hanging, still attached by the rooted spinal cord. More tendrils unfurled, frilling over the brain.

The other body also cracked open, tremoring its length on the table.

Closer at hand, the violence worsened in the tub. The spinal cord lifted from the saline solution like a cobra. With a final wrench, its length split into three pieces that tangled and whipped against one another.

"Get back!" Captain Tse shouted into the airlock.

Still transfixed by the sight, Heng could not move. Min retreated, and Junjie grabbed Heng's shoulder and tugged him away from the window. The motion snapped Heng's attention around.

Realizing what Tse intended, he shouted, "Don't!"

Tse ignored him. She punched a large red button outside. A low whoosh sounded from the morgue, followed by an explosive roar. Flames shot from nozzles across the roof. The heat, trapped by the cement block walls, seared past the airlock's inner door.

Heng shielded his eyes from the blaze and backed with the others. A fire door lowered over the window, transforming the morgue into a crematorium. The roaring inferno raged for several long minutes.

When the incineration ended, the morgue remained sealed.

Heng panted through his respirator. The airlock had turned into an oven. Before exiting, he had his group strip out of their biohazard suits. They abandoned their gear inside, and Heng closed the door behind them.

He then glared at Captain Tse in the hallway. "There was no need for that overreaction. The morgue was well contained."

"You don't know that. The safety of this installation is *my* responsibility. Until we better understand what we're dealing with, I will proceed with utmost caution." She pointed a finger at him. "Any loss here is due to your ineffectiveness, for failing to offer any insight into what happened to these men."

One of the newcomers—the young man in a uniform—fixed Heng with his gaze. The PLA major looked to be in his late twenties. His dark hair had been buzzed short. His eyes had an intensity that was hard to stare at for long.

"Not everything was destroyed by the fire," the man reminded Heng. "There remains another subject for study. Petty Officer Wong."

"My son is right," the older gentleman said. "With all that we've witnessed, the submariner has become critically important. We must see him."

Heng glanced between the two men, recognizing now the family resemblance in their strong jawlines and sharp cheekbones. "He remains in a coma," Heng warned. "But you can view him from the main lab."

As Heng led the party into the next room, introductions were made. The young man—Major Choi Xue—stayed beside him. Tse whispered with the man's father, a former lieutenant-general with the PLA Strategic Support Force and now a consultant with a Chinese space agency.

Heng struggled to understand what members from such groups were doing here. Min shared a worried look with him, too. He gritted his teeth, again panged by guilt for involving her in a matter that had grown more tense and involved. It felt as if they were falling deeper into quicksand that had no bottom.

Xue must have noted his consternation. "We will explain as best we can," the man promised with a solemnity that felt authentic. "Perhaps first you could share what you've learned about the strange affliction."

Heng nodded. He still had trouble meeting the man's eyes. He sensed a brilliance behind that intensity. This assessment grew clearer as Heng related all that his team had learned. Xue listened with his head tilted, as if memorizing every syllable. Unlike Tse, the man asked pointed questions, inquiries that required intuitive leaps of understanding.

Xue leaned over the computer and studied the various polymorphs of carbonate on the monitor. "The afflicted bodies are infiltrated by *aragonite*." He pointed at the orthorhombic crystal on the screen. "And carbonate crystalizes into aragonite in the presence of seawater. To me, that suggests that whatever afflicted the men likely came from the seas versus a biotoxin loosed upon the crew prior to them shipping off."

Heng lifted a brow. "That's my current hypothesis, too. A seaborne pathogen. Nothing else makes sense." He grabbed the mouse and shifted through files. "Let me show you this. I performed a punch biopsy on Officer Wong's skin, then vacuum desiccated the cells to getter a better view of the pattern of calcification. This is what scanning electron microscopy revealed."

On the screen, a grayish layering of the crystallization appeared. It formed distinct thin crinkled sheets.

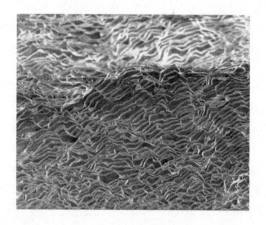

Heng started to explain, but Xue nodded.

"It looks like the layering of aragonite found in seashells," the major said.

Heng glanced quizzically at the man. "That's what I thought. Mollusk shells or maybe the calcareous skeletons of corals. They're all comprised of aragonite."

"Which would further support a seaborne source of this disease." Xue looked in the direction of the morgue. "It's as if the process is using our body's raw materials—our salty blood, our calcium-rich bones—as a means of propagating itself. Turning bone into an exoskeleton of aragonite, while simultaneously preserving the neurological tissue as a media to grow . . . something else."

"But what? And what's causing it?" Heng stared pointedly at the man. "I've shared all that I know. What haven't you told *me*?"

Xue met his gaze for a long breath, then dipped his chin as if settled on some manner. "A moment please."

The major shifted higher and lifted an arm, trying to get his father's attention. The older man stood with Captain Tse. The two had been talking together, studying the prone form of Petty Officer Wong through the window.

Inside the med ward, Nurse Lam continued her monitoring and care of the comatose patient. The black hardening had continued its inevitable spread across the patient's body, a black tide that would fully consume the man in another day or two.

Xue winced at the sight. "Why do you allow him to linger in such a state?"

"Not by my choice. We've had to resuscitate him five times. On the orders of Captain Tse." Heng shook his head. "The transformation process will continue whether the man lives or dies. We can observe it just as well without putting Wong through all of this."

The elder Choi finally turned to his son. Xue removed a thumb drive from a pocket and held it up, clearly asking permission to share what they had kept secret up until now. Aigua nodded, trusting his son's judgment on the matter.

Xue turned to Heng and pointed to the computer. "May I?"

"Of course."

Xue popped in the drive and opened the files it contained. He searched rapidly through until he settled on a folder marked 嫦娥五号.

Heng frowned. The file was labeled with the name of a Chinese lunar spacecraft, the Chang'e-5.

Xue pulled up an image from the file and displayed it on the screen. It was a crisp photo of a sharp-edged crystal in an orthorhombic shape.

Heng noted the size of the specimen. *Five microns.* It was the size of a dust particle. "The microcrystal? It's aragonite?"

Xue nodded. "*Shì.* With the same unusual crystalline matrix that you just showed me from your samples."

"Where did you find it?" Heng girded himself for the truth, already guessing the answer from the name on the file folder.

Xue confirmed his fear. "The microcrystal came from particles isolated out of a lunar rock sample."

Heng swallowed. He wanted to declare it impossible, but he knew what he had witnessed next door. "What are we dealing with?" he mumbled.

Xue simply shook his head.

Min approached, drawing both their attention. She kept her voice low. "Something is wrong with Sublieutenant Junjie."

Both men looked over to where the team's videographer was uploading the morgue recording into the system. He shook one of his hands and rubbed it on his trousers. Even from here, it was easy to see the graying hue to the man's index finger.

Heng hurried over. Min and Xue followed.

Once there, he grabbed Junjie's wrist and brought the sublieutenant's hand more fully into the light. The man's finger was clearly discolored.

"What are you doing?" Junjie asked.

"Did you damage your suit when we were in the morgue?"

Junjie tried to pull his arm away. "Just a pinprick. On one of the electrode needles."

"Did you handle one of the bodies afterward?"

The sublieutenant's eyes took on a wild look. "I . . . no, I'm sure. Maybe I touched the table where you cut the body up. But that's all."

Xue backed away, as if fearful of being near the man. "He could've come in contact with particulates that were cast off during your dissection."

Heng rolled the finger, examining it from all angles. The tip was distinctly darker, nearly black around a point that could be a needle prick.

By now, Captain Tse and Aigua had been drawn over by the commotion.

"What's wrong?" Tse asked.

Heng continued to study the finger. "Sublieutenant Junjie may have contaminated himself. Through an open wound. But it makes no sense. Others have handled the bodies without getting sick."

Before arriving here, Heng had watched the video of recovery of the sub's jettisoned pod. When the men's corpses had been removed, the rescuers had not even been wearing gloves. Still, the disease had not spread among them.

Afterward, Heng had performed a battery of tests on lab mice, exposing them to blood, saliva, and tissues from both Wong and the dead men. None of the animals had become ill. This stubborn lack of transmission made it harder to determine the cause of this affliction.

So why is Junjie sick now?

He pictured the horror in the other room. Had the bodies become contagious once the process had advanced enough to cause the neurological malformation? Had Junjie come in contact with a splattering of cerebrospinal fluid, allowing something pathogenic to enter his body?

Xue pushed past his father. Focused on the medical mystery, Heng had failed to note that Xue had crossed the lab and returned. He now carried a fire axe in hand.

"Hold his arm to the tabletop," Xue ordered.

Heng understood and gripped the sublieutenant's wrist tighter.

"No, no, no . . ." Junjie moaned.

"Better to lose your finger than . . ." Heng nodded to the next room. "The contaminated digit must be removed."

The sublieutenant's eyes got huge. He stopped struggling and allowed Heng to pin his hand to a nearby workbench. Junjie turned his face away.

"Keep your fingers splayed wide," Heng warned.

Xue came up on the other side and raised the axe. "Fetch Nurse Lam," he ordered Min. "Prep a tourniquet."

Min fled to the lab's airlock.

Xue lifted his axe higher, took a deep breath, then brought it down hard. The edge cleaved through bone and skin—and took off not just the finger, but the entire hand.

Junjie screamed at the pain, at the mutilation.

Heng clenched the man's forearm, trying to cut off blood flow. He looked over at Xue for an explanation.

The man lowered his axe and threw Heng's words back at him. "Better to lose a *hand* than . . ." He tilted his head toward the med ward.

Heng felt sick, but he knew the man was right.

Xue looked down at the severed hand. "And even this amputation may have been too cautious."

4:04 P.M.

Captain Tse Daiyu paced the length of the conference room table, trying to dispel her irritation and frustration. She took some measure of satisfaction from the dismay on Heng's face as Xue shared the information that Aigua had already gone over with her, a tale of a malfunctioning lunar lander, of exotic particles in moon rocks, of chunks of an ancient planetoid that threatened the world, and the real reason the *Changzheng 24* had been lost.

Xue went into far more technical details, but it failed to hold Daiyu's attention. She eyed Major Choi's father. He stood out in the hall, talking animatedly on the phone. Something was amiss. She enjoyed his consternation, finding the man too full of himself, too proud of a son he had coddled into his current rank. She had no doubt that the conversation he was having pertained to this matter.

Her eyes narrowed.

If something is wrong, can I turn it to my advantage?

They had already left Sublieutenant Junjie down in the lab's med ward. He would be closely monitored for any further sign of contamination. Even his hand rested in a saline bath for further study.

But none of it interested her any longer.

Greater matters were afoot in the world at large, along with a chance for incredible glory.

She remembered Aigua's claim.

A weapon that would make the world's nuclear arsenal obsolete.

Aigua finally lowered his phone, stood quietly for a full minute, then returned to the conference room. All eyes turned to the man, who swept his gaze over them.

"The strike team in Singapore reported in," he announced. "They were able to secure the museum artifact. A steel box from 1823."

Xue stood up. "What did it hold?"

Daiyu knew the young man had been the one to uncover this historical angle. His eyes shone with anticipation.

Aigua sighed. "Not much that makes sense. It contained a single branch of coral. Maybe it was once a *finger*. It's hard to tell. To know for sure, we'll need to examine it in greater detail." His gaze settled on his son. "But if so, Xue, it could prove you were right—that this has happened before. During the eruption of Mount Tambora."

Xue stepped forward. "Did the box hold anything else?"

"One other artifact, one that makes even less sense." Aigua frowned. "According to the strike team leader, it held an old painted wooden spearhead, all tied in knotted twine. I don't understand how it's involved, or if it was added by mistake."

"What about any papers?" Heng asked, glancing at Xue. "I saw the old museum log that your son discovered. The entry listed more than just a box."

Aigua's frown turned into a scowl. "We lost those."

"What?" Daiyu asked. "How?"

"American agents intervened. A group we tried to secure the night before."

"So others are on this same trail," Heng said. "If we asked for cooperation—"

"It's too late at this point." Aigua stared pointedly at Daiyu. "Too much blood's been spilled."

Clearly the man was keeping his ambition for a new weapon from Dr. Luo maybe even from his own son.

Aigua continued. "But the strike team leader believes she has leverage to coerce the U.S. agents into giving up the papers. A hostage she hopes to exchange for what was stolen from her."

"When will this happen?" Xue asked.

"At midnight. In the city of Jakarta on the island of Java."

"Where Stamford Raffles was once lieutenant-governor," Xue noted.

"I recommended the location for that very reason. It was where the man collected those artifacts, where he resided during the Tambora eruption. Even now, Raffles has a great historical presence there, with contributions across many of the city's museums. If we're to make a quick assessment, the proximity to where this all started could prove valuable." Aigua faced his son. "To that end, Xue, I want you there for the exchange."

Xue nodded. "Of course."

"And I'd like you to take Dr. Luo with you."

Heng backed away. "Wait! What?"

Xue turned to the physician. "I would value your input."

Before Heng could even respond, Aigua forged on. "I'll be sending you both with a squad from the Falcon Command Unit. As protection and further support."

"Why such a force?" Xue asked.

Aigua frowned. "The strike team I hired before were *mercenaries*, employed to keep our involvement at a distance. That no longer matters. Too much is in motion to play such games. On multiple fronts."

"What do you mean?" Heng asked.

"We've received word that an international research ship is headed to the Tonga Trench. Which will prove problematic. Another of our submarines—a Yuan-class attack boat—is scheduled to arrive in the region sometime after midnight. As is the *Dayangxi*, our new Type 076 helicopter landing dock."

Daiyu stiffened. She knew the *Dayangxi*. The ship had been designed using technology from her work on the AI-driven vessel, the *Zhu Hai Yun*. The new landing dock was outfitted with a complement of autonomous drones and submersibles. It even had an electromagnetic catapult and arresting gear for deploying unmanned aerial combat vehicles. She had helped design it all.

Aigua noted her reaction. As if reading her mind—and her heart's desire—he said, "It is why I've requested that Captain Tse oversee operations at the trench. We need those seas locked down. Which includes commandeering the incoming research vessel—along with the site where it had been dispatched."

Daiyu straightened her back. In her head, she pictured her decade-long plan to achieve the rank of admiral. Success here could bring the star and bars to her shoulders in half that time—maybe less.

Still, she wanted the scope and parameters of this mission better defined. "If there proves too much resistance or threat from those out at sea . . ."

Aigua understood what she was asking. "Make it look like an accident."

THIRD

The Hadal Zone

14

Phoebe Reed headed down the spiral stairs. It cored through the center of the thirteen-story glass orb, dubbed Science City. The sphere sat atop the stern end of the three-hundred-yard *Titan X*. Even at this hour, the place bustled with activity. More than a hundred researchers labored across the City's state-of-the-art labs.

She had to keep side-stepping past other men and women on the stairs, all of them in matching navy jumpsuits. The only differences were the insignia that denoted their field of study, along with sewn-on name badges.

Ahead of her, Adam led the way with the DARPA scientist, Monk Kokkalis. She felt like a third wheel. The two men spoke rapidly, keeping their voices low. She heard mention of a museum and Singapore, but it was hard to make out their words amidst the clamor around her.

As they passed the fifth floor, Phoebe cast her gaze across the four passageways heading off in cardinal directions. Each hallway ended at the orb's curve of glass, which offered expansive views of the Pacific Ocean. The hallway to the west was blinding, ablaze from the sun sitting low on the water.

Sunset was an hour away.

And I'll be missing it.

They were due to embark on their dive in twenty minutes. Her group was returning from a safety class, which included a rudimentary practice session inside a simulator. Normally there would have been weeks of pre-dive preparations, but the situation was so dire that they were circumventing it. They wouldn't even wait until the morning before departing—not that the time of day would make any difference once they descended into the sea's sunless depths.

Phoebe's group had arrived aboard the *Titan X* in the early afternoon. It took the ship another two hours to reach the Tonga Trench. She had been ready to head immediately to the DSV—their deep-submergence vehicle. The submarine had been specially commissioned by William Byrd, who must have dug deep into his pockets to have the leader in submersible design, Triton Submarines, build a custom-made vehicle for the project.

Its pilot—who had ultimate command—had forced them all to spend the afternoon and early evening prepping for the mission.

But now we're good to go.

She and the two men reached the bottom of Science City and crossed to an elevator. It would take them down to the stern hold, where the submersible's launch-and-recovery system was mounted.

As they entered the cage, another scientist in a navy jumpsuit waited for them. His patch—a fish floating over the earth—marked him as a member of the biology team. She didn't recognize him, which meant he must have spent most of his time aboard the *Titan X*. The Asian man looked to be in his late twenties. His jumpsuit hung on a bony frame that reached at best five-foot-two. Still, what he lacked in size, he made up for with enthusiasm.

His smile brightened the cage. He bobbed on his heels, as if trying to increase his height. He swiped a fall of hair from his eyes, only to have it drop back, nearly knocking off a pair of glasses from the bridge of his nose. He pushed the eyewear back in place and swept his gaze over them.

"You must be Drs. Reed, Kaneko, and Kokkalis." He thrust out his hand, jabbing it all around, as if unsure who to offer it to first. His accent was distinctly British. "I'm Dr. Datuk Lee, a biochemist from the Universiti Sains Malaysia."

Phoebe was the first to shake his hand as the elevator closed. "Wonderful to meet you, Dr. Lee, but how do you know us?"

She could guess the answer. Like any fraternity house, Science City was a rumor and gossip mill. The abrupt repositioning of the *Titan X* to these waters was surely a matter of much excited discussion.

But that was not the answer.

"I'm replacing Dr. Ismail on your dive."

Both Adam and Monk looked sharply at each other.

"What happened to Dr. Ismail?" Phoebe asked.

"She became ill. GI-upset. I was asked to take her place as I had already completed my DSV training. Plus, my specialty is piezophiles."

Both Adam and Monk looked to Phoebe for an explanation.

She nodded, understanding now why the man had been selected as a replacement and why he had already undergone prior training. "Piezophiles are organisms that survive under extreme pressures. Like in deep-sea trenches."

"I've been studying such species to better understand how our planet's geology coevolved with life. But my main funding supports a search for—"

The elevator bumped to a stop.

Monk used the moment to ask a question of their new member. "Who *is* funding your research, Dr. Lee? Your university?"

"Of course, but also a generous grant from PLASSF."

Phoebe didn't recognize the acronym.

Adam did. "China's Strategic Support Force?"

Datuk nodded. "Along with NASA."

Monk matched Adam's confused expression. "You're funded by *two* different space agencies?"

Before the biochemist could respond, the elevator doors opened into the noisy chaos of the stern's open hold. Men and women piled inside the cage, pushing them all out.

Phoebe followed the others, struggling to keep abreast of the men and to understand this sudden addition to their crew. The air reeked of saltwater and diesel fuel. They headed past the climate-controlled hangar where the ship's DSV was housed during transit. The vehicle had already been pulled free and hung in a steel A-frame over the water.

As it came into view, Phoebe forgot all about the others.

What man can compete with that?

She stumbled out onto the stern deck and gaped at their means of transportation. Their pilot—a muscular, auburn-haired Aussie named Bryan Finch—stood atop the vehicle. He bellowed and gestured to the support crew as the vessel was lowered into the water.

Phoebe studied the DSV. The submersible had been built on the frame of a Triton 36000/2. Only this one had been designed slightly larger, big enough to house five people instead of the standard two. It retained its boxy shape, all to protect a hollow sphere of Grade 23 titanium at its heart, which would carry its passengers. The forward edge of the sphere protruded out the front, forming a clamshell made of thick acrylic glass and framed by the same titanium.

The other unique feature of the DSV was a pair of gull wings that lay flat against its flanks. They could be swept upward once underwater. Their undersides were loaded with additional lights and cameras. When deployed at depth, the wings allowed the craft to glide with precision, driven by the vehicle's ten thrusters.

It was those wings that also gave their vehicle its name—the *Cormorant*—a seabird capable of diving fifty meters underwater.

Phoebe grinned.

Only this bird will be going far deeper.

8:15 P.M.

Adam sank into his seat inside the titanium sphere. He had never considered himself claustrophobic. It was not a good trait for a geologist, a profession that often required one to be underground. But when their pilot sealed the hatch overhead, his breath caught in his throat. His heart pounded harder.

His reaction had less to do with being sealed inside a three-cubic-meter titanium ball and more about *where* that ball was headed.

Six miles down.

The pilot—Bryan Finch—shimmied past the passengers and took his place behind the controls. Phoebe had commandeered the copilot's seat to the man's left. Monk sat behind her, flanked by Datuk Lee.

It left the lone seat at the back for Adam, which he didn't mind. He wanted to keep an eye on the Malaysian biochemist ahead of him. The man's sudden inclusion rankled Adam's suspicions, especially upon learning of the scientist's connection to the Chinese and knowing the wreck upon which they were about to dive.

He had already been on edge after hearing Monk's story of what had befallen his comrades in Singapore. From the bloodshed and subterfuge, the resources committed, there had to be more going on with the Chinese than just the cover-up of a missing submarine.

"Flooding the trunking and ballast tanks," Bryan reported after finishing an inspection and system check.

A muffled gurgling sounded all around the *Cormorant.* Each of the back seats had its own window at knee level, and the pair in front had a more panoramic view through the domed clamshell. As the DSV sank, the water level rose across the glass and swamped over the top of the vehicle.

"Down we go, mates," Bryan said with a big smile.

Adam breathed heavier, fighting another wave of panic. He eyed the row of carbon-fiber oxygen tanks. He had been told there was enough air for three days, which should be plenty as the *Cormorant*'s batteries would only last sixteen hours.

Bryan guided their descent via a joystick. This afternoon, they had all practiced inside the submersible's simulator. Maneuvering the craft was like piloting a helicopter. Still, Adam had crashed his vehicle five times. Both Monk and Phoebe had shamed him with their own skills. Monk had explained how he had flown helicopters during his stint with the Green Berets, so he had felt comfortable with the *Cormorant*'s systems. Likewise, Phoebe's background in deep-sea exploration had made her a natural.

Maybe it's best that I'm seated back here.

Bryan radioed in with the *Titan X*, keeping the ship abreast of their descent. The pilot also monitored a swath of switches, lights, and LCD panels and surveyed data coming in from a navigation array.

The *Cormorant* was actually only *one* component of the Hadal Exploration System. Besides the massive ship overhead, two DriX USVs circled the area like a pair of steel sharks. One used its multibeam echo-sounder to continue a bathymetric contouring of the terrain below. The other was outfitted with a communications modem, a redundant system for the one aboard the *Titan X*. It would allow the *Cormorant* to stay in continual contact with the world above—though, the deeper they traveled, the longer the lag time would stretch. Once at the bottom, it would take seven seconds for an SOS to reach the surface, and another seven seconds for the *Titan X* to respond with a sincere *we'll miss you*.

The final component of the Hadal Exploration System was a trio of box-like landers that had been deployed after the *Titan X* had arrived here. The heavy landers had descended in a freefall all the way to the bottom. The trio had been named *Huey*, *Dewey*, and *Louie*, after the Disney ducks—because scientists considered themselves capable of humor. This proved otherwise.

The landers would aid in navigation and double as scientific platforms. They were loaded with scoops, sediment corers, and sample collection gear. They even had a deployable bait box for luring in sea life.

"Everyone settle in," Bryan said. "It'll take us three hours to reach the bottom."

He demonstrated this by leaning back and twisting open a bottle of Diet Coke. Knowing the efficiencies built into every bit of the design, Adam imagined the plastic bottle would serve later as a redundant system for collecting bodily wastes—at least for those with good aim.

No one spoke during their initial descent. All remained lost in their own thoughts or perhaps they were fearful of distracting the pilot. The latter precaution seemed unnecessary as Bryan pulled out a cell phone and began watching a downloaded Netflix movie.

After several minutes, Phoebe finally broke the ice among them. She had her nose pressed to her window. "This is amazing."

By now, they had fallen out of the brighter waters into a twilight world. Adam failed to appreciate her sense of wonder. The landscape outside was a featureless wash of dark blue, except for swirls of snow lit by the vehicle's lamps. He knew the *snow* was a mix of krill, microshrimps, and plankton. Occasionally a curious fish would burst into view, then vanish away. A few jellyfish lingered longer, until the *Cormorant* fell past their floating bells.

Soon, twilight became night.

"We're exiting the thermocline," Datuk reported, staring at a colorfully lighted display of data.

"Which means what?" Monk asked.

Datuk readjusted his glasses and pointed to a screen. The information glowing there came from the vehicle's external Niskin water sampler and CTD sensor. The screen ran with a slew of real-time readings: depth, outside pressure, temperature, conductivity, salinity, pH, and oxygen levels.

"The thermocline lies between the ocean's sunlit layers and the colder depths," Datuk explained. "The temperature dropped rapidly when we first descended. But now out of the thermocline, it'll drop much slower. We're at *four* degrees now. It'll drop only another two or three degrees before we reach the bottom. Ending at just above freezing."

Adam looked over Datuk's shoulder. While the temperature reading on his screen had slowed, the depth and pressure gauges continued to rise. It was the only evidence that they were still descending. Inside the DSV, there was no sense of motion.

Phoebe was drawn into the conversation, twisting around. "We're now entering the bathypelagic—or midnight—zone of the ocean. Between one thousand and four thousand meters. After that, we'll drop into the abyssopelagic zone."

Datuk nodded. "And below six thousand meters, we'll reach the bottommost region of the ocean—the hadal zone—named after Hades, the Greek god of the underworld. These unexplored depths make up nearly half the ocean. Yet, until a short time ago, more people had walked on the moon than had visited these extreme depths. Currently, though, the score stands at *twelve* on the moon and *twenty-two* who reached the bottom of the ocean's deepest trenches."

Even in the dim light, Phoebe's eyes shone with her excitement. "And those numbers are about to change today."

Adam wished he could appreciate their enthusiasm. During their safety class, he had learned the two greatest dangers during a descent: a fire or a leak. At these pulverizing depths, there would be no chance of a rescue. Their best defense was early detection.

As they continued down, Bryan interrupted his movie every fifteen minutes to give their topside monitors an update. Adam listened attentively each time—not so much to the technical details, a majority of which was over his head anyway, but to the tone in their pilot's voice. Adam strained to hear any note of distress or alarm.

Still, after another hour, it was hard to maintain that level of concentration and tension. To his surprise, Adam found himself drifting into a light drowse, his eyelids slipping closed.

Phoebe's voice—sharp with surprise—stirred him back to full attention. "I think we're entering a brine layer," she said.

Adam sat straighter. Beyond the front window, the black waters were illuminated by the exterior lamps. Only now there was a distinct haziness to the view, as if they were sinking through cloudy chicken broth.

Datuk spoke up from his station. His eyes were still glued to the screen next to him. "You're right, Dr. Reed. The salinity spiked eightfold. It's definitely a dense layer of saltier water."

"Is it a reason for concern?" Adam asked, leaning forward.

"Not for us," Phoebe said. "But such spots are kill-zones for marine life. Due to the water's hypersalinity and lack of oxygen."

Datuk nodded. "But these brine stratifications host all manner of strange chemosynthetic organisms. Due to their unique enzymes, they've been studied for pharmaceutical and industrial uses. Much like the piezophiles that I study."

Monk stared at the biochemist. "You mean those organisms that survive under high pressure?"

"That's right." Datuk smiled. "These brine layers also show heightened electrical conductivity. Such a unique property will be used to harvest water from the atmosphere of Mars. Something that the Exo-

Mars lander—the *Kazachok*—will attempt to demonstrate when it's sent there in a year or two."

Monk turned to Adam, lifting an eyebrow. They had both avoided raising the subject of the scientist's connection to China's space agency. If the man was a mole, they didn't want to spook him. But Datuk had just offered them a perfect opening to broach the subject.

Besides, where could he go now?

9:50 P.M.

As Phoebe studied the murky brine layer, movement in the window's reflection drew her eye. She noted Adam leaning forward from the rear seat.

"Dr. Lee," he said, "you mentioned earlier that your study into high-pressure organisms had interested the space industry. Why?"

Phoebe had been wondering the same. Intrigued, she twisted around to face the others.

Datuk grinned, his eyes sparkling. Like most scientists, he was happy to extol about his research. "I'm part of an investigative team called LAB. The Laboratory for Agnostic Biosignatures. We're funded by astrobiology programs from around the world. Our mission is to explore beyond the current understanding of what constitutes *life*—to expand its definition. It involves studying the far corners of our planet, to search for life in places it shouldn't exist."

Phoebe glanced out the window. "Like where we're headed."

"Certainly. The search *below* offers unique ways of looking *up*—beyond our world. It offers new approaches to search the stars for novel biosignatures of extraterrestrial life. So far, we've limited ourselves to looking for water on foreign planets or for the presence of methane or other organic compounds. LAB hopes to expand the scope of such searches."

"That's why you're studying these extreme depths?" Monk asked.

He nodded. "Our team has been trying to break through the walls of accepted dogma. For example, it has been believed for decades that the emergence of life happened on Earth's *surface*, where water and atmosphere are exposed to sunlight and UV radiation. My goal is to prove otherwise. To show that life could have started in the subsurface environment, fueled by chemical energy. It's what sparked my interest in Earth's *piezosphere*—a layer that covers the deep sea and five thousand meters below the sea floor. In deep marine sediments, miles underground, we've found life where it shouldn't be. Life that is so metabolically slow that one cell division takes a thousand years."

Phoebe frowned. "And your study of such strange life hopes to expand the search for extraterrestrial biosignatures?"

"I believe it can. I'm convinced we have a greater chance of discovering life on another planet by searching for *slow* life, buried deep. *Fast* life on the surface comes and goes quickly. While planetary surfaces receive plenty of energy from their suns, they're also susceptible to annihilation by meteoric impacts or stellar flares. Whereas subsurface life is protected and preserved from such disruptions, and thus more stable."

Phoebe blinked as she absorbed this information.

Datuk stared past her shoulders and nodded toward the window. "Looks like we're back in open water."

Phoebe swung around.

The murkiness had indeed cleared.

Datuk reported from his bank of sensors. "Salinity has dropped back to normal." A quizzical note entered his voice. "And it keeps dropping. And oxygen levels are also rising."

Phoebe stared out at the dark ocean. By now, they had dropped below seven thousand meters, well into the hadal zone. "That's expected at these depths," she said. "The water in these deep ocean trenches is richer in oxygen due to the lowered salinity and higher pressure."

"But look at these numbers," Datuk said.

Phoebe drew her gaze from the seas to his small glowing screen. The DO reading—dissolved oxygen—steadily climbed. It crossed 12 mg/L as she watched—20% higher than expected. Similarly, the salinity had dropped below 29‰. Seawater typically stayed above 33‰, even at these extreme depths.

She shook her head. "Something must be wrong with the external sensors. Those numbers can't be right."

Bryan spoke from the pilot's seat, interrupting them. "What's that rising under us?"

Phoebe turned around. The others bent to their respective windows. She stared between her knees. The lower curve of the dome allowed her to look straight down.

Gasps rose around her.

She simply choked, strangled by astonishment.

Below—and rising swiftly toward them—the world shimmered and glowed. Traceries of emerald and cerulean fire lanced across the view, shooting off in hundreds of directions. Other areas pulsed through a radiant kaleidoscope.

She knew what she was witnessing.

Bioluminescence.

They continued to drop toward the shining, unearthly landscape. As they did, the expanse stretched in all directions, fading into darkness at the edges. She pictured walls towering to either side, the cliffs of the Tonga Trench. They had dropped down its center, not wanting to risk brushing against its rocky sides.

"Is that what I think it is?" Adam asked behind her.

Phoebe remembered the spread of black oil noted on the bathymetric map of the trench. It had marked the presence of a vast coral forest, a thousand feet tall and covering two hundred square miles.

Only this forest wasn't *black*.

As the *Cormorant* dropped toward the bottom, the bioluminescent jungle grew into focus. It was a fiery wonderland of dark branches that blinked, shimmered, and glowed in radiant hues. Trunks of coral, as thick around as redwoods, climbed from below. Their roots were so deep that not even the forest's brilliance could illuminate them. Directly under the *Cormorant*, the weave of branches formed a continuous canopy that rose and fell across the field of view.

"Dumping ballast," Bryan said. "Going for neutral buoyancy."

He hit switches, ejecting five-kilogram weights, one after the other.

As their descent slowed, Phoebe could not shift her gaze away. The *Cormorant* lowered until it hovered above the shimmering canopy. Past the glow, she discerned the fringes of polyps that crowded the nearest black branches.

The polyps were all a uniform emerald, sprouting from the hard black skeleton of the coral.

She flashed to the day before, picturing the lone sentinel of coral that she had sampled outside *Titan Station Down*. Was this the same species? They were still too high to say for sure. Yesterday, she had judged the tree by the station to be an ancient giant. If the forest below *was* the same species, then that tall specimen was a mere seedling.

She wished Jazz were here, to witness this firsthand, too.

Datuk murmured behind her, *"Akah Bahar."*

"What was that?" Adam asked him.

"It's the Malay name for black coral—which seemed appropriate."

Phoebe kept her gaze outside. "Why? What does it mean?"

"It means *Root of the Sea.*"

Phoebe stared at the vast expanse and corrected him. "This looks more like the Root of the Entire World."

15

Jasleen Patel rubbed her eyes as she leaned back from the optical microscope. She had spent two hours reviewing slides from the seventeen specimens she had collected with Phoebe. A headache knotted behind her eyes. She blamed it on a dip in blood glucose from skipping dinner. But she had not wanted to disappoint her boss.

She stretched a kink from her neck and checked the time on the open laptop next to her. Phoebe should be at the bottom of the trench by now. A flicker of envy traced through her. She threw cold water on it.

I'll get my own chance soon.

She reached over to the laptop and reviewed her work. She had spent the day cataloguing the specimens' morphological and physiological details. It required delicately extracting centimeter-size cores from the chunks of coral secured inside the station's high-pressure benthic chambers. Before they could be studied, each tiny sample had to be slowly equilibrated to the station's one atmosphere of pressure.

The work had been painstaking.

Over the course of the day, she had studied each specimen, counting the number of polyp tentacles, noting their coloration, measuring their lengths and dimensions. She had run samples through a NovaSeq 6000 DNA sequencer. She had even used the lab's dissecting microscope to tease out nematocytes—the venomous cells—from the tentacles. The latter were all unique, like fingerprints, and could help substantiate taxonomy.

A chime sounded from her laptop, and an email alert popped up. *Finally . . .*

She shifted over and opened the attached file. It had been sent from the team running the station's scanning electron microscope. She had sent over samples of each coral to have their sclerites—their calcareous endoskeletons—recorded from multiple angles. It was yet another means of classifying each species. No two corals were alike in their carbonate structure.

She sifted quickly through the scanning photos, but in particular she searched for Specimen A17, named after the quadrant from where it had been collected. She pictured the towering black giant, festooned with emerald polyps, a lone Christmas tree slowly growing in darkness.

She brought up the scan of its sclerite. It showed the specimen from multiple angles. The micro team had done a wonderful job.

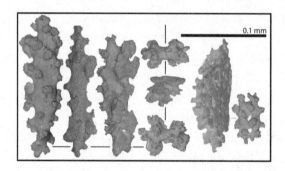

She brought her nose closer to the screen, shifting her glasses higher. "What are you?" she whispered to the mystery before her.

Specimen A17 continued to confound, baffle, and intrigue her. It had all the characteristics of a black coral, but its polyps had eight arms instead of the expected six. Plus, its sweeper tentacle had been monstrously long, tipped by a stinging nematocyst that was four times the size of any others. Even this scan of its sclerite showed a density of polyp cupping that she had never witnessed before in another coral.

No wonder you little green guys evolved an escape method. You're all too crowded in there.

She pictured the little polyps jettisoning in alarm when Phoebe had collected a sample, even attacking the extraction claw.

Still, the most frustrating part of the day had been her attempt at analyzing this specimen's DNA. She kept getting an error code on the sequencer. Knowing she had the other specimens to record, she had finally given up. She had planned on waiting until Phoebe returned to try again.

She checked the time.

Maybe I should give it another go myself.

Jazz hated to fail her friend. She had wanted to complete her study today and send her results to Phoebe on the *Titan X*, to have them waiting for her when she finished her dive.

Decided on the matter, Jazz rolled her chair away from her station. At this late hour, others were still working across the biology lab, all bent in various postures of concentration. She stood up with a jaw-cracking yawn and headed out of the lab. She crossed the central hub and descended to the next tier. The department's wet lab and high-pressure benthic chambers were on this lower level. It was also where the curve of ROV stations were located.

Even at this hour, every ROV cubicle was occupied.

She turned her back and pushed into the high-pressure room. It was like walking into an aquarium. The tanks were stacked four high and ten across, all fronted by the same glass that ringed each tier. Under each chamber, a set of caliper controls stuck out, not unlike those that operated a claw machine at an amusement park. It allowed a researcher to manipulate a set of drills, corers, and suction tubes inside the pressurized tank.

Before rerunning the DNA sequencing on Specimen A17, Jazz wanted a fresh sample. Two other biologists were already at work in here. Luckily, no one blocked her tank, which would have required her to wait her turn.

She stepped to the benthic chamber. Their names—Reed/Patel—had been scrawled in an upper corner of the tank's glass, written in erasable black marker. It was how each researcher staked a claim to a tank. It was crude but effective.

Only now a new name had been written under theirs: 김종석. Though she was not that familiar with the various Asian alphabets, she was fairly certain it was Korean *hangul*. The researcher had to be Dr. Kim Jong Suk, who studied crustaceans, specifically shrimp species. The man was equally known for his foul temper and rude manner, especially toward the female researchers.

Inside the tank, Jazz had meticulously sectioned off each of her coral samples into separate plastic trays and positioned across the tank's bottom. Dr. Kim had simply dumped in two dozen large shrimp with translucent pink shells. Jazz recognized them as a species of *Lucensosergia lucensi*, or Sakura shrimp, named after the Japanese cherry blossom. They swam, kicked, and crawled throughout the tank. Their excrement dotted the bottom as if an overzealous waiter with a pepper grinder had seasoned the chamber.

She huffed out her exasperation. The scientists had been warned that these high-pressure chambers would have to be shared among them, but currently there were four others that remained empty. It required hours to prep one, and clearly Kim hadn't wanted to bother with those extra steps and simply threw his samples into their tank.

"What a jackass," she whispered as she grabbed the manipulator controls.

Phoebe would be equally pissed.

Jazz stared across the trays, which had been shifted into disarray by the antics of the busy shrimp. One of her specimens—G5—had been tossed out of its place. She used a claw to return the chunk to its proper tray. She then shifted over to A17, ready to get to work, bringing up a pincer and drill.

At least A17 remained unmolested. Only a few pepper grains marred its plastic tray. She shook her head at the sight of three pink shrimp lying on their sides nearby. Their legs were not moving, nor their antennas.

Dead.

Clearly Kim treated his specimens no better than he treated his fellow colleagues. His rough handling must have killed these specimens.

He hadn't even bothered to separate the living from the dead. The other shrimp avoided that corner of the tank, as if fearful of their dead brethren.

Jazz nudged one of the bodies with her pincers. A flurry of small green blebs blasted off the pink shrimp. *Polyps.* They pulsed and spun back to their home, the black branch of spiky coral.

She grimaced. *Had they been feeding on it?* She rolled the shrimp over. Its normally translucent legs were all black. One limb broke and drifted away. The shrimp must have been dead for days, further proving Kim's lack of attention to his work.

She sighed and focused on her own task. She grasped the thick branch of A17 and drilled out a core sample, making sure to capture several of the polyps, which required chasing a few with the suction tool. She then collected everything into an extraction receptacle. Once the tiny chute was sealed, she pressed a button to slowly release the pressure inside it. The decompression took four long minutes.

As she waited, she leaned her forehead against the tank. She watched the antics of the pink shrimp. It was hard to be angry at these visitors. Like a passel of rowdy brothers, they cavorted and rolled around the tank. One got too near to A17. A dozen polyps burst off the black stalk and unleashed furls of sweeper tentacles. They battered at the trespasser, whipping it savagely.

The shrimp writhed in place, legs kicking, carapace flinching. It slowly sank to the bottom, joining the others below. A few polyps followed it down; the rest returned to their roosts inside the coral. As the assaulted shrimp landed on its back, she spotted a fiery glow through its translucent carapace, as if it were burning from within. She shifted for a better view, but the belly went dark.

She scowled. *Must've been a trick of the room's light off the glass.* Still, she repeated the question that had been plaguing her all day, staring at the obstinate piece of black coral.

"What are you?"

Someone else had a similar question. "What are you doing to my specimens?" a voice asked sharply.

Startled, she jerked around.

Kim Jong Suk frowned at her. Anger narrowed his eyes. He stood only three inches taller than her, but he carried himself as if he were taller than seven feet.

Jazz didn't back down. "Your specimens? I thought you collected these for a late-night snack. Clearly no researcher would mishandle their research subjects in this manner."

Kim's lips paled to a hard line under a thin black mustache. He was a professor from KAIST—the Korea Advanced Institute of Science and Technology. He was clearly unaccustomed to someone challenging him, especially a post-grad student, and a woman to boot.

"Ms. Patel," he said coldly, emphasizing her lack of a doctorate. "I have time-sensitive research and found your chamber to be mostly empty. And with Dr. Reed gone, I imagine no real science will be conducted here. The tank might as well be put to good use in the meantime. I'm sure whatever busy work assigned to you by Dr. Reed can wait while real research is being done."

Jazz merely smiled at his condescension, not taking her eyes off him. "We're about to identify an entirely new subphylum of *Cnidaria*. And you're playing with a species of shrimp that have been studied for years. What is your research? To discover a new way to stir fry them?"

"Ms. Patel, I'll have you know—"

"And I see you're still here at *Titan Station Down*. While my boss is six miles under the ocean, exploring an entirely new biosphere. So, whose research is truly more important?"

By now, the other biologists in the room stared toward them. Jazz was sure the story of this confrontation would spread throughout the station.

Kim's hands had balled into fists.

Jazz's smile broadened. *Try it, bub.* She had been raised with three older brothers and knew how to fight dirty.

The conflict was interrupted by a sharp *click* from the tank behind her. She turned as the decompression door popped open near the base of the chamber. Her sample was ready for collection.

She swung around and carefully withdrew the small open-mouthed Nalgene bottle that contained her sliver of coral. While she would have

liked to have knocked Kim down another few pegs, she had real work
to do. She snapped the decompression chamber closed and collected a
matching lid before turning back around.

Kim crowded close, anxious for her to get out of his way, trying to
assert his dominance. Jazz continued to block him, staring down into
the bottle. He huffed loudly, but she stood and swirled the content,
rolling the black sliver of extracted coral in the seawater.

"Can you please step aside?" Kim asked her. It clearly strained him
to be even this civil.

She finally relented, feeling that she had affirmed her place well
enough. But before she could shift out of the way, the floor jolted. The
sharp quake threw her into Kim. On reflex, he grabbed for her hand
to hold her up, knocking the sample bottle away. Its contents splashed
across their fingers.

The ground shook for another five long seconds.

When it ended, she pushed out of Kim's arms, her face heated with
embarrassment. She shook her wet fingers and stared down at the bottle on the floor. She bent to collect it, praying the cored sample was still
inside.

Before she could touch it, something stung her middle finger. It felt
worse than a hornet strike. She gasped and dropped to a knee. The
intensity of the pain grew into a fire. She turned her hand and spotted
a millimeter-size green dot clinging to her finger. She grimaced and
brushed the polyp off.

Kim stumbled back, rubbing his hand on his chest. His face was
fixed in a rictus of pain. He had clearly been stung, too. "What was
that?"

Jazz picked up the bottle, which rattled with the sample piece still
inside. "Just a coral bite," she scolded, acting nonchalant while her finger continued to burn.

She collected the plastic lid and screwed it on. As she did, the pain
slowly ebbed. Kim frowned and headed out of the room; apparently his
time-sensitive research wasn't as urgent as he had claimed.

Jazz crossed to a cleaning station, gathered paper towels and a spray
bottle of antiseptic solution, and cleaned up her spill. She dumped it

all into the biological waste chute, where the contents would eventually be incinerated.

Once done, she headed away, embarrassed and subdued. She was sure this incident would also be shared across the station's tiers. Feeling somewhat defeated, she returned to the lab and stored the sample for the night.

I'll start fresh in the morning.

She headed up toward the women's dorm. She opened and closed her hand, working away the residual heat in her finger. She felt foolish for breaking safety protocol. She should have sealed the bottle as soon as she had taken it from the decompression chamber.

While climbing the stairs, she pictured the little pink shrimp toppling to the bottom of the high-pressure tank, chased by emerald polyps. From the fire of that sting, she now understood how the small crustacean had been felled by the attack.

The polyp's venom was intense.

Thank goodness I'm not a shrimp.

10:44 P.M.

Kowalski had never been one to settle an argument.

He usually *caused* them.

He stood inside the geology lab with a cigar clamped between his back molars. The stogie remained unlit due to strict fire restrictions. Not that he would have smoked it anyway. Doctor's orders. Still, he could appreciate the taste and smell of the dried Cuban leaves.

Before him, William Byrd browbeat the older geologist. Dr. Haru Kaneko sat before an array of monitors, all displaying graphs, charts, and seismic readings. Everyone in the room had felt the last temblor. Apparently, Haru believed it was some final straw, a harbinger of a greater geological event to come.

"I've run multiple projections," Haru declared emphatically. "The entire region is destabilizing at an alarming rate. Faster than even my earlier models predicted."

"But it could also settle just as quickly," Byrd argued. "I've read the assessments from the seismologists at Stanford and MIT."

"Those interpretations are outliers, and you know it. Many more agree with my projections—at least to variable degrees."

"Those variable degrees range from an event *possibly* happening in the next few days to years from now."

"Yet, the grimmest predictions came from *volcanologists*. Like myself. Volcanic eruptions pose the greatest threat. And few geologists have studied this region as in depth as I have, nor have they been involved with monitoring this trench over the past weeks. My modeling shows an eighty-three percent probability of a catastrophic event happening within the next twelve hours, maybe less than that."

Byrd sighed dramatically and ceded ground. "Then let your team continue to monitor conditions overnight. If you're still this worried in the morning, then we'll begin evacuations when the sun is up."

Both men turned to Kowalski, seeing if he was willing to chime in. He had only one recommendation. It was a philosophy he seldom lived by—but it sounded good now.

"Better safe than sorry," he warned gruffly.

Haru nodded.

"We should get the hell out of here," Kowalski recommended. "How long would it take to evacuate this place?"

Byrd calculated in his head and counted on his fingers. "With the contingent of personnel down here, and accounting for the number of submersibles, plus the transit times up and down—about three hours."

Kowalski scowled. "That friggin' long?"

"We're two miles down," the billionaire reminded him.

"Then why are we even arguing?" Kowalski said. "Get everyone packing."

Byrd offered a lame excuse. "If we do, it will take us weeks to reestablish everything. It'll cost us millions. Interrupt countless projects. And if we're wrong, the press will have a field day about our needless panic."

Kowalski pointed to the door. "Better some bad press than a hundred dead scientists."

Byrd sagged under Kowalski's glare. "That's true, of course."

Haru looked greatly relieved, as did the other geologists around the room. It was the *depth* of their relief that worried Kowalski more than all their charts and graphs.

Byrd headed toward the door, but before he could exit, a tall dark-skinned man hurried into the lab, stepping briskly up to the billionaire. He stood as tall as Kowalski. His bulk strained his jumpsuit, which was charcoal gray, marking him part of the station's security team. His only weapon was a collapsible steel baton at his waist. No one wanted to risk bringing a gun down here.

Well, almost nobody.

"Sir," the security chief said.

"What is it, Jarrah?"

"Word from *Up*," he reported. "A large military ship is steaming toward us."

"And?"

"They refuse to respond to our hails."

Kowalski butted in. "What military?"

"It's too dark to make out any details. It could be nothing."

Kowalski frowned, knowing better.

It's never nothing.

"Have topside keep us updated," Byrd said. "Let them also know we're instituting an evacuation down here."

Jarrah's eyebrows rose, but he simply nodded, turned on a heel, and headed out.

Byrd faced the room. "I think you're all right. Until matters calm down, it'll be safer up top for everybody."

Kowalski doubted this. His stomach gave a sour churn—and he trusted his gut. He checked his watch, knowing there were others who also needed to be warned.

He faced Haru. "What about the team diving into the trench?" He pictured Monk and the others. "Maybe you should let them know that the place could explode at any moment."

As if affirming this, the station gave another hard shake. Equipment rattled on tables, glassware tinkled, the floor trembled.

They all waited out the quake.

Once it ended, Kowalski started to speak—when another jolt struck. Followed by another.

Kowalski pointed to the lab's radio. "Do it now."

16

Phoebe leaned forward in her seat. The thrusters thrummed outside, driving the *Cormorant* over the shining landscape below. It was as if they were gliding over a rainforest, only one that had been painted and daubed by a wild artist wielding a palette of phosphorescent oils. Everywhere, the coral jungle flickered and flashed, tracing through its depths with metallic fire.

Bryan had cast off another five kilograms of ballast to draw the vehicle to within a few yards of the wonderland. He had also deployed the *Cormorant's* gull wings, transforming the DSV into its namesake.

Lights blazed from the vehicle, casting down and ahead.

At the back, Adam was monitoring a screen that displayed a scan from the onboard sub-bottom profiler. The hope was, by scanning this low in the water column, that they could finally discover the true bottom of the Tonga Trench.

"Anything?" Monk asked.

Adam nodded. "We're picking up the sea floor. It's roughly five hundred meters below us. Past all that coral."

Datuk bounced a knee in excitement. "That depth would match the deepest part of the Tonga Trench."

"And the bottom continues to steadily drop."

Phoebe stared below her knees, wishing her eyes were as good as the profiler at penetrating the forest. It was difficult to discern much through the dense canopy. Though, it did appear that the emerald-green polyps grew larger deeper down, steadily increasing in size. The population across the canopy's surface must be the youngest, the most juvenile of the colony.

She had also noted that the larger polyps below seemed to be the source for most of the forest's bioluminescence. Their younger siblings did not seem to possess this property. She knew coastal corals formed a symbiotic relationship with microscopic algae, called zooxanthellae, which photosynthesized sunlight to provide sustenance for both. She wondered if there could be a similar mutualism going on here, only with a bioluminescent alga. Or could there be some internalized chemical reaction that developed as the polyps aged?

So many mysteries . . .

As they continued across the forest, something caught her eye. A large shadow appeared to be following the *Cormorant*, flowing deep through the forest, sweeping around the massive trunks of coral. She had caught glimpses of it before, but she couldn't tell what it was. It could even just be a trick of shadows from the passage of their lights. Its presence was only notable as a dark bulk that occluded the bioluminescence, like a storm cloud passing over stars. Even now, she wasn't sure if it was truly there.

Still, it made her wonder.

What sort of life made its home at these crushing depths?

She knew one way to find out and glanced to Bryan. "How much farther is one of the landers? I'd love to deploy a bait box and lure life out of the forest."

He checked a sonar scope. Three lights glowed atop a bathymetric chart. "*Louie* is half a klick ahead," he reported. "It lies along the path to the wrecked submarine. But I don't think you'll have to wait that long to cast out bait."

"Why? What do you mean?"

Bryan goosed the thrusters to lift them higher as they approached a dark hillock in the canopy—only it wasn't part of the forest.

"Whale fall ahead," the pilot reported.

Datuk and Monk both shifted to peer over their shoulders.

"What's that?" Monk asked.

"Just what it sounds like," Phoebe answered. "Dead whales often sink to the bottom of the ocean, becoming a great banquet for deep-sea life."

As the *Cormorant* approached, Phoebe made sure the external 4K cameras were recording everything. The dark hill soon materialized into the bulk of a sperm whale. It lay on its side atop the forest. Even its great weight had failed to crash through the canopy.

Like any whale fall, it had become a feast for life down here, a bounty dropped into these nutrient-starved depths. Half the carcass had already been scoured, exposing arcs of white rib and lengths of jaw bones. Life scurried and thrashed over the remains: picking and tearing, snipping and worming.

"What the hell?" Monk asked. "Do you normally find so many creatures down here?"

"Yes," Phoebe whispered in awe. "And no."

Monk gaped past her shoulder. "What do you mean?"

She pointed to a herd of large corpse-white crustaceans as they ripped into the flesh. They looked like a cross between a lobster and a shrimp. Long antennae waved in front of them.

"Those are amphipods. They've been spotted in deep trenches, capable of surviving at these depths. Their shallow-water counterparts seldom grow larger than your thumbnail. In deep trenches, they can grow to a foot long."

Monk shook his head. "Those giants out there are a *yard* across."

She nodded. "As I said, *yes*, creatures like this can be found down here—but *no*, never this size."

One of the amphipods curled its carapace into a ball—much like pill bugs, their distant cousins—and rolled down the flank of the whale.

"It's like something out of a nightmare." Adam pointed at a bright red crab that stalked over the hummock of decaying flesh. It towered high on jointed legs that stretched fifteen feet across. "Is that creature oversize, too?"

"Actually, no," Phoebe said. "That's *Macrocheira kaempferi*. A Japanese spider crab. They've never been reported at these depths. But then again, less than one percent of these deep ocean trenches have ever been seen by any eyes—human or robotic."

She watched a large stingray sweep over the hump of the whale. It stretched six feet wide and twice again in length if you counted its barbed tail.

Elsewhere, a colony of octopuses—normally solitary creatures—fought and writhed inside the hollowed-out carcass. She recognized them. *Enteroctopus dofleini*—the giant Pacific octopus. They stretched thirty feet long, massing seven-hundred pounds each.

She shook her head in both disbelief and wonder.

How were they surviving down here?

She knew deep-sea trenches functioned like solitary islands. They were so remote and inhospitable that life could not move between them, which meant species were forced to adapt to each locale where they were trapped.

And this is as unique as you could get.

The creatures, isolated here, must have developed their own adaptation strategies to contend with the extreme pressure.

As if proving this, a lone squid rose into view, swelling even larger as it staked its territory. It was a massive specimen of *Mesonychoteuthis hamiltoni*, the Colossal Squid. Easily a ton in weight. Its eyes were black dinnerplates, softly aglow from the luminous photophores around its lenses. Likewise, trickles of bright blue phosphorescence traced its limbs in a threatening lightshow.

As they glided past, Phoebe wondered if some of the shine of the coral forest came from bioluminescent creatures like this who made it their home.

Before she could ponder further, a low rumble shook the *Cormorant*. The coral canopy rolled beneath them, shaking and vibrating. Pieces of it shattered and fell away.

Phoebe braced a palm against the window as Bryan drove the DSV higher.

They were not the only ones to try to escape the quake.

The feasting creatures scattered in all directions. Some dove into the trembling forest to hide. Others sped off into the darkness. A few oc-topuses buried themselves deeper into the whale's belly for shelter. The huge stingray fled over the *Cormorant*, striking the DSV's top with its barbed tail, as if warning them to flee.

Bryan did his best to do that, to put a safe distance between them and the thrashing forest. After a minute, the seaquake ended, and the world settled again. Still, Bryan kept them gliding higher over the coral.

"Everyone all right?" he asked.

He got nods and thumbs up.

"We keep going?" he asked.

Monk leaned forward. "How much farther to the sub?"

"Another three kilometers."

Before descending, Monk had recommended that they not drop di-rectly atop the wreckage. He had expressed concern about leaking radi-ation if the submarine was a nuclear vessel. Adam had agreed with him. From their furtive glances, she suspected the pair knew more about the submarine than they were willing to share. Still, she hadn't objected to this course. It had allowed her more time to explore the coral forest.

With the whale behind them, Monk glanced back, apparently equally intrigued by life down here. "Why is everything so huge down here?"

"It's called deep-sea gigantism," she explained. "Across the taxonomic range, deep-sea animals grow larger than their shallower-dwelling counterparts. It's due to the colder temperatures and high pressure. It makes cells grow bigger and live longer. Food scarcity also contributes. Larger animals have a slower, more efficient metabolism."

"Meaning they need to eat less," Monk said.

"And not just that," Datuk chimed in, ready to demonstrate his own knowledge of life under high pressures. "The size of a marine animal is in direct correlation to the amount of dissolved oxygen. The more oxygen, the bigger the animal." He pointed to his glowing display of sensor readings. "Look at the numbers for these waters. They're off the charts. Thirty percent higher than what's been reported during other trench dives."

Phoebe leaned over to review them. "Salinity has dropped by roughly the same percentage."

Datuk nodded. "These waters are far higher in oxygen and lower in salt. Nearly what you'd find in blood plasma."

"If so, then that must be a giant red blood cell." Monk pointed to the massive rosy bell of a jellyfish to the right. It stretched yards across, rimmed by fleshy arms.

"*Tiburonia*," Phoebe reported. "The Big Red jellyfish of the Pacific. But that specimen is twice the size of anything reported before."

"In these oxygen-rich waters, I'm not surprised," Datuk said. "I'm also not registering any microplastics from the samplings. It's as if the coral forest below has purified these waters into a pristine sea."

Phoebe glanced below. It was an intriguing thought. In South America, the Brazilian rainforest served as one of the lungs for the planet, breathing in carbon dioxide and breathing out oxygen.

Was this coral forest doing something similar?

Bryan sat straighter. "We should be coming up on *Louie*, one of the landers, shortly. Once there, I'm going to slow us and perform a system check before continuing on. Everyone okay with that?"

No one objected.

Phoebe wondered if someone should have.

11:30 P.M.

The change in the timbre of the thrusters drew Phoebe's attention from the landscape passing under them. The *Cormorant* lurched slightly, shifting her forward.

"We're about to reach *Louie*," Bryan reported. "The lander should be just ahead."

The thrum of the thrusters continued to fade. With great skill, Bryan timed their glide to stop where the lander's site glowed on his bathymetric map.

Once halted into a hover, Phoebe stared across the flat expanse around them. "Where is it?"

Bryan pointed down. "Directly under us."

Phoebe leaned forward and stared past her toes.

Ah . . .

The boxy lander had crashed through the top of the canopy and was lodged a couple meters down. It sat crookedly, cradled amidst broken branches. She cringed at the damage to the ancient forest—but it also offered her an opportunity.

As Bryan started a full check of their systems, Phoebe rotated their underwing lights to focus on the lander. She hoped the break in the canopy would offer a deeper glimpse into the forest. She centered a beam atop the steel of the lander.

A slight green haze clouded the water. She realized it came from a swirl of emerald polyps, the millimeter-sized juveniles that covered the canopy. They must have been shaken from their perches by the violent crash of the lander.

She pictured those same polyps attacking the ROV claw back at *Titan Station Down*, when she had snapped off a coral branch. Here was further proof that the two must be the same species of coral. She wondered if she had time to take a sample while Bryan worked. To do so would require them getting closer.

She reached to the controls of the *Cormorant*'s hydraulic arm. "Could we—"

From below, a huge black eel lunged up through the break in the forest. It was as thick around as her thigh, its length pulsing with lights. Jaws opened wide, revealing a maw of three-inch-long needle teeth. It snapped in their direction, thrashing its muscular length in a display of fierce aggression.

The light beam must have lured it out.

And not just it.

In its wake, thousands of polyps swirled up in a dense fog. Already aggravated, they attacked what they could, descending upon the eel. In seconds, its black length turned a corroded green, its skin frosted with polyps. The eel thrashed even more violently, no longer in aggression, but in pain. As it did, its lights flashed in alarm, tracing up and down.

Phoebe winced at the torment, feeling guilty for luring the eel out.

Datuk spoke behind her. "I'm getting a spike in water temperature."

Focused on his screen, the biochemist had failed to note the attack near one of the DSV's external sensors.

"Look outside," Phoebe ordered him. "I think you're registering the eel's body heat."

Datuk bent to his window, holding his eyeglasses in place. He stared for a long breath. "*Ni tidak mungkin*," he mumbled in disbelief. "At this cold depth, the metabolic heat must be incredibly intense for the external sensors to pick it up. If this was happening on the surface, that eel would be frying, if not self-immolating."

By now, the eel's lights had begun to dim. Its writhing quieted.

Phoebe covered her mouth, still panged by guilt. The suffering creature had survived decades, if not longer, down here—*until we intruded.*

From the bower, another shape coiled upward. For a moment, she thought it was another eel. Only this limb was dark green, scintillating in a spectrum of bioluminescent colors. It reached the eel, wrapped around it, and withdrew its catch into the break in the canopy. Another glowing tentacle snaked out, then a third. Their tips gently brushed across the eel's skin.

As they did, the green frosting wafted away. In seconds, the polyps were chased off the eel's black skin. The first arm released its hold. From its underside, smaller tendrils still connected the tentacle to the eel. Lights flashed along those thin strands, beating like a heart.

The eel slowly stirred, undulating under the other's attention. Luminescent lines again trickled across its length. Finally, the eel broke free and squirmed back into the depths of the forest. The glowing tentacles receded with it, vanishing away.

Everyone aboard had witnessed this, even Bryan.

Monk was the first to speak. "Did that other creature nurse the eel back to health?"

"And what was it?" Adam asked. "A hidden octopus?"

Phoebe shook her head, too dumbstruck to speak, but knowing the truth. She swallowed before answering. "No, not an octopus. I think it was a polyp."

Datuk looked sharply at her. "A polyp? From the coral?"

"From deep down," she said. "I had already noted that the polyps grew steadily *bigger* with each descending level of the forest. Down at the bottom, they could be gigantic."

No one looked convinced.

Phoebe didn't care. She trusted her gut and the science. "The polyps have already shown they could be freely motile, capable of leaving their calcareous branches. And those small tendrils that pulsed outward from the tentacles, they could be adaptations of sweeper tentacles, something that I'd witnessed before from this species."

"Witnessed when?" Datuk asked. "And where?"

She told them about the lone coral tree she had discovered outside Titan Station. "I'm sure it's the same species."

Adam frowned. "To me, those tentacles still looked like the limbs of an octopus. Maybe an early form, one that hadn't developed any suction cups yet."

"It's a polyp," Phoebe insisted.

"Maybe it's *both*," Datuk said.

All eyes turned to the biochemist.

He ignored his sensor data to face them. "While octopuses are classified as cephalopods, they make no evolutionary sense. Their huge brains, their complicated nervous systems, their camera-like eyes, even their ability to camouflage—all these features just suddenly appeared on the evolutionary scene. Octopuses can even edit their own RNA to help them adapt to their environment, unlike any other organism. Across the board, they're light-years ahead in evolution compared to all their cephalopod relatives."

"What does that mean?" Monk asked. "What are you saying?"

"That we still don't understand *how* octopuses came into being. They're so strange that scientists have postulated that they could have come from beyond Earth."

"From outer space?" Adam asked in a mocking tone.

"Indirectly. And that's according to a scientific paper that has survived vigorous peer review." Datuk lifted a palm. "But that's not truly my point. What I'm trying to emphasize is that we still don't know *how* octopuses came to be. All we know is that they arrived on the evolutionary scene shortly after the first corals appeared in the ocean."

"That's true," Phoebe said.

Datuk pointed down. "And that is some very ancient coral."

Phoebe nodded. "That's also true."

Adam stared down at the coral. "Are you suggesting those large polyps could be an early precursor to the modern-day octopus? The missing link in their evolutionary history?"

"I'm not suggesting anything. Just speculating."

Phoebe remembered one other aspect unique to this coral. Something that had stymied her attempt to lump it taxonomically with other black coral species.

These polyps had eight limbs.

Just like an octopus.

She pictured the glowing tentacles gently reviving the eel. Such an altruistic action might further support Datuk's assertion. Studies continued to expand the understanding of how complex and intelligent octopuses were. They were extraordinarily nurturing, capable of compassion, of showing affection and empathy. They also experienced emotional pain, even suffered grief.

She stared at the forest below.

Could Datuk be right?

She pictured the juvenile polyps attacking the eel and wondered if such aggression reflected their young age. She knew baby rattlesnakes posed a greater danger than full-grown adults. Baby rattlers struck wildly and unloaded all their venom at once, where mature snakes grew to understand that hiding and caution served them better. Adult rattlers controlled the amount of venom they dispensed, protecting their reserves. Even *dry striking* at times to warn off a threat, biting but not envenomating.

Did we just witness some version of that? Were the adults correcting the aggressive behavior of their young? Were they policing their garden, protecting the denizens of their bower?

Phoebe shook her head, both daunted and awed.

But such mysteries would have to wait.

Bryan straightened in his seat and drew their attention back to the mission at hand. "Green lights across the board, everybody. We're good to head onward."

17

As the *Cormorant* closed on the location of the wrecked submarine, Monk stared out his viewport. The glowing forest stretched in all directions. He found himself rubbing at his left wrist, a habit whenever he grew anxious. At such times, his fingers were drawn to his old maiming, as if unconsciously trying to remind him to stay alert, lest he suffer worse than losing a hand.

Or maybe it was just that his new prosthetic hand chafed.

He had only been wearing it for three months. The latest bit of DARPA tech was attached to his wrist by magnetic contact points, which were wired into his arm's nerves, both motor and sensory. Between lab-grown skin and a wireless cortical implant to control it all, he could barely distinguish his prosthetic hand from the real one. It certainly looked the part. No one aboard the *Cormorant* had given it a second glance.

The prosthesis was also far more than it seemed. The fingers were strong enough to crack walnuts. The palm hid a potent charge of C4. The DARPA engineers had also incorporated a suite of electronic warfare countermeasures, including hacking tools.

In many ways, it was as much a weapon as any sidearm.

Not that any of it helps down here.

Monk forced his fingers away from his wrist and shifted in his seat to study the bathymetric map near the pilot's shoulder. A green triangle marked the position of the submarine.

Another half-kilometer and we'll be on site.

He returned to staring out his viewport, but he kept a sidelong watch on the man seated across from him. Datuk Lee had shown no evidence of being a mole, a Chinese agent. Still, as they approached the sub, Monk intended to keep a closer eye on the man, to spy for any crack in his jovial demeanor.

Behind Monk's shoulder, Adam was doing the same from the rear seat, but with much less circumspection. The TaU agent watched the biochemist steadily, barely looking away. Not that Datuk noted it. The man continued to monitor his sensors, muttering occasionally to himself.

Movement drew Monk's attention below, but it was nothing to be concerned about. A bright red KitKat candy wrapper rolled across the coral canopy, stirred by the current of their passage. He had noted other signs of man's reach down here: a few beer cans, several fluttering plastic bags, a huge tire. It was a sad testament that even at these depths there was no escaping the trash from the world above.

But that was not the worst damage.

Phoebe gasped from the front seat.

Monk saw it then, too.

Ahead, a dark wound blackened the brilliant landscape. It spread in a vast, cancerous swath across the coral.

"We're coming up on the submarine's location," Bryan reported.

The damage ahead looked far worse than could be attributed to the impact of a submarine. Where the lander, *Louie*, had crashed, the forest around it had still glowed.

Unlike here.

The coral fields ahead appeared black and dead. As they drew closer, the dark expanse grew, spreading outward in a widening circle.

Datuk offered an explanation. "I'm picking up gamma radiation."

All eyes turned to him.

"How bad?" Monk asked.

"Eighteen rem," he reported. "Not too dangerous while we're insulated in here. But it's climbing steadily. We should not travel too close to that sub."

Bryan had already cut the thrusters with Datuk's first warning. Momentum still carried them forward, bringing the *Cormorant* to the edge of the dead zone.

"Twenty rem," Datuk sounded off. "Thirty . . ."

"Back us off," Monk ordered.

Bryan reversed their thrusters and set them gliding away.

"Guess we know what killed the coral out there," Adam said. "The wrecked submarine must have a massive leak. Still, water acts as a good insulator. With six miles of ocean overhead, the radiation shouldn't pose any risk to the surface—just to the local sea life."

"Then let's make sure that doesn't include *us*," Monk added.

Phoebe turned to them. "Adam, the radiation might not pose a danger to the greater world, but *something* down here has your uncle worried. It's this section of the Tonga where all the quakes have been clustering. The submarine's crash could just be coincidence, but I'm not buying it. Especially if the vessel went down two weeks ago."

Monk glanced at Adam. They both knew the crash likely happened in that timeframe.

"This forest has been here for millennia on end." Phoebe waved a hand at the dark swath. "This blight is new. Something about that wreckage is to blame. I'm sure of it."

"But we can't get any closer to investigate," Datuk reminded them.

"What about the ROV attached to the underside of the *Cormorant?*" Adam asked.

Phoebe shook her head. "Its tether only stretches eighty meters. We're still a quarter mile off. To utilize the ROV, we'd still have to bring the *Cormorant* in close."

"We mustn't," Datuk warned. "If the radiation level continues to rise at the same rate as I've recorded, it'll be deadly within that range."

"But not *immediately* fatal," Phoebe added.

Bryan concurred, but he didn't look happy about it. "The titanium and the leaded glass of the sphere will offer some protection. Up to a limit."

Phoebe nodded. "Which means we could live long enough to investigate, to find out the reason for the quakes and maybe discover a way to stop them."

"Only to die of radiation sickness afterward," Adam added.

Phoebe shrugged. "If it meant saving millions."

Monk lifted a hand. "We're getting ahead of ourselves. Let's first confirm *where* the submarine came from. Whoever lost it might have answers that won't require us sacrificing ourselves."

Bryan pointed ahead. "We're close enough that we can use our 4K cameras to zoom in on the site and try to identify the sub from here."

"Let's do it," Monk said.

Phoebe and Bryan quickly set to work, shifting through the *Cormorant*'s eight cameras. They also raised an eight-foot light tower.

"The SeaCam looks like it's our best bet," Bryan concluded. "It has the greatest zoom capability, especially in low light."

"I agree."

On the monitor above the pilot station, a blurry image appeared. With some final adjustments, it grew clearer, revealing a close-up of the black stain spreading across the bright landscape ahead.

"Zooming in now," Phoebe said.

The view ratcheted forward, pushing out into the darkness, to the farthest reach of the light array's twenty thousand lumens.

Nothing came into view.

Phoebe huffed and toggled the camera right and left.

"Wait!" Monk called. "Swing the other way."

The image stuttered as it swept back.

"There!" Monk leaned forward and pointed to a duller blot against the blackness. "Zoom on that."

Phoebe nodded. "Hang on."

The view leaped forward again. The blot swelled into a grainy view of a gray tower sticking out of the black coral. The rest of the submarine remained buried, but what was in view was enough. Both Monk and Adam had reviewed the surveillance footage from the Huludao Shipyard. The Chinese Type 096 SSBN had a very distinct sail.

He shared a look with Adam.

A sail just like that one.

Adam gave him a small nod of confirmation, while continuing to stare at Datuk. The biochemist showed no reaction.

"Do you recognize it?" Phoebe asked.

At this point, Monk saw no reason to lie. "It's a Chinese sub."

Phoebe frowned. "Then we'll have to hope that the Chinese are willing to—"

With a great boom, the landscape lurched ahead of them. The coral forest rose in a huge wave and swept swiftly toward them. Bryan goosed the thrusters and shot them higher, trying to escape the quake. Still, they barely got clear in time. The rolling wave of the forest canopy brushed the *Cormorant*'s underside as the wave passed beneath them.

Turbulence continued to rock the DSV like a paint shaker. This quake was far more violent than the other.

But that was not the only danger.

"Radiation is spiking!" Datuk yelled.

Bryan spun the *Cormorant* and fled farther away.

"Eighty rem!"

Monk pictured the quake shattering the shielding around the sub's nuclear reactor, breaking it open wider. They were never going to escape in time.

Not like this.

"A hundred! If it crosses much higher, we risk radiation poisoning. Even in here."

"Blowing all ballast," Bryan warned. "Jettisoning external battery packs, too."

Small booms sounded outside the DSV as explosive bolts were blown, casting off extra weight. The *Cormorant* shot upward like a cork out of a champagne bottle.

Below, the glowing landscape fell away. The dark stain spread wider as the surge of radiation fried more of the sensitive coral.

A new voice intruded, rising from the radio modem. The message was urgent, panicked. "*Cormorant*, this is *Titan X*! Get out of the Tonga. Now!"

Monk knew there was a lag time in communications at this depth. The warning had been dispatched seven seconds ago.

He prayed it wasn't already too late.

FOURTH

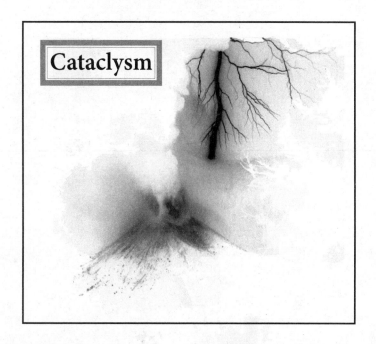

Cataclysm

18

Gray had to appreciate the irony of the location for this hostage exchange. It was called the Love Bridge, a tourist attraction at the Ancol beach resort in northern Jakarta.

He stood at the western leg of the U-shaped wooden bridge as it arced out over Jakarta Bay and returned to the beach nine hundred feet away. Between the two legs stretched a curve of sandy beach. The Love Bridge got its name because the arc of the wooden jetty and the curve of the beach formed the outline of a huge heart at the edge of the city's bay.

"It's gotta be a trap," Seichan said.

"Love usually is." Gray cast her a sidelong glance.

It was *love* that had drawn them here. Valya had captured Seichan's mother in Singapore. The Russian had contacted them through the triad network, showing proof of life and arranging this exchange. In the brief video, Guan-yin's face had been a mask of fury, one eye swollen shut. Valya had given them little time to reach Jakarta from Singapore. Her demand had reached them only six hours ago. Either they came to Jakarta and handed over the papers that Gray had secured at the museum or Guan-yin would be returned to them—piece by piece. The schedule had left them little leeway to do more than scramble to get to the island of Java.

Seichan's anxiety and fury were palpable as she stood alongside Zhuang and a dozen of the *Duàn zhī* Triad members. More gunmen guarded the paths to the bridge on this side. Zhuang carried an H&K assault rifle. His other men bore a slew of firearms.

Nine hundred feet away, the opposite leg of the bridge had been equally fortified by the enemy. Gray had studied them through a set of binoculars. He had easily spotted Valya standing next to Guan-yin. The former Guild assassin had shed her disguise. Her pale face and white hair were a beacon in the dark, aglow in the wan light of a streetlight on that side. She had brought not only a handful of her own men—a mix of Russians and Eastern Europeans—but also a large cadre of Chinese gunmen. From the way the latter carried themselves and their QBZ rifles, they were likely military, possibly one of the PLA's elite combat units.

With the two encampments entrenched on either side, the exchange would happen out on the middle of the bridge, where the wooden jetty pinched inward and formed the top of a heart sitting on the water. There was a restaurant—Le Bridge—located at that picturesque point, but it was closed and dark for the night. The two parties would meet on the bridge near there.

Gray checked his watch. "Ready?"

"Let's go," Seichan said.

They set off, trailed by Zhuang and two triad members, including the steely-eyed triad deputy, Yeung, who was loaded down with weapons.

On the far side of the bridge, a similar small group split off from the larger party and headed for the rendezvous. Valya had been specific about the numbers allowed to meet on the bridge. She stalked toward them with two of her men and two of the Chinese commandos. One of her mercenaries held a pistol against the back of Guan-yin's head.

Under his jacket, Gray carried the payment to free Guan-yin. The sheaf of papers was still sealed in the same acid-free plastic sleeve from the museum. Gray had copied the pages already, so there was minimal cost in exchanging them for Seichan's mother. With the tight timetable, he'd barely had time to do more than glance at them.

A brief reading told of an account of petrified men, a strange autopsy, and a wild claim about a cure and a possible means to appease the gods of the underworld. The rest had been hand-drawn sketches of what appeared to be a type of *coral*, a couple of drawings of an *island*, and what looked like a child's drawing of a *snake*.

None of it made any sense and was likely intentionally cryptic.

But how did all of this hang together?

With no way of knowing, he concentrated on the immediate threat. The dark waters of the bay lay flat around them, reflecting the sickle of the moon. He searched for any sign of a threat, a hidden ambush out in the waters. But this late, there was not a single boat. The waters were too shallow for any submersible. If there were divers in the water, they swam silently, showing not even a bubble. He had also surveilled the small dark restaurant out on the water, watching for any sign of men lurking there. He had spotted no one, even searching with an infrared scope for body heat.

So far, Valya seemed to be sticking to her word.

Still, Gray knew better. Seichan was undoubtedly right.

This is a trap.

But he could not discern how it would be sprung.

Both sides approached the rendezvous heavily armed. The exchange would happen out in the open with no place to hide. The only guarantee of cooperation was their mutually assured destruction.

As Gray reached the closed restaurant, his heart pounded harder. Zhuang swung his assault rifle, guarding against an ambush from in there. But the establishment was small, barely larger than a coffeehouse. Yeung dashed over and searched past its windows, flashing a light mounted on his rifle. No one was hiding in there.

They continued to where they would meet Valya's group.

Weapons bristled on both sides.

Gray had a gut feeling this was going to end badly.

12:06 A.M.

Dr. Luo Heng slapped a mosquito on his neck. The noise made one of the Falcon commandos flinch. The soldier had an assault rifle at his shoulder, staring down its telescopic sight as the two groups converged.

Around him, a dozen men—a mix of mercenaries and military—guarded this end of the bridge. Major Choi Xue whispered with the leader of the counterterror unit, Captain Wen, who glared at the Russians standing with them. The commander rested his palm on a holstered QSZ-92 sidearm. Much depended on the next few minutes going right, and clearly Wen had no respect for their allies in this venture.

Heng understood Wen's frustration. While en route from Cambodia, he had been informed of the plans to regain the stolen papers. While the mercenaries had lost the museum documents, they had secured a hostage—along with an artifact, a dented steel box belonging to Stamford Raffles.

After landing, Heng had briefly examined its contents. On outward appearances, the branch of coral from two centuries ago *did* appear to have the same aragonite structure as the carbonate found in the afflicted submariners, but he could not be certain without studying its crystalline pattern under an electron microscope. He remained entirely clueless concerning the other artifact in the box: the wooden spearhead. It looked old, and it could be unrelated, something tossed into the box over the ages for safekeeping and forgotten about.

Xue shifted over to Heng. "Once we retrieve the papers and confirm their authenticity, I've secured a research lab here in Jakarta so you can work."

"We're not returning to Cambodia?" Heng had left Min at the naval base with the patients—both Junjie and Wong—to continue monitoring the two men. "There's still much research to be done there."

"First, we must confirm if this old account from two centuries ago has any bearing on the present. If so, I'd like to continue investigating this historical angle. Stamford Raffles collected his artifacts here in Jakarta when he was lieutenant-governor. If he left any other clues, they would likely be hidden here."

Heng nodded, accepting this recommendation. In truth, he was also anxious to study the piece of old coral as soon as possible.

He stared across the water. The two parties had reached the middle of the bridge to make the exchange.

Xue watched, too, tapping a finger on his thigh, both impatient and likely trepidatious. One concern kept him edgy.

He whispered it to the dark water. "Who are these Americans?"

12:08 A.M.

Seichan clenched her jaw so hard that she expected a molar to break. She clutched her Glock 45 in her right hand with her finger tight on the trigger guard, ready to fire, tempted to do so now. But she held off.

Her mother was held by a thick-browed Russian with dusky blond hair. He had a fist wrapped in the back of her robe, a gun at her head. Her wrists were bound behind her. Guan-yin's silk niqab had been stripped from her head and face, exposing her purplish scar and dragon tattoo.

Valya had also set aside any pretense. Her snowy hair was tied in a tail, pulling her hairline to a sharp V across her forehead. Her skin was pale to the point of translucency. The woman suffered from albinism. Yet, defying the assumption that all those afflicted had red eyes, her irises were an icy blue. Hatred burned through that ice as she faced Seichan.

It was only in this moment that Seichan recognized how much her mother and this Russian woman were alike, down to the tattooing on the left sides of their faces. Valya's black ink formed a half sun with kinked rays extending over cheek and brow. Only now it also had a scar cutting across it, a knotted line that ran through the sun's center. Both women had led equally hard lives, forced to survive when fate stripped them from their homes. Valya had found her way into the brutality of the Guild; Guan-yin into the cruelty and criminality of the triads. Each had forged a role where they couldn't be hurt again, leading their own organizations.

Gray shifted forward to face Valya, ready to bargain for Guan-yin's freedom. Seichan never took her gaze from the assassin, watching for every twitch of muscle, shift of balance, and flick of eye. Still, she smelled the musk of Gray, heard the huff of his breath, even felt the heat of his body as he brushed past her shoulder. With her gaze locked on Valya, she couldn't help but wonder where she would be if she hadn't found Gray.

Would I be standing on the other side right now?

Gray held up his palms as he stepped toward Valya. His light windbreaker flapped in the sea breeze, exposing the SIG Sauer holstered at his waist—along with the folded sheaf of papers tucked into his belt. He slowly reached down and tugged the plastic envelope out, but he kept them away from the enemy's reach.

"Free Guan-yin," he said firmly. He bent and lowered the packet of pages to the wooden slats of the bridge and stepped back, leaving the envelope behind. He drew his pistol but held the weapon at his thigh.

"I will need to inspect the papers first," Valya warned. "To make sure this isn't a trick. The museum manifest described fourteen pages. They had all better be there."

"I've kept my word. I expect you to do the same."

Valya nodded once, and her mother was thrust forward. Valya kept hold of Guan-yin's elbow, a Beretta pressed into her side. Her two men had their weapons trained on Gray. He took another step back to make sure there were no misunderstandings.

Seichan shifted her finger to her weapon's trigger.

Valya lowered a hand toward the envelope, her eyes on Gray, her pistol still aiming for Guan-yin's heart. She picked up the envelope and shifted her weight onto her right leg. Her eyes narrowed a fraction.

No . . .

Seichan knew what was going to happen—or thought she did. Guan-yin must have suspected something, too. Seichan's mother dropped to a knee and twisted around to face the enemy behind her. Guan-yin swung up a small pistol in her right hand, revealing her wrists had never been truly bound, only appeared to be. Pieces of severed plastic zip ties fell to the planks.

Valya also spun in the same direction.

The two women fired simultaneously.

The two Chinese gunmen both dropped, shot through the foreheads.

Valya thrust off her right leg and lunged at Seichan and Gray. "Run!" she hollered at them, clutching the packet of pages.

Guan-yin followed at her side, trailed by Valya's two men.

"*Pǎo!*" Guan-yin yelled, reinforcing the order to flee.

Gray got swept along with their rush. Seichan followed at her mother's side and pointed her Glock at Valya, who was flanked by her two men.

Guan-yin pushed Seichan's arm down. "*Mh' hóu.*"

Any further explanation had to wait. Gunfire chased them down the bridge, rising from the Chinese contingent on the far side. Rounds blasted into the planks and spattered into the water, but for the moment, the shots were wild due to a fierce firefight at the other end of the bridge. It appeared Valya's men had ambushed the commandos back there, too.

But that battle would not last long.

Already the Chinese were getting the upper hand. Brief glances showed Valya's men fleeing into the dark streets of the waterfront. The gunfire grew more focused on the bridge as Seichan and the others fled past the restaurant and headed toward their end of the jetty. Ahead, the triad forces covered them with bursts from their assault rifles, aimed at the Chinese contingent, keeping the enemy pinned down on that side.

A pair of commandos tried to cross the stretch of beach between their two sides. Zhuang spotted them, too. He ran alongside Guan-yin with his rifle at his shoulder. He fired at the beach, casting up sand. One man fell. The other was forced back.

Seichan pounded down the planks, clutching her Glock hard. She shared a look with Gray. By now, they both understood what must have happened. Valya hadn't come here to trade Guan-yin for the *pages*. She had used Seichan's mother to barter for her own *life*.

Valya must have sensed she was trapped and in danger when the Chinese commandos arrived in Jakarta. The Chinese clearly no longer felt the need to hide behind mercenaries. Knowing that and knowing her team had failed—*twice*, back in Hong Kong and at the museum— Valya must have suspected her usefulness to the Chinese was coming to an end.

Guan-yin had offered her a way out, promising the assistance of the triads to help Valya make her escape.

A life for a life.

As their group neared the western side of the bridge, Seichan lifted her pistol.

I made no such promise.

Even with her back turned, Valya must have sensed the threat. She turned, skidding slightly, and lifted her Beretta at Seichan.

"Don't!" Guan-yin ordered and stopped between the two of them. "I've sworn Mikhailov protection until she leaves this region."

Such an oath was sacrosanct among the warring triads. To break it would bring dishonor to Guan-yin and the entire *Duàn zhī* clan.

Zhuang waved more of his men forward, to shield the bridge during this momentary impasse. Gunfire kept the Chinese pinned, but it would not last long.

"Go!" Guan-yin waved to Valya. Even after putting her body between them, Guan-yin's anger and hatred for the assassin sharpened her words. "Take your men. Zhuang, see that the others secure passage for her group."

Valya crossed the last of the distance, backpedaling the entire time with her pistol raised at Seichan. Seichan held her weapon up, too. She kept her arm steady, even as her body trembled with rage. She matched eyes with Valya. Both women were ready to fire, but both knew their revenge would have to wait.

Still, Seichan could not let the assassin escape yet again. She centered her aim between those ice-blue eyes.

Not this time.

12:21 A.M.

Gray rushed Seichan, fearing what would happen if Guan-yin's guarantee of safe passage was broken. Before he could reach her, the world trembled and jolted hard.

The bridge was tossed high with a great splintering of wood. Sirens burst across the city. The jetty thrashed and tore apart around and under them.

Another quake . . .

Valya fled from the bridge onto solid ground. She was surrounded by members of the triad, including Zhuang.

Gray rushed to Seichan and Guan-yin. With Yeung's help, he herded them toward shore, traversing the quaking shreds of the bridge. "We don't want to be near the coast if another tsunami—"

A thunderous boom shattered over them, sounding as if the world had cracked in half. The ground bucked hard, throwing them all off the bridge and into the water. Gray splashed into the shallows. This close to the beach, the waters were only knee-deep.

He gained his legs and waded to Guan-yin, helping her up.

Seichan joined them, still holding her pistol.

Gray pointed to the shore. They had been tossed to the far side of the bridge and were momentarily shielded by pilings. Despite the quake, gunfire continued on the other side.

They waded across the trembling water. The distance was not far, but the quake's shaking had liquefied the packed sand under their boots, turning it into a sucking muck. With every hard-won step, more booms chased them. Despite the distance, each blast felt like a punch to the gut. They finally reached the beach and clambered out of the water.

Zhuang rushed to meet them and got them moving more swiftly. He must have sent Valya ahead with a cadre of the triad, honoring Guan-yin's oath.

"Where do we go?" Gray asked.

By now, the Chinese had also vanished from their end of the bridge. Gray and the others would need to remain wary, not that his group had anything to offer the Chinese. When Valya had left, she was still clutching the envelope of papers she had grabbed off the dock. Maybe that was her plan all along. To use this entire gambit as a way of nabbing the prize for herself, to sell it to the Chinese afterward.

Gray could not dismiss such a strategy, especially when it came to that woman.

"This way." Zhuang led them off the beach, seeming to know where he was going. Before landing in Jakarta, the man had hinted that the triad maintained a safe house in the city.

Gray hoped that was true.

By now, the quake had ended, but the detonations continued, sounding like cannon fire. Sometimes closer. Sometimes farther off.

"What is happening?" Guan-yin asked, staring back at the bay.

Gray pointed to the east. The dark skies shone with fire, as if the sun were rising. "Volcanic eruption."

And it was not just in that direction. All around, fiery patches dotted the horizon with distant flames. Booms continued, as if marking the end of the world.

They reached the city and fled away from the bay, knowing another tsunami would surely hit. Though the quake had not been fierce or prolonged, it must have set off a chain reaction across the volcanic chain of islands, something the geologists had predicted. Already, a hint of sulfurous brimstone reached him, blown by the stiff wind off the bay, coming from the direction of the brightest flames.

As they fled through the city, the streets grew crowded. Faces stared toward the fiery horizon. Lightning flared in jagged bolts, illuminating a black plume rising from a glowing caldera.

"Over here!" Zhuang yelled.

The triad lieutenant led them unerringly off the streets as panic and shouts grew. He drew them into an alleyway and down a crooked course, before stopping at a nondescript tall gate.

"We'll be safe in here," Zhuang said.

Gray doubted this, but he followed the others into a small courtyard. Three stories of balconied levels surrounded them. He stared up as the stars slowly faded, erased by the smoke rolling in.

A light fall of ash rained down. The flakes stung his cheek and forehead, still retaining the heat of the eruption.

The booming had finally gone silent, but it felt more like the world was taking a deep breath before it truly unleashed Armageddon.

Gray felt a buzzing from the inner pocket of his jacket. He removed the sat-phone—the one supplied to their group back in Singapore. Only one person had this number.

Gray lifted the phone to his ear. "Director Crowe."

"Gray," Painter said. "Thank God, you're still okay. You and the others need to get out of that region. Projections are for a total geological collapse. It's going to become hell on earth over there."

"What about the Chinese, their submarine—"

"It's the least of anyone's concern."

Gray stared toward the streets.

Not to the Chinese.

Still, Gray had his own worry. "Were you able to warn Monk and Kowalski?"

The phone remained silent for a long stretch. Gray feared he had lost the connection.

Painter finally spoke. "Kat has tried to reach them since she landed in D.C. Both the *Titan X* and the project's base station in the Coral Sea have gone silent. We're trying to access an NSA surveillance satellite, but neighboring islands—both the Kermadec chain near the Tonga Trench and the Solomon Islands near the Titan Project—started erupting two hours ago."

Gray swallowed. That was long before the quake here.

"Reports are of heavy ash obscuring the area," Painter said. "At the moment, we have no optical sightlines. Even our SAR satellites—which can normally pierce thick clouds and smoke—are failing to offer any clarity due to the heavy static charge of the ash clouds. Or possibly it could be due to EW jamming by hostiles. Maybe both."

Gray stared up. The stars were completely occluded now. He sought shelter under a balcony as the ash fell heavier, swirling with fiery flakes.

"We'll keep trying to raise them," Painter promised. "Right now, you have to get clear of the area before all flights are grounded."

"It may be too late for that."

"Then get to a boat."

Gray heard a distant rumbling and cracking coming from the direction of the bay. He recognized that ripping growl from yesterday. A tsunami had struck the coast, likely pushed out from the nearby volcanic eruption.

He remembered not only his own experience, but also the accounts he had read from two centuries ago, when Mount Tambora had erupted. He also knew who had been here. Sir Stamford Raffles. History was repeating itself, only a hundredfold worse.

While he had only a short time to review the pages recovered from the museum, he remembered Raffles's words in the introduction of his account: *The only hope for the world lies within the pages that follow.*

"Gray?" Painter asked. "What are you going to do?"

"I'm staying here."

"Why?"

It was a fair question. Though Gray had no time to digest the pages of Stamford's account, he sensed the import. That *strange mind* of his, as Seichan described it, had already begun to work on a puzzle, one with too few pieces yet. But in those pages, Stamford had hinted at a means of salvation, a way to *appease the gods of the underworld.*

Gray listened as more booms echoed over the horizon.

Painter repeated his question. "Why do you need to stay out there?"

Gray answered as best he could, knowing it to be true. "To discover a way to speak to the gods."

19

More than three hours into the evacuation of *Titan Station Down*, Kowalski paced the geology lab. He chewed the end of his cigar, anxious to get moving, all too aware of the two miles of water over his head.

Outside the lab, handfuls of people ran up and down the central hub, shouldering duffels or carrying laptops. Shouts and calls echoed everywhere. Still, a quarter of the station's personnel remained down here. The evacuation was way behind schedule.

What is taking so damned long?

Every half hour, a station-wide klaxon rang out, announcing the arrival of another shuttle of submersibles that would ferry the next contingent of researchers and staff to *Titan Station Up*. William Byrd had used the station's PA to urge everyone to remain calm, assuring them that the evacuation was just a precautionary measure.

It had not helped much.

Especially with the repeated quakes that followed.

Kowalski had been tempted to leave with the first subs, but Haru Kaneko had refused to abandon his post, even though the man had sent the rest of his geology team packing. William Byrd was also down here, along with his security chief, Jarrah. Apparently, the billionaire was determined to adhere to the captain's adage of going down with his ship—even when this ship was already at the bottom of the sea.

The ongoing quakes continued to harangue the evacuation. Most were just tremors. Others had been stronger. One had been fierce enough to rip free two of the six cables anchoring them to the seabed. But even minor temblors had made it challenging for the submersibles to safely dock at the station's airlocks. To make matters worse, reports from topside described a heavy cloud of ash sweeping over the ocean. It rose from volcanic eruptions across the neighboring islands that had started a couple of hours ago. The ash, which was highly conductive, was wreaking havoc with communications due to insulator flashovers and repeated disruptions of the *Up*'s generators.

All in all, it was a clusterfuck.

And Byrd knew it. "Topside comms are still down," he reported from his station next to the geologist. "I'm sorry, Haru. I should've listened to you earlier and not delayed the evacuation. We should all be gone by now."

Haru stood before his monitors, bent over a keyboard. "At least down here, I'm still receiving data from the sonobuoys and seismic monitors."

Kowalski leaned over his shoulder. "Are any of them sending *good* news?"

Haru sighed. "The buoys are showing a major seabed rise along the Tonga Trench. Fifty meters and still climbing. The seabed seismographs and geophones continue to show an escalation in quakes. Only now it's no longer limited to just *one* section of the Tonga. New clusters are popping up along the entire two-thousand-kilometer length of the Tonga-Kermadec subduction zone."

Kowalski frowned. "In English, that means what?"

"That we've not seen the worst of it yet," Haru said. "Not by half."

"How much worse can it get?" Byrd asked.

Haru turned to them. "Volcanic strength is ranked by VEI—a Volcanic Explosive Index. It's open-ended, meaning it doesn't have an upper limit. A VEI of zero is a slow leakage of lava, like you see at Kīlauea in Hawaii. From there, it rises across eight known ranks, from explosive to mega-colossal. The modern world has never experienced an *eight*. The last was seventy thousand years ago, the Toba eruption. It was so devastating that it drove the human population down to a mere thirty thousand people."

Kowalski felt a sickening drop in his stomach. "And now?"

Haru faced his screens and brought up a map of the region that was dotted with hundreds of triangles, marking the volcanoes most at risk.

"At present, twenty-four peaks have erupted over the past two hours. Most in the three to four range, a few sixes, which are still considered in the *colossal* range." He tapped on his keyboard. "Here is what my son's modeling program predicts, what the status will look like in two or three days if the tectonic instability continues to escalate."

He tapped a button.

On the map, a number appeared above each of the volcanic triangles.

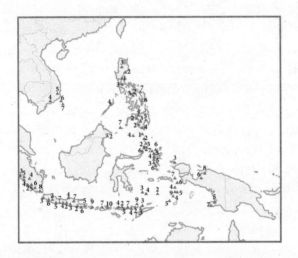

Kowalski squinted at all the fours and fives. A handful of sixes. But there were also several sevens and two eights. But it didn't stop there.

"That can't be . . ." Byrd moaned, as if trying to deny the numbers on the screen.

"There are three *nines* on that map." Kowalski glanced at Haru. "And one *ten*."

The geologist nodded. "That ten marks the center of the Sunda arc of volcanos. Mount Tambora. A peak that erupted in the nineteenth century and killed a hundred thousand people. Back then, it was only a *seven*."

Byrd stood up sharply, knocking his chair away. "What can we do?"
Kowalski knew the answer.

He pulled out a lighter and lit his cigar.

That's better.

No one even frowned at him.

Haru simply shook his head. "Unless this trench suddenly and inexplicably calms again, there is nothing we can do. Beyond the immediate cataclysm, such devastation will raise a planet-shrouding ash cloud. One that will last decades. It'll mark the end of life on Earth. The only hope—"

A loud klaxon made them all jump.

They waited out the three short bursts. It heralded the arrival of the next group of submersibles. Out in the central hub, several stragglers ran upward, hoping for a berth on this second-to-last flotilla.

Kowalski studied a CCTV monitor at the workstation. It showed the tier above them. The last of the personnel crowded and milled in front of the ring of airlocks, all anxious to leave—not that the surface would be any safer for much longer.

Byrd turned toward the door. "I should get up there and organize the next group of evacuees. Try to reassure the rest. Then I'll be back."

Byrd swung around to leave, motioning for Jarrah to come with him to help maintain order. Before the men could step away, Kowalski grabbed Byrd's arm and pointed at the CCTV screen.

"We got company."

By now, several of the airlocks had opened. People crushed forward—but they were forced back as figures in black armor entered the station. They came in with helmets, masks, and rifles. Muffled gunshots echoed from above. Several researchers dropped. Screams followed.

The assailants were judicious with where they fired, clearly understanding the danger of an errant shot at these depths. But that was not their only means of coercion. All their weapons had bayonets mounted on them. Several carried tasers, felling several more researchers into trembling submission.

Kowalski remembered Jarrah's report of an incoming military ship that had refused to respond to any hails. With the evacuation, the quakes, the volcanic eruptions, no one had paid any more heed to the silent vessel as it crossed the seas nearby.

Only it must not have sailed past.

Kowalski now suspected the communication blackout over the past half hour had nothing to do with power outages. The ship must have jammed any transmissions.

Kowalski shoved Byrd toward the door. "We can't stay here."

Jarrah nodded his agreement. He reached to his belt and freed a steel baton, snapping it to its full extendable length. The security head grabbed Haru and yanked him to follow. They rushed out of the lab but approached the central stair warily.

Delphin Tier lay directly above them. They needed to put some distance between them and the assailants. So far, the enemy seemed focused on securing the level above, but their group couldn't count on that lasting for long.

Kowalski reached under his coat and pulled out a Mark XIX Desert Eagle. He pointed the fifty-caliber weapon up and leaned his head out into the stairwell. He spotted shadows shifting up there. A single gunshot made him cringe, but no one appeared to be looking his way. He hissed and waved the others down the stairs.

The three men scurried ahead of him, then he followed. They wound down the long spiral and paused at the next level, which looked deserted—though there could be a few laggards holed up and hiding in labs.

Byrd carried an e-tablet in hand. Kowalski leaned over his shoulder. The billionaire had patched the CCTV feed to his tablet. As more commandos arrived, station personnel were herded at gunpoint into the galley and dorms. Several commandos guarded the top of the stairwell, making no attempt to venture deeper, which Kowalski found worrisome.

"Who are they?" Byrd gasped out.

"Trouble," Kowalski said. "That's all we need to know for now."

"What do we do?" Haru asked.

Byrd lowered his tablet, but Kowalski pulled it back up.

On the screen, a group of commandos clustered around a pair of plastic crates. They began handing out rectangular parcels, each affixed with a knob of electronics.

Kowalski swore, recognizing the threat from his own demolitions background.

Semtex and detonators.

The commandos set about planting charges around the tier. A few headed toward the stairwell. While it would take only one or two bombs to implode the entire complex, the assailants weren't taking any chances.

Kowalski got them moving downward again. "Is there another way off the station? Maybe through one of the emergency airlocks at each level."

Byrd shook his head. "A submersible would need to dock there first."

Kowalski scowled.

That's not happening any time soon.

Byrd hurried down. "Our only hope is to get to the lowest level in the station."

Kowalski followed, though he failed to see how burying their head two levels deeper in the sand was going to help. But the bottommost tier was the smallest and likely the most defensible.

They reached the next level—Kalliste Tier—only to be confronted by a young woman hugging a laptop with a pack slung over her shoulder.

She looked more pissed than scared.

2:38 A.M.

Jazz confronted the group of men. "What the hell's happening?"

"Come with us," Byrd ordered and herded her down the steps toward Tethys Tier.

Confused, she allowed herself to be swept along. She was too tired, too addled to argue. She wiped sweat from her brow and shivered, not out of fear, but due to a slight fever. The middle finger of her right hand throbbed and felt stiff. She opened and closed her hand, worrying about circulation, fearing a clot. The digit had taken on a worrisomely gray hue.

But that was clearly the least of her problems.

A gunshot above confirmed this.

As they all hurried faster, she searched the group around her. She recognized Jarrah and Haru Kaneko. The last of the group towered over her. Though she hadn't been introduced to Joseph Kowalski, his size, demeanor, and hard features had been a point of much conversation. He claimed to be a member of DARPA. His partner—a biomedical expert—had accompanied Phoebe to the Tonga Trench.

Jazz eyed the huge pistol clutched in the man's hand. Earlier, she had thought she had heard gunshots. At the time, she was sealed inside the benthic lab and had dismissed the noise as pops from the stressed walls of the station after the quakes. Anything else made no sense. Who would dare shoot inside a space surrounded by pulverizing pressure?

She looked up at Kowalski's stern face, smoke wafting from a cigar. *This guy would.*

As they reached the bottom of the station, a sharp cry echoed down the stairwell. It was followed by a spate of angry shouting in Chinese.

Byrd headed across the tier. "Hurry."

Beyond the ring of windows, the ocean continued to shine under the exterior lamps. The reef glowed in radiant hues. But now there was an ominous cast to the seas. More harsh shouts echoed, getting closer.

"We need to seal off this level," Byrd said.

"How?" Haru asked.

The trio had left Jarrah and Kowalski at the bottom of the stairs.

Jazz tried to look both ways at once and asked the most important question. "Why?"

Haru explained in crisp sentences. "We're under attack. A military contingent arrived in the last shuttle of subs. They're holding everyone at gunpoint." He saved the worst for last. "And they're planting bombs throughout the station."

Aghast, Jazz looked at the two men by the stairs. Hours ago, she could have left with the first evacuation group. She had been asleep up in the women's dorm when the evacuation order had been announced. Byrd had assured them it was of no concern, that it was a decision made through an abundance of caution. She had taken the man at his word and, rather than leaving immediately, had gone down to the biology lab to secure all her research and collect samples to take with her. It was all too important to abandon.

That's what I get for being so diligent.

She should have taken a page from her older brothers, who believed idleness was a great virtue and that the mere act of getting out of bed should be applauded.

Byrd reached a slanted door along one side of the tier. It lay directly across from the emergency airlock on the opposite side. Jazz knew this door led down to a set of auxiliary controls, a redundant system of batteries and generators, allowing each tier to be self-contained in case of a disaster.

This certainly counted as one.

Byrd hauled open the door and freed a large key hanging from a chain around his neck. He then climbed down the two steps to a dark chamber below.

Haru and Jazz remained at the door's threshold.

"Better do something quick!" Kowalski called over, raising his pistol higher.

Down in the chamber, Byrd inserted his key into a console and gave it a hard twist. Lights flickered, then flared across a secondary bank of controls.

Directly behind her, a thunderous gunshot made her flinch and duck. The blast deafened and stung her ears. Still, she heard a sharp shout of surprise from the tier above.

Behind her, Kowalski shifted around the stairwell, angling for a second shot.

And luckily, he did.

Automatic gunfire sparked where he had been standing. Rounds pinged and ricocheted off the steel floor. They struck all around, even off the glass.

Jazz winced and ducked lower.

Kowalski fired again with the cannon in his hand, then shouted over to them. "Now or never!"

"Hang on!" At the auxiliary controls, Byrd pounded a fist on a red button with FIRE stamped on it.

Immediately, a warning alarm blared across the tiers. Overhead, large bulkhead doors slammed closed, one after the other, sealing off each tier. The force was strong enough to shake the floor.

Two objects tumbled down the steps, bouncing and spraying blood. They landed at the foot of the steps.

A pair of severed legs.

Jazz gasped and nearly fell back into the compartment with Byrd. She realized the shooter must have been perched at the level of the hatch—and suffered for his trespass.

Kowalski stepped over the limbs, as if they were a couple of logs. He had to shout to be heard over the fire alarm. "This trick won't buy us much time. They'll just plant one of those Semtex charges right on top of us."

Byrd shifted over to a pair of red levers. "Then let's not be here when that happens."

He pulled the smaller lever marked with the word ANCHOR. Sharp muffled bursts sounded outside. Beyond the window, thick cables fell away from the station's sides and slithered to the seabed. Freed now of its attachments, *Titan Station Down* spun slightly over the reefs. The stabilizing thrusters kicked in, thrumming loudly as they fought to stop the station's wobbling.

"How's this gonna help us escape?" Kowalski asked.

"Like this."

Byrd flipped four toggles, lighting each up—then hauled on the larger lever. It required both hands and some body weight to pull it down. It was stamped with the word UNCOUPLE.

As he snapped it into place, the entire station shook with a series of chunking clanks. Jazz lost her balance and grabbed the door jamb. The fire alarm immediately ceased. In the silence that followed, the noise of the thrusters grew in volume, tremoring the floor.

Jazz stared out the window as the reefs drifted under them. "What's happening?"

"It's how we assembled the five tiers of the station," Byrd explained. "Piece by piece."

He turned over to a bank of controls that had bloomed into light behind him. Above it, the curve of glass extended in an arc across the space. Below it, Byrd grasped a large yoke that stuck out.

"Each tier is its own self-contained submersible," he explained. He pushed the yoke forward, and the thrusters thrummed louder. "How else could we position and join the tiers together down here? We needed some means of maneuvering them into alignment and stacking them together."

Jazz got her legs fully under her and stumbled to one of the windows. She leaned her palms on the glass and gaped back at the glowing bulk of *Titan Station Down*. It still shone in the dark, only now it was slowly coming apart, the tiers sliding past one another.

"Unless interrupted, each tier will autonomously rise to the surface on its own." Byrd glanced back to them. "Like I told you all, I designed multiple fail-safes and redundancies into this construction."

Haru stared at the fragmenting slide of tiers. "What about everyone else back there?"

"When a tier is in motion, the submersible docks automatically lock down. It's too risky to release them when moving. Could cause a catastrophic leak. There is a manual override, but I doubt the newcomers know about it."

Kowalski crossed next to Jazz and whistled out a stream of cigar smoke. "So you trapped the bastards with the station personnel."

Byrd shrugged. "Unless they're suicidal, it should discourage them from exploding those charges."

Kowalski grimaced and looked up. "It's not them I'm worried about—but whoever sent them. They may not care who dies down here."

20

Captain Tse Daiyu frowned at the sonar array on the bridge of the *Day-angxi*. The data did not come from the equipment aboard their ship, a Type 076 helicopter landing dock. Instead, it had been transmitted to them via an array of sonobouys dropped into the waves around the tall research station floating atop the Coral Sea.

The bright sonar screen revealed a 3D map of the seas beneath the research rig. She stared at the ruins two miles below. The deep-sea station showed up as a scatter of saucer-like blobs, which slowly fell apart as she watched.

"I don't understand," Daiyu said. "Did Snow Leopard Team already destroy the submerged station?"

A radio operator in blue camouflage sat at a console behind her. He held a headphone to one ear. "There remains confusion, sir. The men sent below have not yet surfaced. But so far, no underwater explosions have been picked up by the hydrophones on the sea's surface."

"Then what happened?"

"Unclear, Captain. Current consensus is that there might have been an accident."

Her frown deepened, detesting such uncertainty. "Do we still maintain full control of the upper facility?"

He nodded sharply. "*Shì.*"

She stepped over to the windows facing the stern. The dark seas lay flat around them, as if beaten down by the press of the low, dark skies. Even the *Dayangxi*'s exterior lamps had been dimmed by a shroud of falling ash. Occasional flashes of static discharge snapped through the roiling clouds of powder.

To the west, eighty nautical miles off the stern, a small torch glowed through the pall. It marked the upper tier of the research rig, which still burned following the initial missile attack. Snow Leopard Team had destroyed a helicopter, which allowed one of their own birds, a Z-8 transport chopper, to land and deploy a well-armed assault force. At the same time, a trio of attack boats, each loaded with forty men, had sped out of *Dayangxi*'s flooded well deck. They had reached the station and quickly subdued it.

Daiyu had overseen the attack from afar. Already, the *Dayangxi* was steaming away under the full power of its gas turbine and diesel engines. She had barely slowed the ship as it passed the research rig at a distance. It was of secondary importance. Instead, she continued swiftly toward their primary objective—the Tonga Trench.

Still, she had monitored the assault behind her from the *Dayangxi*'s combat information center. She had been prepared to deploy additional forces, both by sea and air. Even now, a Hongdu GJ-11 Sharp Sword—a stealth combat drone—waited atop one of the flight deck's electromagnetic launchers. She was somewhat disappointed she hadn't needed to dispatch the drone—which was no surprise. She knew the research rig had minimal security and firepower.

As she stood by the bridge window, she watched the site burn for another two breaths, then crossed back to the sonar station.

Once there, she pointed to the radio operator. "Alert Snow Leopard Team. After their divers are clear, blow everything below and have their demolition force sink the rig above. Then rendezvous back at the *Dayangxi*."

"Yes, sir."

Snow Leopard's helicopter and attack boats were far swifter than the two-hundred-meter-long *Dayangxi*. The assault team could easily close the distance while the landing dock made slow passage to the trench.

Within the next hour, she planned to take advantage of another swift vessel, one still stored in the well deck of the ship. She intended to use it to reach the trench well ahead of the *Dayangxi*.

She pictured the boat waiting below her and clenched a fist.

It's only fitting that I command such a craft.

The PLA Navy had taken Daiyu's design specs for the AI-driven *Zhu Hai Yun*, along with its complement of autonomous drones. They had built a militarized version of it and mounted it all atop a *Yema*, a Type 726 air-cushioned landing craft. The boat could sweep across the ocean at eighty knots, nearly three times the speed of *Dayangxi*. It would put her at the trench in roughly five hours. Once there, she would coordinate with the hunter-killer submarine that was on approach. The sub was under a standing order to only *patrol* the waters until she arrived.

Her fist tightened.

No one will steal my thunder.

She refused to allow the hunter-killer's captain to take command of the site where the *Changzheng 24* had gone down. Instead, she intended to prove the military prowess and worth of her autonomous design systems. The modified LCAC waiting in the well deck carried a battle tank and a fleet of her drones, each one unique and deadly. It also held a deep-sea bathyscaphe, a submersible capable of reaching the bottom of the trench, a craft as dangerous as any of her designs.

She smiled at this thought. She would sideline both the attack submarine and the lumbering *Dayangxi*. She would turn both into mere support vessels to her own ambitions. Instead, she intended to prove to Beijing that it was time to look beyond the old weapons of warfare. She would show them a new path—a better one—into the future.

And I will lead us there.

"Captain Tse, sir," the radioman alerted her. "I've passed on your orders to Snow Leopard Team. But communications are growing patchy as the ash cover thickens. Between the charge in the air and physical compromise of our antennas, it may grow worse."

As if emphasizing this threat, a bolt of lightning chained across the sky in a blinding display.

She scowled at the low skies. Off the starboard side, fires glowed out in the darkness, marking the volcanic eruptions along the chain of Solomon Islands. She pondered the mystery—and opportunity—they presented.

Seven hours before, she had landed aboard the *Dayangxi* and taken command as the ship transited these waters. While at sea, she had failed to feel any of the reported quakes. She had only witnessed the volcanic eruptions and the blackening of the night sky, which was concerning enough. Afterward, she had taken a brief call from Choi Aigua. He believed the tectonic activity was further proof of his theory—inflaming his hope for what might lay hidden in the waters ahead.

Daiyu stared at her toes, trying to picture a chunk of a foreign planetoid buried in Earth's upper mantle. According to Choi, it was the source for the spreading chaos and eruptions. She remained unconvinced—though the volcanic eruptions across the region were eroding her doubts.

As with her own ambitions, she knew *what* Aigua hoped would be discovered at the trench. He was convinced that the sinking of the *Changzheng 24* had somehow triggered this cascade of events. If they could learn *how* it happened—how it tied to petrified bodies, crystals from a lunar rock sample, and a strange ELF pulse—it might offer a clue to a great weapon, a way to control the very foundations of the planet. If successful, it would return China to its rightful dominance of the world, to create a new shining dynasty that would last until the sun went cold.

Though she didn't fully accept Aigua's theory, she dared not dismiss it.

If there is even the slimmest chance of it being true . . .

Movement on the sonar screen drew her eye. The broken sections of the underwater station had fallen farther apart. The saucer-like fragments also appeared to be slowly rising upward. But what drew her attention was its smallest section. That tiny splinter remained deep and had drifted away.

She squinted at it, both suspicious and curious.

As she stared, the sonar screen pixelated into obscurity. After a few seconds, it slowly reformed. Only now the image blurred in and out of focus.

"We're getting stronger interference," the sonar operator reported. "Maybe due to the electromagnetic effects from the volcanic eruptions we're passing. The transmission should clear up again after we gain some distance."

"Do what you can," she said.

She straightened and stared ahead, already putting the fate of the research station out of her mind. She trusted Snow Leopard Team could handle matters back there. Besides, she had left extra insurance in the waters around the huge rig. Before departing, she had dispatched four UUVs into the sea. The unmanned underwater vehicles operated autonomously. They were capable of recognizing, following, and attacking any anomalous cavitations in the water. If detected, they turned into self-guided torpedoes.

She pictured the tiny fragment of the station drifting off. If it strayed too far, it would be blown up. Knowing this, she dismissed any misgivings and concentrated on what lay ahead. She pictured the giant research yacht—the *Titan X*.

She smiled at the dark seas.

One more target to destroy, one more step toward glory.

21

Seated at the rear of the *Cormorant*, Adam leaned forward between Datuk and Monk. Cold sweat pebbled his brow—and not just from the tension. The humidity inside the submersible had increased steadily as they ascended.

"How's it looking?" he asked.

Datuk pointed to his array of sensor data. "I'm not detecting any more radiation. It has dropped steadily after we rose through the salt-dense brine layer. It's been holding at zero for the past twenty minutes. We should be safe from here."

Their pilot sat in front next to Phoebe. After the radiation level had dropped to within a tolerable zone, he had halted their ascent at various depths. Each time, like now, he performed a system check. Half of the green lights across his control board blinked an angry red. Even more worrisome were the wisps of smoke rising from several spots. Bryan had assured them it was just some fried circuits and that there was nothing to worry about.

Still, Adam was all too aware of the fire danger aboard the enclosed vehicle. He glanced at Datuk's screen. The *Cormorant* was still a thousand meters underwater.

"We should be able to complete our ascent from here," Bryan said.

"I've bypassed the electrical actuator and manually released the last of our ballast weights."

They began rising again, but it was impossible to tell from looking out at the black ocean. There was no sense of motion inside the enclosed bathysphere. The only evidence was the steadily decreasing number on their depth gauge.

Up front, Bryan toggled a switch back and forth, clearly trying to get the dead section of his board to turn back on.

Monk grimaced at this effort. "Maybe we should have reserved a couple of those extra battery packs, instead of jettisoning them all."

Adam refused to second-guess their pilot. As rapidly as the radiation had been spiking after the quake, he was happy that Bryan had tossed away the extra baggage of those batteries.

Anything to hasten our departure.

Still, it was taking them longer to ascend than it had taken to get down. Once away from the radiation, Bryan had insisted on a more cautious ascent. Especially as the *Cormorant* had been struck by the coral's canopy as the quake wave passed under it. The brief brush had damaged several systems.

"Do we have enough power to reach the surface?" Phoebe asked.

Bryan nodded and wiped the moisture from his brow. "With most systems turned off, the shipboard batteries should suffice."

"What about communication with the *Titan X*?" Monk asked.

Phoebe lifted a pair of headphones. "No luck. I'm still getting interference. It's a common problem with acoustic modems . . . they're highly susceptible to background noise. Whale song from miles away can block sound waves and halt communication for hours."

"What's causing this interference?" Adam asked.

"It could be anything," Phoebe said. "Oceans are noisier than most people realize. I ran into a colony of pistol shrimp when working on the Sur Ridge off California's coast that confounded our sonar efforts. They're considered the loudest creatures on the planet. They each have a huge claw that snaps so strongly it shoots out a vacuum bubble that collapses in a burst of glowing plasma that reaches a thousand degrees.

They literally shoot bullets to kill prey. And very noisily so. Colonies can deafen a sea for miles."

Monk nodded. "DARPA is actually studying the noise of those shrimp, along with the loud booms of territorial groupers, as a means of detecting underwater threats rather than actively casting out a sonar ping from a boat or buoy. The project called PALS—Persistent Aquatic Living Sensors—is seeking an algorithm that would allow searchers to use the natural background noise of sea creatures as a version of active sonar, listening for how those sounds reflect off hidden objects."

Phoebe turned to him. "Truly?"

Monk shrugged. "DARPA is always looking for innovation. The oceans cover seventy percent of the earth's surface, which makes it a huge potential battlefield, one where tensions are increasing rapidly. Especially the seas around this region."

Phoebe's interest visibly soured. She surely did not appreciate the natural world being co-opted for war.

Adam changed the subject, back to what truly mattered at the moment. "So, Phoebe, you have no clue where the noise on the phone is coming from?"

"It sounds like gravel spilling down a hillside. Which makes me think we might be hearing the residual tectonics under us."

Datuk lifted a brow. "The earth grinding its teeth."

Adam did not appreciate the imagery.

Monk waved for the headphones. "Let me hear it." He took the phones and listened for a full minute with his brow crinkled, then passed them to Adam. "What do you think?"

Adam slipped the headphones in place and pressed both palms over its earpieces. The tone filled his head. He closed his eyes and noted it did sound like an avalanche of gravel, only this landslide never ended. The only change was a slight rise and fall in volume. He felt a sickening lurch in his belly.

It can't be . . .

He swallowed and passed the headphones back to Monk. The Sigma operative stared hard at him, his eyes unblinking, clearly asking for confirmation.

Adam nodded.

Monk turned to stare out the front window as the *Cormorant* ascended through the water column. A glance at the depth gauge showed the vehicle had risen out of the midnight seas and into what should have been sunlit waters. But at this late hour, it remained as dark as the depths of the trench.

Still, Monk stared into those black seas, searching for the threat that they both knew must be hiding out there. The gravelly noise could be nothing. It could be, as Phoebe had attested, some residual grinding of the tectonic plates under them. But it could also be a more immediate threat—one close by.

The noise sounded worrisomely like the cavitation of a propeller thrumming through the water around them, circling closer and farther, creating a shifting doppler as it moved.

Adam hoped he and Monk were both wrong, especially considering the nationality of the wreckage under them. He leaned forward and joined Monk's vigil of the seas, but in his gut, he knew they were both right.

There's a submarine hiding out there.

4:12 A.M.

As the *Cormorant* crested out of the water, a thunderous boom greeted their arrival. Phoebe had heard similar muffled explosions for the past two minutes as the vehicle neared the surface. It sounded like they were rising into the middle of a sea battle. The others all crowded toward the front window.

"Dumping the freeboard weight now," Bryan said.

Small bolts blew outside, and the *Cormorant* lifted higher in the water. The seas receded across the glass, stopping about three-quarters of the way down.

Above the waterline, the sight made no sense. It looked as if they had surfaced into another world. There were no stars. The skies lay low and heavy. Lightning and deep flashes coursed through a thick cloud layer—but the source of the booming was not thunder.

To the east, the horizon was on fire. A handful of patches glowed a bright orange through the gloom. The closest danced with a cascade of flames.

"Volcanos," Phoebe said.

Another shattering explosion blasted a distant glow into a fiery spectacle. She glanced over to Adam, remembering the maps she had shown him, along with the cataclysm he had forecast.

Is it already coming true?

Adam pointed toward the view. "Those fires must mark the neighboring Kermadec Islands. A chain that runs alongside the trench from New Zealand to Tonga."

"Does anyone live on them?" Monk asked.

Adam shook his head. "They're all uninhabited. I think there's a field station on one that's periodically occupied."

"Thank god for that," Monk said.

Phoebe felt little relief.

These islands aren't the only ones threatened.

She cast her gaze past Adam's shoulder, picturing the regions west of the trench and the hundred-plus volcanos that he and his uncle had judged to be the most at risk. Adam met her gaze before she could look away.

"Are we too late?" Phoebe asked him.

He simply shook his head. "We need to get aboard the *Titan X* to find out."

She turned around. Already a fine layer of powdery ash settled over the window. Even the waves that washed along the bottom of the glass were heavily clouded by the same.

Bryan pulled the yoke by his seat, and the thrusters hummed. As the *Cormorant* turned, the giant yacht came into view. Its lights shone dully, dimmed by the ash fall. Even the huge glass sphere of Science City was crowned by a layer of dark powder.

The pilot hit a switch, and a Xenon strobe started flashing above, signaling their location. Phoebe knew from her pre-dive instructions that it also ignited an Iridium satellite beacon.

Bryan unhooked a handset. "Now that we've surfaced, I can radio the *Titan X*. Get them to send out a recovery boat."

"Make it fast," Adam said, sharing a worried look with Monk and a guarded glance at Datuk.

Phoebe suspected Adam's concern went beyond erupting volcanos. As the two men faced the window, they both stared across the water, ignoring the glowering expanse of the *Titan X*.

Bryan reached the yacht's radio room and chattered in the arcane language of pilots. All acronyms and shorthanded instructions. Once done, he hauled out of his seat and squeezed over to the heavy wheel of the overhead hatch. He twirled it open, then shoved hard on the hinged door. Once it was open, he climbed up the short exit trunk to reach the exterior hatch. He cracked the door enough to let in fresh air—though *fresh* was far from what it smelled like. The sea breeze reeked of burning sulfur. He didn't open the hatch any farther, to keep ash from contaminating the interior of the sphere.

Outside, a low rumbling continued, punctuated by louder blasts.

"What's the word from the yacht?" Adam asked, as Bryan returned to his seat.

"Most of their comms are down. I likely only reached them because we're practically bobbing in their shadow."

Phoebe frowned, matching Adam's expression. "Do they know what's happening back at Titan Station?"

"Last word was that the quakes were worsening over there, so they instituted an evacuation of the station. Everyone was going to weather out the storm at the topside rig."

Phoebe let out a long breath.

At least, Jazz should be safe.

"And nothing after that?" Monk asked.

"Like I said, comms are mostly down. Can't even get a sat-feed."

Phoebe stared out at the dark seas.

So, we're cut off out here.

4:44 A.M.

Monk stood at the bow of the rescue boat. The rigid-hulled inflatable craft droned slowly through the ash-covered waves, hauling the *Cormorant* behind them. He was flanked by Adam. Behind them, Phoebe and Datuk shared a bench. The two cradled steaming cups of coffee on their laps, courtesy of their rescuers.

Bryan had stayed aboard the DSV as it was towed. He would help get the vehicle hooked back into its launch-and-recovery crane at the stern of the *Titan X*. The plan was to quickly ready the *Cormorant* for another dive, though if it ever happened was another matter. With the radiation levels down there, any approach would be dangerous, if not deadly. Still, the question remained: *What the hell is happening in that trench?*

But Monk had a larger concern, even one that outweighed the fiery horizons and the rain of ash. He watched the seas around them, searching for any evidence of the presence of a submarine. The fact that the sub remained submerged and hidden reinforced his assumption that it must be a Chinese boat.

If one's even out there.

He wanted to get to the yacht's sonar room. As an oceanic research vessel, it had a sophisticated system of exploratory tools, certainly more than what was available aboard the *Cormorant*. Movement snapped his attention to the starboard. Around the far side of the *Titan X*, a tall red mast appeared low in the water, cutting through the waves.

But it was too small to be the sail of a military sub.

Adam confirmed the same. "It's one of the two Drix USVs. It's still paired with its twin. They're programmed to autonomously circle the *Titan X* and surveil the seas." He turned to Monk. "Could those vessels' props be the source of the interference we heard?"

Monk shook his head. "They run too quiet. We would've heard them when we were descending. The only times they revealed themselves were when they periodically pinged their echosounders to monitor our descent. And those pings were plenty loud and distinct."

Adam nodded. "Then what do we do from here?"

Monk narrowed his gaze on the tall red mast. "For now, let's keep those sharks circling out there. Just in case."

"So, you're still convinced we're not alone in these waters."

"Never hurts to keep our eyes open and ears up."

The boat closed the last of the distance to the *Titan X*. They all offloaded and headed into the yacht's stern hold. Behind them, Bryan orchestrated the recovery of the *Cormorant*.

Monk glanced back toward the cascades of fire along the horizon. Rumbles and booms had chased them back to the yacht. The skies had lowered further, the air filling with smoke and ash. Bolts of lightning flashed up there, discharged by the immense energy inside those clouds. Another fountain of flames burst higher from one of the erupting peaks.

He grimaced.

We need to find out what's causing all of this.

He pictured the wrecked sub in the trench, the luminescent coral forest, and the spreading dead zone. Still, he could not dismiss the threat closer at hand.

As their small group crossed toward the elevator, Phoebe stumbled on her feet, clearly exhausted from the lack of sleep. He hated to keep her from her bed any longer, but—

He touched her elbow as the elevator opened. "Phoebe, can I have a word with you?"

Datuk entered the elevator and held the door open.

"We'll catch the next one," Adam said.

Datuk looked confused, but he was too tired to challenge them. His hand slipped from the door, and it closed.

Monk waited until the cage started ascending before facing Phoebe. "Adam told me that you're skilled with driving a DriX USV."

She shook ash from her hair and stared down at him. Her eyes were the color of warm caramel. "*Skilled* may be too flattering a description, but yes, I can manage one."

"How about *two*?"

Her brows lowered, pinching her expression. "Why?" She glanced over at Adam. "What has you both so spooked?"

Monk appreciated her astuteness and saw no reason to lie. "I need you to help us hunt a submarine—and not a wreck this time."

She looked between him and Adam. Her next words proved exactly how astute she was. "You think the Chinese sent another boat. To protect what sank. That's what you thought you heard on the acoustic phones."

"We don't know for sure," Adam admitted sheepishly.

Phoebe shrugged. "Then let's get sure."

Monk smiled as she turned and headed away from the elevator. He and Adam followed her.

The monitoring station for the two DriX units was just off the stern hold. They pushed into the small communication cabin, where a lone operator monitored a spread of glowing screens.

The young tech stood up as they entered, his eyes wide. He searched all their faces. "How was the dive?"

Phoebe offered one word. "Interrupted."

The man pointed to the control station. "I was just about to shut everything down and recall the USVs before those waters get any more covered in ash."

"We can handle it," Monk said. "We wanted to review some data before retiring."

"I'm happy to—"

Adam took him by the elbow and guided him out. "We're fine."

As Adam closed the door behind the man, Phoebe faced them. "Why not have the tech help us? He's probably more proficient than I am."

"For now, we should keep this between the three of us," Adam said.

Monk nodded. "If there is a threat lurking in these waters, we don't want to alert the enemy of our knowledge."

"And if we're wrong," Adam added, "there's no reason to start a panic. Especially as there's plenty to worry about already."

Phoebe frowned, clearly not comfortable with such subterfuge. Still, she took the seat before the console. She quickly scanned the twin set of monitors, one for each DriX. With the multibeam system switched off after the dive, the two sonar screens were dark, but smaller windows showed positional and operational data of the two USVs.

"The pair should be circling in tandem," Monk said. "One on each side of the *Titan X.*"

Phoebe leaned toward a small screen on the desktop that showed the DriX's position in relation to the yacht. "That's correct."

"Can you send them circling wider? Very incrementally. No sudden changes."

She leaned over the control keyboard, tapped a few times, and manipulated a mouse cursor across some menus. "Done. I've set the radius of their transit to increase by five percent with each pass."

Monk nodded. "Can you set up a scheduled pinging of their sonar? As regular as clockwork. As if it's an automated routine."

"Simple enough." She worked the controls again. "I'll set them to alternate their pinging. One after the other. Five minutes apart."

Adam turned to Monk. "Now what?"

He shrugged. "We wait. When it comes to hunting, patience is as important as stealth or firepower."

They all settled in. Every five minutes one of the DriX units would fire its echosounder, casting an expanding wave of sound toward the seabed. On their respective screens, colorful 3D images appeared, showing the water column in gradients of depths and a crisp image of the seabed.

The trench appeared in flashes, revealing its high cliffs and the dark shadow of its bottom. The detail was clear enough to discern the scar across the coral canopy below. Even the smooth contour of the Chinese submarine showed up, crumpled at one end.

But Monk concentrated higher up the water column.

An hour went by, and the seas remained empty.

"Maybe we're wrong," Adam finally offered with a jaw-breaking yawn.

Phoebe cocked her head, narrowing one eye. "That can't be good."

"What?" Monk asked.

Phoebe leaned closer, while blindly tapping the keyboard. She flipped between the image recorded by the *first* ping and the *latest* one. She switched back and forth, like an optometrist testing one's vision.

"What are you seeing?" Adam asked, clearly failing the eye exam like Monk.

"Hang on. Let me adjust the opacity."

Phoebe tapped a few more times, and the two images now over-lapped each other, translucent enough to see both. The trench walls aligned perfectly on both images, as did most of the seabed—but not at its center. The current image showed the coral canopy and the sub-marine it cradled had dropped tens of meters lower.

"What's happening?" Adam asked.

"It's all sinking." Phoebe frowned. "Maybe the radiation weakened the coral forest under it, enough to make it crumble beneath the sub's weight."

"Is that possible?" Monk asked. "The sub's been leaking radiation for more than two weeks. Why would the coral be breaking down now?"

"Could it be secondary to the quake?" Adam asked.

"Maybe."

Another of the DriX pinged its sonar scanner. Phoebe quickly placed the new image on top of the other two.

"It's still subsiding," she reported. "Another eight meters."

As they watched the images over the next half hour, the sinking ap-peared to be accelerating, which made no sense.

Phoebe frowned at the oddity. "If the sub was merely settling atop a crumbling expanse of forest, its descent should be slowing as the debris piled beneath it, braking its fall. But that's not happening. I think I know what's—"

They all gasped with the next sonar firing.

Phoebe leaned closer, studying the seabed.

The wreck of the submarine was gone.

6:30 A.M.

Phoebe ignored the chatter from the two men. They had kept secrets long enough, so she felt little need to answer their press of questions.

Instead, she brought up the sub-bottom profiler on one of the DriX units and ran a real-time scan of the black hole in the coral. She studied the cross-sectional image as it cut down into the darkness, searching for its bottom.

She didn't find it.

With a growl of frustration, she sat back.

Adam touched her shoulder very gently, as if fearful of her reaction. "What happened down there?"

"It's as I feared."

"What?"

"A fissure must have opened under it. Swallowing the sub and a big section of the coral forest with it." She glanced over at Monk and Adam. "I don't know if the quake broke it open, or if it was always there. Maybe the radiation weakened a bridge of coral that had spanned the crack. Until it finally shattered, dumping everything below."

Adam stared at the screen. "But what could be down there?"

Phoebe sighed her frustration. "It's too deep to discern anything."

"Could whatever we're seeking—the cause of all this tectonic instability—be hidden in there?" Monk asked. "It's right at the heart of the strange swarming of quakes."

Phoebe stared over at the two men. "There's only one way to find out."

Adam closed his eyes, knowing what she meant. "Radiation or not, we have to go down there again."

She slowly nodded.

One of the DriX units blasted its sonar again. She leaned forward as its scan appeared, hoping it might offer some further answers to what lay below.

Instead, a shape blocked the right edge of the image. It was the tip of a tapered object that sprouted a set of fins at its end. It hung at a depth of two hundred meters.

Phoebe knew what she was seeing. "You were both right."

They waited out the next pass of the second DriX as it circled to the same position and pinged its sonar. The image on the screen was clear again. The tail of the submarine was gone.

"Does it know we found it?" she asked.

Monk shook his head. "No way of telling. The sub surely heard the ping, but hopefully those aboard just assumed that it was another of the units' automated blasts. For us to have caught a glimpse of its tail, the sub's captain must have let his guard down, overly confident that the *Titan X*—an unarmed research vessel—posed no threat to it."

"So what do we do?" Phoebe asked. "Do we dare dive in the *Cormorant* with that shark patrolling these waters?"

Monk rubbed his chin. "Something feels off."

Adam stepped closer. "What do you mean?"

"Why's the sub just waiting out there? Circling the *Titan X*."

"Maybe it's come to guard the wreckage below," Adam suggested. "Making sure no one else dives down there."

Monk shook his head. "No, it's waiting for something else."

"What?" Phoebe asked.

Monk stared them down, certainty firming his voice. "Reinforcements."

22

From the courtyard balcony of the safe house, Seichan stared out at the shrouded hellscape. Ash rained in a hot powder across the city. Low clouds hugged the island. Four fiery-sloped mountains glowed brightly beyond the city. The peaks were close enough that rivers of lava could be seen flowing down their sides.

She had learned the mountains' names.

Salak, Gede, Cereme, Papandayan.

Other volcanos were surely erupting across Indonesia, but the thick smoke had reduced the world to those four peaks and this beleaguered city at the edge of the Java Sea.

The volcanos continued to boom, at times loud enough to shatter windows. The ground shook in a continual tremor. The tops of the peaks cast out dark plumes lit by showers of fire below and chains of lightning above. The air burned with sulfur. Flames lit large swaths of the city.

Closer by, shouts and screams echoed in a continual chorus of misery. Wagons and laden cars crept through the pall. Faces were masked against the powder and foul air. But where could anyone go? The falling ash had grounded all aircraft. The coastline remained treacherous, continually swamped by tides and surges.

One thing remained clear.

We're all trapped here.

Seichan hoped that included one other. She pictured Valya's smirking confidence when they had all met at the bridge. Though Seichan was happy to have her mother safely recovered, she wondered if such a reprieve would prove costlier in the end.

As if sensing her misgiving, Guan-yin touched Seichan's clenched fist. Her mother stood beside her in the balcony doorway. Despite the blistering heat and burn in the air, she smoked a cigarette.

"There will be another chance," Guan-yin assured her with a long exhale of smoke, clearly knowing what frustrated Seichan. "Remember, my daughter, *wonsungido namueseo tteoleojinda.*"

Seichan lifted a brow, recognizing the Korean adage. "'Even monkeys fall from trees.'"

Guan-yin nodded. "The Russian woman believes herself to be as skilled as a monkey in a tree, but even she will make a mistake. You must be patient enough to take advantage of it."

"Or I can hunt her down and kill her before she gets a chance." Seichan challenged her mother with another proverb, this one from their native Vietnam. "*Việc hôm nay chớ để ngày mai.*"

It was a sentiment Seichan preferred when it came to dealing with Valya.

Don't leave today's work for tomorrow.

Guan-yin shrugged. "For now, let's hope there is a tomorrow."

Seichan glanced back into the room where Gray sat and pored over a spread of papers, the copies he had made of the museum pages. Zhuang stood on the other side, leaning on his fists atop the table.

Seichan crossed back inside. "Let's see if the others have made any headway."

2:49 A.M.

Gray rested his forehead in his palm, his elbow on the table. The room was hot, the air stifling. A low fan stirred a slight breeze.

The colonial-era building was in the Old Town quarter of Jakarta. Outwardly, the structure appeared dilapidated, with a crumbling façade and taped windows. The courtyard was overgrown and weedy. But the place had a modern generator chugging down there, where a triad member fought to keep the falling ash from clogging it. The rest of the city lay dark, lit by occasional flames and loomed over by the fiery flanks of the volcanos.

The nearest—Mount Salak—rose only twenty miles away. It boomed with regular detonations, flaring the skies brighter, as if scolding him for not solving this riddle.

Gray shifted the papers on the table. He had read through them four times, searching for answers in the faded lines of neat script. The account came from Sir Stamford Raffles. It told the tale of his discovery of a pair of petrified bodies. The two corpses had been recovered from a ship sent out to sea following the eruption of Mount Tambora. An autopsy had been performed by a local physician—Dr. John Crawfurd—the same man whom Stamford would eventually assign to govern Singapore after driving off his nemesis, William Farquhar.

Seichan joined him, accompanied by her mother. "Have you learned anything?"

Gray sighed and straightened. "Nothing that makes sense."

"Tell me what you know." She placed a palm on his shoulder. "Talk it out."

He had already told her some of the account, so he skipped ahead. "The recovered bodies belonged to Johannes Stoepker—a member of the Batavian Society—and an Aboriginal cabin boy named Matthew. Dr. Crawfurd seemed certain that Stoepker's corpse—which was only partially consumed by the petrification process—might offer a clue to a cure."

"Did he find one?"

"Not directly. After studying Stoepker's body, Crawfurd became convinced *something* had stopped the petrifying process. Unfortunately, not in time to save the man's life. Still, Stoepker had survived long enough to leave behind a record. His story described toxic seas and a danger lurking in the water following the eruption of Mount Tambora. Whatever that hazard was, it had set fire to his ship and a pirate vessel."

"What was it?"

Gray sat back and shook his head. "Stoepker believed it was a strange coral. I suspect a piece of it might have been in that box that the Chinese obtained from Valya. Something hard had been rattling inside there."

"Why do you think it was a piece of coral?"

Gray shifted through the pile of papers. "Besides studying the bodies, Crawfurd had employed a biologist to help him investigate a stick of coral. Look at this."

Gray slipped out a page. It showed a naturalist's sketch of a branch of coral and a microscopic study of its hard skeleton.

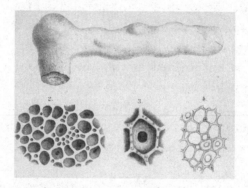

Seichan grimaced. "That coral almost looks like a finger."

Gray conceded the point. "You could be right. From the pathology findings, Crawfurd believed the bodies were mineralized in the same manner as the coral." He pulled out a sheet and read from it: "*The bones of the deceased appear to have been dissolved away and reformed into a new crystalline pattern throughout the surrounding tissues. Thus casting the flesh into an unnaturally brittle texture.*"

Zhuang frowned with distaste. "Is that possible?"

Gray shrugged. "I can't discount it. Considering what the researchers at the Titan Project discovered in the Tonga Trench—a huge coral forest—it could be significant."

"What else did Stoepker or Crawfurd write about all of this?" Seichan asked.

"That's just it. The story ends there. To me, it feels as if it had been purposefully edited. Stoepker's account seems incomplete. And Crawfurd draws no further conclusions."

Zhuang waved to the pages. "What about all those drawings?"

"I don't know. It's as if they were left as clues to the rest of the tale. If Stamford had been worried that someone like Farquhar might expose his secret, he might have taken some of the pages and hidden them elsewhere."

"Didn't want to keep all his eggs in one basket," Seichan said.

"Maybe. But if so, I keep going around in circles."

Guan-yin joined in. "What do the drawings show?"

Gray shifted a page into view. "This one just shows a detailed sketch of some island and some indigenous people living there."

Seichan frowned at the drawing. "Maybe it was added by mistake. Someone's travelogue that got mixed in over the centuries."

"I might have thought that, too, except for one detail."

Gray slid out the other sketch, which showed a thatched hut, probably on the same island.

"Why do you think it's significant?" Guan-yin asked.

Gray tapped the bottom left edge of the sketch. A figure in colonial clothes sat there, smoking a pipe, and appeared to be consulting with the natives.

"I think this could be Crawfurd," Gray said. "I can't be certain, but to me, it looks like someone from this story went to that island to talk to an indigenous tribe living out there. And these drawings are a record of that encounter."

"But what does it mean?" Zhuang asked. "Why would the doctor go out there?"

"Maybe in search of that cure," Gray said. "The account does hint at some discovery of an elixir."

Seichan scowled. "That island . . . it could be anywhere."

"True. But the last drawing in the portfolio makes even less sense."

He pulled out another sketch. This one was far cruder, nearly childish in nature. It depicted a fire-breathing snake and what appeared to be a rainbow.

"According to the account, this was discovered among Stoepker's handwritten papers in the steel box found with his body," Gray said. "It comes with no provenance or explanation. Or least not in the pages secured in Singapore. Maybe there's more of an account in the part of the story that remains missing."

"Why did Stoepker include it?" Zhuang asked. "There must be a reason."

"If I had to guess, it was not drawn by Stoepker, but by his passenger aboard the tender."

"The Aboriginal kid," Seichan said.

Gray sighed. "Matthew, the cabin boy of the doomed *Tenebrae*. He and Stoepker were found roughly sixteen days after their ship departed Jakarta. I wager the course of the illness took a long time to incapacitate them. During that time, Stoepker wrote his account. Maybe Matthew did the same, drawing the snake and rainbow before he died."

"That poor boy," Guan-yin said. "But why would he draw such a strange picture?"

"It had to be significant for Stoepker to seal it up in his box," Gray said. "Unless he just wanted to preserve the boy's artistry—in which case, it's meaningless. But I don't think so."

Seichan frowned. "Why?"

"From their account, Crawfurd and Raffles did not strike me as sentimental. They're coldly scientific, which is fitting for members of the Batavian Society. If Stoepker had merely kept it as a memorial to the boy, the others would not have saved it."

"Then what does it mean?" Guan-yin asked.

"I can only guess."

Seichan narrowed her eyes. "Guess or hunch?"

"A bit of both, I suppose. While en route to Jakarta, I only had a short time with the papers, but even then, I had suspected that the drawing was done by Matthew." He tapped the detailed sketches of a meeting at an island. "Maybe the indigenous people shown here are Aboriginal, too."

Zhuang picked up the page and squinted at the figures.

Gray tried to explain his reasoning. "Before landing here, I did an internet search for *snake* and *rainbow* and *Aboriginal people*. It was a long shot, but something intriguing did pop up."

Zhuang lowered the drawing. "What?"

Gray reached to an e-tablet where he had stored his research. "According to Aboriginal mythology, one story persists across the hundreds of communities of the Australian First Nations. It's the myth of the Rainbow Serpent. A snake god that went by many names. *Yurlunggur, Tulloun, Kanmare, Goorialla*, and others. Yet, its story remains remarkably consistent. In fact, the myth is considered to be one of the oldest continuing religious beliefs in the world."

"What's the story behind this snake god?" Seichan asked.

Gray stared down at the sketch. "According to Australia's First Nations peoples, the Rainbow Serpent is said to be the creator of humankind. It's a great snake that lives in the water. And while it's considered to be a creator of humanity, it's also said to be a destroyer. It travels the watery pathways beneath the world, popping up here or there and exacting punishment or offering protection."

Zhuang shifted the sketch closer. "Could the boy have drawn the snake as a means to seek his god's help?"

"I don't know. But if this page was some form of an Aboriginal prayer, why did Crawfurd and Raffles—both Christians—preserve it with their records?" Gray stared around the group. "It must be significant."

Seichan crossed her arms, still unconvinced.

Gray pulled free the last page of the handwritten account and read from it. "Here is what Sir Stamford Raffles writes at the end. *'Alas, we have learned how very little we know of our world. And now we must protect a secret that could lead to its ruination if abused by the wrong hand. Perhaps it would be better if we carried it to our grave, but we know it must not be lost. For it equally holds the promise of salvation. A method to appease the gods of the underworld if they should ever grow angry again, which they surely will.'"*

A thunderous boom outside ended his words, as if the gods were punctuating this centuries-old testament. Past the windows, flames fountained high over the crown of Mount Salak.

"The gods are certainly furious now," Seichan mumbled.

"Then we must find a way to appease them," Gray said.

"How?" Zhuang asked.

"By seeking out the rest of Stamford and Crawfurd's account."

"Where do we even begin to look?" Guan-yin asked.

Gray stood up and stared beyond the balcony to the raging skies. "By breaking into another museum."

He reached to his e-tablet and scrolled past the many legends of the Rainbow Serpent—a god of creation and destruction. He brought up an advertisement for a current exhibit: MARITIME TRAILS: PEOPLE, PLACES, AND OBJECTS.

"This is a current exhibition funded by the Australia-Indonesia Museum Project. It's an exploration of the long historical connection between Indonesia and Australia's Aboriginal tribes. Which seems fortuitous, but in fact it has been an ongoing pursuit at this particular museum."

"Which museum?" Seichan asked.

"It's right here in the city's Old Town. The Jakarta History Museum."

Seichan frowned. "I get why that topic might help with your research, but why do you think it has any connection to Stamford's missing pages? Did the guy found this museum, too?"

"No. The museum's building dates back to a century before Stamford's time on the island." He looked across the group. "But when he lived here, it served as Jakarta's city hall."

He stared across the group.

Seichan understood. "As lieutenant-governor, Stamford kept an office there."

"He did. And if he wanted to hide some important paperwork, he might've felt confident enough to secure them there." Gray shrugged. "Seems like a good place to start a search for those missing pages."

Seichan waved toward the balcony, reluctantly accepting his conclusions. "Then best get on with it before the whole city burns down."

Another booming detonation shook the building, reminding him it wasn't just Jakarta that was at risk—but this entire region, maybe the rest of the world.

Still, as they left, Gray knew they had to be cautious. There was more of a threat out there than just fire and ash.

We're not the only ones trapped on this island.

23

Heng cracked his knuckles as he waited for the scanning electron microscope to finish its assay. His foot tapped, too. He stared about the small research lab in the basement of the Eijkman Institute for Molecular Biology in central Jakarta.

The facility was part of a larger medical research complex, which was likely why it still had power. The building itself dated back to the nineteenth century. Even then, it had been a medical facility, one built to study bacteria. Today it was a state-of-the-art institution, with its own biosafety lab and gas decontamination chamber.

Pray we don't have to use them.

The facility had been closed for the night, but Xue had arranged for the emergency use of the lab due to a cooperative outreach between China's scientific community and the Indonesian Ministry of Research. A lone guard had opened the gate and hurried them inside. He had looked panicked and ready to bolt.

And he was not the only one.

Behind him, just outside the lab door, Xue was arguing heatedly with Captain Wen, head of the Falcon Command Unit. Wen wanted to evacuate his men, along with Xue and Heng, back to mainland China. Apparently, the captain had a boat anchored far enough out in the bay that it had survived the initial tsunami and subsequent tidal surge. Xue refused to leave, plainly frustrated that he had lost those museum papers.

More of Wen's men guarded the hallway and were posted between them and the gated archway that led out of the facility. Regular updates alerted them to the status outside. Not that Heng needed any. Volcanic detonations regularly shook the building. Even buried in the basement, he heard sirens and screams from the panicked city. The stench of sulfur had grown heavier as he worked down here.

While waiting for his work to finish, he had used the facility's wireless internet, which shockingly was still working—further testament to the importance of the medical complex and the two neighboring hospitals. He had looked up the history of the volcanos on this island. Java alone had more than forty active volcanos. The closest—Mount Salak—had last erupted back in 1938, but it had been regularly outgassing, leading to the deaths of six teenagers in 2007 as toxic gas filled its caldera.

The latest report from Jakarta's emergency services was that another dozen peaks on the island had begun spewing fumes from fissures and cracks. It was further evidence that this could be the start of a greater geological catastrophe.

Xue stalked into the lab. His cheeks were flushed, his eyes flashing. "How much longer do you need, Dr. Luo?"

Heng checked the countdown running on the monitor next to the SEM unit. "Less than a minute."

"Perfect. Time is of the essence. We must be off quickly."

Heng understood the danger. He turned back to Xue, again struck by the man's finely sculpted features. It took Heng an extra breath to continue. "And we'll be heading off the island after that?"

Those dark eyes settled on him, a slight smile shadowing his lips.

"That'll depend on your findings here." Xue glanced at the doorway. "And the temperament of Captain Wen. He lost seven men during the firefight."

"But you intend to stay in Jakarta?"

"Despite the danger, there is one avenue of pursuit that I wish to undertake. If your research bears fruit."

"What do you mean?"

Before Xue could answer, the computer chimed, announcing the completion of the SEM assay. Heng twisted around in his seat as a file popped up on the window.

Finally . . .

During the past hour, Heng had sectioned off a sliver of the black coral found in the museum's box and mounted it with double-sided carbon tape to the SEM's aluminum stud, then air-sprayed away particulate debris. It had taken extra time, but he had wanted as clean an image as possible.

Heng opened the folder, which contained a pair of photos at different magnifications. He tapped the first one. The image showed two crusty holes—called *calyxes*—which was where the polyps normally nested within the coral.

Xue placed a hand on Heng's shoulder as he leaned closer. His palm was hot, as was his breath on Heng's cheek. "Does this look like the same type of calcification you found in the afflicted submariners?"

"Maybe." Heng stammered a bit, flustered with the man so close. "Let me be sure."

Heng opened the second image. It revealed a magnified close-up of the crystals bordering one of the calyxes.

Xue's fingers tightened on Heng's shoulder. "They're orthorhombic crystals. Same as those found in the submariners' tissues."

"And the lunar dust collected by Chang'e-5's lander," Heng added.

"Well done." Xue patted his shoulder.

Heng's face heated up. He shifted out of the man's reach before turning around. "But what does this prove?"

Excitement brightened Xue's eyes as he continued to stare at the screen. "It proves that the events of the past *do* have bearing on the present."

"If so, what now? You said there was an avenue of pursuit that you still wanted to investigate on the island."

Xue straightened to his full height. "There is a site that I'd like to check out. Where Sir Stamford Raffles kept an office while he resided here as lieutenant-governor."

"The old governor's office? It's still here?"

"It is. The original city hall of Batavia still stands. It was turned into the Jakarta History Museum." Xue waved Heng up. "Now that you've confirmed that history is indeed repeating itself, we have no more time to waste."

Heng hurried to gather his research material. "Why? What's the rush?"

Xue looked back over his shoulder. "I was told a few minutes ago that the Americans are headed there, too—to the same museum."

"Told by whom?" Heng asked.

Xue ignored him. He was halfway across the lab, striding toward the exit, ready to rouse Captain Wen. Heng suspected the chance to confront the Americans again would be enough to convince the captain to remain on the island.

More than survival, Wen surely had a greater desire, especially after losing seven of his men.

Revenge.

FIFTH

Hunter/Killer

24

Kowalski lost count of the number of times he had stalked around the circumference of Tethys Tier. It had to be more than a thousand.

At least, it felt that way.

It had been three hours since the station had uncoupled into pieces. Frustrated, he ground the stub of his cold cigar between his molars. The others had made him snub it out, complaining about the limited air in the twenty-yard-wide tier—which *was* a growing concern.

They couldn't stay down here forever. While each level could become its own saucer-shaped submersible, the oxygen reserves were limited. Normally the carbon-fiber tanks were replaced from topside shipments. But Tethys Tier had been late for its replenishment due to the recent quakes. According to Byrd, they had maybe another six hours of reserves left before they'd all asphyxiate.

Still, they dared not head straight back up.

From the sonar screen in the auxiliary control station, they had all watched the four other tiers rise to the surface. Their group had followed upward at a wary distance, then settled into a neutral-buoyancy hover about a quarter mile down. Once in place, the thrusters were turned off, making them look dead in the water.

No one dared to even speak.

Then a series of huge explosions erupted overhead. The sound carried to them. Shortly thereafter, the sonar showed debris raining down. Fearing that they might be hit, Byrd had glided them out of the way, before returning them to a dead hover. Worry plagued them as they hung in the water—and not for their own safety. It was impossible to tell if the station's personnel had been offloaded to *Titan Station Up* before the tiers had been destroyed.

That had been an hour ago.

It was now a tense waiting game.

The hope was that the assailants would depart these waters, allowing them to safely rise to the surface. Byrd's plan was to wait for as long as possible, to only ascend once their oxygen tanks were depleted. They had no other choice. The onboard batteries could at best get them a half mile away before dying, leaving them stranded and in full view of the station.

Knowing this and feeling like a caged lion, Kowalski made another pass around the floor. The petite researcher—Jasleen Patel—sat alongside the curve of glass. Her laptop was open on her knees, but she ignored the screen, leaning her head against the wall. Her complexion was pale, her brow damp. She shivered from a spiking fever. The geologist, Haru, knelt beside her, holding her hand—no, *examining* her hand.

Kowalski stopped next to them. "What's wrong?"

"I don't think her fever and chills are from a flu bug." Haru waved him down. "Look."

Kowalski dropped to a knee as the geologist held out her arm. Her palm was gray and three of her fingers were even darker.

Jazz lifted her head to stare down, too. Her teeth chattered as she spoke. "It . . . it's a toxic reaction. Some type of envenomation. From a sting I suffered. Feels like my hand is on fire. I can barely move my fingers."

Kowalski shrugged out of his wool duster. "Put this on."

He helped her draw his coat over her shoulders and pulled it around her. She set down her laptop and burrowed deeper into its warmth. "Thanks."

"What stung you?" Haru asked.

She sighed with exasperation. "A coral polyp. Stupid of me. I wager Dr. Kim Jong Suk is feeling as crappy as I am. If he's still alive."

Haru looked at Kowalski. "She needs medical attention."

"There's only one place she can get it." Kowalski stared up. "And it's a quarter mile away."

With a grunt, Kowalski stood and crossed over to the doorway that led down to the auxiliary controls. Jarrah stood at the threshold, guarding over Byrd inside.

"Gotta talk to your boss," Kowalski said.

Jarrah shifted aside.

Byrd heard him and turned from where he was studying various information on the board: oxygen levels, exterior pressure, depth gauge, battery charges. Past his shoulders, a curve of windows showed only black seas.

"What is it?" Byrd asked.

"That woman is sick and getting worse. She needs help. And she's not going to find it down here."

"And what do you propose we do?"

Kowalski pointed a finger up. "We take our chances now rather than later."

"We don't know what's happening topside. We could end up getting her killed—and us—much quicker."

"I don't think waiting a couple more hours is gonna make any—"

A series of booming detonations reached them, strong enough to shake the hovering tier. Kowalski ducked and looked across the curve of windows, expecting them to crack.

Byrd turned to the sonar screen.

Kowalski crowded in behind him. "What the hell was that?"

Byrd pointed to four shadows near the top of the sonar monitor. They marked the pylons that kept *Titan Station Up* floating on the surface. Only now those crisp outlines were blurry blobs.

"The bastards are trying to take the station down," Byrd said.

As they watched, huge shapes tumbled through the water, marking sections of the massive complex falling toward them.

Byrd ignited the thrusters and got them moving. The engines fought the dead weight of their sub.

Kowalski watched a large piece—easily thirty or forty meters across—cleaving straight toward them. "Not going to clear it in time."

Byrd pushed his yoke forward. "I don't dare burn out our thrusters."

"Better that than being sliced in half."

The tier gained more speed.

Kowalski winced, expecting to be struck at any moment. Movement elsewhere on the sonar screen drew his eye. It rose from the right side. It sped toward them, angling downward. He had spent enough years in the Navy to recognize that signature.

He shouted it to Byrd. "Torpedo!"

25

Two hundred feet *above* the ocean, Monk struggled to hide from what lurked *below*. He stood on the bridge of the *Titan X*. It was housed in an observation platform—a glass-walled wedge—that sat atop the lofty bow of the yacht. The windows offered a panoramic 360-degree view of the ship and ocean.

Behind him, the thirteen-story sphere of Science City sat like a black sun on the yacht's aft end. It glowed from its interior lights, but a thick coating of ash shrouded its upper levels. Ahead of him, to the east, five fiery mountains glowed. They marked the chain of the volcanic Kermadec Islands. Fed by those smoking plumes, the skies had fallen lower, about to smother the *Titan X*. Lone bolts and long chains of lightning flashed up there in a code known only to the gods.

Otherwise, the ocean lay dark and menacing all around them. The rolling waves were dull and heavy with powder. Farther east, the sun had surely risen, but there was no sign of it. The world was stuck at an eternal midnight.

The captain of the *Titan X*—a squat Aussie in a beige jumpsuit—called over from bridge control. "We're picking up something on radar. A big boat. Coming in bloody fast. Seventy knots."

Monk winced. "How far off?"

"Fifteen kilometers and closing."

Monk did some fast math.

It'll reach us in six minutes.

He swore and leaned a palm on the communication station. His other hand—the prosthetic one—clutched a radio. He had to refrain from crushing it in his grip. He stared at the CCTV monitor. It showed a view out the stern hold. Men scrambled around and on top of the *Cormorant*, looking like a NASCAR pit crew. The vehicle still hung in its A-frame over the water.

Monk lifted his radio. "Bryan, we have company coming. We need to launch *now*. Do you copy?"

Monk swallowed, waiting for the pilot's response. When it did come, it was preceded by a string of expletives that would make a Marine blush and ended with a firm declarative.

"I need at least another twenty minutes!"

"You have *two*. There's an unknown craft speeding toward us. It's not likely to be friendly. You want to be well gone by the time that boat gets here."

Bryan's next words were neither agreement nor dissent, just anger. "Fuck it then."

On the screen, the activity around the *Cormorant* sped up.

Monk turned to the bridge control. "Captain Stemm?"

"Twelve klicks out," the Aussie reported. His face was as red as the shock of hair trapped under his cap. "I'm cutting engines."

"Do that. And be ready on my mark."

An hour ago, Monk had informed the bridge crew of the threat patrolling the waters under them. He had shown them the glimpse of the Chinese submarine. Captain Henry Stemm had served in the Australian Navy for two decades before retiring and signing on to this project. He had enough encounters with trespassing Chinese subs to recognize the fin assembly on the sonar. He deemed it likely to be a Yuan-class diesel-electric boat, a hunter-killer of the Chinese submarine fleet.

Monk had also shared with the captain his concerns about what lay six miles under them and its relation to the spreading quakes and eruptions. Someone had to go down into the trench and take another look.

But first, the *Cormorant* needed to slip past that steel shark. Adam and Phoebe had volunteered, both to take that risk and to face the danger in that bottomless trench.

Monk had wanted to go, too, but he knew someone had to guard these waters. It would do no good if the others were successful, only to be apprehended or destroyed upon surfacing. Monk's role in the hours ahead was to play defensive lineman. He stared at the rest of his team, which included the captain and the five bridge crew.

Us against the Chinese Navy.

Monk shrugged. Not the best odds, but as someone once said, *you go to war with the army you have.*

Monk felt and heard the engines cut off.

The next part was risky.

Twenty minutes ago, Monk had sent the *Titan X* into a slow circle, stirring and rumbling the ash-choked waters. He hoped that the noise had lulled the submariners into complacency. Until now, he had wanted no outward indication that anyone aboard the yacht was aware of the boat below.

What came next was an entirely different tactic.

He turned to Captain Stemm for an update. The Aussie's lips were bloodless lines of tension. "Eight kilometers," he reported from the radar station. "Are you certain it's the Chinese?"

"With this entire region burning, all military forces are likely bogged down in rescue operations. Including the U.S. Pacific Fleet. So, that's no random ship, especially coming at us so fast. It's gotta be hostile."

Monk had expected Chinese reinforcements. He had been waiting for them, but he had hoped for more than an hour's reprieve. He hated to rush Bryan in re-outfitting the *Cormorant*, but he had no choice.

On the screen, the pilot ushered Adam and Phoebe through the DSV's upper hatch. The submersible still hung by its chains.

Monk raised the radio to his lips. "Now or never, Bryan."

The pilot was too busy to respond, at least over the airwaves. Bryan lifted an arm toward the CCTV camera and flipped him the bird, then dropped after the others. He yanked the hatch closed over him.

Monk turned to Captain Stemm and held the radio at his lips. "On my mark!" His instruction was for many listeners, not just the bridge. "NOW!"

The captain shouted to his crew. "Starboard bow thrusters! Portside stern thrusters! Full power!"

The *Titan X* vibrated hard as the maneuvering thrusters on both sides of the yacht fired up simultaneously. With a great surge, the ship started a slow turn while still holding its position, making an eighty-thousand-ton pirouette.

Monk imagined that burbling cacophony if heard from below.

But that still wasn't enough to satisfy him.

A moment ago, his command had also reached the lone technician in the DriX control station in the stern hold. The man set both units to pulsing their sonars in a continual cavalcade of pinging.

On the CCTV monitor, the *Cormorant* dropped from the A-frame and crashed into the water. There was no time for a gentle lowering into the sea. The craft bobbed up once, then quickly plunged away.

Safe travels, Monk wished them.

But he should've saved some of that hope for himself.

Captain Stemm swung around. "Picking up another bogie! At the outer reach of our radar. Coming in at eight hundred kilometers an hour."

The captain had barely finished his warning when something shot over the yacht, low enough that it swept ash from the top of Science City in its wake. The bandit tilted its nose up and blasted into the ash layer and vanished.

"Lost it," the captain shouted over.

Monk had briefly glimpsed its triangular shape, the V of its wings.

A stealth drone.

Probably a Hongu Sharp Sword or maybe a Flying Dragon.

Either way, it was likely heavily armed.

He stared to the west, from the direction it had come. The boat speeding toward them couldn't have launched it. The drone had to have come from another, likely larger, ship out there.

Monk stared at his toes.

Maybe I should've gone with them.

7:43 A.M.

Adam pulled himself fully back into the rear seat of the *Cormorant*. The jolt—as they struck the water, bobbed back up, then plummeted into the depths—had left his heart pounding in his throat and his stomach somewhere near his knees.

But it wasn't just the impact that had him shaken.

He glared at the seat ahead of him.

Dr. Datuk Lee had braced himself, with a grip on his chair and a palm on the curve of titanium overhead. The only evidence of their hard plunge was that the man's eyeglasses had slipped to the tip of his nose. With the *Cormorant* stabilizing into a steadier fall, Datuk settled into his seat and secured his glasses.

"What is he doing here?" Adam called forward to Phoebe and Bryan.

"I asked him to join us," Phoebe said.

Bryan nodded. "I agreed to it, too. I added three more ballast weights to our exterior, but we could use every extra ounce. The heavier we are, the faster we'll fall."

Adam swallowed and gazed out at the dark water.

When he had entered the submersible behind Phoebe, he had found Datuk already seated there. Busy elsewhere, Adam had failed to note the Malaysian biochemist boarding the craft. By then, it had been too late to protest. Bryan had clambered in after them, took his seat, then ordered the crane's emergency releases to be blown, dropping them into the sea.

Bryan was now checking the *Cormorant*'s systems. His board was all green, except for two dark lights. The repair crew had swapped out the fried circuits, refitted in new oxygen tanks and batteries, and inspected the rest. Still, Adam knew Bryan wasn't happy.

I'm not either.

Phoebe must have noted his anger at her invitation. "We don't know what we'll be facing down there," she explained. "We need all the expertise we can scrounge. We're lucky Datuk was willing to risk this descent."

Adam wouldn't call it luck.

Phoebe rolled her eyes and turned to Datuk. She knew what worried Adam and addressed it point blank. "Dr. Lee, are you a Chinese spy?"

The man stiffened, looking aghast. "What? Me? Why would you ask me that?"

Phoebe turned to Adam. "See. Nothing to worry about."

She returned her gaze forward, clearly settled on the matter.

Adam, though, was not persuaded by Phoebe's interrogation methods in the least. But there was no going back.

Bryan reminded them of the more immediate danger. "Maybe we should all keep quiet for a few minutes rather than squawking about."

All eyes turned to the windows. Phoebe picked up the acoustic headphones and donned them. She winced at whatever she heard.

Adam stared up. Monk had offered them plenty of sonic cover to make their escape. Between the thrusters, the rumbling waters, and the sonar pinging, the hope was to mask their descent, to momentarily blind and distract the hunter-killer.

But was it enough?

They needed to reach six hundred meters. After that, the sub—even its torpedoes—could not travel any deeper.

Or so we had better hope.

Naval intelligences were notoriously cagy when it came to revealing the true crush depths of their submarines and ancillary weapons.

Datuk monitored their depth gauge.

So did Adam.

Three hundred meters . . .

Phoebe kept an eye on a small screen that showed a glowing schematic of their location. Their navigational position was fixed by the three landers on the seabed: *Huey*, *Louie*, and *Dewey*. The screen was fuzzy and flickering with interference. The *Cormorant* appeared as a winged blip dropping along a gradient. The seabed glowed below in bright colors, courtesy of the last echo-sounding. The fissure was also evident, showing as a gaping black scar.

Adam watched the winged dot speed toward there.

Four hundred meters . . .

Phoebe gasped and ducked lower in her seat.

Adam leaned forward. "What?"

She glanced back. "A huge ping just struck us. Far louder than the repeated blasts from the DriX. Hurt like hell."

Datuk's eyes got huge. "They found us."

Five hundred meters . . .

Adam waved for the phones. Phoebe passed them over. He quickly pulled them over his ears. He closed his eyes. Noise filled his skull—a disharmony of tonal frequencies from Monk's efforts overhead.

Adam tried to push it all aside, straining for one tell-tale signature.

As he did, an ear-piercing ping struck the *Cormorant* again, strong enough to ache his teeth. He flinched and waited as it faded into a receding doppler—then a new noise cut through. It was a low rumble that grew steadily in volume. A slightly louder bump interrupted it, confirming his worst fear.

It marked the slam of a torpedo hatch.

He opened his eyes and stared over Datuk's shoulder.

Six hundred meters . . .

The rumbling escalated rapidly.

Phoebe stared back at him. He tried to mask his reaction, seeing no reason to panic everyone. Still, her eyes narrowed, and her lips tightened.

She knows what I'm hearing.

He held his breath.

The rumbling quickly drowned out all else—then suddenly stopped. He girded himself for an explosion, but nothing happened. The torpedo must have reached its crush depth and been disabled by the pressure. He pictured it toppling inertly into the depths.

He leaned forward and checked their position.

Seven hundred meters . . .

He sighed with relief and stripped off the headphones. Monk's ploy had proven successful. The diversion had bought them enough time to escape into the deeper water—but just barely.

"We should be safe from here," he said.

Datuk glanced back. "I wouldn't be so sure of that."

The man sounded ominous enough that Adam half expected him to pull out a pistol and point it at Phoebe's head. Instead, he motioned to his screen.

"Sensors are already picking up radiation."

26

Kowalski slid on his belly across the tilted floor. Above him, Byrd crouched in the auxiliary control room. Jarrah braced in the doorway. Haru and Jazz tumbled along with him.

"Hang on!" Byrd called out.

To frigging what?

Kowalski clawed at the steel floor and dug with his toes. The tier was tilted nearly vertical.

Seconds ago, he had spotted the torpedo speeding toward them. Upon his shout of warning, Byrd had yanked on the yoke, sending the nose of their submersible high. By then, they had been under enough speed that the sudden maneuver tumbled Kowalski out of the doorway and across the floor.

"What're you doing?" Kowalski hollered over.

Byrd was too busy to answer. Kowalski slipped all the way to the far side. His boots hit the curve of glass behind him. Out the windows, lit by the exterior lamps, a huge shape fell past the underside of the tier, covering it completely. It filled the world out there. Kowalski recognized the giant section of decking from *Titan Station Up*. It was the chunk of debris they had been trying to avoid a moment ago. It cleaved through the water past them like the fall of a huge dark axe.

But that was not what Byrd intended it to be.

Rather than escaping it, the Aussie took on more ballast, sucking in ocean water. Their submersible sank alongside the fractured chunk of decking.

Kowalski understood.

The guy's trying to use it like a shield.

That's even crazier than—

The explosion shattered the ocean with a blinding flare of fire. The shockwave blasted the chunk of decking into their submersible and drove them through the water, sending them tumbling end over end.

Kowalski flew through the air, slamming into steel and glass, sliding wildly.

They all suffered the same.

It seemed to go on forever—until finally the spinning slowed. The tier made one last turn, then settled crookedly in the water.

Kowalski lay on his back, aching and rattled. His ears rang. He tasted blood on his tongue. He rolled to a shoulder. Jazz lay unmoving against one window. Haru sat up, cradling an arm that hung crookedly. Blood ran from his nose.

Jarrah and Byrd had ridden out the storm inside the control room. The limited space had kept them somewhat protected.

Kowalski groaned and wobbled to his feet. He glanced to Haru, who waved that he was all right, though his face was a mask of pain. Kowalski turned and stumbled over to Jazz. Along the way, he searched for any leaks, any cracks in the glass.

"How are we still alive?" he called over to Byrd.

The man checked his systems while explaining. "Submersibles are built to withstand up to twice the expected pressure of a dive. I achieved this with Tethys Tier, but only because it was the smallest section of the station. It's why I picked this level to make our escape. She can withstand pressures of four tons per square inch. Despite appearances, she's a glass-and-titanium tank."

Jarrah sat heavily on the top step and added his own assessment. "The shielding from that chunk of decking probably blunted some of the blast, too."

Kowalski reached Jazz, who moaned and slowly pushed away from the windows.

"Wh . . . What happened?" she asked blearily.

"Someone left an attack dog in these waters," Kowalski said. "We must have strayed into its territory, and it caught our scent."

Jazz shook her head, addled and still feverish, struggling to make sense of his words. "Dogs? Underwater?"

Kowalski checked her pupils. One was dilated to twice the size of the other. She had a concussion, if not a cracked skull. "Don't worry about it."

Haru stumbled over to them, still clutching an arm to his chest. "Go. I'll watch her."

Kowalski eyed him skeptically, but Haru hissed him out of the way. Knowing there was nothing he could do for either of them unless they reached the surface, Kowalski crossed to the control station.

The floor remained crooked and drifted slowly in a circle.

"Lost half our thrusters," Byrd reported. He pointed to where bubbles rolled across one section of the windows. "And we're leaking oxygen from one of our reserve tanks."

"Then we head up," Kowalski said. "After that explosion, whoever's up there knows someone's down here. They won't leave until they confirm that blast killed us."

"The torpedo," Byrd asked. "Does that mean there's a sub in the area?"

"No." He stared out into the darkness. "It was likely a UUV left in these waters. There could be more."

Jarrah turned to him. The security chief still had hold of his steel baton. He looked like he wanted to hit something with it. "What's a UUV?"

"Unmanned underwater vehicle. China tested a few recently in the Taiwan Strait. They can autonomously patrol a region. Once they detect an enemy in their zone, they close in and fire a smart torpedo, which will fix on any cavitation, chase it down, and blow it up. Luckily, those torpedoes are usually smaller than conventional armaments."

"And maybe another reason we're still alive," Jarrah added.

"Let's not give them a chance to correct that," Kowalski said. "We'd better keep under what's left of the rig. The UUVs are likely patrolling the waters around it, keeping everything fenced in."

Byrd waved at the large shadow on his sonar screen. "It looks like most of the station is still afloat on top of us. The enemy's first attempt to sink her failed. She is one stubborn girl."

"Then let's go see how she's faring," Kowalski said. "Before we run out of oxygen."

Byrd swallowed and nodded.

"No thrusters," Kowalski reminded him. "Let 'er drift up on her own buoyancy. We play dead for as long as possible."

7:30 A.M.

Jazz leaned on the doorframe of the control room. Her head pounded, narrowing her vision. Nausea churned her stomach, while her right arm burned like a torch. She used the pain to keep focused.

"You shouldn't be standing," Haru warned on the other side of the threshold.

She tried to firm her voice, but it still came out raspy. "If I'm going to die, I'll do it on my feet."

She eyed him up and down, noting his broken arm and the dried crust of blood under his nose. She felt guilty forcing him to follow her. He had helped her up and over to the control room as Tethys Tier made their final ascent. She still had Kowalski's long coat over her shoulders and hugged it tighter around her.

He nodded at her words, her determination. "Very well then. We'll meet our ends together."

Byrd called from the control room. "Blowing the last of our ballast. Everyone brace for surfacing!"

A great rush of bubbling rose along the windows. As it did, Tethys Tier surged upward with a heavy heave. It thrust high out of the water. Waves sloshed and washed across the glass as their makeshift submersible rocked drunkenly in the ocean.

Jazz grabbed tight to the control room's doorframe—not because of the swaying, but because of the view outside. She gasped. Byrd swore. Haru sank down to his knees.

Beyond the windows, the massive ruins of *Titan Station Up* leaned crookedly in the water, shrouded by smoke, topped by patches of fire. Its decks—what was left of them—canted steeply. Debris bobbed in the dark water: yellow HOVs, chunks of the pylons' syntactic foam, shattered boats, glassy pieces of other tiers.

And bodies, so many bodies.

Aghast at the horror of it all, it took Jazz four full breaths before she realized the smoke was not just from the burning wreckage. The morning sky was sunless, cloaked by low clouds. Dark powder sifted in a continual rain, along with fiery flakes. Silent lightning flashed up there. Farther out, cascading fountains of fire dotted the horizons, churning with black smoke. Distant booms rolled over the water in a continuous cannonade.

Movement and a sharper whine drew her attention. A large pontoon boat—painted in blue-and-black camouflage—sped around the wreckage. Shadowy men in battle gear crowded its deck. From its bow, a huge gun pointed toward them. There was no mistaking this as anything but an attack craft.

Byrd shouted from his station. "Engaging all thrusters—or what's left of them."

Water burbled outside the window, and the tier retreated across the debris field. It slowly gained speed, but it would never outrun their pursuers. In clear warning, gunfire spattered off the titanium and glass. Byrd ignored the threat and kept them moving faster. The bulk of the station's burning wreckage slowly receded. They finally bumped clear of the last of the debris.

Just a little farther . . .

"Contact made!" Byrd shouted and cut the thrusters.

The tier drifted farther under its own momentum, but the thrum of the engines went silent. The hunters closed in, only thirty yards away.

Jazz held her breath. Everyone cringed, expecting the worst.

Then a huge explosion blasted the incoming boat, sending it upward in a flume of water and fire. It shattered in half and flew high. Several pieces rattled over the tier as a huge wave shoved them farther out.

This had been Kowalski's plan.

To sic the attack dogs on their own masters.

Their group had needed to lure the enemy away from the station—out into the waters patrolled by the hidden UUVs. As before, the cavitations of the tier's thrusters had triggered an automated attack. According to Kowalski, once a smart torpedo was deployed, it would constantly watch its target, reengaging as needed if it lost contact. With their thrusters silenced, the incoming torpedo had done just that—retargeting on the only remaining cavitation in the water.

Pieces of the boat and bodies rained out of the sky.

Byrd kept them dead in the water, using the hunters below to protect them. Another amphibious craft was still moored at the lower level of the burning station, likely the support boat for a demolition team that was planting another round of charges to sink the stubborn station. The enemy had surely witnessed the explosion, recognized the threat hidden in the depths. They would be leery to come out here.

But the boat wasn't the only danger.

Jazz spotted a lone helicopter off in the distance, lit by its lights. It was headed east, running low under the ash cloud. She prayed it didn't turn back. The UUVs below could not defend them against a missile attack from the air.

Knowing there was nothing to be done about it, she turned her gaze to the wreck of *Titan Station Up*. The middle level, the crew quarters, remained mostly intact. She prayed some of the researchers and staff were still alive in there.

She glanced back across the empty floor of Tethys Tier—toward the airlock on the other side.

She prayed Kowalski and Jarrah reached the station in time.

7:44 A.M.

Kowalski swam the last of the distance to a shattered section of the lower decking. It was overshadowed by one of the floating pylons that

slanted half out of the water due to the station's tilt. He grabbed hold
of a strut and reached back to pull Jarrah to him.

He gave the man a hard, questioning look.

You okay?

Jarrah panted heavily but nodded.

Kowalski looked past the man's shoulder. Tethys Tier floated a hundred yards away, barely discernible in the midnight gloom. Its location
was marked by burning pieces of the attack boat and a flaming pool of
diesel fuel.

So far, so good.

With the others momentarily out of harm's way, Kowalski clambered up. He had stripped down to his skivvies for the swim. Jarrah
had done the same. While the tier had been rising, they had exited out
its flooded airlock when it was ten meters down. They had surfaced into
an apocalyptic hellscape. The two of them had used the floating debris
to help cover their fifty-yard swim to the station. As they crossed the
distance, they had watched Tethys Tier surge up and lure one of the
two amphibious boats to its doom.

Now it's our turn.

Kowalski crouched atop the decking and removed his Desert Eagle
from a waterproof pouch that was tied around his waist. He quickly
inspected it, while Jarrah snapped his steel baton to its full extension.

"Ready?" Kowalski whispered.

Jarrah nodded. "Let's go."

They set off across the ruins of the lower level, wading and hop-
ping over the wreckage, circumnavigating its edge to reach the moored
boat on the other side. The darkness hid their approach. The craft was
under minimal guard as the enemy assumed they had the place fully
locked down. The two soldiers left aboard weren't even watching the
station. Their gazes were out toward the shadowy Tethys Tiers, likely
still baffled as to what had happened.

Across the breadth of the ruins, voices reached them, echoing from
above as the various demolition teams finished setting up their second set
of charges. The eight or nine sites were easily spotted and avoided in the
darkness due to the flashlights the enemy used to illuminate their work.

Kowalski concentrated on the target at hand. He eyed the boat's wheelhouse that rose midship. It was lit from within and showed no movement inside. Satisfied, he leveled his Eagle at one of the two guards, the one closest to the huge gun that was mounted at the pontoon's bow. The other soldier stood a couple yards off.

Before he could fire, Jarrah pushed Kowalski's arm down. The security chief, a glistening ebony statue, stepped past Kowalski and motioned him to stay put.

Jarrah lifted his baton, crossed the last of the distance, and hopped aboard the boat. Even knowing the guy was there, Kowalski still had a hard time picking him out of the shadows. Jarrah waited until both men were looking in opposite directions—then he dashed out of hiding.

Kowalski covered him with his Eagle.

Jarrah swung his baton like a broadsword, cracking it into the side of the man near the bow gun. Before his target could even topple, Jarrah spun around on a toe. The second man heard the strike of steel on bone and turned with his rifle—only to meet the upswing of the baton to his jaw. The man's head flew back. The blow looked forceful enough to decapitate him. His body crumpled to the deck.

Jarrah waved to Kowalski.

With a nod, he leaped to the bow and ran to the weapon mounted there. It was a three-barreled 12.7mm Gatling gun on a swivel mount. He got behind its steel shield and swung the weapon toward the station.

Jarrah ran to the wheelhouse and started its engine with a roar.

As the boat set off, Kowalski aimed for those lighted sites along the station and strafed each spot. The rotary cannon could fire two thousand rounds per second, but he flipped to low mode, reserving his ammunition. The rounds lanced in bright tracer streaks through the darkness and pummeled those spots, tearing through steel and flesh.

He paused between sites as Jarrah guided the boat around the station, sticking close. Kowalski heard screams in the wake of his blasting. Return fire pinged off the armored flanks of the boat, its wheelhouse. A few rounds ricocheted off the gun shield. A huge blast erupted from a corner of the station as one of the charges was mishandled.

Bodies flew through the air.

Kowalski ignored it all and continued strafing any shadowy movement.

Jarrah made two full passes around the station until there were no more screams or return fire. Fresh smoke billowed. Kowalski waved an arm for Jarrah to take them back in. He was under no misconception that there weren't a few commandos still alive.

The boat bumped against the flank of the station. Kowalski offloaded, armed with his Eagle and a QBZ assault rifle he had pilfered from one of the guards. Jarrah followed, but not before sending the boat jetting away into the dangerous waters beyond the station. They dared not risk it being used against them.

Kowalski faced the smoky mass of the station.

Time to go hunting.

Behind him, Jarrah had grabbed a sidearm of his own, but he poked Kowalski with his baton, then pointed it at the skies. Off in the distance, the bright speck of a helicopter glided around and headed back to the station.

Kowalski swore, suddenly wishing he hadn't sent the attack boat and its huge gun away.

An explosive boom and fiery flume of water ended any hope of recovering it.

Jarrah grimaced. "What now?"

Kowalski waved at the dark station. "One problem at a time."

27

With a small army at his back, Gray crossed the city square that fronted the Jakarta History Museum. The air scorched, and their faces were masked like bandits to keep the powdery ash from their lungs. Still, his eyes watered, and the occasional fiery flake burned his exposed skin.

The museum's columned façade rose ahead of him, spreading out in Dutch-colonial wings that flanked a rear courtyard. It climbed in two stories of white plaster with rows of small windows, all sealed behind green shutters. The red-tiled roof was covered in several inches of ash. Directly ahead, carved into the triangular pediment of the second story, was a single word in Dutch: GOUVERNEURSKANTOOR.

It translated as "Governor's Office."

That's what we need to find in there.

As Gray headed across the plaza, he was surprised to discover that there was no cordon of defense around the museum. Then again, the entire island was coming apart at the seams.

Earthquakes continued to rattle with sudden jolts. Another two volcanic peaks had erupted over the past hour. Tidal surges struck the coastline in unending volleys. All around, the streets had become roadblocks of cars and wagons, most simply abandoned. People crowded past with their lives piled on their backs or dragged behind in carts.

The military and police forces were scattered and strained. Especially as it wasn't just this island that was under siege. The Indonesian archipelago encompassed seventeen thousand islands, six thousand of which were inhabited.

Gray stared at the dark face of the unguarded museum.

Right now, no one is worried about the past—only their futures.

Gray turned to his group. Seichan marched with her mother. Zhuang led a force—twenty strong—of triad fighters. Gray had tried repeatedly to raise Painter on his sat-phone. He had managed a few sporadic connections, none that lasted longer than thirty seconds. Still, he had tried his best to share his intent, to ask for support. While he knew Governor Raffles had kept an office here, Gray had no clue where to find it.

Cut off and operating on only tidbits of information, he felt as if he were flailing in the dark. Breaking into the museum was a long shot, but it was the only move he had left.

Seichan drew closer and pointed between the columns ahead. "Looks like we're not the only ones who had this idea."

Shutters had been ripped off a window flanking the main entrance. The glass had been shattered and brushed away. Gray raised an arm to slow his group. As he approached, he heard angry shouts and spats of gunfire from inside.

Gray shifted next to Zhuang. "We go in swift and shut that down."

The shots sounded like small-arms fire. He studied their group's automatic weapons and hoped it was enough. He gripped his SIG Sauer and Seichan raised her Glock. Zhuang carried a pistol in one hand and his antique saber in the other. Gray was unsure which was the deadlier weapon for the man, especially in a close-quarters battle.

Only one way to find out.

Gray pointed ahead. "Let's go!"

They set off in a tight group and flowed through the broken window, crunching over the shards of glass as quietly as possible. They hurried across the dark entry lobby and into the museum proper. Doors opened in all directions.

Gray led his group to the right, to where the gunplay and shouts continued within a side gallery. So far, no one seemed to have noticed their trespass. Gray flanked to the left of the gallery entrance with Seichan and her mother, along with the triad deputy Yeung, who carried an arsenal of weapons. He was a veritable walking tank.

Zhuang took a post on the doorway's far side with the rest of his contingent.

Gray poked his head around the corner. The gallery's long hall was lined by tall display cabinets and dotted by pedestals. A few emergency lights glowed in the darkness. One of the cases toppled with a shatter of glass. More shouts erupted in Indonesian and Javanese. A pistol cracked off four shots.

Gray counted six or seven shadowy figures nestled among the cabinets. They were masked like his army. On the gallery's far side, a clutch of men and women hid behind a low marble pedestal that supported a reclining Hindu goddess. Those defenders wore matching beige shirts. They were likely museum staff trying to guard the place.

From the attackers' disheveled nature and disparate weaponry, they must be looters who had come to take advantage of the chaos.

Gray scowled and motioned Zhuang to take the gallery's far side. He led his group along the closest wall. He paused until Zhuang was in position, then their two groups swept in tandem down the hall's edges and ambushed the looters from both sides.

A brief firefight ended the standoff. Bodies fell, glass shattered. Finally, the last of the attackers fled down the center of the gallery and out the far door. Zhuang sent a handful of men after them to make sure they left.

One of the staff members called over from their hiding spot.

Guan-yin responded in kind, proving her fluency in the Indonesian language. After some back-and-forth, the others revealed themselves. Gray crossed with Guan-yin to meet them.

The leader of the defenders stepped forward. He was a tall stern-faced Indonesian. He had to be in his late sixties, but he looked capable of wrestling someone half his age to the ground.

"I'm Kadir Numberi, the museum director," he said, introducing himself in English. "Thank you for helping us."

"Glad to be of assistance," Gray said.

Kadir frowned at the masked army behind Gray. "But how did you come to be here?" he asked with clear suspicion.

Gray tried his best to explain an abbreviated version of their story, one that connected to events two centuries earlier.

Even with this explanation, the suspicion in Kadir's eyes dimmed only slightly.

"We need to find where Sir Stamford Raffles once kept his office," Gray finished.

"Back when he was governor?"

Gray nodded. "That's why we've come. Nothing more."

Kadir turned to his staff and spoke rapidly. He got nods back, then turned to Gray. "In truth, I have no idea where his office was, but there are old schematics and records going back to the building's founding in 1710."

"Can you show us?"

"Certainly." He turned and set off down the wing. "The records are in back."

Before they followed, Zhuang ordered Yeung and a cadre of their forces to take up posts behind them, to guard the museum and their backs.

As Gray drew alongside Kadir, the man glanced to him. "I'm sorry. I don't know much about the building when it was a city hall. My area of expertise is in anthropology."

"In that case, Director Numberi, you could be of help. The museum has an exhibit regarding the history of Indonesia and its relation to the Aboriginal people."

"We do." Kadir raised an eyebrow at Gray. "It explores Australia's First Nations peoples and their nautical ties to our country. I put together that exhibit myself."

"You did?"

"I'm from West Papua. But my great-grandfather was a member of the Yolngu People from northern Australia. So the merging of our histories—like my bloodline—is of particular interest to me."

Gray now understood *why* this museum had a long history of covering this corner of Indonesian history.

Kadir's stiff demeanor softened. "Why are you interested in the subject? I know Sir Raffles had a similar long-standing fascination when he was governor, but I know little else about him."

"Raffles had an interest in Aboriginal people?"

"And in ethnography in general. Besides being a naturalist, he wanted to raise awareness and appreciation of the region's peoples."

With these words, Gray felt something shift inside him. That sense of flailing subsided.

We must be on the right track.

As they crossed into the next gallery, gunshots rose behind them. At first just a few pops—then a flurry of rattling blasts. Shouts and breaking glass echoed to them through the darkness.

More looters.

Gray drew Seichan to one side, raising his weapon. Zhuang guarded over Guan-yin. The rest of the triads took up positions flanking the gallery's entrance, aiming weapons toward the long hall that they had just exited.

Yeung and a group of men came bustling back, sheltering a handful of Kadir's staff. A sharp explosion lit the hall from a grenade blast. Automatic fire chewed through the smoke.

Gray and the others flattened to the sides.

These were no looters.

Zhuang called to Yeung in Cantonese. The triad deputy shoulder-rolled across the threshold and fired a grenade from a STK 40 launcher. The blast shattered into the hall. Yeung reached their side. Blood streamed from a cut over his eye, but he slapped a fresh 40mm grenade into the weapon's breech.

Flames glowed out in the hall now.

The firefight momentarily halted as both sides reassessed the situation.

A shout rose from the far end of the hall. "Leave the museum! Leave the papers you secured! And you can walk free."

The man's English had a British lilt to it, but he was no doubt one of the Chinese commandos, part of the contingent that had chased off Valya.

Exasperated and frustrated at the stupidity of this battle, especially as the world burned outside, Gray took a deep breath. The fire in the gallery was quickly spreading. The old building was all wooden floors and beams.

Enough.

Someone had to make the first move—and not with a gun.

He cupped his mouth and called back. "We're equally matched and determined! We can keep killing each other until the world ends. Or we can take a step back. Call a momentary truce!"

Seichan hissed at him. Guan-yin scowled.

There was a long pause, then, "What do you propose?"

"To find a way to save the world," Gray called over. "Together if need be. If you're willing. Or we keep this war going and watch the world burn."

A fierce argument rose on the other side.

At least, someone over there seemed amiable to this pact.

Gray supported whoever that was. "You see what's happening outside! On this island. Across this region. Both our sides have pieces to a centuries-old puzzle. One that could either end the world or save it. Yet, we keep fighting, clinging to our scraps. If we keep doing that, it'll only end in destruction. But it's your choice!"

The squabble slowly died over there.

The same speaker called to them. "You believe there is a way to stop what's happening?"

"Stamford's papers—the pages we have—hint at it." Gray quoted from memory. "He states at the beginning, *the only hope for the world lies within the pages that follow* and ends with a promise, *a method to appease the gods of the underworld if they should ever grow angry again.* But I believe he hid part of his secret at this museum, dividing it up to better secure it."

"In his old governor's office," the shouter called back, proving his own knowledge of the historical angle to all of this. "Do his papers mention petrified bodies?"

Gray stiffened.

What the hell?

Seichan glanced at him, looking less angry and more confused.

"They do!" Gray admitted. "An illness that dissolves bones and recalcifies into bodily tissues."

More mumbling followed this admission.

A new voice called over, higher pitched and anxious, "Is there a cure?"

3:46 A.M.

Heng was hauled back by Captain Wen. The soldier's fingers dug down to bone. Even Xue scolded him with a frown. He was pushed back into the cadre of Falcon commandos.

Still, his hastily shouted question was answered.

"Raffles does mention an elixir!" the American called back. "But that remedy is buried in riddles. It will take the recovery of those other pages to know more."

Wen shifted over to Xue. "I have men circling to the rear courtyard. Keep the Americans talking until we're in position."

"No," Xue ordered. "Hold your forces in place. Our opponents are no fools. They'll be watching their backs. They could easily burn those pages before any raid shuts them down."

Wen looked ready to object, stepping closer to do so.

Xue turned his shoulder to the man. "For now, I say we consider their offer. We could perhaps learn what they know, get them to share it—then decide what to do."

Heng let out the breath he had been holding. He pictured Petty Officer Wong and Sublieutenant Junjie in the medical ward back in Cambodia.

If there was even the slimmest chance of a cure, we must find it.

Heng shook free of the fingers holding him. "The Americans are right. We either cooperate fully, share what each side knows—or we risk losing everything. If this geological collapse continues unchecked, it will bring down the world."

As Xue pondered this, his eyes reflected the firelight from their brief battle. To Heng, the spreading flames was a microcosm of the greater threat.

As the house burns around us, we're still arguing.

"Please . . ." Heng begged.

Xue slowly nodded, having come to a decision. He stepped forward and called across the hall. "I agree to a truce!"

Wen shook his head with a scowl.

Heng listened as further exchanges finalized the parley. The representatives of their respective sides would meet in the middle of the long hall. While these details were worked out, a handful of the museum staff rushed forward and fought the flames with extinguishers.

Smoke fogged the room and filled the rafters.

Once the fires were out, Xue headed across with Captain Wen and another two commandos. Heng followed, carrying the old steel box from the Singapore museum.

Through the pall ahead, a group approached. They were led by a tall man with a ruddy complexion and dark hair, likely the one who had made this deal. He was accompanied by a slim Eurasian woman holding a pistol and a severe-faced older man with an assault rifle. Behind them, two other gunmen followed.

At each end of the gallery, their respective armies bristled with weapons, encouraging their continuing cooperation.

The two parties finally reached a waist-high marble table in the middle. It divided their two camps. A broken and blasted piece of statuary lay to one side. Heng felt a twinge of guilt at the destruction wrought here, but fear burned it away—both for himself and the world.

Xue stepped forward, facing his opponent.

Except for their nationalities, the two looked a match. In height, in determination, in icy-eyed intelligence. It was no wonder the Americans had confounded them at every turn. This opponent was no one to trifle with.

Xue leaned his palms on the marble. "Let's begin."

4:01 A.M.

With her Glock in hand, Seichan kept close watch on the captain of the commandos. The man's countenance was a stone wall, shadowed by a helmet. He clutched a QSZ-92 pistol and had an assault rifle slung across his chest.

At the marble table, Gray and his Chinese counterpart, Major Choi Xue, started their exchange. Information flowed in fits and starts, both sides clearly reserving as much as possible.

Gray leaned over and stared into a steel box.

Seichan remembered the fight over it at the Singapore museum. She studied it from the corner of her eye. The box held a stick of black coral. It matched the one sketched in Raffles's pages. The other object made no sense—even Gray's eyes narrowed at the sight of it.

"What is that?" Gray asked, glancing up from under a lowered brow.

Seichan recognized his tone, his manner.

He knows something and is testing the other.

Xue picked it up, examined it, and placed it on the marble. "As far as we've been able to determine, it appears to be a wooden spearhead. Bound with twined rope. It's clearly old, but we have no clue how it ties to anything."

Seichan gave it a second glance and reluctantly agreed with him.

It did look like an old spearhead, painted with ceremonial symbols.

Gray glanced back to their group. "Do you mind if I have someone else join us? Someone who might confirm my suspicions about this object."

"Certainly. That's fine."

Gray motioned for the museum director to join them. Kadir did so with some reluctance. He shook his head at the ruins of the room. Once he arrived, introductions were quickly made.

Gray pointed to the spearhead. "Director Numberi, I wanted to make sure that's what I think it is. That it's an Aboriginal bullroarer."

"It is." Kadir picked it up. "From the markings, it's likely the work of the Kaurareg people, also called the Torres Strait Islander peoples. They lived among the islands between Australia and Papua New Guinea and were renowned for their nautical skills."

"What's a bullroarer?" Xue asked with a perplexed but interested expression.

Kadir unwrapped part of the twining, as if ready to demonstrate how to use it. Instead, due to the confined space, he pantomimed and pretended to whip the bladed piece of wood through the air by its string.

"When spun rapidly," he explained, "the plane of wood creates a very loud and distinctive roaring noise. Hence, its more common name. Among the First Nations peoples, it goes by many different names, but all of them roughly mean *secret-sacred*."

Xue stood straighter. "How were they used?"

"Mostly in ceremonies. Sometimes as a means of communication over great distances. Up to ten miles, especially on a quiet night or over water. The sound could reach a hundred decibels. Equivalent of a chainsaw. It could also be modulated by speed and direction to create the equivalent of a Morse code."

Xue's eyes narrowed at this explanation, as if it bore some bearing on what he knew and still kept secret.

Gray pressed the director, too. "What sort of sacred ceremonies was it used for?"

"Mostly to ward off evil spirits or bad tidings."

Gray glanced to the high shuttered windows, likely picturing the flaming skies around Jakarta and beyond. Seichan imagined the same.

This definitely counts as bad tidings.

"There are many taboos surrounding the use of a bullroarer," Kadir added. "To use it without permission was punishable by death. Especially as the First Nations peoples believe the sound of a bullroarer is the voice of the Rainbow Serpent, their most sacred god of creation."

Gray's brows pinched at this revelation. He looked harder at the wooden object.

Xue cocked his head, noting Gray's reaction.

As of yet, neither side was willing to fully share what they knew.

Gray recognized this, too, and challenged Xue. He pointed at the box and its contents. "A piece of coral. An old bullroarer. You clearly have more knowledge about all of this. You mentioned petrified bodies earlier. Which has *nothing* to do with what you showed us in the box. So, clearly you're not being forthright."

Xue stood his ground. "The same could be said of *you*, Commander Pierce. You refuse to show us Raffles's papers, guarding them with the army behind you. You tell us *part* of his tale, but not *all* of it. Clearly you suspect some connection to the Aboriginal people—yet, you do not say why."

They stared hard at each other for several long breaths.

The impasse was broken by the quietest of them. "Why are we here?" Dr. Luo Heng said with acid in his voice. He pointed a finger at Gray. "Tell us . . . *show* us . . . what you know, what you learned, what you suspect."

Xue nodded, folding his arms.

But Heng wasn't done. His finger swung to the major. "And, Xue, you tell the others about our submariners, about the ELF transmission, about the lunar rocks and strange crystals."

Xue's face darkened, looking both shocked and furious.

"Or fucking shoot me," Heng declared with a heavy shrug. "I don't care. Time is running out, and you two are still playing games. Keep this up, and we'll all be dead."

Captain Wen looked willing to take up that offer and shoot the man. His pistol shifted toward Heng, but Xue pushed the weapon aside.

"Dr. Luo is not wrong," Xue admitted after taking a deep breath. "Let us cooperate more openly. To—as you said earlier—save the world."

Xue held a hand across the marble.

Gray stared down at it—then with a nod, he reached and shook the man's hand.

"I have a wild story to share," Gray admitted.

Xue smiled for the first time. "I think I can beat it."

28

A half hour later, Gray stared down at the two e-tablets resting atop the marble table. Each side had laid them down, like poker players revealing their cards. Gray had shown Xue a digitized version of the pages, allowing the man to read through them and review the sketches. Gray had also shared what he knew, what he suspected. Still, as a precaution, he kept the original pages with Guan-yin and the triad force.

Likewise, Xue had closed the steel box and passed it to Dr. Luo for safekeeping.

We might be showing our cards, but we're still not willing to hand them over.

On his tablet, Xue had shared pictures of orthorhombic crystals and petrified bodies, along with glimpses of what could be pieces of a planetoid buried in Earth's mantle. Xue had even played a macabre video of a black skull splitting open and discharging a thrashing, tendrilled mass.

Gray swallowed and did his best to stitch their two stories together. "Let me get this straight in my head. Back in 2020, a Chinese lunar lander drilled into what could be a buried, crystalline vein of Theia, the ancient planetoid that crashed into the primordial Earth and formed the moon. When that happened, an ELF transmission was picked up, coming from a chunk of the same planetoid buried beneath the Tonga Trench."

Xue acknowledged as much with a nod. "Whatever we did on the moon must have been sensed by the pieces on Earth. While no transmission was detected coming from the moon, it could be something unknown to our tech. Tachyon. Gravity waves. Maybe the pieces are still connected via some quantum entanglement, so one immediately knows what's happening to the other."

"But that event—that ELF transmission in 2020—it didn't result in a tectonic disaster like we're experiencing now. It only damaged the lander, disabling its drill. It almost sounds like the Chang'e-5 had been specifically targeted. Maybe to keep it from further attacking that vein."

"Possibly," Xue admitted.

"Then two weeks ago, one of your subs went to investigate the source of the transmission. Once it was in the area, your military sent a matching ELF pulse."

"A strong one."

"Which triggered a quake. And in some way damaged the submarine enough to sink it into the trench. Now, the instability has been steadily worsening, threatening the world."

Xue looked down, clearly pained by his words.

Gray shook his head. "It's not your fault. No one could've predicted what would follow. But together maybe we can find a way to stop it."

Xue nodded once and raised his head.

Gray continued, "Stamford Raffles and Dr. Crawfurd must have experienced a similar event when Mount Tambora erupted. The biomineralized bodies, a dangerous sea, escalating quakes and volcanic eruptions. But they learned some secret, something connected to Aboriginal knowledge and history."

Matthew's drawing of the Rainbow Serpent still glowed on the e-tablet's screen.

Gray pictured the bullroarer and remembered Kadir's words about the sound it generated. *The voice of their god.* He sensed something important there, but he couldn't quite grasp it.

Xue sighed loudly, drawing back his attention. "But how can we be sure Stamford discovered anything significant?"

"We can't, but one piece of this history makes me believe he might have."

"What?"

"It's a detail that continues to baffle geologists and volcanologists who have studied the Tambora eruption." Gray stared toward the shuttered windows. "Stamford even reports this in his papers. After the first eruption, the mountain continued to explode. Each blast stronger than the one before it. Volcanologists have no explanation for why it suddenly ceased. The pattern was inconsistent with known events—both in the escalating eruptions and their sudden end."

"You believe Stamford found a way to quell the mountain."

"Maybe."

Heng stepped forward. "What about the cure to the petrifying disease?"

"Stamford might have found that, too. But none of this speculation does us any good without those missing pages." Gray turned to Kadir, who hung behind them and had listened to everything. His expression balanced between amazement and disbelief. "Director Numberi, can you take us to those old records, so we can figure out which of the museum's thirty-seven rooms was Stamford's office?"

Xue spoke up. "No need. I know where it is." He turned and pointed to the opposite wing. "It's on the second story. Overlooking Fatahillah Square."

Kadir's eyes got huge. "I think you're describing *my* office."

Gray smiled. "If so, that makes sense. The museum director *should* be given the best office."

Kadir shook his head. "But nothing's there. It was stripped long ago. Multiple times. It's been the director's office for more than fifty years."

Gray remained undeterred. "Then let's go see how well Stamford was at keeping a secret." He turned to Xue. "That is, if our truce still stands."

Xue shrugged. "For now."

5:02 A.M.

In the office of the museum director, Seichan stood next to Gray. "I guess it's better than tapping on the walls."

"They came prepared," he admitted.

Kadir's second-floor office was shuttered and dark. Flashlights lit the space and danced along the walls. A wide mahogany desk stood to one side. It was heavy and sturdy, as much an historical artifact as anything in the museum. Even the planks of the floor were scarred and scuffed and nailed in black iron. Overhead, timbered beams held up the roof. One wall was covered in a bookcase that looked melded in place by age and use. It was filled with a private collection of carved figures, small stone idols, woven grass baskets, and other pottery. Books filled every other niche.

Across from Seichan, one of Xue's men panned the wall from floor to ceiling with a screened device he held between two hands. The glorified stud-finder glowed with a vague image of what lay behind the lathe and plaster. The technician had already swept the other three walls, searching for a hidden object, a secret room, or cubby.

As an extra measure, Gray had tested the bookshelves, tugging and searching each shelf and frame—until he finally admitted defeat.

The tech finished the fourth wall and lowered the device and gave Xue his assessment. "*Méiyǒu.*"

Seichan translated for Gray. "Nothing."

Xue crossed his arms and rubbed his chin.

"What about the floor?" Gray asked. "This building—to have lasted from 1710—must be heavily joisted."

Xue nodded. "Of course."

The technician set about scanning the room's planks, sweeping back and forth. There were only a few people to get in his way. Zhuang flanked Gray's other side. Besides Xue, the Chinese contingent included the tech, the sour-faced Captain Wen, and Dr. Luo, who stood in a corner with a worried expression.

They had all felt the series of quakes, heard the cannon fire of more eruptions.

The rest of the city had fallen eerily quiet. The panicked shouts, honking horns, and sirens had died away, as if everyone knew the futility of fighting the inevitable.

Except us.

The tech stopped, retreated a step, then stood for a moment. He started again, this time making a small circle over the rug in front of Kadir's desk. "I found something," he reported in Mandarin to Xue and Wen.

Gray needed no translation and crossed to join the others. The tech spoke rapidly to Xue and pointed to a large rectangular shadow on the screen. It filled the space between two floor joists.

"The engineer believes it's metal," Xue reported.

"We can dig it out." Gray turned to Kadir—more out of politeness than any true intent to bend to the director's will if the man refused.

Kadir nodded. "I'll help roll the rug back."

They all worked to clear the space. The planks beneath the rug appeared no different than those around them. Same rough scuffing, same dark patinating. Yet, from the scan, something was clearly under them.

Kadir pointed to the doorway. "There's a fire axe in the hall."

Captain Wen crossed and barked orders to his men. Out in the hallway, their two armies were entrenched at either end. After some scuffling, one of the commandos rushed in with an axe. Not to be outdone, Yeung followed inside with another.

The two men set to work hacking at the floor. Each splintering of wood made Kadir wince, as if they were axing into his own chest. In short order, a black iron box, two-foot-by-three, was revealed beneath the boards.

Kadir covered his mouth. "That was there this entire time?"

A pair of hinged doors split the box's middle. Gray and Xue knelt on either side and grabbed the knobs and parted them open, revealing the face of a safe.

"The outer doors must be additional fireproofing," Gray commented. "Raffles wasn't taking any chances."

The safe had a drawer along its bottom and two keyholes on its face. Between the holes was an ornate plate of bronze that had been inscribed with an erupting volcano.

Gray pointed to the image. "That suggests we found the right spot."

"But how do we open it?" Heng asked, looming behind Xue.

Xue reached to the slim drawer. It slid out smoothly, revealing a velvet-lined interior. Nestled inside was a large bronze key.

"It can't be that simple," Seichan said. "It's *never* that simple."

Xue tested the keyhole on the left. It fit, but it wouldn't budge.

"See," Seichan mumbled.

"Try the other," Gray said.

Xue nodded and did just that. The key fit there, too. As he turned it, the ornate bronze panel snapped open on a concealed hinge. The secret door revealed seven more holes behind it, each with a tiny window next to it. Enameled letters could be seen behind the yellowed glass.

Gray held out his palm. "May I?"

Xue passed him the key. He tested the row of smaller holes. Only the tip of the key fit the tinier openings, but it was enough to turn the hidden dials. Individual letters spun across the windows.

Gray sat back. "I wager we're supposed to line up those seven letters to form a word."

Seichan counted on her fingers. "What about Stamford's last name? *Raffles*. It's seven letters."

"I'll try, but Stamford was no fool. Using his own name would be like someone using *password* for their password." Still, Gray twirled the letters. "That's odd."

"What?" Xue asked.

"Each dial only has *five* letters. The top dial runs from L to P. The middle four cover the first letters of the alphabet, and the bottom two show the last letters." Gray turned to Seichan. "So, there's no way to spell *Raffles* with those limited letters. It's got to be another word. One, I wager, that's tied to the path we're following."

"Maybe you missed something written on those pages," Seichan suggested. "On their backsides or hidden in their drawings."

"I don't think so. Stamford wouldn't risk burying that code in pages that could be lost?"

"Then what?" Heng pressed him. "What could the word be?"

Xue pointed to the etching on the bronze door. "That has to be representative of Mount Tambora's eruption. *Tambora* is seven letters, too, but you can't spell that name either."

Gray sat back on his heels. He took a deep breath, concentrating with his eyes half closed. Seichan imagined the gears churning in his head, struggling to form a seven-letter word out of those limited letters. The possible combinations were still astronomical.

Xue looked as deeply contemplative.

Heng paced around them in a circle. "If there had been numbers on those dials, the combination could've been the date when Tambora erupted?"

Both men jerked straighter.

"Of course," Gray said. "That's it."

Xue nodded, clearly getting it, too.

Seichan did not.

Gray looked to Xue for permission and got a nod. He reached and dialed a letter into each slot. "It's not a *word*," he stated as he worked and nodded his thanks to Heng. "It's a *date*—like you said—the year of the eruption."

Gray finished and sat back.

Seichan read the letters revealed down the row: MDCCCXV.

"It's 1815 in Roman numerals," Xue explained. "When Tambora blew."

Seichan stared between Gray and Xue. Plainly these two shared the same strangeness of mind. Both seemed equally capable of shaking order out of chaos.

Gray respected his counterpart enough to hand back the key. "I'll let you do the honors."

Xue dipped his head in thanks, then leaned over and inserted the key into the left hole again—this time, it turned with a loud snap of gears. The tight seal of the door released.

"You did it," Heng gasped.

Working together, Gray and Xue pulled the heavy door open and let it drop to the side.

As they did, all of them withdrew at the smell that wafted up. It reeked of salt and rot and alcohol, a cocktail no one would order. They waited for the worst of the smell to dissipate before leaning in closer.

The source of the odor was easy to spot. A glass-lidded tank rested at the bottom of the safe. It still held liquid, though its seal must have weakened enough for some of the fluid to evaporate and condensate inside the airtight safe.

Seichan covered her mouth at the smell—and the sight.

Something dark lay curled inside the tank.

"What is it?" she asked.

For the moment, Gray ignored the tank and reached to an iron shelf next to it. He slid out an oilskin-wrapped pouch. The package was sealed in wax and stamped with an insignia of the British crown.

"This must be Stamford's missing pages," Gray said.

Xue remained fixated on the preserved specimen. "But what did he hide with it?"

Gray used the cuff of his jacket to wipe the condensation from the glass lid. The contents were still hard to make out. It appeared to be a coiled black mass, splotched with gray, all nestled upon itself.

"It looks like a snake," Seichan said. "Maybe the Rainbow Serpent."

Gray tilted his head one way, then the other. "It's not a snake."

He pulled out a penlight and shone it through the yellowed glass to better illuminate the contents. What looked like a single fat coil was actually made up of several tentacle-like strands twined together.

But that was not the true horror.

Gray shifted his light to reveal a mass half buried beneath those tentacles. Its gyrations and folds were unmistakable, but from its surfaces, hundreds of tendrils hung in the fluid.

"Is that a brain?" Seichan gasped out.

"Maybe at one time." Gray turned to Xue and Heng. "This looks like what I saw on your video. From the morgue in Cambodia. Emerging from a corpse's skull."

Heng confirmed with a nod.

Gray reached down and wiped his thumb across a steel tag affixed to the glass lid. It was deeply inscribed. But what was written there was no scientific classification of the specimen—only a grave marker. It was etched with a single name to encompass a life cut short.

Matthew

29

Ninety minutes after setting foot on the ruins of *Titan Station Up*, Kowalski was ready to leave.

He stood atop the rig's mid-deck and stared across the seas. To keep his perch on the tilted floor, he braced a hand against a strut. With his other, he balanced a PF-89 anti-tank rocket launcher on his shoulder. He had confiscated it from one of the Chinese prisoners.

He smoked a cigar and stared down at the fiery wreckage of a Z-8 helicopter. It floated in the ash-choked sea. The bird had been an easy target. Pinned down by the low clouds of ash, it had nowhere to hide during its approach. Kowalski suspected it had returned to the station not to attack it, but to seek a safe harbor. By the time it got here, its engine—clogged by ash—struggled to hold the aircraft aloft. It coughed and stuttered the last of the distance.

Still, Kowalski had noted the helicopter's air-to-surface missiles and gunpods. In an abundance of caution and even more fury, he had shot it down before it could do any harm. It was an easy decision. After he and Jarrah had hunted down the last of the Chinese stragglers, they discovered a couple dozen researchers and support staff locked in the mid-deck crew quarters. The survivors were only a fraction of those who had been aboard the two stations—*Up* and *Down*.

So, Kowalski had not been feeling especially merciful. Still, he had spared the lives of the handful of commandos who had surrendered or who were too injured to be a threat. They were bound and locked up. Jarrah had gathered discarded weapons and armed the remaining survivors.

While he did that, Kowalski had swum out to the seaplane. It was the Twin Otter that he and Monk had flown aboard to reach the station. It had been set adrift in the debris field, but it was still intact. Once he recovered it, he used the plane to retrieve Haru, Byrd, and Jazz from the foundering Tethys Tier. Gliding over the waves, with no cavitation of props in the water to trigger a UUV, he was able to safely ferry them back to the station.

The Otter now rocked below, moored to the lower level. It still had another trip to make. Kowalski squinted to the east, toward where the Chinese helicopter had been headed. He had learned from the survivors that a large military ship had steamed off in the same direction.

Kowalski knew what lay out there.

The *Titan X*.

And Monk.

Despite the risk of flying through this foul air, Kowalski wasn't about to sit idly by. While he had some satisfaction in downing the helicopter, he was not sated. His heart pounded as he stared down at the bodies floating among the debris.

A hatch slammed behind him.

He turned as Byrd marched toward him. He was shouldering a pack and carrying a rifle. The billionaire had his own score to settle. Plus, the man knew the *Titan X* better than anyone.

Down at the mooring dock, Jarrah was loading more gear. The security chief was determined to continue his role. He had found one of his teammates, injured but alive, among the survivors. The lone man would do his best to guard the station after the three of them left.

Byrd joined him. "Jazz and Haru are both resting in the med ward. But there's no doctor, only a nurse."

"That'll have to do for now. I'll keep trying to reach someone. Get them to send help."

"If you do, warn them about what's in the water around us."

Kowalski nodded. "The UUVs will lose juice after a day or so. But until then, they'll help keep the station protected."

The radio chirped at Kowalski's neck.

"All set down here," Jarrah reported. "We can depart any time."

Kowalski turned to Byrd. "Ready for some payback?"

Byrd's expression remained grim. "I'm more than happy to return the package they left us."

Kowalski looked past his toes to the Twin Otter. Earlier, he had collected all the charges that the commandos had been planting, along with their extra satchels of Semtex. Leaning on his demolition background, Kowalski had crafted a special care package for the Chinese.

"Then let's go play mailman," Kowalski said.

Byrd set off down the steps.

Kowalski followed, while still staring to the east. He recognized a major obstacle to his plan.

First, we have to get there.

With every passing hour, the world steadily shrank. The skies lowered. The horizons, aglow with distant fires, closed around them. Lightning shattered across dark clouds. Distant thunder rumbled—not from the skies, but from deep in the earth. And ash fell in a continual hot wash of powder, filling the air and sea.

Still, he was determined to fulfill the postman's credo about completing a route.

Neither snow nor rain nor heat nor gloom of night . . .

Kowalski scowled at the world and added his own postscript.

Or motherfucking volcanic eruptions.

9:55 A.M.

Buried under blankets, Jazz shivered in the small medical ward. Her head throbbed. To fight the chill, she had piled on Kowalski's long coat, too.

When Jazz first got to the ward, a slim red-haired nurse with a thick Aussie accent had passed her a couple tabs of Tylenol. Due to her concussion, Jazz couldn't take anything stronger, not even aspirin, as it might aggravate any intracranial bleeding.

Best to just rest, the nurse had suggested.

She glanced to the neighboring bed. Haru had gotten jabbed with the good stuff while his arm had been splinted. He drowsed in a drug-induced haze, snoring slightly through his open mouth. She was happy he was finally able to get some sleep.

On her other side, the bed was occupied by someone she was less keen to see.

Swallowed up by blankets, Dr. Kim Jong Suk suffered like her. He quaked and trembled. His face was ashen, his eyes bloodshot. His brow ran with sweat, and his lips were cracked and bloodless. The man had left with the first shuttle of evacuees. Already ill, he had ridden out the attack in the ward.

His left arm rested atop his blankets. From the elbow down, his arm was dark gray. His fingers were black, as if afflicted with some stony gangrene. He moaned and occasionally thrashed. But the nurse had established a morphine drip. It still trickled and kept him in a restless haze.

The man was clearly afflicted worse than her. He must have been stung by more than one coral polyp, inflicting a stronger envenomation, making him get sick faster.

She tugged out her hand and inspected it. Half of her palm was gray. Two fingers were even darker. She could not move the middle digit at all.

"What sort of poison is this?" she whispered.

Seeking answers, she rolled over and grabbed her laptop. She had taken it with her when Kowalski had ferried them back in the seaplane. Even with everything going on, she had refused to abandon her research. To distract herself from the fever and aches, she opened the computer and pulled up her files, specifically those pertaining to Specimen A17, the chunk of black coral with those vicious free-swimming emerald polyps.

She set about reviewing it all, going through the macro- and microscopic data and images. She searched for any explanation to the severity of her condition—and Kim's. In retrospect, she wished she had examined the coral's venomous nematocysts in greater detail. All she had done was note the cells' morphological features—which could be summarized in two words.

Damn big.

Frustrated, with her head pounding worse, she pulled up the DNA data. The little that there was of it. She remembered the reason she had gotten stung. She had been collecting a second sample to re-rerun the problematic assay, one that had kept popping up with errors on the DNA sequencer.

Still, some information had been gleaned on the first run. Normally the screen would fill up with a kaleidoscope of data, but A17 had large gaps everywhere. It was no wonder the NovaSeq sequencer had thrown it all back in her face. She studied the missing swaths, struggling to understand why the sequencer had failed to read those sections of code. If a second assay showed the same errors in the same places, it would indicate that the problem was not with the machine or her technique— heaven forbid—but due to an abnormality in the DNA itself.

Jazz licked her dry lips and brought up her second run.

This was why she had been still working when Kowalski and the others had come running down. With the second sample already collected—and no one was using the NovaSeq during the evacuation— she had quickly run a second sequencing.

Unfortunately, during the rush to leave, she hadn't had any time to analyze the results.

Got plenty of that now.

She pulled up the second screen of data and compared the two runs. A small gasp escaped her, encompassing surprise, delight, and some deep satisfaction.

I knew it couldn't be user error.

The two data sets aligned perfectly. Both times, the sequencer had run into problems digesting identical regions of the genetic code.

She glared at those blank spaces.

"What are you hiding?" she whispered to them.

Before she could ponder it further, a hard thrashing rose from the neighboring bed. She turned to find Kim Jong Suk convulsing with his head thrown back, his mouth frothing. She glanced at a screen that monitored his vitals. His heart rate was higher than two hundred beats. His temperature had spiked to 105.

The nurse came running up with a syringe.

Kim's temperature climbed to 107. Another staff member rushed over to hold the man down.

The nurse secured the IV line and poked a needle. "Administering diazepam."

As she pushed the plunger, Kim's convulsions died down to trembles, then a slack-limbed lassitude. His heart rate slowed. But one vital kept rising.

His temperature was now 110.

"We need an ice bath," the nurse said, noting the spiking fever.

"I'll check the commissary." Her assistant ran off.

Jazz shook her head as Kim's temp rose to 112. It was as if he was burning up from the inside. She placed a palm on her own damp forehead, checking her status. She stared at Kim's arm. The blackening of his skin had spread over his entire hand.

Jazz clenched a fist—but two more of her fingers refused to bend.

She lowered her arm.

What the hell is happening?

30

"Is there any mention of a cure?" Heng asked.

Gray tuned out the physician as he finished reading the last page in the stack. He concentrated on piecing the tale together. Once done, he slid the page to Xue, who sat beside him at Kadir's desk. Besides the handwritten account, more drawings were spread across the mahogany, extending the story and the mystery.

Gray waited for Xue to finish.

On the far side of the room, Seichan whispered with Zhuang and Guan-yin. In the opposite corner, Captain Wen had his head bowed with one of his men. At the doorway, Yeung stood guard next to Kadir.

It had taken more than an hour to read through the pages, and tensions continued to mount in the room. Gray didn't know how long this truce would last, but he hoped it would stretch enough to glean some answers.

Heng crossed to the open safe, staring down with crossed arms at the macabre remains of Matthew. Even Stamford had offered no answers about the transformation of the Aboriginal lad's body—or at least, his central nervous system. Raffles had described Crawfurd's horror at the discovery of the still-living tissue inside the mineralized shell of the boy's skull. Mercifully, it had only survived twenty minutes before finally going slack with death. Afterward, Stamford had interred the remains in the hopes that some future scientist could make sense of the boy's death.

Xue finally shoved the last page aside.

Gray watched him stare contemplatively off into the distance and waited for the man to return. It was a frightening story and still left many questions unanswered.

Like the condition of Matthew.

Xue sighed and turned to Gray. "What do you make of it?"

The others in the room gathered closer.

"What did you learn?" Seichan pressed them both.

"The story picks up where Stamford and Crawfurd left off. Following the autopsy of the two bodies." Gray waved to the buried safe. "We all know how one of those post-mortems ended up."

"What about the other?"

"Stoepker." Gray sighed. "Crawfurd discovered strange welts over the man's body. On those regions of the man's flesh that had been untainted by the biomineralization process. He believed those welts were the source of whatever cured him."

"Or at least, *halted* the advancement of the disease," Xue corrected him. "I doubt it could reverse it. To reform bone that had been dissolved."

"True," Gray acknowledged. "Crawfurd found more information about those welts in the account that Stoepker wrote. While dying, Stoepker had related the events that followed after he and Matthew had left the *Tenebrae* in a steel-hulled tender."

"What happened?" Heng asked.

"Shortly after boarding the tender and escaping the burning *Tenebrae*, a fierce quake struck. Their boat nearly capsized. The tender got swamped with broken branches of coral that stung and burned. Stoepker also discovered a strange sight in the ash-covered seas. *Hundreds of spiny balls of coral*, as he described them. They seemed to spin and churn on their own."

"What were they?" Heng asked.

"We'll get to that," Gray said and continued the account. "Over the course of a dozen days, the pair got sicker and sicker. Unfortunately,

Matthew went downhill faster—maybe due to his body size or perhaps he took on more of the venom. They also witnessed how those spiny balls, even fractured pieces of them, could set fire to any combustible material. Wood, clothing, oil."

Xue nodded. "Stoepker wrote of rowing past a small bay that was entirely aflame."

Gray eyed the others, stressing the significance of this next part of the story. "But it wasn't just *coral* in the water. Stoepker described seeing lights flashing under and around his boat. Though the source would never reveal itself, Matthew insisted they were Rainbow Serpents. He told Stoepker that if they prayed to them, the serpents might intercede."

"Did they?"

"Matthew tried his best. Over the course of two days and nights, he drew his picture and sang to the waters. He so exhausted himself that he fell into a coma afterward. Still, something heard him, or maybe it was happenstance. But one night, those glowing serpents rose around the tender and probed with long shining tentacles, revealing themselves to be some type of bioluminescent cephalopod—or so Stoepker believed at the time."

"If they weren't that," Heng asked, "what were they?"

Xue lifted a palm. "I'm not entirely sure we have an answer, but let's finish Stoepker's story first."

Gray nodded and continued. "Those tentacles didn't have any suckers, but they did—to quote Stoepker—*flail with stinging threads that flamed through cloth and skin, as if reaching for my very bones.*"

"Which must have created those welts," Heng said. "Whatever chemical was in those stings, they likely acted as a counteragent to the coral's poison."

"That is what both Stoepker, and later Crawfurd, believed. Sadly, the Rainbow Serpents hadn't arrived in time to save the boy, and their intervention only delayed the inevitable in Stoepker, as he was already too far gone by then. And so ended their tragic tale."

"But it was picked up by Raffles and Crawfurd after that," Xue said.

"Wanting to know more about those Rainbow Serpents, Raffles sought out Matthew's people."

Gray lifted his chin to stare over at Kadir. "Matthew hailed from an island in the Torres Strait."

"He must have been a member of the Kaurareg People." Kadir stepped closer, drawn by this aspect of the story. "It makes sense that the boy was from there. The nautical expertise of the Torres Strait Islanders was well known at the time. Many of them ended up serving aboard British and Dutch ships. But what did Raffles learn from Matthew's people?"

"While seeking them out, Raffles heard about a great gathering of Aboriginal folk. They had come from across Indonesia and traveled in a large flotilla to the seas near the island of Sumbawa. This was weeks prior, when Tambora was still erupting. There, they performed a ceremony to appease the angry gods. They used bullroarers during the ceremony. Hundreds of them. According to Raffles, after that ritual, the mountain finally quieted down."

"And whatever fouled and poisoned the waters vanished, too," Xue added.

Seichan scowled. "But no one actually *witnessed* this. Right? No one but the Aboriginal people who told this story afterward. For all anyone knows, it could have been fabricated, a tale to boost their mystical esteem."

"Maybe, but Raffles and Crawfurd did speak to their elders. From them, the pair learned the legends of the Rainbow Serpent. It was a tale that goes back to what the Aboriginal elders called the *Dark Dreaming*, the dawn of humanity—or at least to the arrival of the Aboriginal people to Australia and the neighboring islands."

Kadir rubbed his chin, looking like he wanted to comment, but he remained quiet.

Xue picked up the story for the others. "Up until then, this ancient story and how it bore on the present world was a closely guarded secret among the Aboriginal people. But Crawfurd convinced the elders to share it with him. According to their legends, the world's crust is *thin* in several places, so thin that it allows access to the underworld of the Rainbow Serpent, a god who could travel the globe along deep rivers beneath the world."

Kadir nodded at this description.

"The Java Sea around the island of Sumbawa was one of those thin places. When the gods were angry, they could burst through there to exact punishment."

"But that wasn't the only spot." Gray reached to the set of drawings found with the papers from the safe. "There was another. One far more significant. What the Aboriginal elders claimed was the true home of the Rainbow Serpents."

"Where was that?" Seichan asked.

"As Crawfurd writes, *it lies well beyond all islands, in seas rarely seen*. Still, he kept a record of his journey there, even commissioning sketches."

Seichan squinted. "You're talking about those drawings of an island with some indigenous people."

Gray nodded. "Which we now know was the Aboriginal party who took Crawfurd to that other *thin* spot of the world, the home of their gods. When he was there, he had shipboard artists draw renditions of the island. I think the ones secured in the safe were hidden there because, unlike the first set, the coastlines were drawn with enough detail that the island could be identified."

Gray slid a sketch that showed one such coastline with a prominent cratered mountain.

"I wager this is the silhouette of a volcano on that island. The equivalent of Tambora out in those *rarely seen seas*." Gray drew forth a second sketch. "And here you can see another view of the island, on its other side. There's also either a map of the island's edges or maybe the reefs around it."

"Does this place have a name?" Kadir asked, plainly intrigued by this secret tied to his great-grandfather. "Or do you have any idea where it might be?"

"Not yet," Gray answered. "But I have some thoughts."

Xue looked at him, but Gray waved for him to continue with the story.

Xue cleared his throat. "Crawfurd spent three months on that island, learning all he could. He witnessed for himself how the Aboriginal elders could summon Rainbow Serpents with their bullroarers. He learned more about the strange coral and how the two were connected. He even examined specimens of both in secret. Those efforts were later discovered and considered deeply sacrilegious by the elders. He barely escaped with his life. Still, he did manage to secure one of their sacred bullroarers, along with the pages he had drawn."

Before continuing, Gray studied the spread of sketches that encompassed Crawfurd's investigation on the island. He shifted their order, trying to piece them together like a jigsaw puzzle. Xue helped him, offering some suggestions and even sharper insights.

Once they were ready to present Crawfurd's work in the best light, Gray faced the group. "Our intrepid doctor began his investigation with the *coral*. So let's follow his example. Here is his detailed drawing of the specimen in all its glory, what Crawfurd dubbed *Perfidia lithia-sis*, meaning *treacherous stone*."

Gray slid over a handsome sketch of a tree of black coral. In the upper corner was a close-up of its eight-limbed polyp.

Xue stared at the page. "From the level of detail that follows, Crawfurd's ship must have been well equipped with microscopes, dissecting instruments, anything that the Batavian Society could provide to assist his efforts."

"Here's more of his handiwork." Gray laid out a selection of pages. They showed another schematic of the coral tree, a cross-section of its stony skeleton, and a large peek at its stinging polyp.

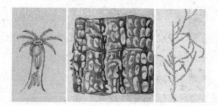

"While on the island," Xue continued, "Crawfurd experienced an eruption. A fairly violent one. Enough that he fled to his ship. During that quake, he spied in the waters what Stoepker had described as *spiny balls of coral*. Having read Stoepker's account and knowing the fiery threat they presented, he beseeched his Aboriginal guides for help. Again, they spun their bullroarers atop the ship's deck and summoned the Rainbow Serpents. The tentacled beasts rose and cleared the seas of the danger, whisking the threat back into the depths. At the same time, the volcanic eruption also subsided, as if their efforts had soothed the angry gods of the underworld."

"Or it could be a coincidence," Seichan reminded them.

Gray ignored her skepticism and withdrew another sketch from the pile. "Here is a drawing Crawfurd made of that strange mobile version of the hard coral."

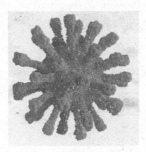

"It looks like a floating mine," Zhuang said sternly.

"Or a viral particle," Heng added.

Gray conceded both points with a nod. "If the tale is true, they could possibly be *both*. Like any naval mine, those spiky balls would pose a fiery threat to any passing ships. And maybe that was their function. A means of defense for the species. Whenever a danger rose, the spiny corals would be dispatched, sent out as a biological attack against a threat."

Heng studied the spread of drawings with a furrowed brow. "But how does this aggressive and dangerous coral connect to the Rainbow Serpents, a species that seems relatively benevolent?"

Gray turned to Xue. "I'll let you share what you came to believe from studying the sketches."

Xue nodded. "I'm convinced the two are actually the same species. With the Serpent being a more mature version of the other. Crawfurd seemed to suspect the same. Whether he learned this on his own or was instructed by an elder, I don't know. But he did draw this sketch."

Xue pulled forward a picture that showed a series of iterations—from an eight-limb polyp to a version that appeared motile to a larger independent beast with eyes.

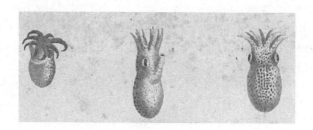

"I believe he's demonstrating the life cycle of the species," Xue explained.

Heng squinted at the last image. "Ending with the Rainbow Serpent."

Gray nodded. "Like with the coral, Crawfurd also studied this adult form of the species. He suspected it lived deep in the sea, only rising when called or needed. Which in most cases meant mitigating the damage done by their younger versions and removing them once their attack was deemed to be over."

Xue pulled up the last two sketches. "He did anatomical drawings of those smooth-limbed serpents. Here's one that details its circulatory system and the papules that cast out those stinging threads."

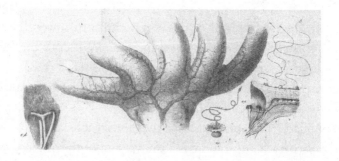

"I suspect he did more drawings," Xue said. "But this was all he was willing to share. Leaving behind the barest clue to what he and Raffles were trying to protect. Still, he spent considerable time examining and drawing those stinging *tendrils*. As a physician, Crawfurd must have found them the most intriguing."

Xue showed the last sketch. It detailed the anatomy and conformation of those potent-tipped tendrils.

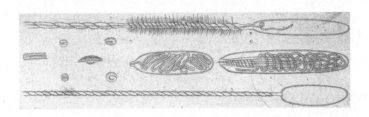

Heng stepped closer, demonstrating the same keen medical interest as Crawfurd. "Those tendrils could be modified versions of a coral's stinging cells. Maybe it was how they conveyed the cure, dispensing a counteragent to their younger version's toxin."

Gray gathered the pages. "That's what Crawfurd was told and believed. But we don't know if he ever had a chance to confirm it himself."

Seichan scowled at this admission. "So all of this could be *hearsay*, like the claim that bullroarers could calm eruptions."

Gray couldn't argue against this. A healthy skepticism might be warranted.

Xue had taken on that thousand-mile stare again.

Gray waited it out.

Xue finally leaned back. "What I find naggingly consistent across these stories is the role of *harmonics*. It was an ELF transmission that started all of this, back when our lunar landing was drilling into a deposit of what could be a piece of Theia's crystalline crust. It makes me wonder if that particular frequency and wavelength is the species' equivalent of a *distress call*. Maybe it blasted out that signal when it sensed our drilling, taking it as the threat."

"But how had it known what was happening on the moon?" Seichan asked.

"As I said before, it could be a means of communication that is unknown to us, a quantum entanglement between all the pieces of Theia—both under our mantle and beneath the moon's dust."

For now, Gray ran with this hypothesis, seeing where it might lead. "If you're right, maybe everything remained quiet back in 2020 because there was no confirmatory *Help!* from the moon after the distress call." Gray turned to Xue. "But what's happening now?"

"I can only hazard a guess. Two weeks ago, we sent out that same ELF transmission. A very loud one. Maybe they took it as another distress call. Originating deep in our mountains."

Xue's countenance tightened as if coming to a concerning realization.

"What?" Gray pressed him.

A note of panic entered his voice. "Our geologists. They had been studying the quakes over the past two weeks. From the pattern and intensity, they believe the vectors of force were aiming from the Tonga Trench straight to our coastline."

Xue turned to him. "Maybe what we're experiencing is a response to that distress call, the one buried in our ELF transmission. Maybe all of this is an effort to reach the source of our signal in the mountains."

"And they're ripping through the world to get to it," Gray added.

"But what's behind it?" Heng asked. "How does this strange species—these old gods of the Aboriginal species—tie into all of this?"

Xue shook his head, more than willing to admit his ignorance.

Gray dismissed this question, too—for now. "Xue, if you're right about this being all about *harmonics*, then maybe the tonal frequency of a bullroarer—a very specifically crafted one—is the species' equivalent of an *All Clear*. A signal to stop whatever is causing the tectonic disturbance and to halt the spreading attack by those viral mines."

Xue stood up. "There is only one way to find out."

Gray frowned.

"We have an aircraft and can secure a boat," Xue explained. "It's risky, but Mount Tambora is not far away."

Gray followed him up. "You want to *test* this theory? In the shadow of a mountain that nearly broke the world before?"

Xue faced him. "If this threat is truly aiming straight for China—and taking the world down with it—I can use your help."

"So our truce continues?"

Xue shook his head as he left. "No."

Confused, Gray hurried after him.

Xue glanced back. "It's a partnership now."

SIXTH

Dark Eden

31

Monk sat at the communication station on the *Titan X*'s bridge. He wore a beige jumpsuit, disguising himself as one of the yacht's crew. Captain Stemm stood before the helm. The other men worked silently around him.

All were under the watchful eye of three commandos in body armor and helmets. Their battle gear was painted in black-and-blue camo. They patrolled the floor, armed with QBZ assault rifles. But the trio were not their true captors. The ship and all those aboard were trapped in a net—both above and below the sea.

Monk searched the panoramic view out to the ocean and skies. Three hours ago, a huge amphibious boat had sped into these waters. It was a Chinese Type 726 LCAC—an air-cushioned landing craft— nicknamed *Yema*, which meant *wild horse*.

And that stallion had quickly proven its name.

On arrival, even at a hundred feet in length and half as wide, it had proven its nimble-footedness. It had jetted several times around the *Titan X*, skimming the ash-covered waves on fat pontoons, nearly floating atop a cushion of air. Its gas-turbine engines churned a pair of seven-meter-tall fans mounted on the boat's aft end.

Such crafts were meant to ride up onto land, even maneuver over shores on those air cushions. An LCAC could carry sixty tons of personnel and equipment, dumping hundreds of marines onto battle lines. But that wasn't this boat's main objective. It had a Type 96 battle tank, commonly deployed with such boats, sitting atop its deck, but this vehicle was capped by an armored dome stubbed with antennas.

Monk guessed the tank had been modified into a drone, like all the other equipment aboard the LCAC. Its deck had been altered from its usual configuration of two fixed hull structures running parallel down either side with a gap between for tanks, landing docks, and infantry vehicles. All that was left of those twin structures was a pilothouse mounted forward-left. The rest of the deck was festooned with cranes and electromagnetic air-launchers.

From those frames hung all manner of UUVs and AUVs. He recognized what looked like Sea Whales and Hidden Dragons, both of which were designed to operate autonomously underwater. Same with the rows of torpedoes, stacked like cordwood atop launching racks. In addition, fixed-wing and VTOL drones dotted the deck.

Someone had transformed this LCAC into a fully automated attack boat.

Earlier, Captain Stemm had helped Monk understand what was facing them. As a former Aussie naval man, he had recognized much of the technology, having followed the development of China's AI-controlled naval forces.

As they had watched helplessly from the bridge, the LCAC had launched an array of drones into the air and dumped more into the sea, forming a web of surveillance devices and armed weaponry all around. The *Titan X* had no choice but to surrender and allow an armed force to board the yacht. The LCAC had arrived with only a couple dozen marines. The other fifty commandos had come from the attack submarine that surfaced shortly after the LCAC's arrival.

The submarine's sail still stuck out of the water, plying a slow circle a quarter mile off. It looked dejected and redundant. Beyond sending support troops, it was not needed. The LCAC and its complement of autonomous equipment had the yacht locked up tight. The AI-driven boat sat out there, crewed by maybe two or three. Its systems had clearly been designed to operate with minimal, if any, supervision.

Captain Stemm wandered over, drawing the eye of two commandos, but they quickly lost interest. The gunmen knew the handful on the bridge offered no threat. The passing hours had further dulled their attentiveness.

Stemm drew alongside Monk. "Radar is picking up a distant shadow to the west," he mumbled under a fist as he feigned a yawn. "I know some Mandarin and overheard the bastards mention an LHD."

A landing helicopter dock.

Monk bit off a groan and stared off to the dark skies to the west. Jagged bolts lanced through the low clouds, but the lightning failed to illuminate that threat.

It was still too far off.

"How long?" Monk asked.

"At its current speed, it'll be here in an hour."

Monk winced. He remembered the large V-shaped drone that had buzzed the yacht hours ago. It must have come from that larger ship. The Chinese were clearly not taking any chances. Whatever they were trying to hide or discover six miles under them had to be important.

Since commandeering the yacht, the Chinese had been brutally interrogating the researchers, trying to discern how much they knew. It was likely the only reason the yacht hadn't already been sunk.

From his station, Monk could only watch impotently as the Chinese took control. He had flipped through the CCTV cameras that offered views into Science City. Bodies lay in the hallways, demonstrating the cost of resistance. Interrogators had beaten and maimed many others.

Monk had noted a Chinese woman who appeared to be orchestrating this line of inquiry. Beyond her gender, she stood out because of the deference shown to her and the fact that she was the only one not dressed in camo. She wore a navy jacket with prominent epaulets over a white shirt and tie.

Voices rose from the hallway.

A contingent pushed onto the bridge, led by that same woman. She was flanked by a hulking brute in helmet and armor. His knuckles were bleeding and torn, marking him as one of the interrogators. The three commandos on the bridge snapped to attention.

As Monk kept his gaze down, he heard her addressed, naming her and her rank.

"*Hǎijūn shang xiao Tse.*"

He gritted his teeth. *Captain Tse.* She must be the leader of this task force. He watched her sidelong as she made the rounds across the bridge. She crossed to the front and stared out the forward window, surveying all that she had subdued.

Drones buzzed like gnats around the ship or sped by on fixed wings. The layers of ash on the water stirred with the tiny sails of her AUV and UUV weaponry. More patrolled deeper. She placed her hands on her hips, clearly satisfied with the view.

She turned back around. Even shadowed by the brim of her hat, her eyes glinted under a straight line of black bangs. Her hair had been close-cropped and oiled flat to the sides. Her suit and shirt remained as crisp as her manner. The only blemish was a spatter of blood on her collar.

Must've gotten too close to the handiwork of her bloody-knuckled interrogator.

She consulted with that same man before coming forward to confront Captain Stemm, who had returned to the helm upon her arrival.

She switched to English. "Captain Stemm, I understand that a submersible was launched shortly before our arrival. It was detected by our submarine and confirmed by those we spoke to aboard your ship."

Stemm swallowed and nodded. "It was a scheduled dive. That's all."

"I don't believe it was," she said coldly, taking another step forward.

Stemm tried to retreat, but he was blocked by the bulk of her interrogator, who pressed a pistol into the captain's back.

"According to the commander of our submarine," the woman said coldly, "you all performed quite the noisy dance when it dropped—as if you were purposefully trying to mask its descent."

Stemm clamped his lips, refusing to respond.

"I also heard of the discovery of a forest of giant coral and strange life down at the bottom of the trench where one of our boats sank. And rumor of a fissure opening up, swallowing that submarine and a large portion of the forest."

Captain Tse's eyes shone with malice. Clearly her interrogator had done his job, and she now enjoyed lording it over her new target. From her stiff spine and thrown-back shoulders, she was carrying a four-ton chip on her shoulders. As a woman in the PLA, she likely had to claw her way to her current position, to be harder willed, more callous and cunning than her counterparts.

Monk tried to find pity in his heart for her, but he pictured the bodies in the halls, the pummeled faces of the researchers.

Screw that.

Tse pressed Stemm for more details. "What did your submersible hope to find down there? I suspect it must be nearing the bottom by now. Were those aboard seeking to steal our new submarine's technology or were they investigating the source of the quakes?"

Stemm must have known it was futile to prevaricate with this woman. "The only interest we have in your nuclear submarine was how it pertained to those quakes." He waved to the glower of flames in the distance. "Something must be done to stop this. You must recognize that."

"I *recognize* that when it comes to operations such as this, there should be only one captain." She nodded to the hulking interrogator.

The man shifted his pistol to the back of Stemm's head.

Monk took a step forward.

The gunshot deafened and stung his ears.

Captain Tse had stepped aside at the last moment—to avoid the spray of blood and gore as the round tore through Stemm's skull. The man toppled to the floor as the rest of the crew gasped and fell back in horror.

Monk's fist clenched hard enough that his knuckles cracked under the strain.

Tse looked his way, as if she had heard this. But she ignored the threat of his fist and stared him in the face.

"Dr. Kokkalis," she said. "We, too, will have a conversation. I am very much interested in DARPA's involvement in all of this."

Monk refused to look away.

So much for trying to blend in with the crew.

Once again, the skill and handiwork of her interrogator had paid off. Too many of those aboard had known of Monk's background—or at least the story that had been told to them. At present, as cut off as they were, he doubted the Chinese knew of his connection to Sigma. He had to hope this knowledge was kept from this woman for as long as possible.

She waved to her commandos and barked orders. Two came forward with rifles and motioned for him to head toward the door.

Before he left, Captain Tse had some last words and a promise.

"We'll continue our discussion shortly, Dr. Kokkalis." She stared down toward her toes. "But first I must attend to another matter. One that I'll address personally."

As Monk was marched off, he looked out windows to the LCAC. There remained one additional vehicle still aboard that attack boat. It hung over the stern. From its boxy shape and the sphere of glass at the front, there was no mistaking it.

A deep-sea submersible.

Only this one was being loaded with fat torpedoes. The weapons were likely engineered to operate at extreme depths.

Monk glanced back to Captain Tse, who was looking down from the bridge at the same sight. He winced and turned his gaze miles down and sent a warning.

Careful, guys, a new shark's about to enter your waters.

32

"Blowing ballast," Bryan called out. "Slowing our descent."

Phoebe startled out of her drowse, shocked to find her chin resting on her collarbone. After being up all night and sinking silently and motionlessly through black waters for three hours, she had fallen into a light slumber.

A few bubbles raced over the scallop of glass in front of her. As their descent slowed, she twisted in her seat. She didn't even have to voice her concern.

"Reading hundred-and-thirty rem out there," Datuk reported, leaning to his sensor screen.

"What about in here?" she asked.

For this descent, Datuk had secured a portable radiation monitor so they could track the amount of their exposure inside. Insulated by the thick titanium and leaded glass, they had some protection, but it wasn't absolute.

He nodded. "So far, we're still okay. Only picking up eight rem in the sphere. But you definitely don't want to go swimming out there."

Adam spoke behind her. "I expected it to be worse by now. We've crossed nine thousand meters. Almost to the bottom."

Phoebe stared out the window and knew the radiation was bad enough. Far below, as they slowed their descent, the coral field remained a dark forest under them. Off in the distance, a luminescent shimmer marked the distant fringe of unaffected coral. The dead patch was easily four times as large as before.

They continued sinking toward the center of that black hole.

She knew the darkness directly under them was not due to deadened coral, but the mouth of the fissure that had opened. Bathymetric measurements showed the crack to be two kilometers long and a quarter as wide.

She reached to her controls and pinged their sonar down into the depths.

Adam noted her effort. "Any better luck?"

She leaned back in her seat. "See for yourself."

On the screen in front of her, the *Cormorant*'s multibeam sonar showed the walls of the fissure below. While the trench bottomed out at ten thousand meters, the crack through the seabed delved far deeper. Its sides dropped away in sheer cliffs and broken escarpments. According to the gradient scale on the screen, those walls fell at least another two thousand meters, more than a full mile. Beyond that, it was impossible to judge how much farther it dropped. The image blanked out past that point.

"I'm still getting nothing," she said. "Something is either absorbing our sonar ping or keeping it from reflecting back to us."

"What could be causing that?" Datuk asked.

Phoebe ticked off the possibilities. "Changes in water density, sonar from another source, noisy sea life." She shook her head. "But none of that presents as a blank zone like that. We should still be picking up *something*. Instead, our ping simply vanishes."

Adam offered one frightening possibility. "Unless it's so deep that our sonar failed to find its bottom."

"That would only happen if the bottom was hundreds of miles down."

Adam shrugged. "Do you have a better explanation?"

She scowled and turned to Bryan. "Keep us dropping at this rate. It's slow enough that if the radiation worsens, we can still head back up before getting overexposed."

Datuk reported from the back. "Hundred-and-eighty rem outside. Ten inside."

"Maybe the reason the radiation is less than we expected is because the Chinese sub dropped into a far deeper hole," Adam said, clearly trying to support his theory. "Like I said before, water is a great insulator, especially at these pressures."

By now, the *Cormorant* had reached the top of the forest. They started to drop through its ruins. To either side, the coral spread in a dark ominous deadfall of shattered branches and toppled trunks. Nothing moved out there. Nothing shone or flickered.

As if in respect for the graveyard they were passing through, a heavy silence fell over the group. Phoebe's chest tightened. Her breathing grew harder.

So much destruction.

As they descended, the boles of the black trees steadily thickened. At a thousand feet in height, the surrounding forest rose as tall as the Empire State Building. She could only imagine the age of this coral field. Considering the slow growth of black coral, it had to be millions of years old.

She gazed in awe at the majesty and mystery around her.

After another ten minutes, the *Cormorant* neared the bottom of the forest. Here, the trunks were forty feet wide. They formed a giant colonnade around them, a dark cathedral six miles under the sea.

"Here we go," Bryan whispered as they descended past those roots and dropped into the fissure.

"Two hundred rem," Datuk noted.

Adam leaned down to peer out his window. He studied the rock wall falling alongside them. "I'm not seeing anything growing on those cliffs."

"Not even algal mats," Datuk agreed, peering past Adam's shoulders.

"The rock is still crumbling in places, running with trails of sand." Adam straightened. "There's no way this is some ancient crack that has been hidden by a bridge of coral. This is a *new* fissure."

Datuk nodded. "Definitely opened with the last quake."

Phoebe frowned at the view. "But why? And why right here?" She glanced over her shoulder. "It can't be pure coincidence that it swallowed that leaking sub."

Datuk speculated, shrugging as if trying to discount his own words. "Maybe the clustering of quakes over the past two weeks was some attempt to get rid of the sub, an effort to drive it off. Then with that last spike in radiation, it'd finally had enough and decided to deal with it directly."

"If you're right," Adam challenged him, "what could do that?"

"No idea." He motioned to his sensors. "But I still find it odd how *clean* this water is after we passed through the brine layer. I'm not picking up any microplastics. The dissolved oxygen levels are through the roof. The salinity is way low. There's a purity that makes no sense unless something is actively making it so."

Phoebe remembered pondering this mystery on their last dive, when she compared these vast coral fields to the Brazilian rainforest, one of the lungs on the planet's surface. Was this forest the equivalent down here? Was it somehow keeping these seas pure, actively fighting to make it so? Did this support Datuk's conjecture about something trying to physically rid the trench of the leaking, toxic boat?

Bryan interrupted this reverie. "We're about to break a record."

Phoebe turned to him. "What do you mean?"

He nodded to the depth gauge on the screen that monitored their descent. The tiny, winged blip of the *Cormorant* on the bathymetric screen continued to fall along a gradient marked along one side.

"We're approaching eleven thousand meters," he said. "Victor Vescovo holds the world's record for the deepest dive. Just more than ten thousand, nine hundred meters. In a Triton-designed submersible like ours."

They all gathered closer and watched the *Cormorant* fall past that record.

Tired smiles spread amongst them.

"We should've brought champagne," Bryan mumbled.

Adam sighed. "Let's hope we get a chance to tell the Guinness people."

Datuk asked an important question: "How deep can the *Cormorant* go?"

"She's been overengineered," Bryan said. "Like most submersibles. She was designed to withstand pressures deeper than any known trench."

"Which means what?" Adam asked. "What is her crush depth?"

"Fourteen thousand meters." Bryan turned to them. "But that was based on lab tests, not a real-world challenge."

Adam stared down. "Looks like we're about to test that."

Silence again settled over their group as they continued their plummet into a bottomless darkness.

12:07 P.M.

Daiyu climbed into the seat of the *Qianliyan*. The deep-sea bathyscaphe was named after a Chinese demon, whose name meant *far-seeing eye*. According to legend, he challenged Mazu, the goddess of the sea, but she tamed him and he became her guardian, protecting the depths of the seas.

It seemed a fitting name, especially as she had chosen it when she and her team of engineers at the Guangdong Southern Marine Science and Engineering Laboratory had built its prototype. The PLA Navy had taken her early design and built this vehicle for their amphibious attack boat. She had inspected the *Qianliyan* while en route here and took great satisfaction in what she found, noting the PLA had adhered to her every engineering spec, down to the titanium and acrylic passenger compartment, which had been machined to within 99.978 percent of a true spherical form.

But best of all . . .

They kept my name for the vessel.

She took it as a testament to her achievement. The two-person sphere was surrounded by a matte-black outer shell shaped like an elongated teardrop with a glass scallop protruding out its front.

The *Qianliyan* had been primarily engineered as a surveillance-and-reconnaissance vessel. But it could also serve a role in anti-submarine warfare. To that end, four *Dú-yá* torpedoes were being loaded under it. The weapons' name meant *venomous fangs*, which they definitely were. Their sleek shapes and piston-driven engines, fueled by a solid-fuel rocket propellant, were built to withstand extreme pressures. The weapons were slow at maximum depth, but they were deadly and dogged in their pursuit once a target was locked.

A grunt overhead announced the arrival of her co-pilot, Lieutenant Yang Háo. He dropped through the exit trunk and down into the sphere. He secured the hatch behind him and squeezed his large bulk into the neighboring seat. His torn knuckles had been treated and stained with an iodine solution. As her second-in-command, he had proven his skill aboard the yacht, and he would do so again below the seas.

Together, they silently performed a system check.

Once done, he turned to her. "Captain Tse, I'm trained in operating the *Qianliyan*. I would be proud to pilot her myself. There is no need for you to travel down into the trench."

She scowled back at him.

There were *plenty* of reasons.

First and foremost, this vehicle was her design. She would allow no one else to pilot it on its first true mission. She had spent most of her career—except for a brief stint as a navigator aboard an aircraft carrier—in research and development. She knew intellectual prowess alone would not gain her the rank of admiral. She needed to hone her combat credentials, to whet her sword with the blood of China's enemies.

Plus, her goal in these seas was to show proof-of-concept for all her autonomous designs. By leaving control of the surface to the militarized clone of her AI-driven ship, it showed her level of confidence in her work. If the systems required supervision and babysitting, what would be the point of her design?

Diving in the *Qianliyan* further emphasized her self-assurance. It demonstrated that she was willing to put her life behind her research.

Still, there remained a final reason.

Before leaving Cambodia, she had been given orders to destroy the wreckage of the *Changzheng 24*. They dared not leave anything behind for a foreign power to salvage and gain knowledge of their naval advancements.

But more importantly, Choi Aigua had wanted to repeat his prior experiment. Upon Tse's word, he would send another ELF pulse to this trench—as proof-of-concept for his own endeavor. It could be the first step in the advent of a new weapons system, one that could shake the foundations of the world.

To that end, someone needed to observe the effect down there—and survive it.

The *Qianliyan* was both smaller and more heavily shielded than the submarine that sank. It was a fortress built to withstand extreme pressures. Even its electronics were locked in a Faraday cage to protect against any EM blast. She felt confident the *Qianliyan* could be safely present to witness Aigua's repeat firing of the ELF signal.

Her act in doing so, especially if such a formidable weapon could be secured, would assure her position as a future admiral of the Chinese fleet.

But before all that, she had another objective to address first: to destroy the other deep-sea submersible. It was unarmed and unaware. The *Qianliyan* was far heavier, especially with its load of torpedoes. It would make the descent in half the time. She planned to quickly dive into the trench, hunt the other submersible down, and destroy it, adding more blood to her sword.

Satisfied with her plan, she radioed for the *Qianliyan* to be lowered into the sea. She then turned her hard gaze upon Lieutenant Yang and finally answered his question.

"This is *my* mission," she declared emphatically. "I will allow no one to cast a shadow over my glory."

33

Four hours after leaving the Jakarta History Museum, Gray stood at the bow of a fast-interceptor boat as it raced away from the Bali coastline. Seichan kept next to him. For the moment, they had this spot to themselves.

"I don't trust any of them," she said, glowering past her shoulder to the pilothouse.

"We don't have much choice in the matter."

A loud boom emphasized this.

Behind them, a peak atop the island of Bali—Mount Batar—fountained fire into the sky. Ahead, the dark seas rolled under black clouds, chained through with lightning. Their boat skimmed at sixty miles an hour across waters choked with ash. Floating rocks of pumice rattled off the fiberglass hull. The breeze smelled of sulfur from the eruptions and woodsmoke from the burning forests.

Earlier, with time running out, their group had to risk flying through the ash-choked skies. Their small transport—a Chinese Harbin Y-12 turboprop—was the same aircraft that Major Xue's forces had flown aboard to reach Jakarta. The plane had taken off from a deserted airstrip and hopped over to the city of Denpasar in neighboring Bali.

While flying here, they had all borne silent witness to the destruction below them. Mountain after mountain had gushed with smoke, adding weight to the skies. Around them, huge bombs burst from flaming calderas. Rivers of lava circumscribed the landscape. Where those fiery streams flowed into the sea, the water boiled up into wide chimneys of steam. The flight had been turbulent. The aircraft's twin props hummed raggedly through the falling ash. By the time they reached Bali, the engines had started faltering. Their descent to the dark airport had been more of a freefall than a controlled approach.

The island city had fared worse. It lay in flames, bombarded by fiery rocks from the eruption of Mount Batar. The forests along the peak's flanks had been set afire by pyroclastic flows. The only saving grace was that the city's bay was well protected and had been sheltered from the worst of the tsunamis. Once there, bribes and threats had gained them possession of the marine interceptor. The boat was a patrol craft used to fight pirates and intercede in drug smuggling. It was now their means of transportation to the seas mentioned in Stoepker's account, where the *Tenebrae* had sunk two centuries before.

Still, by the time they boarded the boat, they had all recognized the importance—and likely futility—of their efforts. But there was nothing else to do but try.

Gray checked his watch. It would still take them another forty minutes to reach those waters. "Let's head below," he said. "There are some final details I'd like to settle."

Seichan stopped him with a hand on his arm. He turned and saw the worry in her eyes. He pulled her closer. He tried to squeeze with as much reassurance as he could. She seldom showed any hesitation or apprehension. Those stoic walls rarely lowered. It was an aloofness born of necessity, instilled into her after decades of hardship and brutality.

"We'll get back home," he promised her. "We still have Jack's true birthday to celebrate."

He felt her smile more than saw it. She relaxed just a fraction. "That's today," she mumbled. "I had nearly forgotten."

"Actually, since we're on this side of the international date line—"

"Shut up," she told his chest. "Just hold me."

He obeyed her.

"And make sure Kowalski doesn't bring another grenade," she mumbled.

He sighed. "I wish I could."

He held her until the muscles of her back and shoulders hardened. Her legs pushed straighter, girding herself for the dangers ahead. He held her a moment longer—not because she needed it, because he did.

He finally let go, and they headed back across the bow. Still, he kept a grip on her hand, but as they passed the wheelhouse, they were slowly drawn apart by the forces ahead of them.

The stern deck and wheelhouse were crowded with twenty men. Half the group were from Gray's contingent. The remaining forces were those of Xue and Wen. The small Harbin transport plane could hold no more. Both sides had to leave some of their men behind. At Gray's request, those left back at Jakarta would continue to protect the museum.

It was the only way he could thank its director, Kadir Numberi, for agreeing to accompany them on this dangerous outing. Much of the story they were following was tied to the secret history of the Aboriginal people, and Gray had wanted the director's continuing expertise. He still had many questions and hoped for some answers before they reached the waters where the *Tenebrae* sank.

To that end, Gray waved to Xue and Heng as he entered the wheelhouse. "Could you bring Stamford's steel box down to the galley? I've had some further thoughts that I'd like to discuss with Dr. Numberi."

"Certainly," Xue said.

The pair followed him to the steps leading below deck.

At the helm, Captain Wen stood next to the boat's pilot. He glanced back, but he made no effort to accompany them. He'd clearly had enough of their historical discussions.

Gray remembered Seichan's warning about not trusting anyone.

That certainly applies to Wen.

Seichan stayed in the wheelhouse, stepping over to Yeung, who carried weapons over both shoulders. She intended to keep close watch on the others.

With his back guarded, Gray descended into the galley. Guan-yin and Zhuang sat at a small table. Across from them, Kadir was reading through Stamford's account with a furrowed brow.

Gray crossed to the table. "Dr. Numberi, I was wondering if I could pick your brain about your great-grandfather's people."

Kadir pushed the pages aside. "Of course."

"We're placing all our hopes on this lost Aboriginal history. But there's one aspect I was hoping you could shed further light on."

Kadir shifted to face him. "Concerning what?"

Gray remembered back at the museum how Kadir had responded strangely to a part of their discussion. He had looked as if he had wanted to say something but had been reluctant to speak.

Gray raised that topic again. "In Stamford's records, he mentions a span of time that he called the Dark Dreaming. It seemed important, but he never elaborated further. Do you know anything about it?"

"Maybe." Kadir sat straighter. "The Aboriginal concept of *Dreamtime* or simply the *Dreaming* is difficult to put into words. It encompasses their origin stories, a time of gods and heroes, but it also includes the past and present. It's a merging of time into one single continuum. Sometimes referred to as *Everywhen*. Truthfully, I was surprised to see it mentioned in Sir Raffles's account."

"Why is that?" Gray asked.

"During Stamford's lifetime, the terms *Dreaming* or *Dreamtime* were never mentioned. They only appeared in more common usage decades after his death. So his mention of the *Dreaming* is odd. As is his use of the word *dark* to describe it."

"What do you think Raffles was referring to?"

"I can only guess, but it must tie to the earliest history of the First Nations peoples." Kadir looked contemplative for a moment before continuing. "The typical date that most archaeologists assign to the populating of Australia is around sixty thousand years ago. That's been accepted for some time. But as further studies have been done—something that's been sorely neglected until very recently—anomalies surrounding that date have come to light. The examination of an Aboriginal fishing site in Warrnambool, Victoria, was recently dated to 120,000 years ago. Another ten locations have similarly shown to be far older than the accepted 60,000 years. Some critics have questioned those numbers, but the initial research was done by respected academics."

Xue frowned. "Regardless, what does the *date* have to do with a time called the Dark Dreaming?"

Kadir turned to him. "Many of the earliest stories of Dreamtime are apocalyptic. They speak of a giant wave sweeping far inland and killing almost everyone. And of fiery gods warring in the earth and bursting forth or raining down fire, killing thousands."

"That does sound *dark*," Xue admitted.

"And very much like *now*," Gray added.

Kadir nodded. "Which made me wonder. There was a volcanic event a thousandfold worse than when Tambora exploded. It happened 74,000 years ago. With eruption of the supervolcano Toba in northern Sumatra. It laid waste to hundreds of miles in all directions, and its volcanic winter lasted decades, driving humanity to a scant few in number."

Gray began to understand. "You think Stamford's Dark Dreaming is an account of that time, buried in legends and myths."

"If that eruption was witnessed by the Aborigine people living here at the time, then the apocalyptic description makes sense. The fires, the tidal waves, all of it. I've wondered for a while if that event might have been what finally drove the Aboriginal people to the Australian continent."

"If so," Xue said, "it would support that they've lived in this region for a far longer time. Maybe it was such a prolonged history that eventually led them to understand the source of the volcanism in this region—or at least some part of it."

Xue stared over at the box in Heng's hands, likely picturing the bullroarer inside it and the promise it held.

Gray kept his focus on Kadir. The man's lips had firmed into harder lines, his eyes had turned downcast, as if he was afraid of broaching something.

"What is it?" Gray pressed him. "What are you holding back?"

"It may be nothing," he said, but the shine in his eyes suggested otherwise. "I read a paper a few years back. It challenged the accepted Out-of-Africa model for the origin of humanity. One of the foundational papers supporting that claim was written by two biologists—Wilson and Cann—back in 1987. They tested and studied mitochondrial DNA and were able to trace our human origins to a single female."

"Mitochondrial Eve," Heng said with a nod. "I remember that from my premed biology courses."

"A woman whom the biologists stated probably came from Africa."

"That's what I was taught," Heng confirmed.

"But that's not where the story ends." Kadir glanced around at those gathered in the galley. "Years later, both Wilson and Cann *refuted* their arguments. This happened after they came to Australia and studied the mitochondrial DNA from hundreds of First Nations people. The results astounded them, so much so that they recanted the central tenet of their prior paper. They concluded emphatically that *Homo sapiens* originated in *Australia*, not Africa. To paraphrase Cann's admission, *mitochondrial DNA puts the origin of humankind much further back and indicates that the Australian Aborigines arose 400,000 years ago.*"

Kadir let that sink in.

"Why have we not heard any of this?" Heng finally asked.

Kadir shrugged. "Since then—and all the way to today—there's been evidence of genetic anomalies and archaeological dating that makes no sense. It all further refutes the accepted story of our origin. Even that first paper by Wilson and Cann clearly states that Africa was *probably* the origin of Mitochondrial Eve. It was never a *certainty*. But once that theory was set in stone, it has become unmovable. Even when those same biologists later refuted it, they were ignored."

"If those scientists were right," Gray said, "then maybe we should consider the myths of the Rainbow Serpent in a new light, especially as their god is intimately tied to their origin stories."

Kadir nodded. "We should. While reading through these old papers, I've noted many similarities between events related by Sir Raffles and the myths of the Rainbow Serpent."

"How so?" Xue asked.

"According to legend, the Rainbow Serpent could appear in many forms and in many places, often at the same time."

"So it wasn't a *single* entity," Gray said, "but a *legion*. Possibly a new species."

"Yes, but despite all the variations in these stories, there is a common thread. The insistence of a *single* huge snake that slumbers deep beneath the earth and whose Dreaming shakes the world."

Gray turned to Xue. "That almost sounds like a description of the pieces of Theia buried in Earth's upper mantle."

"And when that huge snake truly rages, it brings fire and flooding." Kadir cast his gaze upward to the world burning outside. "You've already mentioned how the Rainbow Serpent—or at least, its smaller multitudes—were said to be capable of traveling from waterhole to waterhole beneath the earth, from one *thin* spot to another, bringing destruction or salvation. Digging deeper into those same stories, you can find its actions more *specifically* described."

"Like what?" Gray asked.

Kadir faced him. "When a Serpent punishes someone, it swallows them whole, digesting away their bones and regurgitating them out as stone."

Xue's brows pinched. "That sounds exactly like the petrifying toxin."

"In this process," Kadir continued, "it plants tiny seeds of itself into a body. *Little rainbows*, they're called, that can grow in that stone and be reborn anew, carrying the soul of the afflicted back to the sleeping giant under the earth, where it joins the Dreaming and lives again forever."

Gray pictured the video he had been shown from the morgue in Cambodia. Heng and Xue shared a look, likely making the same correlation. Had they all witnessed one of those rebirths? Was that what had happened to Matthew?

"But according to those same legends," Kadir said, "the Serpent can also stop this process if caught in time. It could burn away the poison and make one whole again."

"Like what caused those welts on Stoepker," Heng said, looking around the group.

Kadir sighed. "Clearly, the early Aboriginal people—whether they traced back to the Toba eruption or to the dawn of humankind—they experienced something that they could only describe in mythological terms, an ongoing understanding between two species, maybe one that traced back to a distant common origin."

Gray searched the faces around him. He had a thousand more questions, but a shout in Mandarin rose from the wheelhouse above.

Xue straightened, listened, then shared the news. "We're nearing the waters where the *Tenebrae* sank."

Gray looked up. "Then let's go see if the past can save the present."

9:48 A.M.

As the boat slowed to a trolling pace, Seichan gripped the butt of her holstered Glock. She kept vigil at the stern and appreciated the pistol's cold steel as she faced the fiery destruction.

Off to the east, the horizon had been set ablaze, but above it all towered a black peak. Its flanks streamed with rivers of lava. Its caldera gushed with arcs and sprays of molten fire. Those flames lit a black column of smoke. Lightning flashed in a continual corona of energy throughout that ominous cloud.

She knew that monster's name.

Mount Tambora.

Seichan breathed through the damp cloth over her mouth and lips. Still, she tasted and smelled the fiery brimstone. Her eyes watered from the falling ash. But she had no reason to complain.

Closer at hand, their boat crept along the coast of West Nusa Tenggara, passing the outlying islands of Panjang and Saringi. Small villages burned along the shoreline. Out on the water, fishing boats had become floating torches, both near the coasts and out to sea.

There had been no escape for the villagers.

She spotted no movement along the shores, no shifting shadows limned against the flames. All lay quiet and dead. They were the only ones still moving, a lone sentinel in the dark.

Is this what the entire region will soon look like?

She cast her gaze farther out.

What of the rest of the world?

Hopelessness weighted her shoulders, dragging her eyes down, too. This close to Tambora, the sea was covered in great rafts of floating pumice. Some rocks were still red and smoldering. They scraped the hull and scratched in a continual chorus.

The rest of the sea was blanketed by ash. She tried to pierce that veil to the waters under it. As she did, something small poked into view, pushing through the powder from below. They looked like a handful of black sticks. They cut through the ash, rolling and spinning, revealing themselves to be balls of coral, the same as Crawfurd had sketched.

Brought to her attention now, she spotted dozens of others, all across the sea, cutting briefly into view, then away again. One rattled out of the water, riding atop a pumice raft, trying to beach itself, then tumbled off.

Seichan returned her attention to the burning skiffs and fishing boats. They were all wooden. Such vessels had no chance of crossing this fiery minefield. She imagined the bodies hidden under the ash or sunk into the depths. An ominous sense of foreboding settled over her.

We shouldn't be here.

A commotion drew her attention from the watery graveyard. Gray led a party from the wheelhouse to the stern deck. He waved to clear a space.

"We need a good ten feet," Gray called out.

Seichan stayed at the stern as others pressed toward her. Her mother spotted her and elbowed over to her side. Zhuang followed. A majority of triad members kept close around them. The Falcon commandos remained on the other side, framing the doorway into the wheelhouse where Captain Wen watched with darkened brows.

He clearly had little faith in this endeavor. She had caught him grousing earlier to his teammates, forgetting that she was fluent in Mandarin. Or maybe he hadn't cared who heard him.

In truth, she shared his pessimism.

"We had better pray this works," Guan-yin murmured through the fold of cloth over her face.

"It won't," Seichan said. "We're chasing ghosts out here."

She pictured the sunken wreckage of the *Tenebrae* somewhere below them.

Xue and Heng came forward with the steel box and opened it.

"We should have Kadir wield the bullroarer," Gray said. "He's the most familiar with the tool."

Xue nodded and offered the open box to the museum director.

Kadir hesitated—then Tambora boomed with a thunderous blast and a great gout of fire. The director plucked out the bullroarer and unwound its tether.

He stepped to the center of the deck. "Even if Stamford and Craw-furd were correct in their judgment, we can't know if a certain pitch or tone needs to be achieved with the bullroarer. Or maybe a code has to be generated by a pattern of cadence."

Gray tried to reassure him. "If there was, we have to trust that Stam-ford would've hinted at it in his papers."

Xue agreed with a nod. "I noted that there were small holes drilled through the wooden paddle—as if the sacred totem that Crawfurd stole had been specially *tuned* for this role. I wager the noise we want to achieve will be created when the bullroarer reaches its maximum speed and volume."

"I'll do my best," Kadir promised.

By now, he had fully untied the bullroarer. He held the rope's looped handle and let the paddle hang at his ankles. Everyone pushed a step farther back. Kadir took a deep breath. Xue lifted his phone and re-corded the action as the director began a slow spin over his head.

A low hum rose from the twirling blade.

"Faster," Gray urged him.

Kadir needed no such direction. He clearly had some skill, manipu-lating his wrist and arm to keep the plane of the paddle's flight at a perfect angle. The blade grew into a blur. Its noise climbed in volume to that of a giant beehive.

Still, Kadir increased his pace.

Everyone looked on with expectation. Even Seichan's heart beat harder, as if trying to match that tempo.

Then the bullroarer's old cord snapped.

The paddle spun high over the deck.

They all watched their hopes fly with it.

Yeung leaped up with a raised arm. He caught the paddle in mid-air, demonstrating his swift reflexes. Seichan wasn't sure she could've caught it so deftly.

Yeung landed and lowered his arm. He crossed into the open and held out the wooden piece, offering the prize to Kadir.

"Thank you," the director said. "I should've thought to replace the old cord." He turned to Xue. "I can make a new one. But it must be the proper length."

This was quickly accomplished. A fishing line was found and threaded through the drilled hole in the paddle. The length was mea-sured, and a looped handle crafted at one end.

They tried it again. In moments, Kadir had the bullroarer spinning. He flailed his arm, expertly guiding the blade's flight with his wrist. The tool soon proved its name as the timbre of the paddle rose into a deafening roar.

The noise cut through Seichan's ears with its sharper undernotes, while its bass tones could be felt in her chest. It did sound like an angry chainsaw—but was it loud enough?

Kadir panted, and his brow ran with sweat.

Gazes shifted from the man's efforts to the surrounding seas. But there seemed to be no reaction out there. To the east, the fiery monster continued to blaze. Distant booms echoed out of the gloom from other eruptions. A small quake trembled the waters.

"Nothing's happening," Guan-yin moaned.

Seichan was disappointed but not surprised.

She stared down as one of those spiky balls rose into view next to the hull. It battered its branches against the boat's side, but the fiberglass resisted its fiery touch. A few spikes broke off. They looked nearly a match to the coral branch resting inside the museum box.

Stirred by the flailing ball, the powdery waters opened enough to offer peeks into the sea's depths. A swirl of lights writhed down there, shimmering in electric blues and fiery crimsons.

She squinted at it—then a sharp splintering snap made her jump. She twisted around as the roaring had cut off at the same time.

Kadir cried out. Pieces of wood scattered into the crowd. The largest flew high, passing over their heads and out to sea. It struck one of the pumice rafts, then skidded across the surrounding ash before coming to a stop.

As they all watched, one of the spiky mines rolled up, brushed against it, and spun back underwater. At its touch, the shard of wood kindled with a puff of smoke, then a moment later, it ignited into flames.

Kadir sank to his knees. "The paddle must have been too dry or had a hidden crack in it."

Heng tried to console him, but his words were not reassuring. "It wasn't working anyway."

Seichan glanced back to the stirring ash, remembering the glimpse of lights. She turned around to say something, to offer a bit of hope—a role that fit her awkwardly.

A shout silenced her.

Captain Wen yelled in Mandarin. "Enough of this bullshit. Kill them all!"

Gunfire erupted.

Seichan ducked low, yanking out her Glock.

Zhuang threw himself in front of Guan-yin. A round clipped his shoulder, spraying blood. The impact jarred him backward—into Seichan's mother.

Guan-yin tumbled over the rail and crashed into the sea.

34

With his wrists cuffed behind him, Monk marched down the long hall that crossed through the bowels of the *Titan X.* Two commandos flanked him, both with QSZ-92 pistols in hand and rifles slung over their shoulders. They wore full battle gear, including helmets.

He knew the ominous reason he had been hauled out of the yacht's small brig. An hour ago, he had heard the arrival of the massive ship— the helicopter landing dock. The LHD's lumbering engines had reverberated through the hull of the *Titan X.* One of his captors had been fluent enough in English to explain why Monk was being moved.

Once Captain Tse returned from her dive, the Chinese forces were going to blow up the yacht and sink it with all aboard. But Monk—as a member of DARPA—would be transferred to the landing dock, destined for some Chinese black site.

Still, he was not about to resist.

I've waited two long hours for this opportunity.

With his arms behind him, he unlatched his prosthetic hand from its magnetic attachments to his wrist. Like everyone else, his guards had failed to recognize the lab-grown skin over a titanium skeleton as anything but a normal hand.

The cuffs fell away from his left wrist. He coughed to cover the slight jangle of the steel chains. With his prosthesis gripped in his real hand, he willed its mechanical fingers to flex. Even with the hand detached, a wireless cortical implant allowed him to communicate with and manipulate the prosthesis.

Satisfied all was operational, Monk moved swiftly. He whipped to the guard on his left and jammed the prosthetic hand at the man's neck. The fingers clamped to his throat, strong enough to crush bone. The strangling throttled away any scream.

The sudden attack, especially from a bound prisoner, caught his other captor by surprise. Monk grabbed the first man's pistol, shoved it under the second guard's chin as he turned, and fired a muffled blast. His helmet kept the gore from splattering the wall.

Both men slumped to the floor at the same time.

Monk pushed the pistol into his belt, retrieved his hand, and snapped it into place. He then hauled both men into a side cabin. Once there, he stripped the strangled soldier of his battle armor and helmet and quickly donned the gear. If he kept his face down, he hoped the black-and-blue camo would hide him.

Out in the hall, he faced the aft end, picturing the giant glass sphere of Science City. All the prisoners were under guard there.

With a shake of his head, Monk turned and headed the opposite way, while making a silent promise.

I'll do what I can.

Still, he knew there were others whom he could not help at all.

1:52 P.M.

How could this be?

Phoebe gazed in awe out her window.

Throughout the last hundred meters of the *Cormorant*'s freefall, she had held her breath. Ninety minutes after entering the fissure, they neared its bottom. The sonar had warned them what to expect, but the sight still drew gasps from them all.

The walls of the crack fell away to either side, revealing a hollow, cavernous void. It opened under and around them. It was as if they had dropped into outer space. Dazzling lights blinked and flashed all around. They formed shining constellations that defied the eye.

"Can you slow us to a hover?" Phoebe asked Bryan.

"Gladly. Dropping ballast now."

Phoebe had incrementally lowered their rate of descent once the end of the fissure had come into view on their sonar. She had good reason to be cautious. They all did.

Datuk reported behind her. "The sensors are picking up more than four hundred rem out there. Enough to trigger acute death if it climbs much higher."

"What about inside here?" Adam asked.

"We're just shy of a hundred. Not immediately fatal. But in a few hours, we'll start experiencing mild radiation sickness. Fatigue, vomiting." He shook his head. "Let's not stay down here for that long."

Bryan had his own concern. "We just crossed thirteen thousand meters. We don't dare go much deeper."

Phoebe understood. The crush depth of the *Cormorant* was only another thousand meters down. She leaned forward as they came to a hover. Amazement kept her fears at bay. The cavern, while vast, was not empty.

"How could all this coral still be growing down here?"

She gaped at the sheer expanse, trying to comprehend it, to take it all in. According to the sonar, the cavern stretched miles in all directions. The coral hidden here had to be ancient, far older than the forest above. The trees rose from the bottomless depths to the arch of roof overhead, as if holding everything up.

But that was no longer true.

The earlier quake had not only split the rock overhead, but it shattered this section of forest. The tumbling crash of the submarine had further damaged the area, ripping through as it all fell. The leaking radiation had done even greater harm, burning a far larger swath.

The nearest stretches of forest were shadowed and dark. Beyond the dead zone, seen in glimpses between the giant boles, distant regions still glowed and shimmered.

Phoebe longed to pass through this blight to what beckoned so brightly.

Datuk had his own opinion. "The growth down here looks less like a forest and more like *roots*."

She appreciated this sentiment. Unlike the straight trunks of the coral field above, the boles down here rose in twisted columns, forking out into curling branches, casting out questing rootlets.

She studied the forest in this new light.

Could Datuk be right? Was this vastness the wellspring of the forest above? Or was it simply another coral field, one trapped by the confines of the cavern to form such a twisted landscape?

Adam reminded them of a more immediate concern. "Where is the Chinese submarine?" He leaned forward. "Phoebe, have you been able to detect the bottom of this cavern?"

Focused elsewhere, Phoebe had momentarily ignored the sonar. "I'll try pinging again."

She reached to her controls and directed a sonic wave toward the bottom. As it returned, the screen showed glimpses of the surrounding walls, which were indeed miles away. But the view was patchy. Some areas were blocked by the heavy coral, others showed up as endless black spots. Directly under the *Cormorant*, the sonar continued to show a black eye, a bottomless well of darkness.

"Wait." She squinted at the screen. "I'm picking up some haloing far below us. Only a few small spots. As if the sonar is registering *something*. Maybe peeks at the true bottom."

"How deep?" Adam asked.

Phoebe sat back with a grimace. "Sixteen thousand meters."

"That's at a total depth of ten miles," Bryan said. "We'll never reach there."

Adam scowled. "If the submarine fell that far, we might as well give up."

Phoebe refused to accept this. "We could drop to fourteen thousand meters." She turned to Bryan. "The *Cormorant* could handle that, right?"

"Theoretically," the pilot warned.

"Once at that depth, we could use our cameras and zoom in. Search what's down below. Like we did before. Whatever's there might explain what's causing the Tonga's swarm of quakes."

Datuk nodded, while working diligently at his station. "We've come this far."

From Adam's deep frown, it looked like he wanted to argue, but he stayed silent.

Satisfied, Phoebe turned around—then flinched back in her seat, startled by movement right outside the glass. She calmed herself once she recognized it was the *Cormorant*'s hydraulic arm. It extended out into the water.

Datuk must have taken control of it from his seat.

"What are you doing?" she asked.

The arm swung farther out. Its claws snagged something and drew it closer. It looked like a limp snake, but she recognized its smooth glistening surface. It was one of the glowing tentacles that they had spotted earlier. Only now, ripped away from its body, it had dimmed to this lifeless gray husk.

"I was hoping to test it," Datuk explained. "To try to understand how such a species could survive at these depths, under such pressure."

Phoebe had forgotten about the biochemist's interest in piezophiles and their relationship to exotic biosignatures of alien life. She watched him draw the sample closer. This lifeform could certainly be considered *alien*, if not in the exact context of Datuk's research.

"What are you testing for?" Adam asked, his voice still tinged with suspicion.

"Before all this started, I had the *Cormorant* equipped with a MinIon sequencer. It's a new tool for genetic analysis. It requires no amplification to detect DNA or RNA. It's sensitive enough to discern between standard and modified bases, even differentiate polypeptides from other polymers."

"Which means what?" Adam asked.

Datuk shrugged. "The nanopore sequencer was designed to search for the rudimentary signs of biological life. Besides using it for my own genetic studies, I've been commissioned to test it in real-world challenges. Like under extreme pressures. And now, unfortunately, under heavy radiation. It's all to see how the MinIon might fare as an investigative tool aboard future exploratory spacecraft."

"To help search for biosignatures," Phoebe said.

"Exactly."

Adam frowned and returned to the original topic. "While you do that, we'll proceed with Phoebe's suggestion. Try to get our eyes on the submarine through the cameras." He gave them all a stern look. "But we drop *slowly*. If Bryan believes there's any danger, we go straight up."

Bryan grunted his acknowledgment. "Trust me, mate. I won't be asking for permission."

With the matter settled, Phoebe shifted her attention fully forward. As they started to descend again, she cast another ping. The *Cormorant* followed that pulse down. On her screen, the new depth sounding appeared.

The haloes were still down there—but they had shifted positions.

She squinted at the oddity. The change was surely due to sonar ghosting. But a more troublesome worry popped into her head, especially considering the enormity of those haloes.

Is something moving down there?

35

At the bow end of the *Titan X*, Monk climbed over a huge red anchor. It rose twice his height and filled the small hold on the starboard flank of the massive yacht. A huge chain was spooled behind it.

He crossed to the open hatch of the anchor bay and leaned out, hoping no one noted when the door had swung open. No doubt somewhere on the bridge a warning light was likely blinking. Hopefully if any of the crew noted it, they would remain silent.

At least for a few more minutes.

Before opening the bay, he had stripped down and donned a set of scuba gear: an air tank and buoyancy vest, along with a mask and fins. He had been prepared to make the swim without them, but he had found the equipment stored in a neighboring locker. It was likely kept there in case someone needed to dive down and troubleshoot an anchoring problem.

It was a small bit of good fortune.

And I'll need every bit of it.

From the open hatch, Monk stared out at the dark water, illuminated by the muted lights of the yacht. Waves washed a few yards below, covered in a thin layer of ash. He hoped it was enough to hide his passage. He eyed his target. The amphibious LCAC floated three hundred yards away, resting atop its huge pontoons. Its water jets idled to hold its position.

Past it, the Kermadec Islands blazed with distant fires.

With a deep scowl, he searched for the Chinese submarine. The attack boat could have submerged after their helicopter landing dock had arrived in these waters. Or it could be cruising on the far side of the yacht.

He leaned out and peered past the ship's stern.

A large city glowed a quarter mile away. The helicopter dock—which he had learned was named the *Dayangxi*—was a formidable sight. It stretched half the length of an aircraft carrier. Since arriving, it had hung back. Like its hunter-killer counterpart, it seemed to be only serving a support role, a backup for the autonomous net that had snared the *Titan X*.

As Monk studied the threat, a bolt of lightning cut across the skies, bright enough to drive him back into hiding. He waited for the flash to pass, for the world to fall darker, especially to any eyes peering his way.

Now or never.

He crossed to the hatch, sat down at its edge, and dropped smoothly into the water, trying to minimize any splash. He fell beneath the waves into a black abyss. He quickly adjusted his buoyancy vest and stopped his descent at three meters. He dared go no lower—and for very good reason.

I'm not alone down here.

In the darkness, the ocean hummed with the deep-throated burble of the idling LCAC. Sharper pings and eerie caterwauls reminded him of the UUVs and AUVs that also plied these waters.

As Monk set off, he hoped he would register on any sensors as normal sea life, just a wandering dolphin. Though, if that were the case, maybe scuba gear wasn't the wisest choice for this mission. The hunters could be drawn by the metal of his air tank. Still, even if he had swum naked, he would've had to haul steel with him. He wasn't about to raid the other ship unarmed.

He had a QBS pistol secured in a waterproof pocket of his vest and an assault rifle hanging from his chest.

With no other choice, he continued a slow swim, using the sound of the LCAC's engines to guide him toward his target. He tried not to stir or thrash too much. He also prayed that the frequent volcanic booms, the electrical discharges in the sky, and the persistent electromagnetic surges would cover his passage.

It proved to no avail.

He had barely crossed a hundred yards when a sharp ping struck him from below. It was loud enough to stab his ears and pound his chest. Something had detected him. He pictured a lurker in the depths under him.

One of the steel sharks had found him.

2:27 P.M.

Daiyu tried to comprehend what lay around the *Qianliyan*. The bathyscaphe slowly dropped through a dead forest of coral. The towering field was a shattered ruin of branches and broken trunks, as if stamped through by a giant.

Through the darkness, she could make out glimmers of a shining forest off in the distance. Earlier, as the *Qianliyan* had descended toward the bottom, she had observed the breadth of the coral field. Beyond an irradiated zone, its shimmering brilliance had been breathtaking. It had rippled with iridescent cobalts, flaming crimsons, glowing jades.

As she had stared, she had flashed to her childhood in the city of Mohe, at the northernmost tip of the province of Heilongjiang. On rare occasions, her father would take her to the rooftop of their apartment, away from the squalor and bluster below. Those winter nights had been frigid, with snow underfoot and icicles hanging like glistening daggers. In the skies, the aurora borealis had swirled in great waves of shimmering emerald fire and shining eddies of glowing blues.

At those moments, her father would take her hand and whisper to her, using her pet name—*Xiǎo Hǔ*. He seldom called her his *little tiger* anymore, but he always did then. He declared the skies were on fire for her and had promised that they heralded a great destiny.

Daiyu squeezed her hands together now. Though far from superstitious, she took the sight of the glowing corals to be further evidence of that future destiny. It was as if the aurora borealis had descended here to remind her of her father's promise.

Lieutenant Yang had a more prosaic take on it all, showing little inter-est beyond his personal stake. "The radiation levels are steadily climbing."

Daiyu dismissed his fear. "We're adequately insulated. And those we hunt are three thousand meters deeper. Yet, we're still picking up their sonar pings. They clearly have not succumbed."

She had ordered Yang to keep their descent silent. They had already closed the distance significantly due to their swifter plummet in the heavier vehicle. The others—believing they were alone—made no ef-fort to hide themselves. In addition, the *Qianliyan*'s onboard systems used their target's pings to reveal the landscape below, piggybacking on their bathymetric soundings. The other submersible—which she knew was named the *Cormorant*—acted like a flashlight in the dark, leading the way.

For now.

As the *Qianliyan* continued its descent, the coral forest vanished out-side, replaced by sheer cliffs and broken rock. They had entered the fissure.

Yang turned to her. "I already have a target lock on the other vehicle. Upon your command, we can fire one of the *Dú-yá* torpedoes."

He was plainly eager to test the weapon—as was she.

But not yet.

"Patience," Daiyu warned him. "Let them face any threat first. They continue to serve us well—as canaries in this dark coal mine."

Yang acknowledged her with a grunt, but he was clearly not happy.

"There is no need for haste," Daiyu assured him and stared up. "We are plenty protected."

2:35 P.M.

Struck by another deafening ping, Monk spun in the water. Trapped in the open, he knew he could never make it back to the *Titan X*. He searched for some refuge. He knew he had moments before the hunter judged him to be a threat and attacked.

The darkness added to his terror.

Then a small glow bloomed in the blackness, a fiery red eye. At first, he thought it was some feverish delusion. Then he heard an engine. A steady thrumming through the water.

He twisted that way, fearing the worst. As it drew closer, it revealed itself to be a small sub-shaped vessel. It sped along the surface, its underside lit by a blinking red light. A long stalk protruded into the water, ending in a football-shaped shadow.

Monk kicked toward it, putting himself in its trajectory. As it sailed toward him, another loud ping hit him. He was certain—or mostly so—that it hadn't come from the vehicle sweeping toward him, but from below.

He kicked faster.

The blinking red eye sped toward him.

As the vessel swept overhead, Monk hooked his arms around its long stalk, just above the football-shaped sonar device. It was going fast enough that he almost lost his grip, but he hugged tighter. The vehicle dragged him along as it continued its pre-set course.

He stared up, wanting to pat the underside of the DriX. It was one of the two support vessels for the *Cormorant*'s dive. In all the tumult, with the seas buzzing with similar autonomous crafts, no one had bothered to recall them.

He allowed the DriX to sweep him out to sea.

As it did, another ping struck him. He hoped that the patrols in the waters had already identified the two DriX as noncombatants and had learned to ignore them.

Keep doing that.

He held his breath and counted. The prior pings had come at regular intervals as the hunter investigated the anomalous shape in the water, trying to judge whether to attack or not. It was likely programmed to be judicious with its limited onboard armaments, not to shoot haphazardly at any moving target.

Like me.

Monk waited a full minute. When no follow-up ping struck him, he finally felt safe enough to shift his position. He got his fins under him and balanced atop the sonar buoy. He leaned out and pushed his head above water.

The LCAC loomed fifty yards away. Unfortunately, DriX would not circle that far out, but its path should brush close enough. Monk waited until the vehicle swept near the boat's stern—then shoved off underwater.

Kicking hard, he swam the last twenty yards.

He safely reached the stern. Cables hung into the water, dropping down from an A-frame above. The launch-and-recovery system awaited the return of Captain Tse's submersible.

Monk ripped off his mask and grabbed hold of a cable's hook. Hauling himself up, he shed his fins, tank, and vest—but not before securing his pistol in his waistband. The boat's idling water jets helped cover any noise. Overhead, two tall fans flanked either side, but their blades were not moving.

Monk shifted the shoulder strap of his rifle higher and set about climbing the cable. Once close enough, he swung back and forth, then leaped to a perch behind one of the giant fan assemblies. He crouched there to catch his breath and peered between the blades.

The long deck spread ahead of him. He searched for any movement among the scatter of equipment and drones. A large battle tank loomed next to the pilothouse. He waited five full breaths, squinting for any shift of shadows, listening for any whispers.

The deck appeared eerily deserted.

Then movement above forced him lower.

As he watched, a VTOL drone dropped out of the skies, hovered a moment, then descended and locked itself into a charging station. It was all done without supervision. Monk waited for its lights to go dark, relieved he hadn't been inadvertently spotted.

Then again, the LCAC was not the target of the drone's surveillance.

Monk stared over at the *Titan X*. It was a dimly lit mountain covered in ash. Small shadows buzzed around it, silhouetted against the glow of Science City. He hoped that airborne force kept its attention focused on the yacht.

Knowing he dared not wait any longer, Monk stayed low and headed across the deck. He stuck to shadows, stopping often to surveil his surroundings, then continued on. He kept his rifle pressed to his shoulder, his cheek against its stock.

As he neared the pilothouse, voices carried to him. He edged to the door at the rear, staying below the sightlines of the windows. Crouched and listening, he heard three distinct voices, joking and chattering aimlessly.

Laugh it up, assholes.

One of the side windows had been cracked open. Someone blew a stream of smoke into the air. Monk caught a glimpse of the glowing end of a cigarette.

He shifted to the door and used a pinky to test the latch, ensuring it was unlocked. Everyone was far too confident in these automated systems, too secure that these seas were locked up tight.

Monk decided it was high time to correct them of that assumption.

He braced his legs, firmed his grip on his weapon, and yanked the door open. Three faces spun in his direction. The men froze in momentary surprise. Monk didn't wait for them to move; he didn't care they were empty-handed. He fired a trio of short bursts. Three bodies fell to the ground. A lone cigarette flew through the air and struck the steel floor with a scatter of red ash.

Monk stalked inside and ground it out under his bare foot.

He then climbed over the bodies and crossed to the cabin's far side. The space looked less like a pilothouse and more like a computer clean room. He ignored the helm controls and turned to a spread of monitors off to the side.

The largest screen in the center showed a 3D view of the surrounding ocean, both above and below the waves. Everything was delineated in graphic lines and polygons, forming detailed outlines. The *Titan X* glowed on the screen, perfectly rendered, as if drawn by a meticulous architect. The yacht's lines and shapes were a bright emerald against the black lines of the surrounding sea.

The shape of a helicopter dock—the *Dayangxi*—was similarly rendered by lines and triangles, only its outline was a dark blue, making it barely discernable from its surroundings.

Monk searched the monitor's field of view but failed to spot the submarine. Either the attack boat was out of range, or it was able to hide from the radar that rendered these images.

Monk returned his attention to the *Titan X*. On the screen, smaller dots circled the yacht, both above and below the ocean's surface. From each of them, small blinking lines connected them to the ship.

Monk understood what he was viewing.

It's a targeting array.

Whoever had set this up had selected the *Titan X* as the primary target. The fleets of autonomous drones were fixed to it. The system was likely in some guardian mode, keeping the yacht trapped by its sensors and threatened by its many weapons.

Monk sought some means to shut it down, but he was clearly locked out.

He grumbled his frustration.

Built into the desktop was a palm reader. It glowed a muted red. Knowing it was probably useless, he dragged each of the dead men forward and pressed their hands against the screen.

Nothing.

He was not surprised. He could guess whose handprint was needed here. He pictured the dead-eyed Captain Tse. The woman did not strike Monk as someone who liked to share. The death of Captain Stemm had made that clear enough.

Frustrated, he considered strafing the control unit with his rifle, but he feared that doing so would immediately turn those guardians into attack dogs. Such a fail-safe was surely built into the command ship. If anyone tried to blow up the LCAC, the deployed forces would mete out immediate revenge.

Instead, Monk held out one hope. It was why he had swum here. He knew pulling the plug on the system was at best a long shot. His fallback position was even more tenuous—and worse, untested.

With a big inhale, he reached and placed his prosthetic hand atop the palm reader.

As soon as he did, the radio by the helm barked out an inquiry in Mandarin. He jerked his arm away, fearing he had triggered the call. But it was only someone checking in on those left aboard the LCAC. Monk knew only a smattering of Mandarin, certainly not enough to impersonate one of the soldiers.

He ignored the call and returned his hand to the reader. As his palm touched the glowing surface, he silently activated the new electronic warfare module built into his prosthesis. The module was equipped with its own brain. Kat had joked that despite its diminutive size, it was far smarter than him—which was probably true.

The unit had not been designed by DARPA. Sigma had its own deep pockets when it came to independent resources. An old friend, Mara Silviera—a Spanish genius when it came to AI—had owed them a favor. In the past, Sigma had helped her battle an evil doppelganger of one of her creations. She, in turn, had agreed to design and program the tiny module in Monk's hand.

He activated it with a command from his cortical implant. The only sign it had responded was a slight uptick in the heat sensor in his palm. As he waited for the module's AI to address its Chinese counterpart, another inquiry rose from the radio, this time more commanding.

He stared down at his hand.

"C'mon already."

The warmth under his palm grew to a hot ember. He suddenly regretted the sensitivity of his prosthesis, especially as the ember became the searing burn of an open flame.

The screens in front of him fritzed and swam with pixelation.

Over the radio, the timbre of the caller changed from inquiry to threat.

Monk tried pressing his hand harder on the reader.

Like that's going to help.

But it did—or maybe it was just good timing.

The palm reader flashed twice, then turned an emerald green as the system was successfully unlocked. Monk gasped his relief and grabbed the mouse next to a built-in keyboard. He wasn't sure what to do. All the screens, even the keyboard, were in *hanzi* characters.

As he swiped the mouse, the cursor swept across the central screen. He tapped at the various threats swimming and flying around *Titan X*. But it was like trying to swat wasps. Still, it failed to do anything.

Frustrated, he shoved the mouse. The cursor swept out to sea, reaching the *Dayangxi*. The outline of the helicopter dock changed from indigo to yellow. The color blinked as if impatient with him.

To the side, the *Titan X*'s silhouette dimmed to a darker green.

Monk remembered what he was staring at.

A targeting array.

He kept the cursor on the *Dayangxi*. A popup menu appeared, again in an indecipherable script—but it was color coded. He scrolled down the list, highlighting each. As he did, the hue of the helicopter dock changed to match each selection. One made the *Dayangxi* blink a bright emerald. It was the same color that the *Titan X* had been.

Green must mean guardian mode.

"That won't do."

Monk scrolled to the next line item on the popup's list. The helicopter dock changed again—to a fiery crimson.

He smiled.

That has to be attack mode.

He clicked on his selection. Another box appeared, clearly asking for confirmation. He picked the green icon, which surely meant one thing.

"Yes, indeed," he said as he tapped his choice.

On the screen, the *Dayangxi* glowed a solid crimson. The *Titan X* darkened to an indigo blue. The swarm of wasps abandoned the yacht and sped toward the helicopter dock. Below the water, UUVs and AUVs lumbered in the same direction, while a dozen smaller shapes speared through the water, jetting at maximum speed.

Monk stepped away from the console and peered out the window.

The *Dayangxi* remained quiet, unsuspecting the danger coming its way. At the last moment, a siren rose from over there, echoing across the water. But it was too late. From the waves, long shapes burst out of the water. Wings snapped wide, and flames flashed from tails. The torpedoes had become airborne missiles.

Monk gaped at the sight. He had heard the Chinese had been developing torpedo-shaped drones capable of such a feat. They were dubbed *flying dragons*. The monsters slammed into the hull of the *Dayangxi*, striking nearly in unison, all along its flank. Fires exploded with thunderous detonations.

Overhead, airborne drones swept down and fired missiles with deadly precision at the deck. Helicopters and fixed-wing aircraft exploded, flying high, dumping into the water. Smaller drones sped lower through the smoke, chattering gunfire at fleeing personnel.

More flying dragons swept around and attacked the ship's far side.

The *Dayangxi* started to fight back. Railguns strafed the skies with bright lines of tracer fire. Some ripped through targets as the battle picked up steam.

But the AI warrior aboard the LCAC was prepared and compensated.

A loud blast drew Monk's attention around. From the open deck, another four drones were electromagnetically launched, heading off to replace those lost. More torpedoes tumbled down racks into the sea, ready to join the fray.

Movement closer to the *Titan X* drew his eye from the firefight. A huge sail rose out of the water a quarter mile off. It steamed toward Monk. It was the Chinese submarine. Left untargeted, it was still free to roam the waters. It must have come to investigate the attack.

Monk glanced to the targeting array. He dared not let up on his attack upon the *Dayangxi*. The huge ship remained the greater threat. Besides, Monk wasn't sure if it was even possible to select *two* targets. And even if it was, he had no clue how to do it—and no time to learn.

A watery boom reached him. From the bow of the hunter-killer, a wake of water shot toward him. Clearly, the boat's captain had recognized the source of this treachery.

Monk swung for the door. He knew such subs carried Yu-4 torpedos, which reached speeds of fifty miles an hour. He ran, calculating distance and speed.

Got less than ten seconds.

He reached the open deck and came to another conclusion.

No way I'm getting clear of this boat in time.

36

As the firefight broke out, Gray grabbed Kadir and rolled him to the side. Across the deck, Gray watched Guan-yin get knocked over the stern rail. Zhuang dove after her. Unable to reach them, Gray did what he could. He bowled Kadir to the deck and shielded him with his body.

He had his SIG Sauer in hand and fired into the kneecap of a Falcon commando. As the man screamed and toppled down, Gray shot him in the face.

Chaos reigned as the two sides fought across the deck. Gunfire sprayed. Bodies fell. Captain Wen snatched Xue, his commanding officer, and hauled him into the boat's wheelhouse. Its windows and superstructure were bulletproof.

Heng was shoved in there, too, by another soldier.

The door slammed behind them.

Hot iron ripped through Gray's thigh as a round hit him. Another whined past his ear and splintered the fiberglass behind him. He rolled and fired back, dropping another commando.

He kept low as the crossfire continued for another ten seconds. Then it was over. The survivors huddled in various wary postures. A quick scan showed five Falcons down. One still moaned, but he was no longer interested in fighting, only surviving. The rest of the Chinese were holed up inside the wheelhouse's fortress.

At the stern, Seichan crouched shoulder-to-shoulder with Yeung. They were somewhat sheltered behind a steel bench near the stern. Elsewhere, three triad members bled out on the deck.

"Get your ass over here!" Seichan hollered to him.

He pushed up with a groan, his left leg on fire. He limped and dragged Kadir with him. The director looked shell-shocked and dazed. One of his ears was torn and bleeding.

Then sharp *pops* of a pistol sounded behind him.

Another round grazed his shoulder, shoving him a step forward. Kadir cried out and fell to a knee.

Ahead, Seichan dove low, sliding on her shoulder. She fired back at a commando sniping through a wheelhouse window. A muffled scream followed.

Another Falcon down.

Gray carried Kadir under an arm and got him behind the steel bench.

Yeung briefly strafed the wheelhouse for good measure, then dropped next to Gray. The deputy let his rifle hang and swung up a grenade launcher that was slung over his other shoulder. He was a veritable Swiss Army knife. The man lifted the weapon with an inquiring look.

"Not yet," Gray gasped out.

He wasn't sure if the grenade would do any damage to the wheelhouse. The blowback from the blast could damage their group.

A strained shout rose past the stern, from the water.

Zhuang.

Seichan sidled low to the stern.

Gray followed her, leaving Kadir with Yeung. Once at the back, Gray lifted high enough to peer over the rail. Down in the water, the fingertips of Zhuang's outstretched arm had snagged the edge of a bumper. His shoulder was black with blood. His good arm held Guan-yin's head above water.

Around them, spiked balls of coral battered at them. Each strike drew pained flinches. Zhuang looked upward in agony—but not from the sting of the attackers. He clung hard to Guan-yin's limp body.

"We must get them out of there," Seichan warned.

Gray nodded, but he knew doing so would leave them exposed. He stared back at the wheelhouse, then turned to Yeung. The deputy understood and switched back to his assault rifle. He would cover them as best he could.

"We go quick," Gray told Seichan. "On my mark."

10:52 P.M.

In the wheelhouse, Heng knelt beside one of the Falcons. The man's hand was a mangle of bone and blood. Heng cinched a tourniquet around the man's forearm, using his own belt.

Captain Wen stood guard by the door, his assault rifle held high. He kept his gaze fixed outside, clearly waiting for a moment to ambush the stragglers out there.

But Wen had left his own back unguarded.

Xue stormed up behind him. "What were you thinking? I gave no orders to shoot, to break our truce."

Wen ignored him. "I have my standing orders. From higher in command. To destroy the enemy when given the chance."

"From whom?"

Wen shook his head, refusing to give out this information. Heng knew there were competing factions within the PLA. Some leaned toward accommodation and compromise. Others were obdurate and bloodthirsty. It was an internal war, waged behind the scenes as fiercely as any battle against a foreign power.

"I gave you as much leeway as feasible," Wen said with a scowl. "But this was clearly a waste of time, and it ends now."

"This insubordination will not go—"

"The lives lost will be placed at your feet, Major Choi. The blood is on your hands for pursuing such a folly."

Heng finished his ministrations and stood up. He stared out the rear window and spotted a commotion at the stern. Half hidden by a low steel bench, Gray and Seichan lunged into view. They leaned over the stern rail, their arms reaching down.

"Now to put an end to this," Wen said.

He cracked the door open and pointed his weapon.

Outside, a figure popped up from behind the bench and shot three-round bursts into the window and frame. It drove Wen back. Behind the shooter, Gray and Seichan dragged a limp and sodden figure to the deck. The group dropped back out of sight.

Wen sneered. "That won't work a second time."

10:54 A.M.

Seichan crouched beside her mother, who was sprawled at her knees. She rubbed one of Guan-yin's hands between her palms. "*Mẹ*," she moaned, her voice that of a plaintive child. "*Mẹ, thức giấc.*"

Her mother slipped in and out of consciousness. Her head lolled to the side, her eyes dazed. She had lost her niqab and scarf. Her dark hair clung in damp strands across her face. The purple scar and tattoo stood out starkly as shock drained blood from her face.

"Stay with your mother," Gray said. "I'll get Zhuang."

Seichan lowered Guan-yin's hand to the deck. "We do this together. On my mark this time."

Gray's upper arm seeped blood from a deep graze. He could hardly bear weight on his left leg. His pant leg was dark with blood. He couldn't do this alone.

Seichan turned to Yeung. Kadir was propped up next to him. The director held an arm tight around his lower abdomen. He had sustained a belly wound. The right side of his face was covered in blood.

She stared from the bench to the wheelhouse, knowing the ground they held was unsustainable—and it wasn't just here on the boat.

Beyond the rails, the world worsened. Mount Tambora had started a brilliant round of eruptions, as if echoing their gunfire. The seas trembled with each blast. Lava flowed over all its flanks, turning the black peak into a flaming mountain. Steam shrouded the island, but it could not dim that blaze.

It seemed futile to continue this battle.

But that's never stopped me in the past.

Seichan returned her attention to Yeung.

He met her gaze.

She nodded. "On my mark."

Heng watched the standoff from the wheelhouse. Though he spotted no change in the party outside, Wen did. He was a skilled warrior. He must have noted something.

Wen hissed under his breath and firmed his grip on his rifle, his eye fixed to the scope. Through the crack in the door, he squeezed out a spatter of rounds.

Heng struggled to understand. There was no target—at least not to his eyes.

Then he heard a scream.

The captain's barrage had ricocheted off the stern rail and struck the shooter who was hiding behind the bench. Wen must have anticipated the man was about to lay down suppressive fire. It all happened so fast that Gray and Seichan were caught by surprise. They were already lunging up, committed to plucking someone else from the water.

With the enemy exposed and vulnerable, Wen burst out of the wheelhouse. He fired his rifle one handed, strafing the bench, keeping the shooter down. With his other hand, he ripped out his pistol and aimed it at the two rescuers.

Gray and Seichan flopped backward, using their bodyweight to haul another figure over the rail. The soaked man fell headlong to the deck between them.

Still firing his rifle, Wen crossed another two steps and swung his pistol at them.

The loud gunshot made Heng flinch and duck.

He turned to see Xue holding his sidearm extended.

Out on the deck, the back of Wen's knee exploded. Somehow, the captain kept upright, but his pistol tumbled from his grip. He bellowed and turned his rifle upon Gray's group.

Xue fired twice more, but Wen had spun on his good leg. Both shots grazed off his body armor.

Movement low on the deck drew Heng's eye.

The rescued man lunged up with surprising speed. He dove forward, then tucked his knees under him. He slid across the blood-slick deck.

Wen fired at him, pelting his chest with rounds.

It failed to stop the man. Momentum kept him sliding.

He reached Wen. With his last breath, he swung a length of silver up from his side. It flashed across the air. The blade cleaved through Wen's elbow. His limb went flying in a spray of blood, along with his rifle.

Wen screamed in horror and backpedaled, struggling on his good leg. He hit the starboard rail and tumbled backward into the water.

On the deck, the swordsman leaned on his blade, his forehead on its hilt, as if in prayer. Blood pooled heavily around him.

Then he toppled to the side, his duty done.

37

Ten seconds . . .

Nine . . .

Monk ran the countdown in his head as he fled across the LCAC. He stared at the V-shaped wake of the torpedo surging toward the amphibious boat. The conning tower of the hunter-killer submarine loomed in the distance. Beyond it, the fiery battle continued to be waged across the breadth of the *Dayangxi*. The helicopter dock was awash in flames, bombarded on all sides. It listed badly, taking on water. Its stern had begun to sink.

Eight . . .

Seven . . .

Past the destruction and flames, the line of Kermadec volcanos exploded with great gouts of lava, splattering high. Along the plumes of black smoke, lightning shattered in great crowns of electrical fire. Thunderous detonations muffled even the missile blasts, making the nearby battle seem petty and unimportant.

But not to Monk.

Six . . .

Knowing he could never swim clear of the torpedo's blast, Monk rushed to the only refuge at hand. He clambered up the side of the battle tank parked atop the deck.

Five . . .

He reached the top of the tank's turret. To the right, a dome sprouted stubby antennas. Its armored shell protected the brains that operated the hulking drone. The tank was meant to be dumped onto some beachhead where it would trundle on its own into battle.

For Monk, it was a port in a storm.

Four . . .

He scrambled to the turret's hatch and yanked on it. It didn't budge.

Three . . .

He feared someone might have soldered it shut, but surely technicians needed to get inside. In his panic, he had failed to note the thick latch on one side. He used the butt of his hand to knock it free.

Two . . .

With a holler of frustration, he hauled again on the hatch. It finally swung up.

One . . .

Monk dove into the cabin, slamming the hatch behind him.

Zero . . .

The explosion was the hammer-strike of an angry god. Even muffled by the tank's armored plating, the blast pounded Monk's head. He hung from the hatch as the vehicle was tossed into the air by the burst of the boat's massive pontoons and the concussion of the detonation.

The tank rolled heavily, going full around. Monk held tight to his handhold and kicked out with his legs, trying to protect himself, but it did no good. He got tossed hard into the wall, against the cabin roof.

Then he felt, more than heard, the impact into the sea. The tank jarred with a resounding clang, then settled into a slow topple as it fell into the depths.

Monk knew he had only moments before the outside water pressure would lock down the turret's hatch. He braced his legs and shoved his shoulders and upper back. The hatch fought him. He growled and pushed harder. It finally popped open.

Water flooded inside with the strength of a fire hose. Monk got blown to the back of the cabin. He lost his breath, bubbling away his air. He clamped his lips and fought against panic. He waited for the tank to fill, for the water to stop gushing, then kicked off the floor and dove through the diminishing tide.

He jettisoned out of the tank. Its dark shadow fell away under him. He paddled and kicked for the surface. His lungs ached. He fought harder and finally reached the surface. He popped up high, higher than he intended. He gasped and sputtered and got lower in the water. He prayed he hadn't been spotted.

Treading in place, he eyed the submarine. It rose like a black shoal a hundred yards away. Lights danced over its length. Small figures moved atop the conning tower, directing actions below. The forward and aft hatches in the main hull had been thrown open. Pontoon boats were tied alongside the sub and offloaded men onto it. Another zoomed from the stern of the *Titan X*.

The Chinese forces were evacuating the yacht.

It could only mean one thing.

They're going to sink it.

The bow of the submarine was already pointed toward the target. The boat's commander must have ordered the evacuation before even firing the torpedo at the LCAC. With the *Dayangxi* doomed and the master of these forces absent, the commander must have taken it upon himself to take down the *Titan X*.

Monk spun in the water, knowing there was nothing he could do. His efforts to save the yacht had only delayed the inevitable.

But apparently, it had been long enough.

Around the bulk of the *Titan X*, a seaplane dove low into view. It tilted on a wing and turned sharply upon the submarine, diving toward its target.

Monk recognized the Twin Otter.

How did it get here?

He gaped in confusion, adding another question.

What is it doing?

3:12 P.M.

Kowalski leaned out the side door of the Twin Otter. He kept a grip on a handle inside. The seas swept low under him. The Chinese submarine rose ahead of them.

In the pilot's seat, William Byrd shouted, "Get ready!"

The plane coughed and choked, stifled by ash. It dropped a full yard.

"Hold it together!" Kowalski hollered back. "Keep us steady!"

The Otter swept over the length of the sub's hull. Spatters of gunfire shot at them. Rounds tore through the wings, pinged off struts. The sail of the submarine appeared dead ahead. Byrd fought to hold their line, to keep them aloft.

"C'mon," Kowalski moaned.

The Otter swept at the conning tower, low enough that the men on top ducked out of the way.

"Now!" Kowalski yelled.

To the side, Jarrah shoved his shoulder into a waist-high stack of Semtex 10. The load rested on a wheeled pallet. The package toppled out the open door and fell heavily downward.

As the seaplane passed onward, Kowalski leaned farther out. He hung by the handle and bellowed, "You left something behind, assholes!"

He watched his care package strike the top of the sail and smiled.

This is what I do best.

In his other hand, he pressed the detonator.

Two hundred pounds of Semtex exploded with a fiery flash. The blast thundered. The concussion shook the air and shoved the plane. Huge gouts of flames burst out the sub's forward and aft hull hatches. Pontoon boats flew high, burning and crashing.

The Otter spun a half circle to view the damage.

The conning tower burned like a torch. The craft slipped sideways. Some seams must have burst lower down. Another explosion rocked the boat. Maybe from the torpedo bay inside. The submarine slowly sank away.

Farther out, a helicopter landing dock burned its way into the sea. Missile fire still blasted into its steeply canted deck, as if making sure it stayed down. Kowalski didn't know who was attacking the ship, but he was grateful for the assist.

Byrd yelled from the pilot seat. "Losing engines!"

Kowalski pulled back in and tapped a fist on the Otter's door frame. "Don't you worry! She'll last!"

He was wrong.

Their engines coughed twice more and conked out.

Byrd shouted into the unnerving quiet. "Hold tight!"

The Otter dove for the waves. Byrd fought their descent, trying to get as much glide out of their bullet-riddled wings as possible.

Kowalski kept his perch by the open door, tightening his fist on the handle.

The ocean sped under them—then the floats skimmed the water. The nose dipped and the floats dug deeper. The Otter tipped high, skidding on its tips.

Kowalski held his breath, expecting to flip over.

But the seaplane crashed down onto its floats and slowly came to a stop.

Kowalski called to Byrd. "Told you she'd make it."

Byrd scowled back.

Jarrah shifted and pointed past the door. "Swimmer! Coming this way."

Kowalski turned and swung up the QBX carbine from behind his back. He wasn't about to take on any hitchhikers.

From the waves, an arm waved. A pale bald head lifted higher. He heard his name called.

Kowalski cupped his mouth. "Monk, what're you doing? Did you fall overboard?"

SEVENTH

Serpent's Roar

38

Gray groaned as Heng tightened a wrap around his upper thigh. "The bullet passed clean through," the doctor scolded. "But you need medical attention as soon as possible."

"That can wait."

Gray sat inside the boat's wheelhouse. The carnage was over, but there was much to be done. Heng did his best to minister to the other injured. Thankfully, the patrol boat's med kit had been well stocked.

Out on the deck, Seichan stayed beside her mother, who hung over the draped body of Zhuang. Guan-yin pressed her head against his chest. Her shoulders shook, but it was not from weakness or fever. Grief crippled her far worse than any poison. Still, she had no doubt suffered a fatal envenomation. Her hundreds of stings had begun to blacken, but Guan-yin ignored them. She looked ready to follow Zhuang in death.

Knowing he could do nothing to help, Gray left them to their grief and hobbled over to Xue, who stood at the helm. From his position, the man stared out at the end of the world.

"Thank you," Gray said.

Xue looked down at his holstered pistol. "I didn't save you."

Gray cast a glance back at Zhuang. "But you bought him enough time to act."

Xue shrugged and returned his gaze outside. "But how much time do any of us have? The bullroarer was a failed effort. In that regard, Captain Wen was correct."

Gray refused to agree with anything that bastard said. "Our efforts were interrupted. We didn't give it a fair trial."

Xue frowned at him. "What do you mean?"

Gray glanced toward the steps that led down to the lower hold. Kadir had been treated and retired to one of the cabins below. "According to Stamford's account, when Mount Tambora last erupted, it was tamed by the Aboriginal people who gathered here. He wrote that it was not a small group, but *hundreds* who had arrived in these waters, all winging their bullroarers through the air. Plainly, even back then, with only Tambora erupting, a single bullroarer wasn't enough to quiet it."

Xue sighed. "Which we don't even have any longer. The bullroarer was destroyed."

"We don't need it."

Xue took a step back and sized him up. His expression clearly questioned Gray's sanity.

Gray pointed to Xue's pocket. "Earlier, I saw you recording Kadir's attempt with the paddle. You should have a copy of its roar on your phone."

Xue's eyes got huge. He pulled out his cell phone and stared down at it.

Gray pointed to the helm. "This is a patrol boat, used for running down pirates and traffickers. There's a huge LRAD speaker mounted on the wheelhouse for ordering boats to heel."

Xue understood Gray's plan. "If we feed that roar through the system—"

"We can broadcast far more than a *hundred* bullroarers. It would sound like *thousands*."

11:21 A.M.

As the final preparations were made, Seichan carried her mother into the wheelhouse. Guan-yin hung limply, barely able to hold herself upright. Her skin burned, hot enough to be felt through her clothing.

Gray met Seichan at the doorway and helped guide Guan-yin to a seat inside. He handed Seichan a set of earphones. He had found them stashed next to the radio alcove. The patrol crew must have kept them handy for their own deafening attacks on pirate ships.

"Keep these on your mother," he said. "It's going to get rough."

She nodded.

He gave her a quick hug and cast a concerned look toward Guan-yin, who slumped sideways in her seat, fading away again.

"This had better work," Seichan said, with a glance toward her mother.

And not just for the world.

"We'll do our best."

He turned away, but she dragged him back and kissed him. She needed to feel his lips, the taste of his breath, to feel his solidity to help ground her. She wasn't gentle. She took what she needed. He did not object.

Once done with him, she pushed him away. "Get to work."

He set off toward Xue and Kadir.

The plan was for their group to ride out the sonic storm inside the cabin, hoping that its armored superstructure and bulletproof windows would offer further insulation.

Gray and Xue spoke in urgent tones. They tested a few blasts, then once satisfied, Gray donned his headphones.

"Here we go!" he shouted.

Seichan made sure her mother's ears were covered, then pressed her headphones tighter to her own skull.

Gray looked around and gave a thumbs-up to Xue. The major hit a switch on the radio console. The man's cell phone had already been plugged into the system. As his recording played, Xue turned the volume dial. He started with a low roar, broadcast through the long-range-acoustic speaker mounted atop the wheelhouse.

Xue glanced to Gray, who nodded for him to continue.

The sound quickly escalated, growing louder and louder. Even directed outward from the speaker, the noise shook the roof. Seichan might as well not have been wearing earphones. The roar filled her skull, rattled her teeth, vibrated her ribs.

Gray checked on them again.

He waited until he got thumbs-ups from everyone, then jabbed a finger in the air.

Louder.

Xue turned the dial all the way up.

Seichan cringed, trying to duck from the sound, but it was everywhere. In her bones, in her blood. Nausea grew. Her skin prickled with heat. Her heart pounded, fueled by an indescribable panic. The roaring filled the air, making it hard to breathe.

She knew it was her imagination, but it felt that way.

Gray leaned toward Xue and pointed out the forward windows.

Seichan pushed out of her seat. At first, she failed to see what had excited him—then she noted the change in Mount Tambora. The fountains of fire had collapsed into the caldera. The lower flanks of the mountain had grown darker, no longer fed by fresh flows of molten rock.

She searched the other windows. The fiery horizons had also dimmed to a dull glow. Gray caught her eye, his expression easy to read.

It's working.

But he didn't just mean with the volcanos.

He waved around the ship. She lowered her gaze to the surrounding waters. They were still dark, but lights now swam through the ash, appearing and disappearing.

The Rainbow Serpents . . .

Gray turned to Xue and made a slicing motion across his throat.

Xue dialed down the volume. In the absence of that roar, the world fell deathly quiet, as if holding its breath.

Gray stared out at the stirring lights in the water. "We've clearly succeeded in summoning them."

Xue's expression remained guarded. "But is it enough?"

11:40 A.M.

Gray stood at the boat's rail and studied Mount Tambora. It continued to remain quiet. During the past ten minutes, the peak had steadily darkened, fading into the ashy gloom. He searched the rest of the horizons. As those distant fires flickered out, the world closed around him. Still, a few spots continued to burn, marking the farthest volcanos.

Xue stood next to him, evaluating the same.

Booms reached the boat, no longer as loud as cannon fire, more like thunder over the horizon. Still, it was an indication that the tectonic instability persisted.

Gray pronounced his judgment. "We managed to quiet this immediate region, but not all of it."

"Not by far," Xue concurred. "We've stuck our finger in the dike, but that's all. If the volcanic activity across the greater region continues to escalate, these seas may start up again."

"Still, what we've done proves there is efficacy to this method."

Gray turned to the waters around the patrol boat. Swarms of bioluminescent creatures swam through the ash, luminous in the darkness. They flickered and blinked with hues of every color. It was no wonder the Aboriginal people had called them *rainbows*.

The creatures were plainly busy out there. Smooth tentacles rose and swept the sea. They grabbed coral balls, combed up broken pieces and branches, and pulled everything away. They were meticulously clearing the waters of the fiery threat.

Gray again wondered if those spiky mines were a biological defense. Were they utilizing their young, aggressive forms to protect their domain?

But that aspect of their biology was not important at the moment.

By the stern, Yeung and Heng had discovered a lever that could extend a dive platform over the water—a feature that Gray wished he had known about earlier when he had rescued Guan-yin and Zhuang.

Yeung called over to him, announcing all was ready.

Gray nodded and crossed to the steel bench that had sheltered them during the firefight. It now held Guan-yin's slack body. The woman had slipped fully unconscious, only stirring to moan and thrash. Her skin was pallid and patched with black stings.

Gray met Seichan. Together, they lifted her mother. Guan-yin felt weightless, as if impending death had hollowed her out.

Yeung stepped forward to help, but Seichan warned him away with a scowl, protective of her mother in this debilitated state. Guan-yin was still the triad's dragonhead. To show weakness risked humiliation. Seichan intended to guard her mother's honor.

A small door opened down to the dive platform. Once extended, the small deck sat even with the sea. They gently carried Guan-yin down to it. The others stayed atop the deck. They lowered Guan-yin to the edge, dropped to their knees, then lifted her out over the layer of ash.

Resting in the sea, buoyed by the water, she felt even more weightless, nearly insubstantial. Her robe billowed outward into wings. She sighed, as if the cool water offered some relief from her fever.

Gray and Seichan supported her there, though it took little effort.

They waited, silently praying for a miracle, for the promise of a cure hidden in old papers and ancient rituals. Unfortunately, their efforts were ignored. The shining creatures rode the waves and surged through the ashy water, but they came no closer.

"Why aren't they helping?" Seichan asked.

"I don't know."

Gray avoided voicing what was in his head.

Maybe they don't deem her worthy.

Guan-yin had a noble honor, but her name—*goddess of mercy*—was more sardonic than factual. She had lived a hard life and exacted the same from those around her, especially her enemies. Her hands had been deeply stained by blood, some of it undoubtedly innocent.

Then again, so are mine.

He had demons of his own that might chase away such gentle creatures.

A noise rose behind him. He turned to find Xue holding up his cell phone. He played his recording of the bullroarer. It wasn't the thunder from before. The lone call sounded forlorn and mournful.

Gray turned back to the sea.

The motion of the serpents slowly stopped, as if listening. One by one, they sank into the sea. The ash settled over the water, erasing them from sight.

Gray frowned.

Had we inadvertently dismissed them?

Seichan gasped, stiffening in surprise.

All around her mother's body, tentacles rose into view, weaving through the air, looking very much like snakes. Their bioluminescent shimmering slowly grew in synch, spiraling one radiant color after another, from one tentacle to the next. It formed a whirlpool of shimmering beauty—as if a rainbow had settled to the water.

The tentacles slowly lowered and gently probed, running over Guan-yin's pale skin. Smaller tendrils sprouted from their lengths and touched her all over. Each dab rose a welt that spasmed her flesh. They fell everywhere, snaking under her robe, over her face. They seemed to concentrate on those blackened marks from the venomous coral stings.

As they worked, Guan-yin gasped in stuporous agony, her eyes pinched with pain.

Still, the serpents continued their ministration.

Unable to restrain himself any longer, Heng stepped down to the platform. He intervened with much apology and bowing. He explained himself: "If this is a cure, more will need it."

They shifted aside to accommodate him. Gray knew the doctor had patients back in Cambodia, but it wasn't just them he was worried about. Guan-yin was surely not the only one who had been envenomated in these waters. The region needed the cure as much as Heng's patients.

As the doctor knelt, he held out a glass collection dish. He must have had it in his pack of supplies. It was why he had come on this journey, in the hopes of discovering a cure. Several of the tendrils probed the glass, dotting it with their fiery solution. He waited until the glass was wet and running with the tonic. He got stung several times in the process, his eyes wincing, willing to suffer for this cure. Once he had enough, he withdrew his hand and sealed the container. He repeated this process with a second dish, then set the sample next to Gray's knee.

"I will share whatever we find," Heng said. "If you'll do the same."

"Of course," Gray promised.

Heng withdrew with a small bow.

Guan-yin's fiery baptism continued for another few minutes, demonstrating the creatures' attentiveness and thoroughness. Finally, as if obeying some unknown signal, the tentacles all drifted away.

Once they were gone, Gray helped pull Guan-yin back onto the dive platform. He let her rest there, watched over by Seichan. He stood and stared across the dark sea.

The creatures failed to reappear, apparently done with their responsibilities, both here and in the surrounding waters.

Unfortunately, that only applied to this immediate area.

Distant booms still echoed, and fires continued to glow along the horizon.

Gray frowned and knew the truth about their efforts.

It's still not enough.

39

Through the acoustic headphones, Phoebe listened to an eerie chorus of undulating calls and sharper cries. They echoed out of the blighted forest, rising from where the glade shimmered and glowed.

The song was interrupted by muffled explosions, which faded in and out. She didn't know if they marked a firefight or if they rose from volcanic eruptions. She stared up. The *Cormorant* was approaching a depth of fourteen thousand meters, but the upper world felt much farther away. Its troubles seemed petty and unimportant, having no bearing on these quiet and peaceful depths.

Datuk huffed behind her, slightly kicking her seat.

She removed her headphones. "What's wrong?"

"I'm still getting the same anomalous results from the nanopore sequencer," he said. "I don't know if the pressure or the radiation is affecting the MinIon unit."

"What's the radiation reading out there?" Adam asked.

Datuk sat back and cringed slightly. "Eight hundred rem. Bad enough to cause acute death."

"What about in here?"

"Hundred and sixty."

Phoebe swallowed. She had begun to feel nauseous, but she didn't know if it was an early sign of radiation poisoning or if it was simply due to tension.

Bryan grimaced. "Approaching fourteen thousand meters. Between the pressure and the radiation, I'm only keeping us down here a quarter hour. After that, we're heading up."

From his tone, he would brook no argument.

No one tried.

None of them wanted to stay down here any longer than possible. For the past hour, the *Cormorant* had begun to pop and groan under the increasing pressure.

It had kept them all tense.

Phoebe had tried to distract herself by listening to the forest, seeking solace in the quiet chorus around her. With that same goal, she twisted and faced Datuk.

"What problem are you having with your sequencer? Maybe I can help?"

Datuk gave a frustrated shake of his head. "I keep getting the same error. The MinIon is normally very precise, able to pick out and differentiate individual DNA and RNA bases. Same with polypeptides and other polymers. But in the DNA I collected from the specimen, I'm registering adenine, guanine, cytosine, and thymine."

Phoebe shrugged. Those four bases—abbreviated as AGCT—composed the four-letter code for most life on the planet. "So what's the problem?"

"According to the MinIon's results, those four bases make up ninety-eight percent of the sample's DNA. I've repeated the test and keep getting the same number. Plus or minus a few decimal places."

"What makes up the other *two* percent?"

Datuk frowned. "That's just it. They're still registering as AGCT, only they've been tagged as *anomalous*."

"Why?"

He stared at her. "Though those bases are configured the same, those AGCT molecules are composed of *silicon* atoms instead of *carbon*."

She frowned. "Is that even possible?"

"Maybe. In labs, they've created microorganisms that can enzymatically produce organo-silicon properties. Even RNA- and DNA-like bases." Datuk sighed. "But the error I'm reading could just be due to contamination, a confusion from silt or sand being present on the sample. Silicon is everywhere. It makes up thirty percent of the earth's crust. It's hundreds of times more abundant than carbon. Silicon-based lifeforms had been theorized, but carbon is more versatile and why life on Earth is based on that atom."

"Maybe not all life." Phoebe stared out at the seas. "Could this lifeform be some sort of chimera? Sharing both types of DNA bases—carbon *and* silicon."

"I don't know. But it might explain how these creatures survive down here. Few species of fish can live at these extreme depths because the protein produced by normal DNA ceases to function under these pressures. Maybe the organo-silicon genes produce unique proteins that help them survive."

"Maybe," Phoebe agreed.

Datuk sighed and sat back. "It's all speculation. Without more research, it's impossible to say."

Adam interrupted them. "Look to the left."

Phoebe faced her window. A shimmering movement drew her eye. A glowing streak sped across the dark forest. It undulated and twisted. Tentacles flared, then contracted. Lights flashed and traced through like fire. The panic of its flight and the distress of its blinking were easy to read.

"It must have accidentally brushed into the irradiated area," Phoebe said. "Then in alarm, it fled the wrong way. Deeper into the dead zone."

The polyp-like creature rushed out of the forest's fringe and into the open space. It flailed and spun, rushing at them.

"It's heading for our lights," Datuk said.

The beast sped up to them and circled the *Cormorant*. Its head was bullet-shaped, somewhere between squid and octopus. Four globular eyes ringed its edge, using each to study this strange foreigner in its midst. It flared out eight arms and wrapped them over the glass scallop, as if begging to be let inside.

But there was nothing they could do.

It clung there, flashing and blinking, pleading. Through its translucent skin, four hearts beat a timpani of clear panic. Over a long minute, the glow faded from its body. The fearful squeezing of its hearts slowed as it succumbed to the radiation.

Phoebe placed her palm over the glass.

I'm sorry.

It finally fell away, its glory dimming, fading back into the gloom, becoming part of it.

Closer at hand, Datuk extended the *Cormorant*'s hydraulic arm toward the specimen, trying for another sample.

Phoebe reached back to him. "Don't. Please don't."

Datuk nodded and retracted the arm.

They sat in silence for several breaths.

Datuk spoke first. "It definitely appeared to bear characteristics of a rudimentary octopus. Maybe it truly is the progenitor of the species. The missing link. An explanation for what has baffled evolutionists when it comes to an octopus's anatomy, physiology, and intelligence."

"But what about those bits of organo-silicon DNA?" Phoebe asked.

Datuk sniffed. "Maybe we shouldn't entirely discount the paper I mentioned during the first dive. The one about octopuses coming from space."

Adam turned to him, clearly skeptical. "What did the article claim?"

"The main argument is that our planet could have been seeded by extraterrestrial retroviruses—which are very mutagenic—during a cometary bombardment that struck Earth during the Cambrian period. The date *does* correspond to the emergence of retroviruses in vertebrate lines, viruses that seemingly came out of nowhere. The paper speculates that it was those mutagenic retroviruses that sparked the Cambrian Explosion of life—an event half a billion years ago when nearly all the major phyla of the modern world came into being. The paper also postulates it was those viruses that produced the unique and inexplicable biology of octopuses."

"So extraterrestrial viruses gave us octopuses?" Adam said, clearly scoffing at such a statement.

Datuk shrugged. "What I find most interesting in retrospect—

especially with what we've witnessed here—is what marked the *beginning* of the Cambrian Explosion. It was a pivotal event. A critical advancement that allowed life to spread across oceans and onto land. It immediately preceded the arrival of octopuses and squids."

"What was that critical advancement?" Adam asked.

Phoebe knew the answer. She stared out at the dark forests around them. "It was the emergence of *hard* body parts in animals. Starting with the skeletons of coral."

3:45 P.M.

Adam kept close watch on the bathymetric screen. "We're approaching fourteen thousand meters."

"Blowing ballast," Bryan said. "Going for neutral buoyancy."

Solid weights were jettisoned off the *Cormorant's* exterior. The vehicle's descent slowed to a crawl, then finally stopped.

Adam noted the depth reading.

13,978 METERS.

That's close enough.

"What's the sonar showing?" Adam asked Phoebe.

She pinged the bottom. "The haloing from before is still there, only more distinct. Some portion of the seabed is a mile under us. But I'm still seeing lots of blank spots, gaps in the sonar sounding."

"Then let's take a look," Adam said.

Bryan rotated the underwing cameras, pointing them straight down. Their eyes had been rolled up during the descent to protect their lenses. "Pulling up the feed from cameras one through four."

He tapped switches, and the large monitor over the helm bloomed to light. It was divided into four zones, one for each camera. But their views were stitched together to form a single large image.

The view was blurry, but Bryan zoomed in and out, focusing each lens until a crisp image of the seabed revealed itself.

Gasps rose from the group.

Adam hadn't known what to expect, but it wasn't that hellscape. The bottom of the cavern appeared to be a moth-eaten ruin. Massive pockets, fissures, and gaps split up the landscape. They must be what formed those blank spots on the echosounding. If sonar couldn't penetrate those dark depths, then they must be impossibly deep, maybe delving all the way through Earth's crust.

Adam dismissed this thought and focused on what he could see. The intact sections of the seabed were blistered with huge calderas, all fuming with black smoke.

Phoebe pointed a finger at one. "What is that?"

From his geology classes, Adam knew the answer. "Submarine volcanos. But these don't spew *magma*. Instead, they blast out liquid *carbon dioxide*. There's one in the Philippine Sea. The Eifuku volcano. It reaches temps of more than two hundred degrees. But those down there, that deep and large, who knows how hot they get?"

"What about those dark yellow spots on the seabed?" Datuk asked. He reached over Phoebe's shoulder and waved a finger across a series of pestilent-looking blemishes, ending at a huge pool of the same.

"I don't know," Adam admitted.

He squinted at them. The largest looked to be a good mile across. A black crust rimmed its edge. The shoreline was a dark umber that grew lighter until at the center it was a glowing yellow sun.

Phoebe leaned closer. "They're lakes of molten sulfur. I've seen pictures of them elsewhere but never in person. And certainly never that huge. The largest looks as if it's eddying around a central pool of molten rock."

Bryan pointed to the bottom-right corner of the monitor. "Is that the tail end of a submarine?"

They all shifted their attention, reminded of why they were down here.

"Can you adjust the cameras?" Adam asked.

Bryan slid the four lenses in that direction. As he did, the full length of the lost submarine came into view. It looked like a crumpled child's toy abandoned on the ground. It was framed and half covered by shattered trunks and branches of coral that had fallen with it. The rest of the collapsed forest must have rained down into those bottomless gaps or been burned up in the volcanos and molten pools.

Too bad the sub hadn't met the same fate.

As if summoned by this thought, something massive shifted out of the neighboring forest. It burrowed under the deadfall, remaining mostly hidden. Brief glimpses of it showed a tunneling black mass patched by rough spots, as if it was carrying a carapace of rock with it. It was huge, three times the diameter of the submarine, dwarfing the crumpled boat.

It bulged upward at one point, breaking through the broken coral, shrugging the tonnage aside. Its dark skin pulsed with a deep glow. It wasn't the bright bioluminescence of the creatures inhabiting the forest. Instead, there was an ancient quality to it, the glow of a dying sun. It shone from deep within it.

Still, there was no mistaking what it was.

Phoebe admitted as much. "It's a tentacle."

At the edges of the forest, shadows shifted, shining with the same somber glow, marking the locations of other tentacles. The lead one reached to the sub and shoved it away. It then retreated, curling as if repulsed. The inner glow dimmed. Even it was struggling with the level of radiation.

Another limb snaked out, no longer hiding. Its length was heavy with patches of rocky carapace. Still, it took its turn to push the submarine farther out into the open. Then spasmed back, burned by the radioactive ember.

They watched as this effort continued. Tentacles pushed, then retreated, again and again, slowly shifting the submarine across the hellish landscape.

Phoebe was the first to understand the ploy, noting the determined trajectory. "They're trying to drive it into the molten lake. To destroy it."

Adam glanced to Datuk, remembering his claim that the local quakes might not have been random, but purposeful. That the shaking could've been an attempt to drive out the hot splinter that had lodged in their forest—and when that didn't work, they broke the crust under it and dropped it into this hellscape.

Is that what we're witnessing?

Datuk seemed to believe so. "It looks like a toxic clean-up job."

"But what is *it*?" Adam challenged them. "Those tentacles down there. They look somewhat like those octopus-like creatures, those overgrown coral polyps. But it's clearly different."

"It must be far more ancient," Phoebe said. "Maybe a great ancestor. It could be hundreds of millions of years old." She turned to Datuk. "I wager if you tested its DNA, you'd find many more silicon-based sections."

"What do you mean?" Adam asked.

Phoebe returned her attention below. "I think we're looking at a blurring of geology and biology. A mix of silicon and carbon life."

Adam wanted Datuk to argue with her, but he remained silent.

Phoebe continued, "Over untold millennia, the polyps of the coral forest probably started shedding the silicon in their DNA, the stone from their bodies, evolving and becoming more free swimming."

"Until there were just traces of silicon in their DNA," Datuk mumbled. "Enough to sustain them at these depths."

"Then eventually those last vestiges were cast off, too. As life swam freer, venturing into less hostile waters, the silicon DNA and its proteins were no longer needed."

"Until the creatures became the baffling oddities we know today," Datuk said. "The octopus."

"Or possibly they're the source for *all* life," Phoebe expounded. "Either way, some of that past has endured. Down deep. And I wager even deeper there could be greater mysteries, ones that we may never fully comprehend."

Adam remembered her description.

A blurring of geology and biology.

As they watched, those rocky tentacles finally rolled the submarine to the edge of the molten lake. The boat's weight cracked through the blackened crust at the rim. It slid down into the depths, vanishing beneath the sulfur.

Adam pictured it falling ever deeper, rolling toward the molten rock at the center. That realization sat him straighter. "We need to get out of here."

"We have a few more minutes before we have to leave," Bryan said, still transfixed by the sight.

"No. We don't."

Bryan glanced at him.

Adam pointed down. "The Chinese sub was likely armed with ballistic missiles." He faced everyone. "Equipped with nuclear warheads."

Datuk gaped at him. "Will they explode?"

"It's not likely, but let's not take the chance."

Bryan shut down the cameras and began hitting buttons with clear anxiety. "Dumping all ballast."

The *Cormorant* started to ascend.

Phoebe stared up. "We have a long way to go."

More than eight miles.

"We can do it," Adam said, though he was unsure what sort of reception they'd get up top. There continued to be no word from the *Titan X*.

A loud grumbling arose around the vehicle as it shot upward. It shook the *Cormorant* and grew steadily in volume and strength. They all shared worried looks, knowing what it was.

Another quake.

"How much farther until we reach the fissure?" Adam asked.

"Pinging sonar up there now," Phoebe said.

Adam waited breathlessly.

"Another half mile," she reported.

He leaned forward to view her screen. It showed a bottom-up view into the crevice. Once they reached it, they still had to climb another three thousand meters to clear it. He prayed he was wrong about the nuclear warheads below.

But if I'm right, we need to be well away from here.

Phoebe continued to ping the roof over their head.

Adam sat back, knowing there was nothing he could do. They were at the mercy of buoyancy and pressure.

"No, no, no . . ." Phoebe moaned.

Adam leaned forward again. "What's wrong?"

She shook her head and hit the sonar button, casting another wave upward.

He studied the image and spotted a small dot dropping from the bottom of the fissure. He pointed at it. "What's that?"

"Can't tell. Likely some falling debris. Maybe a rock dislodged from the cliffs overhead."

"A damned big rock," Adam warned.

"It doesn't matter." She studied the screen. "We have a far bigger problem."

"What?"

"The fissure." She faced them all. "The quake is closing it."

Datuk jerked forward. "What?"

Adam stared up. "If so, we need to get moving faster."

All eyes turned to Bryan, who shook his head. They were already ascending as quickly as they could.

"Can we reach the fissure in time?" Adam asked.

"Yes," Phoebe said, "but it'll do us no good."

Datuk frowned. "Why?"

"The fissure is two miles long," she reminded them. "At the rate it's sealing, we'll never make it through in time."

40

Gray climbed from below into the patrol boat's wheelhouse. Yeung manned the helm and guided the interceptor through seas still choked with ash. Upon Gray's orders, they were trying to get upwind of Mount Tambora, to clear its heaviest pall.

Though the volcano remained quiet, it still steamed and smoked. Bright lava showed through cracks in its cooling crust. It was a reminder that danger still lurked close at hand.

Not that the damage wrought hadn't been devastating enough.

Gray frowned as the boat swept past the ruins of a fishing camp on a tiny atoll. It was smothered by ash. Boats had been washed by tsunamis deep into the ramshackle town. A pair of goats stood on a rooftop and bleated at their passage, the noise sad and forsaken. Nothing else appeared to be living on the tiny island.

Gray felt defeated.

The level of human suffering and loss was already incalculable. Still, he knew they were only in the eye of this tectonic storm. If left unchecked, the eruptions would not only resume, but grow a hundredfold worse.

We've only bought ourselves a brief window of time.

He crossed through the wheelhouse to the stern. Out on the deck, Xue and Heng had rolled the bodies to the side and covered them with tarps. While they had worked above, Gray had helped Seichan get Guan-yin settled below in a cabin. Seichan remained at her mother's bedside. Kadir was resting in a neighboring cabin in case she needed any help.

Though Guan-yin's fever had broken, the woman hovered at the edge of a weary delirium. Her body sweated heavily, as if trying to force the last vestiges of poison out of her skin. Seichan had bathed her mother's brow and arms with a cool, wet cloth. It had seemed to help. A moment ago, Guan-yin had stirred, her eyes opening. She muttered under her breath and stared around in a daze, as if looking for someone.

Both Gray and Seichan had known who that was.

Even that effort took too much out of the woman. Her eyes had slipped closed, and she had sunk away again. Gray suspected a part of Guan-yin found it too painful to wake, preferring oblivion to facing the loss she had suffered.

Out on the deck, Gray stared past the bow of the boat. Though it was midday, the heavy smoke layer still masked the sun. But in the distance, the clouds looked more gray than black. He hoped they had enough time to reach there.

Xue noted where he was looking. "What is your plan, Commander Pierce? You've not been clear about it."

"I'm sorry. I wanted to get the boat moving."

"Why?" Heng asked. "Do you hope to move to a new location and broadcast the bullroarer's call again?"

Gray pictured them sailing throughout this region, trying to hammer those tectonic plates into submission in a massive game of Whac-A-Mole.

"No," he answered. "We'd never be successful. According to Stamford's account, the waters around Mount Tambora were one of the Aboriginal *thin* spots of the earth. Only at those specific locations could a bullroarer work. And while there are supposedly many, we don't know where they are."

"But we do know of *one* other," Xue said.

Gray agreed. "The most important one. The thin spot that marks the *home* of the Rainbow Serpents. According to Crawfurd, it was in the waters around the island that he had sketched."

Xue nodded, grasping his plan. "If we could repeat what we did at that site, it might stop what's been started."

"But where's that island?" Heng asked. "How do we get there?"

Gray lifted up the e-tablet that he had retrieved from below. "Crawfurd's description of the place was vague, saying *it lies well beyond all islands, in seas rarely seen.* But considering all that has happened, I have a fair idea of where it might be found. Or at least a general idea."

He woke the tablet and showed them Crawfurd's sketches—the coastal views of the island and its general shape.

Gray explained, "Crawfurd left enough clues for me to start a search."

"Where?" Heng asked.

Xue answered, already moving a step ahead. "The island must be somewhere along the Tonga Trench. Where the clustering of quakes first started. And where we first picked up the ELF transmission during the Chang'e-5 mission."

Gray nodded. "There is a chain of islands that borders the length of the Tonga. The Kermadec Islands. I checked each one and compared their shape to Crawfurd's drawing and found this."

Gray swiped the screen to reveal a satellite photo of an anvil-shaped island.

Xue studied the photo, then looked up. "How far is this island from where the quakes were clustering?"

Gray lifted a brow. "Less than ten miles."

"Then that *must* be the island," Xue concurred. "The home of the Rainbow Serpents."

Gray prayed it was. "If we could transmit the sound of the bullroarer at that location, it might shut everything down at its source."

"But how do we get there?" Heng asked. "It's thousands of miles away."

"More than four thousand. And with all the ash in the skies, getting there by air would be impossible. We barely made it from Jakarta to Bali."

Xue frowned. "We must do something. Our geologists predicted the tipping point for this region is less than half a day away, possibly far less."

"Then what do we do?" Heng asked.

Gray looked up. "We need to reach clear air, away from the static energy of these heavy ash clouds. I've tried using my sat-phone for the past half hour. I managed a connection, but it lasted only seconds."

Xue stared toward Mount Tambora. "Some of the interference may be from the electromagnetic effects of the volcanic eruptions. Now that they've subsided, transmissions may open up again."

"Even so," Heng said, "who do you plan on calling? Who could get there in time?"

Gray faced the others. "There's a research ship in the area. If we could send them the bullroarer's recording, get them to broadcast it, maybe the gods will listen."

Xue looked at his toes.

"What?" Gray asked, sensing his consternation.

He looked up. "We have forces there, too. Or at least they were on the way before we lost communication. They were supposed to lock down the area."

Gray scowled at the man for not sharing this before. He pictured the huge research yacht—and who was out there.

Monk.

He pointed at Xue. "Then we *both* try. No matter who is in control, someone must do what we cannot."

Xue nodded, but he still looked worried.

"What else?" Gray asked.

"My father," Xue said. "Once the area was secured, he had been planning on sending out the ELF signal again. To confirm that it can indeed trigger earthquakes. He's waiting to hear from the commander of that mission."

Gray closed his eyes. "If he does, it will bring down the world."

"We know that now."

Gray turned to Xue. "You must stop your father, convince him of the threat. Or pray that the mission commander never makes that call."

Xue swallowed, looking sickened, as if he knew the commander.

Heng swore under his breath, indicating he did, too. "Then we're surely doomed."

41

Daiyu lowered her acoustic headphones and scowled upward.

"Any more updates?" Yang asked, his brow damp with sweat, his face deathly pale.

The lieutenant stared out the window. They had just dropped out of the fissure when a massive quake started. Sand, pebbles, and larger rocks continued to rain down. Several struck the *Qianliyan* with resounding clangs.

Yang cringed and ducked at each one.

"I'm hearing nothing from topside," Daiyu reported. "The quake's noise is blocking all communication."

"Then we should blow ballast and head back up."

Earlier, they had received a frantic message from the submarine's commander, detailing the destruction of the *Dayangxi*—by Captain Tse's own weaponry. Daiyu had been awaiting further word. Anger and humiliation warred within her.

"Captain Tse," Yang pressed her, his voice anxious.

"No." She shook her head. "We stay on mission."

Another large stone struck the *Qianliyan*.

"Fuck that," Yang blurted out.

He lunged to the row of ballast switches. He managed to flip one.

Piston-driven pumps pushed water from one of the tanks. The *Qianli-yan*'s descent slowed.

Daiyu had been expecting such a rash act, noting Yang's growing panic. His fingers scrabbled for another switch. Daiyu swung her arm. She already had a dagger in hand—a QNL-95 knife. She stabbed the long blade into Yang's neck.

He jerked back in shock, his hands grabbing for his throat.

She twisted the blade and blood sprayed across the sphere, soaking her uniform. Yang struggled and gasped. His body slid down the seat, as if trying to curl away from his pending death.

There would be no escape.

She held onto the hilt until Yang stopped moving. His mouth opened and closed a few more times, then stayed wide, his expression shocked.

She left the blade there and wiped her palms on her pants. She intended to complete her mission. She needed a win below to make up for her failure above.

I can still salvage this.

She knew that if she could help secure Aigua's new weapon system, one that could change the destiny of China, the loss of a single ship would not matter.

She reached to her controls and reversed the ballast tank's pistons. Water refilled the space. With the added weight, the *Qianliyan* dropped faster, plunging her toward her destiny.

She had no need for Yang. The submersible had plenty of eyes of its own. It was equipped with multiple detection devices: side-scanning and forward-looking sonar, a dozen underwater cameras, even space-based sensors.

She employed them now as she searched below the *Qianliyan*. She fell swiftly toward her target, which continued to reveal its position with repeated pings. The other craft—the *Cormorant*—had reversed course and swept up toward her.

As the two parties closed on each other, she saw no reason for further subterfuge. The enemy was toothless and unprepared. She targeted their vehicle with her acoustic system. They were close enough now that even the background rumble of the continuing quake could not block their communication.

She pulled the headset on and raised the microphone to her lips. "*Cormorant,* this is the *Qianliyan.* Do you copy?"

She waited for a response. With only a half kilometer between them, there should be no lag time.

A voice reached her, full of wary confusion. She noted the heavy Aussie accent, marking the speaker as the vehicle's pilot. "This is the *Cormorant.* What are your intentions, *Qianliyan?* Over."

"The People's Liberation Army has full control of the surface," she lied. "The *Qianliyan* is equipped with deep-sea weaponry. Stop your ascent. Tell us what you learned below. What you know. If we're satisfied, you will follow us to the surface."

"We cannot comply, *Qianliyan.* Your submarine has been destroyed. And—"

She cut him off. "Destroyed how?"

"Sunk into a magma lake."

She heard the panic in his voice. Maybe he feared a nuclear explosion. She sneered at such foolishness. As an engineer, she knew molten fire would not ignite a warhead. At worst, it might blow the missile's fuel tanks.

Still, the pilot was plainly alarmed and explained why. "The quake is closing the fissure overhead. We leave now or not at all."

Daiyu searched up, trying to confirm this threat with her own eyes. She hit her sonar, pinging it for the first time. Focused below, she had failed to watch her backside.

She lowered her gaze to her sonar screen. She pinged three more times, just to be certain. Her breath caught in her throat as each image refreshed, showing the incremental squeezing of the walls overhead.

The others weren't lying.

She used the heel of her hand and flipped the ballast toggles—all of them. The *Qianliyan* trembled as its pistons emptied all its tanks. Explosive bolts cast off more weight. She also dumped batteries and three of the heavy torpedoes.

The vehicle's descent braked so hard that it threw her low. She felt a thousand kilos in weight. Then the *Qianliyan* reversed itself. It slowly rose, quickly gaining speed.

The molten destruction of the navy's nuclear submarine had completed one task assigned to her. Once the quake quieted, she could still send a message above, to be passed to Aigua Choi, to have him transmit the ELF signal. She could still observe its effect from the seas above the fissure.

First, I must reach there.

To ensure that, she needed to lighten the *Qianliyan*. Doing so would also complete her final mission in this cavern. She reached to the weapons console and used a joystick to fix her target. The *Cormorant* continued its noisy ascent. She settled the system's crosshairs atop it and squeezed the trigger.

The last of *Qianliyan*'s fangs shot away from the vehicle's undercarriage. The *Dú-yá* torpedo sailed off into the darkness.

At these depths, where the pressures turned the water leaden, its pace was sluggish at first, but its speed steadily increased. She followed its path as it pinged a continual barrage at its target, doggedly fixed to it.

It was a slow dagger aimed at the heart of her enemy.

The torpedo swept wide, then spiraled down toward the *Cormorant*.

Satisfied, Daiyu turned her attention upward. According to her onboard computer, she still had time to make her escape.

But just barely.

4:28 P.M.

"I'm picking up a target lock," Bryan said.

Adam needed no such warning. A rapid pinging had started bombarding the *Cormorant*. It was loud enough to sting his ears and was rising steadily.

"They fired something at us," Adam said. "Likely a torpedo. We must find cover."

"Where?" Phoebe asked.

Recognizing the approaching threat, Bryan had already begun sucking water into their ballast tanks. Their ascent rapidly slowed, hard enough to lift Adam off his seat.

He braced an arm and pointed out the window. "Into the coral forest. It's our only hope."

And not much of one.

Bryan engaged the vehicle's thrusters and angled them to the side. He used the vehicle's wings to swing them around.

"I've got the weapon up on our sonar," Phoebe said. "Its speed is rapidly increasing."

"Steepen our angle of descent," Adam warned. "We have to get into that forest."

"What do you think I'm trying to do?" Bryan quipped.

On the screen, the blip of the torpedo closed on them. The pings of its targeting system repeatedly struck the sphere, ringing it like a bell.

Bryan made a grim assessment. "We're not going to make it."

4:31 P.M.

Daiyu sped upward in the *Qianliyan*. The fissure's cliffs swept past on both sides. More rocks pummeled the vehicle's exterior shell, but it continued to shield the passenger sphere. A couple of stones bounced off the unprotected glass, making her jerk away.

A moment ago, she had increased her rate of ascent by shedding the vehicle's extra oxygen tanks, stripping the *Qianliyan* down to its barest essentials. At this point, all that mattered was getting clear of this fissure.

To either side, the walls steadily pinched toward her. Through the acoustic headphones, she listened to the constant grinding of rock.

I will not die like this, an ignoble and solitary end.

She glanced at Yang's corpse. He had voided his bowels and the stench filled the sphere with a putrefying rank.

Not like this.

She tried casting up a call to her forces miles overhead, to both alert them to her distress and to prepare Aigua to ready the ELF array in the

Dabie Mountains. But all she got back was that ongoing rumble. The quake continued to deafen and mute her efforts.

She clenched her jaws, taking solace in the fact that her onboard systems continued to show she had just enough time to clear the fissure.

Then a loud cracking boom shook the *Qianliyan*. Out the window, a large slab of the cliff fell away, like an iceberg calving from a glacier. It tilted toward her.

She cringed and goosed the thrusters on that side.

She held her breath. Rock scraped down the *Qianliyan's* shell as the vehicle shied past the slab's top edge. Once free, she raced upward again, heaving out a sigh of relief.

Below her feet, the massive shard fell away and knifed into the darkness. She returned her gaze skyward and repeated her promise to herself.

Not like this.

4:32 P.M.

"Hold tight," Bryan called out.

Phoebe braced a palm on the curve of the roof. Adam had suggested this maneuver. She prayed it would work.

Bryan unloaded their ballast again.

It had quickly become evident that their angled descent would never allow them to reach the coral forest before the torpedo struck. Adam had offered a desperate alternative. *A sudden reversal of their flight.* He hoped it might throw off the torpedo's targeting system, requiring it to reestablish a lock. And if not, the weapon was weighted down by the eight miles of water. Any sudden change in its trajectory could slow it.

Maybe just enough.

The *Cormorant* shot upward again. Bryan tucked their wings tight to the side, streamlining their profile. He lost some maneuverability, but he compensated by driving the thrusters at full power. As they climbed, the vehicle aimed for the forest.

The curving trunks and twisted branches filled the world on that side.

Adam leaned between the front seats. He ignored the view out the window and concentrated on the sonar. "The torpedo's swinging around. It's noted our change."

"It's fucking smart," Datuk said.

"But it lost some speed making the turn," Phoebe reported.

"Still, it's quickly compensating." Adam pointed to the accelerating blip.

Bryan yelled again. "Going to try something."

No one had time to ask him what it was.

He hunched over his controls, tweaked some toggles, then yanked on the control yoke. A shadow rose to the left. The wing lifted on that side. The sudden drag, especially in the rapidly ascending *Cormorant*, threw the vehicle sharply toward the tree line. Bryan fought the thrusters to maintain their trajectory.

Adam gulped in Phoebe's ear. "I think it's working."

"Don't jinx us," Phoebe warned.

They all held their breath for the last twenty seconds—until the *Cormorant* shot into the forest like an injured bird with a broken wing.

Adam announced the inevitable. "Torpedo's still locked on us, following us."

Bryan tucked the wing again, fearful of it being ripped off if the vehicle swayed too close to one of the coral trees.

Phoebe leaned on her window. Lit by the *Cormorant*'s exterior lamps, the irradiated woodlands spread around them in a black colonnade. Bryan glided them swiftly through the forest. He adjusted buoyancy and thrusters to keep them weaving through the trunks.

"Torpedo just entered the forest," Adam reported.

The pinging had fluttered for a spell, but now it steadied.

"It's still got us tagged," Adam said. "We bought some time, but as it speeds up, it'll start closing on us again."

"Where do we go?" Datuk moaned.

Phoebe pointed ahead, where the forest shimmered and shone. "If nothing else, I want to see what's out there before I die."

They all settled in, except for Bryan, who continued to work his magic. The dark forest swept around them. A few branches scraped and scratched at their outer shell, like the claws of the dead.

After a few minutes, it was clear that Adam had been right. The torpedo gained on them—first at a steady pace, then ever faster.

Phoebe stared at the glowing expanse beckoning ahead. By now, the radiant hues had brightened, differentiating into swirls and eddies of bioluminescence. It was as if they were sweeping from the dark fields of Kansas toward the splendor of Oz.

But they would never make it.

Trapped by the press of trees and branches, Bryan had no room for some clever last-minute maneuver. All they could do was keep going, driving across the forest. She remembered the lone creature sweeping through the coral trunks, desperate, terrified.

She felt the same way now.

That poor—

She jerked straighter in her seat.

"What's wrong?" Adam asked.

She turned to Bryan. "Blink all our lights. As rapidly as you can. Raise the lamp pole, too."

He frowned at her, clearly busy.

Right.

She set about doing it herself. Adam helped. So did Datuk.

In moments, the exterior lights strobed the darkness. The lamp pole extended, flaring brightly with its twenty thousand lumens.

Despite the blinding brilliance, Bryan kept them moving. But the Aussie was not Phoebe's intended audience.

Earlier, the lone creature who had fled through the dark forest had been drawn by their lamps. Phoebe prayed their lightshow now might do the same for the denizens of that radiant glade.

She waited and watched.

Adam concentrated on the sonar screen. "Torpedo is closing fast. It'll be on us in under a minute."

Phoebe refused to take her eyes off the shimmering forest. "C'mon . . ."

After a few more seconds, she spotted a subtle change, so faint it could be wishful thinking. Tiny trickles of light flowed into the darkness.

"Look." She pointed—more to make sure what she was seeing was real.

Datuk leaned over her shoulder.

The trickles became streams, then radiant rivers.

"They're coming," Datuk whispered at her ear.

The *Cormorant* rushed to meet them. In another two hushed breaths, the vehicle was swamped by their flowing shapes, their sweeping arms. The flock circled in a candescent eddy of curiosity.

"I can't see anything," Bryan said.

Hopefully that's true of another.

Bryan cut the thrusters before they crashed. The *Cormorant* was bombarded by the cries and calls of the creatures. It grew so loud that it drowned out the torpedo's pinging.

Phoebe prayed the chorus would act like a sonar blanket. Military submarines sometimes took advantage of a similar situation, using the loud bubbling from colonies of pistol shrimp to hide their boat from searchers on the surface.

She pressed her palm against the glass. Her movement drew a swirl of luminous black eyes, peering back at her.

Adam reported with awe. "The torpedo lost its lock. Its path is erratic. I think it might—"

A thunderous boom shook the *Cormorant*. A shockwave shoved the vehicle hard, crashing them sidelong into a coral trunk.

As they bounced off, the polyps continued to swirl around.

A loud splintering echoed behind them. It sounded massive. More of the same followed, sweeping closer. The crackling sounded like a forest fire rushing toward them.

Phoebe knew what she was hearing. The torpedo blast must have felled one of the coral giants. She pictured the huge tree toppling toward the *Cormorant*.

"We're moving," Bryan said.

"What do you mean?" Adam asked.

Bryan lifted his hands from his controls. "It's not me."

Phoebe pressed her nose to the glass, meeting a large eye staring back. She recognized the bright intelligence shining in that luminous glow.

"It's them," she said. "They're pushing us through the forest, trying to get us out of the way."

The crackling grew louder—then thundered into a mighty crash on their left. The impact shook the *Cormorant*. Still, they were carried forward.

The waters slowly brightened, even through the press of creatures. Finally, the view opened up as the swirling mass swept aside. The polyps had accomplished their mission. They had rescued the beleaguered strangers and drew them home.

Phoebe laughed. She couldn't help herself. "It's so beautiful."

A glowing wonderland surrounded them. Giant black boles twisted through the water, casting out huge canopies of branches. The trunks were streaked and painted with shining mats of algae. Elsewhere, waving bushes marked the presence of giant anemone-like creatures, which glowed in hues of every color imaginable.

But it was the keepers of this garden that held Phoebe's attention. Everywhere, radiant and flickering polyps jetted throughout the forest. They swirled into and out of nests, tussling and rolling. Others spun joyously across the water. They came in sizes as small as her fist, to massive giants that hung shyly back.

Phoebe leaned her forehead to the glass, wishing she could swim among them. She remembered the joy she experienced freediving, both in her native Barbados and along the California coast. To be one with the ocean and its creatures. To accept the limitations of her species, while honoring life in all its myriad forms.

Adam offered sobering words. "We're too late."

With great effort, she tore her eyes from the view.

He was looking over his shoulder, back the way they had come. "We can't make it to the fissure. Not in time." He turned to them. "We're trapped down here."

42

Monk took in the view from the bridge of the *Titan X*. The only sign of the battle two hours before was a flotsam of debris: sections of broken boats, orange jackets that still held dead bodies, life preservers that had failed in their duty. Oil barrels rolled in the chop. Pools of petrol burned in patches.

The largest of the latter was a flaming lake. It marked where the *Dayangxi* had sunk. The wreckage was continuing to leak fuel, feeding the funeral pyre above. There were no such markers for the sites where the hunter-killer sub and the amphibious LCAC had gone down.

A gruff complaint announced Kowalski's arrival. "Screw that. I don't care who's on the bridge. I'm not putting out my cigar."

Monk turned as the big man marched in, trailed by redolent smoke. He was flanked by Jarrah, the head of security. They both carried assault rifles and holstered sidearms.

"How are our guests?" Monk called over.

"All tucked into their beds," Kowalski said. "Sweet as can be."

The new captain of the *Titan X* called from the helm. "How many total?" William Byrd asked.

"Eighteen," Jarrah answered crisply. "That should be all of them."

"We crammed them into the two brigs," Kowalski added. "It's tight quarters, but better than a long walk down a short plank."

Monk shook his head. They had rounded up the last of the Chinese soldiers. The injured had been moved to the ship's medical ward, where they were handcuffed and under guard. Their treatment was better than they deserved—more of their comrades floated out in the water. But Monk had held off recovering the bodies.

And for good reason.

He stared out the windows. Several drones circled the flaming lake. They were still guarding the waters where the *Dayangxi* had gone down. No doubt the ocean's depths were similarly patrolled.

Monk feared sending out any of their boats to retrieve the dead. He didn't want to attract the attention of those automated weapons. They likely remained on target, but he wasn't taking any chances. It was one of the reasons he had kept the *Titan X* at its current position.

To wait out the enemy.

Monk pictured the VTOL drone that he had watched land on the LCAC to recharge. With the base ship sunk, the drones would eventually lose power. Once everything was quiet, he would entertain moving.

Kowalski had informed him that there were a couple dozen people alive on the wreckage of *Titan Station Up*. They would have to wait. The safety of the hundred-plus aboard the yacht was his priority.

Plus, four others.

Monk stared down at his toes.

Not much I can do for them.

He crossed to the sonar station. "How do things look down there?" he asked the bridge tech.

Byrd joined him.

"The seaquake seems to be quieting," the man said. "There are some continuing tremors, but they're not as violent."

"And the fissure?" Byrd asked.

"According to the sonar, it's nearly closed up." He swallowed and turned to them. "I've still not heard anything from the *Cormorant*."

Monk scowled. "Captain Tse is down there, too. Her bathyscaphe is armed. Keep a close watch for her. We don't want her ambushing us."

The tech nodded. "Will do."

The radio operator shouted from across the bridge. "Sir! I've got a satellite call." He turned and lifted a handset. "They're asking for you, Dr. Kokkalis."

Monk hurried over. The ship had been trying to reach someone for the past two hours, but they'd had no luck. The heavy ash, the constant static energy, and the EM interference from the raging volcanos had continued to stifle communication.

How did anyone get through to us?

He took the receiver. "Dr. Kokkalis here," he said.

"Monk, that's quite formal. I think we're better friends than that."

"Gray!"

Kowalski shoved forward in a cloud of smoke. "Of course, he calls after all the heavy lifting is done."

"I don't have much time," Gray said. "I can't count on this connection holding. We found some clean air, even a bit of sunshine."

Monk wished for the same. He stared at the midnight gloom smothering the ship. To the east, a line of volcanos cast up fountains of fire. It looked as if those islands were being blasted apart.

"I need you to do something," Gray said. "Right away."

"What is it?"

During the next twenty minutes, Gray shared a digital recording and a wild tale. Monk did his best to fill in his side. He put the conversation on speakerphone so everyone could hear. It seemed they all had pieces to a two-century-old puzzle.

But it came down to one urgency.

"Get to Raoul Island," Gray finished. "As swiftly as you can. Broadcast that recording as loudly as possible. Keep it playing."

Even with Gray's explanation and assurances, Monk found his claim hard to believe. But if Gray and the others had managed to quiet Mount Tambora, it was worth a shot.

Raoul Island was only eight miles from their current location.

Monk squinted and picked out the fieriest of those peaks.

That's gotta be it.

Gray had a final warning. "Major Xue still hasn't been able to reach his father. If the Chinese send out another ELF signal—"

Monk didn't need Gray to finish his statement.

It's game over.

Monk signed off and faced the bridge crew. They all knew what they needed to do.

"What about Dr. Reed and the others?" Byrd asked.

Monk turned to the sonar operator. "Keep trying to reach the *Cormorant*. For as long as we're in the area. Share that recording. Broadcast it down to them." He pointed at the man. "From my pre-dive training, I was told the acoustic modem can send text messages. Is that right?"

The other nodded. "Texts can reach even farther through water than voice calls. And they have a lower probability of interception."

"Perfect. Then you're going to send a message along with that audio recording."

"What do you want me to say?"

Monk told him and stared down at his toes. He prayed his message reached the *Cormorant*.

And no one else.

43

An hour after entering the fissure, the *Qianliyan* neared the top.

Daiyu sweated profusely. The humidity in the sphere had grown severe. She had dumped most of her batteries to hasten her ascent. To conserve what was left, she had shut down circulation, utilizing only the CO_2 scrubbers.

The space also reeked from Yang's body, tainting the heavy air. She tasted his bile on her tongue. It filled her nose. She longed for fresh air.

Through the acoustic phones, she listened as the grinding of rock slowly ebbed. The cliffs had closed to within a meter of either side. Much of her perspiration was not due to the humidity, but from her anxious attempts to keep her ascent fixed between those walls. She had to constantly tweak the thrusters to guide her climb, avoiding outcroppings and falling boulders.

She risked a glance down to check her sonar screen.

Almost there.

A harder tremor shook the *Qianliyan*. The walls surged toward her, closing half the distance.

She grimaced and swore.

I will not die down here, she promised herself for the hundredth time.

She concentrated on the cliffs. The sonar screen showed a clear ride to the top. She prayed for more speed, trying to will it so.

Only a hundred meters to go.

She stared up, hoping to see the exit. But the seas remained dark. Somewhere up there was a glowing forest of coral. To her, it was a mirror of the aurora borealis that heralded her bright future. She searched for any telltale sign of it.

The grumbling of the earth dimmed in her phones. She prayed it meant the quake was finally coming to an end.

As she strained to listen, a new noise rose. It was a low-frequency roaring, a steady hum that sounded angry. She squinted upward, trying to discern where it was coming from, what it could be.

The perpetual blackness above slowly brightened to a lighter gray. She swore she could see swirling hues at the edges.

My aurora . . .

Anxious to confirm this, she switched off the *Qianliyan*'s exterior lamps. The world closed around the vehicle as it swept upward.

I was right.

She smiled as the halo of brilliance grew.

I'm coming.

Then the earth shook with another violent tremor. The *Qianliyan* jolted hard, striking one of the cliffs. She was thrown to the side. She switched the exterior lamps back on.

The walls were pinched tighter now.

The vehicle rebounded off the opposite wall. She fought the thrusters, but the *Qianliyan* rattled back and forth. She was tossed about in her seat. Something got damaged. The exterior lamps snuffed out, leaving only the interior lights. The CO_2 scrubbers died with a sharp grinding whine.

A moment of claustrophobic panic flushed through her.

She held her breath until the tremor settled. She stared up at the aurora borealis shining even brighter now.

Less than five meters away.

The *Qianliyan* swept upward.

Four . . .

Three . . .

A scream of metal on stone ground the *Qianliyan* to a sudden halt. Daiyu twisted and spun in her seat.

No . . .

The vehicle was stuck, pinned by an outcropping she had failed to spot. She checked her sonar.

Only another two meters.

The top of the fissure was right there. The shine of the glowing coral forest mocked her. Still, she refused to relent.

She took on more ballast. If she could drop the *Qianliyan* a meter or so, she could maneuver around the blockage. She filled all her tanks, weighing down the vehicle. She regretted dumping all her torpedoes.

"*Gāisǐ de!*" she screamed, swearing at the world.

She shoved around in her seat as if trying to wiggle herself free.

Something finally did give.

The *Qianliyan* lurched with another screech of tortured steel. The heavy vehicle broke free with a jarring jolt. It dropped swiftly.

She hollered in great satisfaction and stared up, momentarily mystified by the view.

A huge shadow fell through the glow toward her.

She squinted, trying to understand what it was. It crashed onto the top of the fissure, accompanied by a loud metallic gong. Something poked down at her. It was a muzzle and a long barrel. She recognized what had crashed.

The battle tank from the LCAC.

Full of residual air, it had taken the armored vehicle two hours to plummet the six miles. She frowned at this testament to her failure, as if it were mocking her.

A rock fell from the cliff's edge, dislodged by the impact. It bounced between the walls and struck the scallop of her window. It was hard enough to break a seam between the glass and the titanium.

A pencil-thin stream of water shot inside. It hit her stomach. Under the extreme pressures of the deep, the force drilled through her belly, severed her spine. Fiery agony nudged her hand and shifted the throttle.

The *Qianliyan* rolled, throwing her to the side.

The watery laser cut her open, slicing her nearly in half.

Her life spilled into her lap.

She struggled to push it back in.

Not like this.

The sphere imploded, crushing her last thought away.

44

"How much oxygen do we have left?" Adam asked.

Bryan tapped a gauge. "After jettisoning our reserve tanks by the fissure, we have at best four or five hours. Same with the batteries."

Adam gritted his teeth.

Just enough time to write our obituaries.

Phoebe seemed unperturbed. She continued to study the life around her. She had a notebook in her lap and drew rough sketches. Over the past hour, she and Datuk had been whispering, speculating, theorizing about everything. He suspected—at least on Datuk's part—that it was to distract from the inevitable.

Phoebe pointed to a shining swirl of hundreds of polyps. They swept past and cascaded in a complicated, coordinated dance. "That behavior looks less like the *schooling* of fish and more like the *murmuration* of starlings."

Datuk leaned closer. "They must be using a combination of bioluminescent patterns and sonic calls to synchronize their movements. Such behavior could explain why the species appears to be more intelligent than the average octopus. With rare exceptions, octopuses live solitary lives. Intelligence is whetted far better in a societal structure, which requires honing communication skills and cooperation."

Adam tuned them out and sighed heavily. He turned the other way.

He looked toward the dark forest and pictured the fissure back there. They had monitored it with their sonar and watched the lowermost edge close to a narrow gap. It looked like the fissure might be wider up higher, but there was no way to get through the squeeze at the bottom.

Motion drew his gaze to the edge of the black forest. Flocks of the bioluminescent creatures swirled at the fringes, darting among the trunks, as if wanting to enter but still wary of the radiation. As he stared, more and more gathered at that edge, a frustrated army of them.

"What are they doing?" Adam mumbled.

Phoebe glanced back. "What's wrong?"

Adam swung to Bryan. "Can you spin us around?"

The Aussie nodded and boosted the thrusters to turn the *Cormorant.* They all watched the gathering at that blackened fringe of forest.

"It looks like something's calling to them," Datuk said. "But they don't dare cross the irradiated area to get there."

Phoebe pulled up the acoustic headphones. As she listened, two deep lines creased her brow. She turned to Bryan and pointed at an earpiece. "Can you put this on speaker?"

He flipped a switch, and a low roaring filled the sphere.

A few passing polyps spun and circled back to the *Cormorant.* Luminous eyes peered inside, studying them.

"They hear it, too," Datuk said. "It's clearly attracting them."

Phoebe nodded. "Someone's broadcasting it. From above. It must be echoing through the gap in the trench."

"But what is it?" Adam asked. "Who's sending it?"

Bryan pointed at a monitor to the right of his helm. "It's coming from the *Titan X.* It's accompanied by a text message." He glanced back. "From our old shipmate Monk."

Adam leaned over, nearly crawling atop Bryan.

The Aussie elbowed him back. "I'll send it to all your screens."

Adam returned to his seat and read a long missive from Monk. It told a story that went back two centuries. He was clearly trying to share as much intelligence as possible.

"Bullroarers?" Datuk said. "That's what we're hearing? That's what's agitating these creatures?"

Phoebe looked unsurprised. "The species communicate via harmonics. Maybe it's due to the silicon in their DNA or some amplification through the crystalline structure of their coral skeletons. No matter the reason, it's clearly a powerful tool for them."

Adam turned as the roaring dimmed in the sphere. The sonic communication slowly faded. He pictured the *Titan X* sailing away from these waters, heading for Raoul Island.

They've moved out of range.

Frustrated, Adam turned to the others. "Does any of this help us with our situation? Monk clearly has no idea if we're trapped or not. He must have dispatched as much as he could, letting us know where to look for him if we ever made it out of here."

Phoebe ignored his question and played with the sonar array, casting out pings. She leaned over Bryan and checked their positional reading and compass.

"What are you doing?" Adam asked.

Phoebe turned to him. "I know how to get out of here."

"What?" Datuk frowned at her. "How?"

She pointed to the sonar screen, which showed a forward-looking scan of the far wall. The sounding showed a patchwork of solid rock and black spaces that failed to return a ping.

She pointed to the largest. "That's got to be a tunnel. It's heading in the direction of the coordinates that Monk sent us for Raoul Island."

"You think it'll lead us there?" Bryan asked.

"Maybe. That account spoke of the Aboriginal myth of the Rainbow Serpent, how it could travel around the globe via a secret watery world." She waved to encompass this cavernous space. "From waterhole to waterhole, from one thin spot to another."

"And Raoul Island is its legendary home," Adam said.

"Then—like Rome—all roads must lead there."

"But how can we be sure we pick the right path?" Datuk asked. "It could be a maze once we leave this cavern."

Phoebe shrugged. "We either try—"

"Or we die," Adam said, finishing her thought.

6:17 P.M.

With a walkie-talkie in hand, Monk crossed the stern hold of the *Titan X*. Its rear door lay open to the sea. Ahead, the western side of Raoul Island filled the view. The yacht had dropped anchor a mile off the coast. Two spits of land reached toward them, framing a wide bay.

Directly ahead, a tall volcano seethed and boomed. Lava bombs blew in huge fiery arcs from its flaming caldera. They slammed into the bay with sizzling blasts or crashed into the gutted forests. The island had once been a lush atoll covered by dense jungle and dotted by tiny lakes. It was now a flaming coal in a dark sea. Blackened trunks prickled its slopes. Solitary torches burned in the smoke-shrouded gloom.

To the south, volcanos marched off into the distance, heading toward the coast of New Zealand. The closest was as fiery as Raoul, but the others faded with distance into smoldering glows.

Monk stepped out onto the apron of decking.

Kowalski waited to one side. "Don't want to go swimming out there," he warned, knocking red embers from his cigar into the sea, adding to the thick layer of ash. Several patches of the sea flickered with flames.

But it wasn't the pall or fires that concerned the big man.

Across the bay, hundreds of spiky balls spun through the ash. Gray had warned them about those fiery mines and the dangers they posed.

Monk raised his walkie and radioed the bridge. "Kokkalis here. I'm in position. Do you copy?"

Byrd responded. "All set at our end. On your word, we'll pipe that recording through the ship's sirens and emergency speakers. It's going to get loud. You sure you want to be out in the open?"

"Light the cannon," Monk said and lowered the walkie.

He intended to be on hand to witness any change.

Kowalski was down here on a smoke break.

A moment later, a low roaring rose around the ship, echoing over the sea. It quickly rose in volume. Monk winced at the noise. Kowalski clamped his large hands over his ears.

It grew into a resounding alarm. The noise reverberated throughout the ship. It vibrated the decking underfoot and shivered the layers of ash in the water.

The *Titan X* had become the world's largest tuning fork.

The noise shook through Monk's frame, prickling his skin.

He took a step deeper into the hold, trying to escape the onslaught.

Some frequency in that roaring spasmed his prosthetic. The EW module burned under his palm, hot enough he thought it might melt through his skin. His head throbbed. The pain lanced across his scalp, rising from the scar behind his ear that marked where his cortical implant had been placed.

Monk remembered how Gray had mentioned that the ELF signal had knocked out the electronics in a lunar lander and maybe the Chinese nuclear submarine.

Does this roaring contain some wavelength just as damaging?

He stumbled backward, his sight blurring.

Shouldn't have come outside.

Then Kowalski was there. He grabbed Monk and held him upright. Kowalski pointed past the stern.

Monk blinked and squinted. Raoul Island still smoldered and smoked. Its caldera remained fiery. But the cascade of flames had died away. The flows of lava down its flanks appeared to be petering out. The mountain gave one last burp of fire, then stayed quiet.

Monk shifted forward, still beaten down by the roaring. He searched to the south. The line of volcanos had similarly subsided. The distant glows had vanished. The nearest peak slowly disappeared into the gloom.

He raised his walkie and yelled into it. "Byrd, cut it off!"

He was deaf to any acknowledgment, but the sirens and speakers wound down, finally dying away.

With his ears still ringing, he turned to Kowalski. "I didn't think it would work," he admitted. "Especially that fast."

"What are you talking about?" Kowalski scowled at him. He lifted his cigar, which had burned down to a stub. "It's been nearly an hour."

"What?"

Kowalski dug a knuckle into an ear. "Don't know if I'll ever hear right again."

Monk stared at his prosthesis and rubbed the side of his head. Time had slipped for him. He opened and closed his fist. All seemed fine now.

"Look!" Kowalski pointed across the bay.

Without the torch of the volcano, the world had grown darker. Across the water, the layers of ash glowed, suffused with soft lights from below. The patches grew steadily brighter, skimming and gliding. More and more rose, until the bay was swarming with them. A few broke through the powder, shining in brilliant flickers of emerald and cobalt.

The Rainbow Serpents.

Monk stepped out onto the deck, awed and breathless. Still, he felt wobbly and caught a hand on the steel A-frame that hung over the stern. It was the launch-and-recovery system for the *Cormorant*.

Reminded of the others, he raised his walkie to his lips. "Bridge, any word from the *Cormorant*?"

He waited for a response. It was slow coming, dragged by the grim news.

"No," Byrd said. "We may have to consider them lost."

6:45 P.M.

"Do we have any clue where we are?" Adam asked.

Phoebe heard the desperation in his voice and understood it. They had been traversing this labyrinth for more than an hour. They would soon be running out of oxygen.

She shook her head and studied the sonar. The *Cormorant* hovered in a large cavern. It was full of coral, flowing with vibrant, radiant life.

By now, even her enthusiasm had dimmed for this lost landscape.

"Four tunnels and chasms extent eastward," Phoebe reported. "I can't tell which one might lead to Raoul Island."

"If any of them do," Datuk added, exhausted and defeated.

Bryan offered the only option open to them. "We can always flip a coin."

Phoebe frowned, unwilling to accept defeat.

After leaving the first cavern, they had discovered a maze of crisscrossing tunnels, jagged rifts, and bottomless chasms. Even their compass betrayed them, at times spinning wildly in some magnetic flux. She was not sure she could even trace their way back to where they started.

The only hopeful sign came from their external pressure reading. It had been steadily dropping. Bryan had to keep blowing ballast to adjust their buoyancy. It indicated that they must be edging upward. The external pressure was currently at 15,000 psi, which would place them at a depth of around ten thousand meters.

"We have to be close," Phoebe said. "The island was only eight miles from the *Titan X*'s position. And by the time we exited the first huge cavern, we had already crossed two miles off that distance. We must be nearing the island's waters by now."

"Even if that was true," Adam said, "how do we get up there? The sonar's not picked up a single gap, crack, or seam in the roof over our heads. Just endless rock."

Phoebe sighed and pointed. "Then we keep going. We have no choice."

Bryan engaged the thrusters and set them gliding forward. Their motion drew the attention of a few passing polyps. They spun closer, casting an inquiring eye inside at the sphere, then sped off with a whip of their bodies.

More followed and cascaded around them, flashing and streaming with lights. She read some urgency in their pattern, but it was likely only a reflection of her own tension.

"Must be rush hour," Bryan mumbled.

Phoebe grinned—then noted that he was right. She ignored the sonar and studied the growing river running alongside them. She might have dismissed it, except the polyps were all blinking the same urgent pattern as the first couple.

Bryan started to drift the *Cormorant* away, to get out of the traffic flow.

Phoebe reached over and pushed the yoke back. "Follow them!"

Adam leaned forward. "What is it?"

She ignored him and donned the acoustic headphones. The chorus of the coral forest filled her head. She squinted, trying to pick up a deeper tone, but it was too noisy.

Ahead, a branch of nesting polyps shot high and dove into the flow.

Adam touched her shoulder. "Phoebe?"

She pulled off the headphones and turned to him. "The way the polyps are flashing, the army that's building. It's like back at the first cavern, when they bunched at the fringe of the irradiated forest."

Datuk understood. "They're responding the same way. Likely to the same signal."

"The roaring that Monk transmitted to us," Adam said.

"He was planning on broadcasting that same signal over the waters of Raoul Island." Phoebe searched ahead. "I think the creatures are hearing it now, heeding that siren's call like before."

Adam sat straighter. "Then they could lead us out of here."

"I'm not waiting." Bryan tilted the *Cormorant* and maxed their thrusters. "Don't wanna get left behind."

They followed that shining river, chased by rainbows in their wake. The flock swept into a far tunnel, across a smaller cavern, and up a long spiraling rift.

Bryan blew ballast to keep up.

Phoebe flashed their lights, roughly in synch with the polyps, trying to signal her intention: *We're coming, too.*

They reached the end of the spiral and exited into a bowl-shaped cavern. It was full of giant coral, but its nests were mostly empty. Only a few handfuls of polyps spun and drifted through this dark forest.

Adam lunged forward and tapped at the sonar screen. It showed a map of the roof above. "A seam! Right there!"

Bryan eyed the dark shadow and sat straighter. "Emptying all ballast."

The *Cormorant* sailed upward. The vehicle spun as it ascended. A luminous tide of polyps rode along with them. They raced together toward that crack in the roof.

Phoebe watched the polyps. She knew these creatures could travel much faster.

"They're staying with us," she realized. "They don't want us to fall behind."

Adam pointed. "We're approaching the seam. Looks like it'll be a snug fit."

"I'll get us through," Bryan promised.

But the choice was taken from them.

Something bumped them from below. Their ascent quickened. Phoebe leaned between her legs and stared under her. A huge polyp flared and whipped its tentacles below the *Cormorant*. It was the size of an elephant. It propelled them upward.

"We're going too fast," Bryan warned. "At this speed, our thrusters won't be able to finesse any course corrections or adjustments."

"Then let's hope that beast under us has good aim." Adam looked up. "Because there's no turning back now."

Their pace steadily increased.

"Hold tight!" Adam called.

Lit by the shining river above, the rift swept down toward them. Then they were in it. Phoebe sucked in her breath, trying to squeeze herself tighter. The walls swept mere inches to either side.

The passing cliffs were festooned in swaths of waving anemone and thick mats of algae. From all the growth, this rift had to be old.

She understood what they must be traveling through.

One of the Aboriginal *thin* spots.

She imagined there must be a similar one in the seas near Mount Tambora, an ancient window between their two worlds.

A few minutes later, the *Cormorant* shot out of the rift and into open water. Their caretaker gave them another hard push, then swept away. The luminous tide flowed in a glowing river through the black water, heading for Raoul Island.

"Looks like we're on our own," Adam said.

"No worries, mates." Bryan pointed a finger up. "I know the way from here."

Phoebe checked their depth. "Five thousand meters."

"With the momentum we've got," Bryan said, "we should be topside in twenty minutes."

He was wrong.

It took only fifteen.

The *Cormorant* reached the surface and popped high, nearly clearing the water. The vehicle bobbed back down, then up again, until it finally floated atop the waves.

Bryan clambered over them to pop their hatch.

Adam dropped into the pilot's seat, leaning shoulder to shoulder with Phoebe.

They stared across the waves to the smoldering remains of Raoul Island. The bright lights of the *Titan X* glowed a mile off, anchored near the mouth of a bay. The waters there stirred and glowed in the hues of a rainbow.

"Did we do it?" Phoebe asked.

Adam touched her chin and turned her gaze farther west.

The black pall of clouds had dissipated enough to show a peak at the horizon, at the curve of a world that looked new to her eyes.

But one detail remained eternal and full of promise.

The evening sun blazed atop the sea, shining brightly.

She smiled.

Yes, we did it.

45

Several floors beneath the Smithsonian Castle, Gray thumped with a cane down the central corridor of Sigma's buried command center. He checked his watch and scowled. His left thigh stabbed with every step. He passed Sigma's intelligence nest. The spider of that technological web—Kat Bryant—heard his approach and met him at the door.

She leaned on the frame. "You're late."

He shrugged as he passed her. "Physical therapy ran long."

She called after him. "So it wasn't because you stopped for a Starbucks?"

Gray grinned. She was definitely the master of her domain. "That was part of my therapy. Plus, for this debriefing, I could use more than just caffeine."

"A triple espresso wasn't enough?"

He glanced back, but she had already ducked away. Had she tracked his coffee order or was it simply that she knew him so well? He didn't know which was worse.

He continued to the director's office. The door was open, but he still knocked on the frame.

"Commander Pierce, you're late."

"So I've been duly informed."

Gray stepped inside. Monk was already seated and welcomed him with a big grin. Painter Crowe sat behind his desk. The director had shed his jacket and his sleeves were rolled to his elbows. He combed the single white lock in his dark hair behind an ear and waved to the remaining chair.

"Let's get started."

Behind him, monitors glowed on three walls. One showed a map of Southeast Asia. Another ran with silent footage of the ongoing rescue operations. The third was a satellite view of Raoul Island. A large ship was anchored offshore. At its aft end, a tall glass sphere glinted in the sunlight.

Gray settled in his seat. It had been two weeks since the region had quieted down, but the world remained tenuously unsettled. The ash clouds from the dozens of eruptions had circled the planet. A dense haze still persisted. It might take months, if not years, until it fully dissipated, with unknown climatic consequences.

"What's the word out of China?" Gray asked.

"About what you'd expect," Painter said. "They're blaming the civilian deaths and military actions on a rogue unit in the PLA, led by an overly ambitious captain. They refuse to talk about the ELF transmission or their lost submarine."

Monk turned to Gray. "But no one's fooled. The countries that were affected are holding China's feet to the fire. Beijing is funding most of the recovery efforts, trying to buy their way out of what happened."

Painter nodded. "The Chinese have also been chastised enough to open a dialogue and work with NASA's Artemis program when it comes to future lunar missions."

Gray frowned. "I wager that's only so they can share the blame if anything goes wrong again."

"What exactly happened up there?" Monk asked.

"As near as anyone can surmise," Painter explained, "the Chinese were right about Theia—the ancient planetoid that smashed into the primordial Earth and created the moon. It left fragments not only under our mantle but also slivers buried in the lunar crust. Apparently, some force still connects those pieces and responded to the drilling of their lander."

Gray tuned out this explanation. He had kept in contact with Major Xue and had long conversations on this very subject. Much remained unknown. Only it was clear everyone needed to tread lightly from here on out, both on the moon and with the strange ecosystem discovered deep in the sea.

"What's the possibility of someone using that ELF transmission as a weapon?" Monk asked. "Of triggering more quakes?"

Painter sighed. "Nations around the world have been informed about it and will be monitoring for those transmissions. With the knowledge shared globally about the bullroarers, any hostile usage could be mitigated, making any weapon useless."

"We had better hope so," Monk added.

"I also spoke to Dr. Reed about her initial work with the species that was discovered," Painter said. "She's continuing to explore how their morphology seems to blur the line between geology and biology. She believes the species utilizes harmonics as a means of communication and to manipulate their environment. As a vast colony, they seem capable of casting out unique frequencies that vibrate the crystalline nature of the Theia fragments. Thus triggering quakes or eruptions. All as a means to protect their territory."

"If Dr. Reed is right," Monk said, "we'd better not piss them off."

"As a precaution, the seas around Raoul Island have been cordoned off. Research there will be limited. William Byrd is reestablishing the Titan Project in the waters nearby to oversee the effort."

"What about the claim that the species was born out of rock, seeded by those fragments of Theia?" Monk asked.

"Too early to say," Painter said. "According to Dr. Reed, it's a chicken-or-egg situation. Maybe something was already in the crystalline planetoid and emerged out of its fringes, slowly shedding its silicon nature to become what was discovered. Or it could have been some deep-sea coral ancestor that abutted against the fragment and incorporated some of its silicon properties. Either way, the species does seem to have a harmonic relationship with those masses."

Monk frowned. "Could they truly be the great ancestors to the modern-day octopuses and other cephalopod species?"

Painter shrugged. "Dr. Reed is starting to explore that very question with Datuk Lee. They'll be bringing in scientists who have been studying panspermia, the theory that life on Earth may have been seeded—or at least, partially so—by cosmic bombardments. It'll take a lot more research before anything can be substantiated or ruled out."

Gray shifted, his thigh wincing in complaint. It reminded him that he wasn't the only one suffering in recovery.

"I checked up on Kadir Numberi at the hospital in Jakarta," he said. "He's recovering from his belly wound. I talked to him about the Aboriginal connection to all of this. He's already been invited to join the new Titan Project, to further explore the true history of his great-grandfather's people. I think that story has yet to be fully told. He's excited to challenge the Out-of-Africa theory of human origins."

"I look forward to hearing what he discovers," Painter said.

During the next hour, the three reviewed countless other details until the director finally stood up from his desk, clearly ready to dismiss them. But he motioned to Gray. "Commander Pierce, can you hang back for another moment?"

"Of course."

Gray said his good-byes to Monk, hugging and clapping his friend on the back.

Monk pulled away with an amused twinkle in his eyes. "Having to stay after class? Sounds like someone's in trouble."

"What else is new?"

Monk left him with Painter.

Gray remained standing. "What did you want to talk about?"

"This." Painter opened a drawer and pulled out a file that was stamped in red with the words Top Secret. "I was given permission to show you this by the Under Secretary of Defense for Intelligence and Security. It's a deeply classified report by the newly established UAPTF."

Gray frowned at the acronym, not recognizing it.

"The Unidentified Aerial Phenomena Task Force," Painter explained. "The Department of the Navy leads this group, whose mission is to detect, analyze, and catalog UAPs."

Gray stared down at the folder as Painter slid it toward him. "What does it concern?"

"It pertains to the topic we were just discussing. About the possibility that those fragments of Theia might have carried something with them, something that seeded our planet." Painter pointed to the file. "The task force has noted an unusual pattern in UAP activity. It's been noted by the general public, too, even drawing media attention. But it's never been fully investigated."

"Until now," Gray said.

Painter nodded. "In light of all that's happened, the task force believes its results are significant enough to share—at least with us."

Gray opened the folder and read the title of the report: THE PREVALENCE AND PREPONDERANCE OF UAPs IN TECTONICALLY ACTIVE AREAS.

Gray stiffened. "Is this true?"

"The report does show an unusual patterning of UAP activity in volcanic and earthquake-prone regions—especially along the edges of those LLSVP blobs, those regions that could be fragments of Theia."

Gray flipped through the pages of charts and pictures. One showed a ring of blue lights surrounding a fiery caldera.

"It seems like *someone* is monitoring these areas," Painter said.

Gray looked up, his eyes huge, as he understood the implication. "Like gardeners tending a field they seeded."

Painter reached over and closed the folder. "If so, let's hope they don't have a harvest season."

2:00 P.M. WITA
Raoul Island

Standing at the bow of a Zodiac, Phoebe rode across Denham Bay toward the shores of Raoul Island. Her hair was bunched behind her head. The winds brushed her cheeks, and she inhaled the salty spray with each bounce over the waves.

She glanced behind her. The afternoon sun reflected brightly off the blue waters, hiding the dark mysteries below. Closer at hand, the *Titan X* rose like a glossy white iceberg. Its glass sphere, wide decks, and long halls had been polished of any speck of ash. The insides had been scrubbed of blood and were undergoing repairs from the damage inflicted.

It was all overseen by William Byrd, who had forced the Chinese to pay for repairs, along with doling out restitution to the families whose loved ones were killed. China was also funding the new Titan Project. This was achieved not because of Beijing's guilt or sense of justice, but because Byrd was the owner and CEO of ESKY, the shipping conglomerate that orchestrated commerce across the world's oceans. With a word, he could cripple the Chinese economy . . . so he got his way.

Phoebe pushed such matters aside, finding it all disheartening.

She knew what had drawn her to this topic. At the back of the Zodiac, Major Choi Xue and Dr. Luo Heng sat in front of Bryan, who piloted their craft. She did not know them well, but Monk had vouched for them. She had also reviewed Heng's research on the cure for the biomineralizing disease that had afflicted thousands across the region.

Including someone close to her heart.

Jazz shoved up next to her. She carried her right arm in a sling. She had been released from the hospital a week before and had headed straight here. She had lost two fingers to that disease, but she remained in good spirits and was anxious to continue their partnership.

The other researcher afflicted by the coral's venom—Dr. Kim Jong Suk—had not fared as well. He had lost his left arm. Byrd had offered Dr. Kim a place on the new station once it was built. The man had bitterly declined.

"When are you going to tell me why we're headed to the island?" Jazz asked.

Bryan cut them off, calling from the stern. "Better sit down, gals! Might want to grab on to something, too!"

Jazz glanced back as she took her seat. "I know something I'd like to grab on to. That accent of his . . . phew . . ."

Phoebe tried to frown at her but ended up smiling.

Jazz turned forward. "A gal's got to do something with her off time." She eyed Phoebe sidelong. "Speaking of which, I heard Adam's flying in tonight."

"To see how things are going. That's all. It's purely professional."

Jazz cast her a doubtful look.

The conversation mercifully ended as the Zodiac reached the shore and beached high onto the sand with a grating bump. They all offloaded.

Xue and Heng hauled out a large waterproof case and carried it to shore.

Jazz kept alongside her. "What's in there?"

Phoebe knew the answer. Only a few others did. Still, Jazz deserved to be here, having paid in flesh and blood for this honor. If left untreated, her friend might have suffered far worse.

Jazz was about to find out *how* much worse.

2:11 P.M.

Heng lowered the heavy crate to the sand. He wiped sweat from his brow and stared up at the ruins of the island. It was a charred husk of rock and charcoal. The caldera lay quiet but still seeped a curl of smoke.

It was a grim place for a homecoming.

Xue crossed and placed a hand on his shoulder. "Are you all right?"

Heng took a deep breath. "I will be."

Guilt ate at him.

I should've done more.

Shortly after the tragic events, he had managed to distill the antitoxin from the sample they had collected near Mount Tambora. Dr. Reed had aided in this effort, supplying him with several samples of the nematocyst-tipped tendrils. The species had been dubbed *Iridis serpens*, in respect for the Aboriginal people who had first formed a relationship with them. The antitoxin ended up being an organo-silicon enzyme, one that was easy to mass produce via a solid-state fermentation process.

Still, it hadn't been quick enough to save everyone. He had managed to treat Sublieutenant Junjie back at the Réam Naval Base in Cambodia. But it had been too late to help Officer Wong. Heng regretted keeping the man alive for so long, repeatedly reviving him when there was no hope, making him suffer through a long, torturous decline to an agonizing end.

He cursed Captain Tse—wherever she was—for forcing his hand.

Still, I should've stood up to her.

All Heng could do now was attempt to atone for his sins.

Xue's fingers squeezed his shoulder, offering reassurance. Though extremely busy, the major had agreed to travel with Heng to Raoul Island.

Back in Cambodia, Xue had taken over Captain Tse's facility. He was converting it into a new space research center. He was working cooperatively with NASA, trying to forge a more open relationship. It was a challenging assignment, especially with the pushback he was getting from his own father.

They had learned that it was the elder Choi who had ordered Captain Wen to eliminate the Americans. Son and father were on opposite sides of a generational divide. His father adhered to a Maoist philosophy of isolationism and militarism. Xue believed China's future lay in cooperation and mutual respect. It was a friction that might never end until the old guard let loose its grip on power.

Something that would take time and patience to happen.

It could not be rushed.

To help prepare for that long-term goal, Heng had agreed to continue his work at the base. Xue had personally requested that he stay.

Heng patted Xue's hand, thanking him for his support in this venture. They had spent considerable time together during the past two weeks, having long conversations over dinner, well into the night. Heng suspected Xue's request that he stay in Cambodia went beyond academic respect.

But Heng remained unsure.

For the moment, neither of them had voiced anything more.

Maybe that would also take time and patience.

And was best not rushed, too.

Until then, Heng bent and unsnapped the crate's clasps. He pulled open the lid. It was full of a saline nutrient solution. Floating and stir-

ring inside was a gray-pink mass, draped with tentacles that had once
been a single spinal cord.

"What is that?" Jazz asked.

Heng bowed his head in respect. "This is Officer Wong."

Xue stepped aside and lifted a small digital megaphone. He switched
it on, and the warbling call of an ancient bullroarer echoed over the
quiet bay.

To the side, Heng heard Dr. Reed explaining to her colleague about
Wong's fate. Heng had been unable to save him, but he had preserved
what he could.

After a few minutes, Phoebe helped him carry the crate into the water. They waded to their waists and kept vigil. The bullroarer continued
its deep-throated call out to sea.

Heng stared across the bay. "How long do you think—"

"Hush," she said. "They're coming."

Heng saw no change. He shaded his eyes against the sun's reflection
off the water. Finally, shapes shimmered into view, maybe a dozen.
They swam and stirred, flashing with lights. Their pattern looked like a
rainbow trapped underwater.

No wonder the Aboriginal people had named them so.

Iridis serpens.

The Rainbow Serpent.

"Ready?" Phoebe asked.

He nodded, too anxious to speak. Together, they tipped the crate
and spilled the remains of Officer Wong into the sea. The shape rolled
and flailed.

They both retreated.

As they did, the brilliant polyps stirred closer, approaching gently.
Tentacles probed the new stranger, dancing tendrils over its glistening
surface. With each touch, bioluminescence suffused into the other. In
turn, the gray-pink mass extended tendrils of its own. They wove and
danced together, a luminous merging of light and flesh, of energy and
substance.

Slowly, the polyps drew the newcomer along with them, rolling into
the depths, and vanishing.

Heng stared after them. He remembered the Aboriginal legends told by Kadir, concerning how such creatures could plant tiny seeds into a body, and how those seeds helped the afflicted be born anew, to ready them to be carried to the sleeping giant under the earth.

Where life became an endless Dreaming.

Heng didn't know how much of Officer Wong still persisted, but he prayed there was some part of the man still present, who could live forever.

At least, long enough to forgive me.

7:06 P.M. EST
Takoma Park, Maryland

Seichan battled demons inside her living room.

She had pushed aside the sofa and coffee table. She stood barefooted in a black sports bra and shorts. Her taut skin shone as if she were carved of stone. She balanced on the ball of one foot, her other knee held high. She carried the Chinese saber low at her hip in a two-handed grip.

With each breath, she moved through a set of moves in the Qingping Jian-style of sword combat: *Beng, Ci, Mo, Gua, Lan . . .* She dropped, stabbed, pressed, parried, and blocked. She moved faster and faster. The ancient *dao* blurred into a steely haze around her. She lined up the sequences into their ancient forms: *Angel Threads the Spindle, Sun Moon Exchanges the Rays . . .*

She kept her lips clamped and worked until her limbs trembled. She finally collapsed into a panting hunch, the saber across her knees.

Enough.

She stepped away and returned the blade to its matte steel scabbard. It was not a decorative covering. In battle, such sheathes were weapons themselves. She rested the scabbard atop a rosewood stand next to a bowl of white chrysanthemums. To the side, a single candle burned in front of a framed photo of Zhuang.

A week ago, Seichan had returned from the lieutenant's funeral in Macau. The affair had spanned seven days. The entire *Duàn zhī* Triad had been in attendance. Even the Blue Lantern boy, Bolin Chén—who had been initiated into the triad fold, rewarded for the bravery he had shown. Yeung had also been elevated to a lieutenant, standing now at Guan-yin's right side.

During those somber days, Seichan had done her best to console her mother. Guan-yin had put on a stoic face to the public, gowned in white. A sweep of silk across her features had helped to maintain her façade.

But behind doors, she was a broken woman.

In the quiet of the night, her mother had shared Zhuang's past. It was Zhuang who had taken Guan-yin in after she had fled her Vietnamese persecutors. He had been raised by a Buddhist monk after his own family had been killed during the Maoist siege of the city of Changchun. Nearly two hundred thousand civilians had died, including his parents and a younger sister. All he had of his family was his father's *dao*, which he had used to kill a soldier to flee the siege and survive.

Sharing a root of pain and loss, Zhuang and Guan-yin had found a common spirit in each other. They both burned with the same righteous fury, eventually founding the *Duàn zhī* Triad. Over time, while he remained fierce, he had eventually reached a calmness that still escaped Seichan's mother. Guan-yin expressed regret that because of her position she had kept him at arm's length. They were intimate in private, loved each other, but there had always remained a veil between them.

After the funeral, Guan-yin had sent Seichan home with Zhuang's sword. It had been something Zhuang had asked her mother to do. He had wanted the sword kept in the family. While Seichan was not his daughter, he had taken her into his heart. He had taught her the sequences that she had just practiced with the ancient sword. As it sang through the air, she had heard his voice, still teaching her one last lesson.

She touched her fingertips to the photo and readied herself.

With time running short, she quickly showered and donned a black silk dress embroidered with gray roses, each petal outlined in silver thread. She dabbed drops of jasmine on her wrists and pinned her hair back.

She went downstairs and opened a bottle of pinot noir and lit the candles on the table. Jack was spending the night at Monk and Kat's.

Behind her, a key turned in the front door lock. She stiffened, having failed to hear the throaty engine of the restored Thunderbird. A part of her wanted to bolt, but she centered herself, mentally sweeping steel around her.

She checked everything one last time.

As Gray opened the door, she glanced to the memorial table and gave Zhuang a small bow of her head, for teaching her this one last lesson.

Gray called to her. "Why are all the lights out?"

He stepped into the living room and spotted her in the dining room, bathed in candlelight. He stopped in confusion. "What are you—?"

She dropped to a knee and pressed the detonator in her hand.

Out in the backyard, seen through the dining room window, a cascade of fireworks burst into a brilliant splendor, booming with small explosions.

Kowalski—Sigma's demolition expert—had helped set it up.

She opened her mouth to explain, but she was cut off by a huge blast. It flashed as bright as a magnesium flare. The dining room window shattered behind her, scattering glass.

Seichan grimaced, knowing she should have expected as much from Kowalski.

Gray hurried over. "Are you all right?"

She stayed down on one knee. "I'm afraid this moment may not be as good as the Chinese New Year, but—"

She held up the ring box and opened it. The steel circle had belonged to Zhuang, too. She stared up at Gray. She had lived with many regrets. She would not add this one.

She ripped down the last veil between them.

"Will you marry me?"

EPILOGUE

TWO MONTHS LATER

The crisp morning air heralded the first day of spring. The sun shone brightly over the greensward of a wide park. Families strolled. A few dogs bounded. A happy chatter carried on the breeze. Overhead, the sky was an aching blue that looked painted in place.

A gleeful shout drew her attention back down. A child sped toward her, tripping along the sidewalk, half dragged by a string tied to a bat-winged kite.

Valya Mikhailov stepped out of the way. "Careful, *rebenok*."

An arm waved in acknowledgment, but her warning was ignored.

She continued to the far side of the park.

Despite the bright day, her thoughts remained dark. Over the past two years, she had rebuilt her forces as she kept her head low. She had expanded her organization, both in number and expertise, including their intelligence-gathering capabilities.

When the opportunity had arisen to rid herself of a thorn in her side, she had foolishly taken it. In her haste, she had made mistakes. She recognized that and accepted it. Still, she had made one last attempt in Jakarta. She had called Major Xue and alerted him to where Commander Pierce and the others were headed, to the city's history museum. She had hoped by co-opting her former employers that the situation could be rectified.

Again, I was mistaken.

No matter, if she was truthful with herself, she preferred to exact her own retribution. Yet now, the others knew she lived, which was problematic. She refused to be hunted. She was done hiding and biding her time. She was ready to go on the offensive.

If it's a war they want . . .

She glanced over her shoulder and stared up at the spire of the Washington Monument. Beyond it, the redbrick façade of the Smithsonian Castle stood tall.

She paused to listen to the laughter and shouts on this crisp morning—and pressed the transmitter button in her pocket.

The thunderous booms carried like cannon fire.

She continued across the street as the Castle shattered behind her.

. . . *then a war we shall have.*

Author's Note to Readers: Truth or Fiction

It's high time I stepped aside, pulled back the curtain, and revealed how much of this book is based on *fact* and how much is *fabrication*. While the tale I've told is a wild story of exotic organo-silicon lifeforms, lunar missions gone awry, and tectonic disasters, there are indeed plenty of facts upon which this novel was built—and even a fair amount of *fabric* in my fabrications.

So let's begin with where this story starts. In the past.

THE MOUNT TAMBORA ERUPTION

First, I must admit that there was a movie that captured my imagination when I was a boy: *Krakatoa, East of Java*. It came out in 1968 and starred Maximilian Schell and Brian Keith. It was a disaster film dramatizing the eruption of Krakatoa in 1883. The movie stuck with me over the passing decades. It instilled in me a fascination with volcanism. As a writer, I wanted to try to recapture that excitement I experienced watching the movie.

Many of the details that appear in the prologue came from firsthand accounts of Mount Tambora's eruption: the cannon-like explosions that were heard hundreds of miles away, the ash-covered seas dotted by islands of floating pumice, the exploration ships covered in ash. Days turned into night; coastlines crushed by tsunamis.

All of this was related in a wonderfully exciting history book that I highly recommend:

The Year Without Summer: 1816 and the Volcano That Darkened the World and Changed History, by William K. Klingaman and Nicholas P. Klingaman

In that same volume, I learned of Sir Stamford Raffles—the lieutenant-governor of the region—and how he played a pivotal role during the cataclysm, recording many of his experiences. He was also an avid naturalist and had a great interest in the history and culture of the local people. During his stint in Jakarta, he had served as the president of the Royal Batavian Society, a major scientific organization in the region.

Raffles also later established the port of Singapore with William Farquhar. The two famously competed for discoveries in the region and had a dramatic falling-out. In the end, Stamford assigned governorship of Singapore to a physician he knew from his time in Jakarta: Dr. John Crawfurd. Their tangled webs of intrigue, backstabbing, and scientific competition are all true. For me, there surely had to be more to their story—so I wrote it.

One other detail I found intriguing during my research was the discovery that British and Dutch ships in the region often had Aboriginal crewmates. The First Nations peoples of Australia were highly valued for their knowledge and expertise. They served as pilots, trackers, negotiators, interpreters, and guides. So it would not be unusual to find a ship with a cabin boy like Matthew.

Let's explore that latter topic in greater detail.

THE FIRST NATIONS PEOPLES OF AUSTRALIA

In this novel, there was some discussion of *when* the Australian continent was first populated. The currently accepted date is between 50,000 and 60,000 years ago. But that timeframe has come into question by the recent uncovering of older hunting and fishing camps. While the dating remains controversial, I tangentially discovered research articles that challenged the Out-of-Africa theory, shifting the cradle of humanity to Australia. Most astounding was the fact that the geneticists who first proposed the Out-of-Africa model were the very ones who later recanted their own work. The quote that is paraphrased in this novel ("*mitochondrial DNA puts the origin of humankind much further back and indicates that the Australian Aborigines arose 400,000 years ago*") came from one of those scientists.

Moving on to the *legends* among the First Nations peoples, I could only glancingly cover their rich and diverse belief systems. But what is covered in this book is based on true Aboriginal stories. The Rainbow Serpent legends are as written in the novel: the creation myth, the giant snake sleeping deep under Earth's crust, the ability to flow through a watery lair from place to place, the conflicting nature of a serpent that could bring destruction or salvation, even the seeding of "little rainbows"—miniature versions of themselves—into people to wreak havoc.

As to the bullroarers, they are indeed the "secret-sacred" tools of the First Nations peoples. They are considered to be the "voice of the Rainbow Serpent." And that voice is indeed *loud*, capable of traveling miles, of reaching a hundred decibels—the equivalent of a revving chainsaw.

The aspect of the novel that covers the "Dark Dreaming" is a merging of Aboriginal dreamtime mythology with a bit of speculation on my part. I find it intriguing that the eruption of the Toba supervolcano happened in the region 74,000 years ago. I've always wondered if such an event—an eruption that darkened the world for decades and drove the human population to less than 30,000 members—could have been the inciting incident that pushed the Aboriginal people into Australia. Especially as their origin stories speak of a great fiery cataclysm and giant destructive waves. Could this be a firsthand account of the Toba eruption? Someone should research this.

Speaking of research, let's move on to some of the scientific topics covered in this novel.

EXPLORING THE DEEP SEA

I thought I should first cover the *vehicles* used by the characters in this book. I based them on intriguing research vessels—one in development and two that have been well tested and traveled.

The *Titan X* is based on a nuclear-powered gigayacht—the Earth 300—that's currently in production and is scheduled to start its first oceanic research voyage in 2025. If you'd like to learn more, check out the website: earth300.com. The ship will hold a complement of 160 scientists, with the same number of crew. The thirteen-story glass orb (or "science city") has twenty-two state-of-the-art labs, and the yacht will carry a host of underwater expedition vehicles. Upon learning of this ship, I decided to give it a test drive. Note that I barely dented it, even cleaned it up afterward. I'm still waiting for my invitation to its maiden voyage—I'll bring the champagne.

As mentioned above, the Earth 300 will be equipped with underwater expedition vehicles. Maybe even a Triton 36000/2 DSV. The *Cormorant* featured in this book is based on the latter vehicle. I did make it a four-seater instead of two. And I gave it a pair of wings, which I borrowed from another of Triton's submarines: the Titanic Explorer. Otherwise, I stuck to the reality and limitations of the Triton 36000/2. Even the acoustic modem—capable of voice and text communications—is based on current technology and can reach down to the deepest trenches.

The DriX autonomous vessels that were featured prominently in this book are also real, designed by the wonderful people at iXblue.

Moving on to *what* those vessels might find:

DEEP-SEA LIFE

Much of our oceans remains unexplored. We've only crudely mapped about 20 percent of the ocean floor. And if you're talking about finer imaging—sharp enough to detect a plane wreck—that percentage drops to a mere 0.05.

As to what is down there, no one can truly say. New discoveries are made all the time. Giant squids were once considered mythical until they were found washed up on beaches. In this book, I tried to adhere to the biologically feasible. In the opening chapters, I described life at the depth of two miles. That description is accurate. There are wonderful oases that thrive in the sunless deep.

Likewise, the discussions of the unique biology of deep-sea coral are also factual, including the intriguing detail that coral has been growing continually in the Mediterranean Sea for 400,000 years. And while no corals have been found six miles under the sea, we've barely begun to look, and biologically they could be (with a little organo-silicon tweaking).

Exploring further, the conversation about *gigantism* in the deep sea is fascinatingly true. The biological reasons for why this happens (oxygen saturation, salinity, and pressure) are also accurate.

Moving on to some finer points: pistol shrimp are indeed raucous creatures, firing their plasma-charged water bubbles. DARPA is actively researching how to use these natural oceanic noises to develop a new sonar system. In the meantime, military submarines *do* use those boisterous shrimp colonies to hide themselves from the sonar searches of surface ships—like what Phoebe does in this book.

In regards to the geology of the deep sea, I mention submarine volcanos that spew out liquid carbon dioxide and huge pools of molten sulfur. Those both have been found in the dark depths of the unexplored ocean.

And speaking of geology . . .

LARGE LOW-SHEAR VELOCITY PROVINCES (OR "BLOBS") AND THE MOON'S FORMATION

The two huge mysterious fragments under the Pacific Ocean and the African continent are truly there. The growing consensus is that they could very well be pieces of the planetoid Theia that crashed into the early Earth and blasted our moon into orbit. It's also suspected that tiny pieces of the same could make up part of the moon's composition—but that's not been verified. At least not yet.

On a minor note, China's Chang'e-5 lunar lander did mysteriously malfunction while drilling into a strange stratum. The lunar rocks that returned with the mission did indeed show that the moon had cooled far slower than any model predicted. One of the explanations for the slow cooling was the possible presence of an exotic, radioactive material that has kept the moon hot. What could that be? I have my own theory, and you just read it.

Digging deeper, the two "blobs" do seem to be the source for much of the planet's tectonic instability, triggering volcanic eruptions and quakes, especially along their borders. Trond Torsvik at the University of Oslo has linked these blobs to the greatest catastrophe in Earth's history. He believes it was a change in one of those blobs that triggered the Great Dying, a mass extinction event that snuffed out most life on the planet. And he believes it could happen again, that we're all sitting atop an "antediluvian time bomb."

As to the strange prevalence and reports of UAPs around areas of tectonic activity, that's also true. Is someone up there minding a garden that they planted? As Painter says: *If so, let's hope they don't have a harvest season.*

OCTOPUSES FROM SPACE

I thought I'd single out this topic from the general discussion of sea life. I watched the documentary *My Octopus Teacher* and read countless articles about the species' unique biology and intelligence. So I was not entirely surprised to read about challenges to the evolutionary pathway of octopuses. Of late, there has been an uptick in media exposure on this very topic, much of it mocking. But upon digging deeper, I discovered it was based on a peer-reviewed scientific article about panspermia and the cosmic seeding of our planet by extraterrestrial retroviruses. It's titled "Cause of Cambrian Explosion—Terrestrial or Cosmic?" It was authored by astrobiologists from around the globe. I read it and found their conclusions dauntingly convincing. So I decided to extrapolate what that might look like.

And continuing on the topic of extraterrestrial lifeforms and how to find them:

BIOSIGNATURES

Over the past few years, the scientific community has been shifting away from the search for technosignatures (radio signals, etc.) as an indicator of life on other planets. They're now focused more on the search for biosignatures. In his novel, Dr. Datuk Lee touches upon this pursuit. His discussion is based on current and ongoing studies.

The organization he works for—LAB, or the Laboratory for Agnostic Biosignatures—is a real group out of Georgetown University with a global presence. The MinIon nanopore sequencer that he uses in the *Cormorant* is an organic analyzer that is currently being tested for installation into future exploratory spacecraft.

If you'd like to know more about the search for biosignatures, I highly recommend a book written by a Harvard astronomer:

Extraterrestrial: The First Sign of Intelligent Life Beyond Earth by Avi Loeb

It covers the topic of biosignatures in far greater detail, even postulating that the cigar-shaped asteroid, Oumuamua, which passed Earth in 2019, could have been a piece of alien technology. Like with the theory of extraterrestrial octopuses, his thesis has been looked at with a jaundiced eye. But I appreciated his general attitude and conclusion: *Just consider it and look deeper.* It's a philosophy that could serve us all.

CHINA'S AUTONOMOUS FORCES

The PLA equipment featured in the novel is based on actual designs currently in production or already being used. That includes the Type 096 nuclear ballistics submarine (the wrecked *Changzheng 24* in the book), the Type 076 helicopter landing dock (the *Dayangxi*), and the Type 726 Landing Craft Air Cushion (nickname *Yema*), along with its Type 96 battle tank.

Also, the AI-driven vessel—the *Zhu Hai Yun*—is a real boat, one that is believed to be a prototype for a militarized version. In addition, the UUVs and smart torpedoes that plague Kowalski in this story are real and have undergone sea trials in the Taiwan Strait. Likewise, the PLA Navy has developed a deep-sea vessel with militarized applications, from reconnaissance and surveillance to antisubmarine warfare. I based the *Qianliyan* on this design platform.

Moving past the scientific aspects of the book, let's end with areas of special interest.

LOCATION, LOCATION, LOCATION

In Hong Kong, the bar that Kowalski visits—the Old Man—is real, as are the drinks he orders. The elevated park where he tussles with some henchmen is indeed right across the street. Likewise, you could moor your boat at the Royal Hong Kong Yacht Club, and on the neighboring shore, you could play golf—assuming an incoming tsunami doesn't chase you into the clubhouse (like with Gray). The fire roads and hiking trails atop the forested heights of Victoria Peak do form a confounding maze.

In Singapore, the Lee Kwon Chian Natural History Museum does retain the original natural history collection from the museum that Sir Stamford Raffles founded, including discoveries he made himself. The museum's Heritage Gallery also covers the embroiled scientific competition between Raffles and Farquhar. The upper research floors are covered by extensive wet and dry collections, preserving millions of specimens. And in the public spaces, there is indeed a light show highlighting their huge dinosaurs. I apologize for making such a mess of the place.

In Jakarta, the Love Bridge is available for late-night walks (or gun battles). The Jakarta History Museum was once the city hall, where Sir Stamford Raffles kept an office. I doubt there is a coded safe that holds the preserved remains of a dead boy—but you never know. The lab where Heng and Xue do some late-night research—the Eijkman Institute for Molecular Biology—is also a real establishment.

At the Réam Naval Base in Cambodia, China did take over a large corner of the facility. According to an article in *The Washington Post*, the base will be used for both military and scientific purposes—which, to me, is more disturbing than either alone.

Okay, folks, that's it. From that ending, you can imagine that Sigma will be on the warpath. A major battle is about to be fought on a global scale. No one will leave unscathed. To survive, it will require engaging every agent—past and present—including a certain four-legged soldier (possibly even *two* of them).

Rights and Attributions for the Artwork in This Novel

p. 62—Map of Trenches
Drawn by author based on the template of map by Steve Prey

p. 63—Map of Quakes
Drawn by author based on the template of map by Steve Prey

p. 64—Map of Force Vectors
Drawn by author based on the template of map by Steve Prey

p. 65—Map of Volcanos
Drawn by author based on the template of map by Steve Prey

p. 95—Crystals
Secured with an Enhanced License
ID 2166599081 © Yevgenij_D | Shutterstock.com
(image edited by author)

p. 99—Concrete Ark
Jacklee, CC BY-SA 4.0 @https://creativecommons.org/licenses/by
-sa/4.0:, via Wikimedia Commons
(image edited by author)

p. 127—African Blob
Sanne.cottaar, CC BY-SA 3.0 @https://creativecommons.org
/licenses/by-sa/3.0:, via Wikimedia Commons
(image edited by author)

p. 128—Pacific Blob
Sanne.cottaar, CC BY-SA 3.0 @https://creativecommons.org
/licenses/by-sa/3.0:, via Wikimedia Commons
(image edited by author)
Overlaid with partial map from:
ID 1680806881 © Saiful52 | Shutterstock.com
Secured with an Enhanced License
(image composited and edited by author)

p. 144—Argonite layering
Glenn Elert, CC BY-SA 3.0 @https://creativecommons.org/licenses
/by-sa/3.0:, via Wikimedia Commons
(image edited by author)

p. 146—Argonite crystal
Rob Lavinsky, iRocks.com – CC-BY-SA-3.0, CC BY-SA 3.0
@*h*ttps://creativecommons.org/licenses/by-sa/3.0:, via Wikimedia
Commons
(image edited by author)

p. 153—Hadal Zone/Titan X
Iddes Yachts for the Earth 300 organisation, CC BY-SA 4.0
@https://creativecommons.org/licenses/by-sa/4.0:, via Wikimedia
Commons
(image edited by author)

p. 168—Coral Scan
Lau, Yee Wah et al. "Stolonifera from shallow waters in the north-
western Pacific: a description of a new genus and two new species
within the Arulidae (Anthozoa, Octocorallia)." CC BY 4.0
@https://creativecommons.org/licenses/by/4.0:
(image edited by author)

p. 195—Cataclysm
Oliver Spalt, CC BY 2.0 @https://creativecommons.org/licenses
/by/2.0:, via Wikimedia Commons
(image edited by author)

p. 211—VEI Map
Drawn by author based on the template of map by Steve Prey

p. 240—Coral Piece
Public Domain. *The Annals and Magazine of Natural History,
including Zoology, Botany, and Geology* by Albert C. L. G. Günther,

William S. Dallas, William Carruthers, and William Francis (London: Taylor and Francis, Ltd., 1883). Holding Company: Smithsonian Libraries

(Image edited by author)

p. 241—Island Pic #1

Public Domain. *Corals and Coral Islands* by James Dwight Dana (New York: Dodd, Mead and Company, 1890). Holding Company: Harvard University, Museum of Comparative Zoology, Ernst Mayr Library

(image edited by author)

p. 241—Island Pic #2

Public Domain. *Corals and Coral Islands* by James Dwight Dana (New York: Dodd, Mead and Company, 1890). Holding Company: Harvard University, Museum of Comparative Zoology, Ernst Mayr Library

(image edited by author)

p. 242—Island Pic #3

Public Domain. *Corals and Coral Islands* by James Dwight Dana (New York: Dodd, Mead and Company, 1890). Holding Company: Harvard University, Museum of Comparative Zoology, Ernst Mayr Library

(image edited by author)

p. 242—Rainbow Serpent

Wellcome Library, London. Wellcome Images images@wellcome.ac. uk http://wellcomeimages.org, page 34, headed: Et apprehendit Draconem / Serpentein antiquani(?) / Apoc. XX Two drawings: the first depicting a rainbow and a warrior standing on a cloud attacking three monsters (a bird, serpent and a demon); the second depicting scientific apparatus

CC BY 4.0 @https://creativecommons.org/licenses/by/4.0:, via Wikimedia Commons

(image edited by author)

p. 249—SEM Crystal #1

Danielgeounivasf, CC BY-SA 4.0 @https://creativecommons
.org/licenses/by-sa/4.0:, via Wikimedia Commons
(image edited by author)

p. 250—SEM Crystal #2

Danielgeounivasf, CC BY-SA 4.0 @https://creativecommons.org
/licenses/by-sa/4.0:, via Wikimedia Commons
(image edited by author)

p. 253—Hunter/Killer

Secured with an Enhanced License
ID 2181028901 © Studio Melange | Shutterstock.com
(image edited by author)

p. 284—Bullroarer

Secured with an Enhanced License
ID 108145860 © Mushika | Dreamstime.com
(image edited by author)

p. 306—Island Pic #4

Public Domain. *Corals and Coral Islands* by James Dwight Dana
(New York: Dodd, Mead and Company, 1890). Holding
Company: Harvard University, Museum of Comparative Zoology,
Ernst Mayr Library
(image edited by author)

p. 307—Island Pic #5

Public Domain. *Corals and Coral Islands* by James Dwight Dana
(New York: Dodd, Mead and Company, 1890). Holding
Company: Harvard University, Museum of Comparative Zoology,
Ernst Mayr Library
(image edited by author)

p. 308—Big Coral Tree

Public Domain. *Corals and Coral Islands* by James Dwight Dana
(New York: Dodd, Mead and Company, 1890). Holding
Company: Harvard University, Museum of Comparative Zoology,
Ernst Mayr Library
(image edited by author)

p. 308—Coral Collection

Public Domain. *Corals and Coral Islands* by James Dwight Dana
(New York: Dodd, Mead and Company, 1890). Holding
Company: Harvard University, Museum of Comparative Zoology,
Ernst Mayr Library
(image edited by author)

p. 309—Coral Ball

Secured with an Enhanced License
ID 1693692316 © Sharp Dezign| Shutterstock.com
(image edited by author)

p. 310—Life Cycle

Public Domain. *Histoire naturelle : generale et particuliere des
cephalopods acetabuliferes vivants et fossils* by Férussac, A. E.
d'Audebard de baron de, (André Étienne) and Orbigny, Alcide
Dessalines d', (Paris: Impr. de A. Lacour, 1835). Holding
Company: Museums Victoria
(image edited by author)

p. 310—Rainbow Serpent Drawing

Public Domain. *Histoire naturelle : generale et particuliere des
cephalopods acetabuliferes vivants et fossils* by Férussac, A. E.
d'Audebard de baron de, (André Étienne) and Orbigny, Alcide
Dessalines d', (Paris: Impr. de A. Lacour, 1835). Holding
Company: Museums Victoria
(image edited by author)

p. 311—Nematocyst Drawing
Public Domain. *Corals and Coral Islands* by James Dwight Dana
(New York: Dodd, Mead and Company, 1890). Holding
Company: Harvard University, Museum of Comparative Zoology,
Ernst Mayr Library
(image edited by author)

p. 315—Dark Eden
Secured with an Enhanced License
ID 2190950377 © Dav_782| Shutterstock.com
(image edited by author)

p. 371—Serpent's Roar
Secured with an Enhanced License
ID 84245848 © digitalbalance| Shutterstock.com
(image edited by author)

p. 393—Island Pic #6
Public Domain. *Corals and Coral Islands* by James Dwight Dana
(New York: Dodd, Mead and Company, 1890). Holding
Company: Harvard University, Museum of Comparative Zoology,
Ernst Mayr Library
(image edited by author)

p. 394—Satellite View of Raoul Island
Public Domain. NASA International Space Station image ISS002-
E-8883, 2001 (http://eol.jsc.nasa.gov/).
(image edited by author)

About the Author

James Rollins is the #1 *New York Times* bestselling author of international thrillers that have been translated into more than forty languages. His Sigma series has been lauded as one of the "top crowd-pleasers" (*New York Times*) and one of the "hottest summer reads" (*People* magazine). In each novel, acclaimed for its originality, Rollins unveils unseen worlds, scientific breakthroughs, and historical secrets—and he does it all at breakneck speed and with stunning insight. He lives in the Sierra Nevada mountains.